An Uncommon Campaign

Book 3 of the Peninsular War Saga

By

Lynn Bryant

To Richard
With love and gratitude for everything

About the Author

Lynn Bryant was born and raised in London's East End. She studied History at University and had dreams of being a writer from a young age. Since this was clearly not something a working class girl made good could aspire to, she had a variety of careers including a librarian, NHS administrator, relationship counsellor and manager of an art gallery before she realised that most of these were just as unlikely as being a writer and took the step of publishing her first book.

She now lives in the Isle of Man and is married to a man who understands technology, which saves her a job, and has two grown-up children and a Labrador. History is still a passion, with a particular enthusiasm for the Napoleonic era and the sixteenth century. When not writing she waits on her Labrador, reads anything that's put in front of her and makes periodic and unsuccessful attempts to keep a tidy house.

She is the author of the popular *Peninsular War Saga* and the *Manxman series*. The first two books in the Manxman series, ***An Unwilling Alliance*** and ***This Blighted Expedition*** were shortlisted for the Society for Army Historical Research fiction prize in 2019 and 2020.

Acknowledgments

There have been many people who have helped me since I rashly embarked on a career as a writer. Some of them, I did not even know when the first edition of this book was published in 2017 but since then I've received so much help and advice, and what I've learned has gone into the new edition of this book.

Research is a huge part of the writing I do, and I'd like to thank various historians and writers who have helped me with the maddest questions, especially Jacqueline Reiter, Rob Griffith, Rory Muir, Andrew Bamford, Charles Esdaile, Gareth Glover, and many others on social media and in person. There will be some I've missed out and I'm sorry but thank you all.

As always, I'd like to thank Mel Logue, Jacqueline Reiter, and Kristine Hughes Patrone for reading sections of the work and making helpful suggestions.

Thanks to Richard Dawson, my husband, for his amazing cover, for technical help and for endless support and patience during the writing of this book.

Thanks to my son, Jon and his girlfriend Rachael, for sharing my study during lockdown and completely ignoring my historical mutterings and to my daughter, Anya, for helping to keep me on track when I was really struggling to motivate myself.

The re-editing of this and all the other books would never have happened in the way it has without the intervention of Heather Paisley, my editor, proof-reader, and partner-in-crime for more than thirty years.

Finally, thanks to Oscar and Alfie the stars of *Writing with Labradors* for sharing my study and bringing me joy.

And in loving memory of Toby and Joey, my old Labradors who have died since I first wrote this book and broke my heart. You will both always be with me in spirit.

Chapter One

Teresa Cortez was cold.

The temperature in the army prison in Pero Negro was always unpleasant. The prison was located in an old stable block in the village, attached to a stone house which temporarily housed a number of different administrative departments of Wellington's army, including the provost-marshal's office, and it was swelteringly hot during the day and freezing at night. Wearing only a thin muslin dress and without even the covering of a shawl, Teresa had barely slept during her imprisonment.

Conditions in the prison were uncomfortable, but not unbearable and it was not the first time in her twenty-two years that Teresa had been cold and hungry. Over the past year she had grown accustomed to comfort but before that she had been caught up in the first French invasion when Bonaparte's troops had swept through Spain and into Portugal like a plague, destroying the countryside, the towns, and people's lives. Beside the horrors Teresa had endured then, her present discomfort was trivial, and she kept telling herself that this would be over soon.

Teresa had been brought to the prison eleven days earlier, under arrest for assaulting a deputy provost-marshal in the execution of his duty. Teresa had no real defence against the charge. She had always considered herself a reasonable woman, not given to displays of anger, but the sight of Sergeant Parsons with two assistants attempting to drag a wounded man from his bed to send him back to his regiment had caused her to lose her temper spectacularly. She had defended the injured man with the aid of a pewter water jug and although on reflection Teresa wished she had not done so, the swelling bruise on Parsons' bald head had been very satisfying.

There was no separate prison for females. It was unusual for any woman to be kept in prison for more than a night or so, and Teresa found herself sharing the space with a dozen men imprisoned for various offences. On the first evening there had been a barrage of comments and invitations and she had been temporarily frightened. But the gaoler, a big Irishman, had stomped into the gaol and silenced them with a yell.

"Leave the lass alone, you miserable bastards! Look at her, does she look like she should be in here?"

"Well why is she then, Sarge?"

1

"Because she tried to stop the provost marshals dragging wounded men from their beds and sending them back to the lines when they weren't fit. And when they ignored her, she belted one of them with a water jug and gave him a headache."

There was a roar of laughter. "Well done, lass," somebody called.

"And they put you in here for that?" another said, indignantly. "Which regiment you attached to, lass? You married?"

"Betrothed," Teresa said. Her engagement was so recent that it still felt odd to say it, but the word gave her unexpected strength. "The regiment had already marched north with Lord Wellington, but I remained behind to help care for the wounded. The provost-marshal's men came to say that our men were not sick and should join the regiment, which was nonsense. They made the injured men march out. I hope they all made it, one or two were very ill."

"Bloody provost! Does your man know?"

"He does. He was going to the Colonel to ask him to intervene. And he will, I am his wife's maid." Despite herself Teresa smiled. "Danny was furious, but I did not want him arrested, if he had hit the provost, they might have hanged him."

"Which colonel is it, lass? Is his wife good to you? I hope you're right about them because they're going to flog you for assaulting the provost."

"She is very good to me." Teresa did not attempt to explain her relationship with her mistress, who was more like a friend than an employer. "He is Colonel Paul van Daan of the 110th."

There was a short respectful silence. The gaoler grinned.

"Right then, I take it I won't have to come in here again to protect the lassie's virtue? Because if I do I'll be passing your names on to Colonel van Daan. Clear?"

"We're not that stupid, Sarge. I wouldn't want to be in that provost's shoes, mind, when Colonel van Daan finds out he's locked her up. A water jug on the head will be the least of his worries."

Since then, Teresa had been left alone, waiting to be released. She did not know how long it would take for her betrothed, Sergeant Daniel Carter, to reach his regiment with the wounded men and she had no idea what he would find when he got there. If Lord Wellington's army were in the middle of a battle it would take far longer for the Colonel or his wife to intervene to obtain Teresa's release.

In the meantime, the prospect of a trial drew closer and became more real. Under normal circumstances it would have happened much sooner but eavesdropping on the gaolers' conversations, Teresa gathered that with most of the troops up at the lines it had proved difficult to find enough officers to serve on the court. This morning, on the changeover of guards, she heard the unwelcome news that there were enough for a court to be convened, and that the gaol would be cleared by the end of the following day.

Most of the men in the prison had been arrested for theft, looting, or being found absent from duty which Teresa knew was another word for desertion. Her time with the 110th had given her a good understanding of army discipline and the way it worked, or often didn't. With Lord Wellington's army occupied in chasing the French up to the Spanish border there were always men travelling to and from the lines in small groups, either with supply convoys, men returning from sick leave or new recruits on their way to their regiments. Away from their officers and non-

2

commissioned officers it was not uncommon for such men to behave badly. Many were never caught and the complaints of the local population about their depredations remained unanswered. Those who were, could not be tried by their regiment, which might be many miles away, so they were confined in the nearest army prison and left to wait until a local court martial could be convened.

The news came round with the afternoon meal, passed from one man to the next, and into Teresa's stall via a skinny orderly who handed her a mess tin of tasteless stew and a tack biscuit with the words:

"Court's in session tomorrow, miss. Sorry."

Teresa smiled her thanks and set the food down, untasted, her stomach in knots. She had been so sure that a message would come ordering her release that she had not allowed herself to think that much about the alternative. Wives and camp followers were under military discipline and could be punished in the same way as the men, including flogging. Theoretically, the personal maid of the wife of a ranking colonel should not be treated as a common camp follower, but with nobody here to speak up for her, Teresa was beginning to suspect that she was going to have to stand her trial. She also suspected that she would be found guilty.

Teresa had no doubt that if Anne van Daan knew where she was, she would have obtained her release, but she was afraid that a message had been sent and had gone astray. Anne was very attached to her Spanish maid and was fiercely loyal. She would be furious when she found out, but that would not prevent a court from ordering a flogging unless Teresa could find a way to convince them who she was.

Teresa had worked for Anne van Daan for almost two years since Anne had arrived in Lisbon with her first husband. Teresa had been orphaned young and placed as a novice in a convent not far from Salamanca. Growing up within walls she had accepted her lot, not happily but with resignation. She had come from a good family fallen on hard times and what was left of her inheritance had gone to the convent. There was a brother, some years her elder, who had left home in disgrace and not been heard of again. Teresa remembered little of Bruno other than furious arguments followed by frozen silences and her mother's tears. He had been kind to his young sister in a casual way but after her parents died, Teresa had never heard from him and had no idea what had happened to him.

Teresa was eighteen when the French came, battering down doors and dragging the nuns from their prayers. Even now Teresa shied away from remembering those few days of horror. They had slaughtered the older nuns and shared the younger ones around, looting the church and getting drunk on the contents of the wine cellar, and their officers had seemed indifferent to the screams of the girls. Two of the young novices had died, and for a time Teresa had envied them.

Bloody and broken, she watched the French march out, hating them as she had never thought she could hate. They had emptied the food and wine stores and she and the few surviving nuns had staggered to the nearest village only to find that it too had suffered, and that there were also women there shocked and bleeding and crying. Teresa understood quickly that she needed to live, so she had begged and whored and stolen, making her way towards the Portuguese border. When the remains of the Portuguese army came through, fleeing ahead of the French, she attached herself to them, finding them little different to the French except that they paid her or fed her, and did not hit her as much unless they were drunk. Arriving in Lisbon she was appalled to find that the French were close by, and that her survival might depend on her ability to please the army who had made a prostitute of her in the first place.

To Teresa's surprise and relief, the French occupation did not last for long. Instead the English came and with two swift and effective battles, Sir Arthur Wellesley made the English masters of Lisbon. As the tides of war moved away again, Teresa found work in the laundry of an army hospital, sleeping on the kitchen floor, and working for little more than her food, a warm space and freedom from selling her body to strangers although with English troops pouring into Lisbon she was aware that she could have made more money as a prostitute. The thought appalled her, and she resisted any advances made by the stream of British soldiers passing through the hospital wards.

Teresa's experiences had left her frightened and embittered. She was not sure what her future might have been if she had not met the young wife of a lieutenant in the quartermaster's department who had volunteered to help at the hospital. Teresa had heard some of the surgeons and orderlies, laughing about the madness of Dr Adam Norris who was not only allowing the young woman to help with the nursing, but was actually teaching her basic surgical skills. Teresa was occasionally called upon to act as a nurse when the hospital was busy, and she was summoned one afternoon and found herself threading surgical needles for a tall slender girl in a dark dress and white apron, who turned to smile at her revealing the loveliest face Teresa had ever seen.

"You must be Teresa. Thank you for helping, I hope you don't mind. I'm tired of shouting at the orderlies, they think it's fun to ignore me. Eventually I'll take a brick to one of them, perhaps that will improve their manners."

Anne Carlyon was like a breath of fresh air in the filthy, fetid hospital wards, a woman who talked to the enlisted men with the same easy familiarity as she did to their officers, and who laughed readily at the most vulgar of their jokes. Teresa, who had believed herself hardened, was won over within a week and when the girl had asked her if she would consider taking employment as her maid, she had agreed without hesitation. It had been the beginning of a new life for Teresa, a life which had kept her busy and interested, and more alive than she could ever have imagined during her quiet convent days. A life which included Sergeant Daniel Carter of the 110th infantry, who had asked her, very recently, to be his wife.

"Fraulein, you are shivering. Are you all right?"

The voice came from the stall opposite. It was occupied by a soldier from the King's German Legion, a fair young man wrapped in a thick army greatcoat who had not so far troubled Teresa other than with a curious look and a smile. He had been brought in yesterday, and Teresa had noticed his youth and wondered what he had done.

"Come closer, Fraulein."

Teresa sighed and looked over at him.

"I am not interested," she said firmly.

"Fraulein, I am not asking for anything. I am offering you my coat. You are shivering and you have eaten nothing."

Startled Teresa got up and went over to him. He was removing the dark coat and he held it out to her. Teresa tried to smile.

"I am so sorry. You were being kind, and I was rude."

"No, you were not, I understand. This must be very frightening for you. Take the coat, I am warm enough in my uniform."

"Thank you," Teresa said. She draped the heavy coat around her. It was still warm from his body and she felt an unexpected longing for Danny, who often draped his coat around her shoulders as they sat late into the night talking. She sat down at a safe distance and studied the German curiously. His English was very good, but that was true of many of the King's German Legion who had fought under British officers and alongside their men through a number of campaigns.

"Why are you here?"

"I was out of camp without permission."

"Deserting?" Teresa asked.

He grinned. "No. I had not gone very far. And I was not alone. A flogging, possibly, but not a hanging, I think."

"Probably not. Have you been flogged before?"

He shook his head. "No. I am usually much more careful."

"She must have been very pretty," Teresa said, and he grinned.

"She was. The Corporal must have thought so since he let her go before he arrested me. But I do not understand why you are here, surely you are not a camp follower?"

"No. I lost my temper and hit the provost when he came into our regimental hospital."

"You should be rewarded for that. What about your husband?"

"Betrothed. They threatened to arrest him too. And somebody needed to take care of our wounded. I have been hoping the Colonel would send a message for my release. And worrying that he has, and it has got lost."

There was a noise in the corridor, and a voice Teresa did not know called out. One of the other men groaned.

"Oh bloody hell, Lowther is on duty. That's all I need. Thank God it's the court martial tomorrow, I can get flogged and get away from him."

"Stop talking in there, you mangy bastards!" the voice roared. "Private Collins, open this door and let's see what we've got."

He was a short man, overweight with stringy hair and narrow dark eyes. Teresa sat very still and quiet, clutching the German's coat around her. Sergeant Lowther walked slowly up the row of stalls with the thin private stalking behind him. He stopped before each man, barking a question or hurling an insult, and twice she heard a gasp of pain as he kicked an ankle or a leg.

When he got to the end he stood staring down at Teresa and the young German. "KGL?" he asked.

"Yes," the boy said.

"I don't like Germans. Going to put in a very bad report on your behaviour, sonny, make sure they throw in a dozen extra lashes. You won't look so pretty

5

then." His eyes shifted to Teresa. "Or maybe not, since I see you've brought me a present. Get up, girl."

Teresa got to her feet. "I am not a camp follower," she said. "I am..."

"I don't give a shit what you're calling yourself, girl, you're in my gaol and they don't put decent women in here. Outside. Make it worth my while, and I'll even pay you for it."

He reached for Teresa, and she pulled back, suddenly terrified. Lowther took her wrist in an iron grip and began to drag her towards the door. Teresa fought furiously, kicking out at him. He released her, turned, and hit her hard, backhanded across the face.

"Spanish bitch. You don't want to cooperate, that's fine with me. Collins get hold of her arms and help me get her out of here, you can have your turn when I've done with her. I hope they take the skin off that pretty back tomorrow."

Lowther broke off with a yell of pain and released Teresa's arm. There was the crack of a fist on a jaw, and the sergeant swore violently. Teresa fell back against the wall, staring, and realised that the young German was on his feet, fists up. Lowther was straightening up, his face suffused with fury.

"You are dead, you German bastard."

"And you will not be raping anybody tonight." The German moved suddenly and kicked, powerfully with the flat of his foot, straight into Lowther's crotch. The gaoler screamed once and fell to the ground sobbing in pain. The German looked past him to Collins. "If you come close to her I will do the same to you," he said.

Collins looked down at his sergeant and then up at the German. Then he turned and ran to the door, yelling for help. Teresa looked over at the boy. He was white, the blue-grey eyes blazing with anger.

"You should not have done that," she said.

"Ja, I should."

Teresa could hear running footsteps, hear Collins shouting explanations and then four soldiers ran into the room and straight for the German. Teresa stepped back, horrified, as he disappeared under a hail of kicks and blows, while two others got Sergeant Lowther to his feet.

"You all right, Sarge? Christ, he'll wish he hadn't done that tomorrow, he'll be lucky if he doesn't hang."

"If he survives this," another said, watching the beating dispassionately.

Teresa could not bear it. She ran forward furiously, hitting at the back of one of the soldiers. "Stop it! Stop it! You are going to kill him!"

Surprise made him turn. "And who the bloody hell are you?" he demanded.

"She's his whore. Deserves a few kicks herself," Lowther said viciously.

Anger had driven away Teresa's terror. "I am not a prostitute," she spat, furiously. "My name is Teresa Cortez, I am maid to Mrs van Daan, who is the wife of Colonel Paul van Daan of the 110th. And my fiancé is Sergeant Daniel Carter who is going to kill every single one of you for this."

The private stared at her in some astonishment. Then he shouted:

"Davies, Sanderson, get off him. He's had enough."

6

The men backed off and Teresa pushed past them. The German lay very still, his long fair hair soaked in his own blood. Teresa reached for his neck and found a pulse, but he did not stir.

"He needs a doctor."

"Not one in the village. All up with the troops." The soldier was studying her. "Was that true? What you just said."

"Every word, Private, so you had better hope they find you another job before Colonel van Daan gets here."

"And what makes you think he's coming for you?" Lowther said with heavy sarcasm.

"Because I know him."

Teresa sat through the night with the German's head pillowed in her lap. She could find no obvious broken bones, but she was horribly afraid that the kicks to his head had done some serious damage. Occasionally he stirred and murmured, but it was getting light before he finally opened his swollen eyes and looked at her.

"Are you all right?" he said.

"Yes. Thanks to you. I'm so sorry this happened to you. They are animals."

"We are not all that bad," the boy said, trying to smile, and Teresa felt tears come to her eyes.

"They cannot try you like this," she said.

"They will," the German said. "I attacked an NCO. They will have me in court if they have to carry me."

Teresa did not answer, knowing it was probably true. Light was filtering in through the open slots at the top of the stable walls. He shifted and pushed himself cautiously up, wincing, probing at his midriff. "I think I may have a broken rib."

"I was worried they had cracked your skull," Teresa said. "Private, what is your name?"

"Private Kuhn, Fraulein. Theo Kuhn. First company, tenth battalion. And yours?"

"I am Teresa Cortez. I work for Mrs van Daan. Colonel van Daan's wife, the 110th…"

"I have heard of them," Kuhn said. He sounded impressed. "I have not been here long, we came in recently from Cadiz. But I have heard that the 110th are very good. I hope they come for you soon, Fraulein."

"Up! Up, you scurvy bastards! Time for your day in court. Line up!"

Teresa felt her stomach lurch in fear. She glanced at Kuhn. "Can you stand?"

"I will stand if it kills me, Fraulein," he said gravely, pulling himself to his feet. Something about him made Teresa feel stronger. She thought suddenly of her mistress, who had survived two years of brutality from her first husband with such panache, that nobody but Teresa had known how much she was suffering. If Anne van Daan could live through that with her head held high, Teresa decided that she could endure a flogging. She got up and reached for Kuhn's coat.

"Here…"

"Keep it," he said quietly, and Teresa smiled and shook her head.

"No. They will charge you for the loss and you do not get paid enough for that."

7

"Fraulein, I have not been paid at all for five months. But thank you." He shrugged himself into the coat and moved to join the line, limping heavily.

"You – German boy. To the front. Want to make sure they've got time to flog you today while I'm still around," Lowther said. "Or who knows, when they see what you did to my face, they might decide to hang you."

Private Collins shoved the German forward. Lowther looked at Teresa. "Collins keep her here until he's been before the court," he said. "I don't want her mouthing off..."

"You are a pig," Teresa said clearly, and Collins lifted his hand. His sergeant gave a yell.

"Don't hit her. You mark her too much and they'll want to know why."

Teresa watched the men marched away in furious impotence. She could not believe they would hang the young German given that he seemed to have a clean service record so far and she did not think that this court could order a hanging at all, although she supposed they could refer him to a higher court.

"Won't be long now," Collins said softly, watching her. "I wonder if he'll scream. They usually do after a while." He smiled, showing a row of yellow, broken teeth. "I wonder if they'll strip you when they flog you. Wouldn't mind if they do."

Teresa spat accurately, and he swore, and caught her arm, twisting it hard until she cried out. "Don't get clever with me, girl, I don't have to hit your pretty face to hurt you. You know what they do with camp followers like you? They flog them and then they throw them out of camp. And we'll be waiting for you, me and the sergeant, to finish what we started."

Teresa did not respond. The threat did not particularly frighten her. The minute she was free, she had every intention of running straight to headquarters. Most of the staff were up with Wellington and the army, but she was such a familiar sight around headquarters, accompanying her mistress, that she was sure somebody there would recognise her and give her help until a message could be sent to the lines of the 110th.

There were sounds from the parade ground and Collins grinned. "Right, sounds like a flogging for him. I bet it's a good one as well. Let's get you into court and with any luck you'll be out there waiting your turn round about the time he starts to yell."

The prisoner before Teresa was accused of stealing from a local farmer. He had been caught fair and square, the stolen chicken in his hands, its neck already wrung when the sergeant came across him. A skinny lad, probably no more than twenty, his expression was resigned as he stood before the court martial. The chair of the court, a solid major from the guards was quick and short in his questioning, and the boy offered little in the way of defence. The verdict of the court could not be in doubt and the sentence was flogging. The man was led away and there was a brief respite while the officers of the court refreshed themselves and the assistant provost marshal prepared the next case.

"Case of a camp follower, Teresa Cortez, accused of assaulting the provost marshal's deputies."

There was a rustle of interest around the court. Women were often brought up, usually on charges of looting or drunkenness. Wives and camp followers were

8

subject to military discipline and Teresa knew that for battlefield looting they were often worse than their menfolk. But she was aware that she did not look like a typical camp follower even after a week in the prison. Her gown was a gift from Anne, good quality blue muslin, and she had done her best while waiting, to tidy her hair.

The deputy provost marshal was reading out the charges. Teresa listened with immense contempt as the deputy told how she had intervened when her lover had been sent back from his malingering in hospital to fight with his regiment and struck the deputy with a china jug of water, injuring him. She had then bit and scratched several other deputies in the execution of their duty.

The deputy went on to engage in a long and rambling diatribe about the behaviour of the camp followers in the army, of their drunkenness and violence and of Lord Wellington's determination that they be controlled. Teresa was distracted by the sounds of the flogging from outside. It was still Private Kuhn and she wondered with horror how many he had been given.

"Well, girl, have you anything to say in your defence?" the major said finally.

Teresa looked at him. "I was doing my job," she said. "He was dragging a wounded man from his bed. I tried to stop him."

She could see that both her response and the quality of her English had surprised the court.

"The man being your lover?"

"No. I did not know him well. But he was too badly hurt to be moved."

"But your lover was present. A....let me see...a sergeant, is he not?"

"He was there but he was not involved. He is Sergeant Daniel Carter of the 110th." Teresa moved her eyes over the five men on the court. "He serves under Colonel Paul van Daan. I am Mrs van Daan's maid."

There was a shocked rumble around the room. Two of the court members began to converse furiously in low tones and the major looked across at the deputy.

"Is this true, Sergeant?"

"Yes, sir, I believe so. At least, that's what the girl told us."

At one end of the table sat a captain of around thirty. He was dark and intense looking and was studying Teresa with an expression which suggested that he was unsure about the proceedings. Teresa wondered if he was a new arrival. He appeared to be listening to the murmur of voices around the room. "I'm missing something," he said to his neighbour, a captain from an Irish regiment. The man laughed.

"I forgot you're new, Graham. I want to know if this is true, because if this girl really is Mrs van Daan's maidservant, I do not want to be on the court that sends her for thirty lashes. And neither do you."

"Why?" the man said, looking puzzled.

"Because if she's genuinely under Paul van Daan's protection, he is going to go bloody mad when he finds out about this, and trust me, you don't want to be in the firing line."

Graham got up and walked towards Teresa. She watched him come with steady gaze.

9

"What happened to your face?" he asked. "This incident took place over a week ago. That bruise looks more recent."

"It happened at the gaol."

"How?"

"The sergeant of the guards. He was angry with me because I kicked him."

Graham's eyes were steady on hers. "Why?" he asked again.

"I did not like what he was trying to do to me, Captain."

Graham studied her for a long moment. "Did he hurt you?" he asked, very gently.

Teresa met his eyes. "He tried to," she said.

Graham turned back to the court and looked at the Major. "This isn't right," he said. "I propose we adjourn the court until we've looked into this further. Sir..."

"Enough! I'm not backing down just because Van Daan is involved." The Major was more animated than Teresa had yet seen him. "She's not denying what she did. She's guilty."

"Sir..."

"We need a majority. Three votes." The Major looked along the table. "Or are you all too frightened of Wellington's mastiff?"

The atmosphere in the room was tense and uncomfortable. Captain Graham looked at Teresa and then back at the Major.

"I have no idea what you're talking about, sir, being new here," he said. "But I'm not convinced that we have all the information here and I'm not sure this woman has been treated as she ought. At the very least we should postpone the verdict and there should be an inquiry into..."

"Crewe, are you with me?"

"I am. High time somebody brought some discipline into that rabble he commands. If Wellington won't do it, we should."

"One more, gentlemen."

The Irish captain held up his hands. "Like Captain Graham here, I want to know more. If this lassie is really attached to the 110th and employed by the Colonel's lady..."

"Lady?" The final officer on the court gave a short laugh. "She's not a lady. I vote with the majority. The girl is guilty, doesn't matter who employs her."

"Thank you, Cartwright. The sentence of the court is that this Spanish woman be given thirty lashes and thrown out of the camp. Take her away."

"Sir, I protest at this verdict," Graham said vehemently. "I don't know who Colonel van Daan is or why it should matter, but..."

"At some point I will enlighten you," a new voice said. "I can understand your present confusion, however."

The voice came from the door of the room and Teresa turned feeling her terror drain away from her at the sound of his voice. The newcomer came forward. He was above average height and well-built, dressed in uniform with the insignia of a colonel, his red coat sporting silver grey facings. His hair was fair and cut shorter than was fashionable and his eyes were a deep and intense blue. They were resting on the Major and then they moved along the table to the captain called Cartwright.

10

"Good morning, Davy. Interesting to hear your views on my wife. How's yours, by the way?" he said, and there was a rustle of shocked comment around the room. Cartwright did not reply, but his eyes fell to the table. The newcomer turned to Teresa and held out his hand and she wanted to weep with relief.

"Colonel, I am so sorry about this."

"Lass, don't, it's me who should be sorry, this should never have happened to you. Lord Wellington sent a message for your release days ago. Christ knows what went wrong but when he finds out, somebody's balls are going to be decorating his doorway, he's in a foul mood at the moment. Come here. What the bloody hell happened to your face?"

Teresa ran, speechless, into his arms and he held her close. Immediately, she was shocked at herself, but he did not seem to find anything odd about embracing his wife's maid, merely stroked her hair as if she were a child and spoke over her head to the court.

"There is an order for Miss Cortez's immediate release from Lord Wellington," he said quietly. "I have a copy of it here, but when I've nothing better to do I'm going to find out what happened to the original because I'm damned sure it was delivered to somebody. Is Major Courtney here today?"

There was complete silence around the room. The Colonel waited until it became uncomfortable. "Never mind. I'll find him. Don't let me interrupt you any further. I'll have a chat later."

Teresa looked up and stepped back, scrubbing fiercely to wipe away her tears. "I am sorry, sir. I did not mean…"

"Oh stop it, Teresa, you're like family. I feel like punching somebody, I'm just not sure who needs hitting. Come outside and find Carter, he's been frantic about you." The Colonel reached into his coat and withdrew a handkerchief. "Wipe your face, you look like my daughter when she's been in trouble. Captain Devlin."

"Colonel van Daan, sir."

"Good to see you although you're keeping some very bad company these days. Come over to the tavern when you're done here and have a drink. And bring the new lad with you, I'd like to be properly introduced, I've a suspicion he's the man I'm looking for."

He turned to the door and Major Nairn surged to his feet.

"How dare you, sir? You are interfering with the legitimate business of this court and…"

Teresa had known Colonel van Daan for over a year and she was not surprised at the sudden tension in his body. He put her from him very gently and then turned back.

"I have Lord Wellington's orders here, Major, and they'll be placed on the court records, have no fear. Along with my own formal complaint at the provost marshal dragging injured men from their beds and sending them on a six-day march which could have killed them because he doesn't like the way I manage discipline in my regiment. If you want to take this up with Lord Wellington I really suggest you do it in person, I'll escort you myself. Or you could keep your head down and hope that the repercussions of this don't blight what is left of your miserable career in this army. Now piss off and let me do my job, or I will take these orders, knowing

11

that I can obtain a copy of them at any time, and stick them so far up your arse that they will see daylight out the back of your throat. Good afternoon, sir."

***

Outside it was growing hotter, the sun beating down on the main street of Pero Negro. A small crowd had congregated around the wooden frame which had been set up for the administration of punishment. Generally a flogging would be carried out in front of the convicted man's battalion; the point was to warn as well as punish. The men left behind in the gaol at Pero Negro were mostly a long way from their regiments which were up at the front with Lord Wellington. They had either been arrested before the march and had been lingering in the gaol waiting for the next court to be convened or had been picked up away from their regiments, stragglers, sick men, or deserters.

Paul van Daan took a deep breath. It was stuffy in the courtroom and he wondered if it affected the temper of the court to be cooped up inside for so long with a tedious list of mostly trivial misdemeanours. Paul disliked courts martial for a number of reasons and seldom used them except for serious cases such as rape or murder. He preferred to deal with discipline within his regiment and he knew his approach infuriated many of the older officers who considered him too soft on his men and too reluctant to use flogging as a deterrent. Paul did not care what they thought of him but was furious that Major Courtney, the acting provost marshal, had used a woman to make a point, especially Teresa Cortez, who was his wife's maid and companion and the fiancée of his newly promoted Sergeant-Major.

Paul looked around the street. Several months ago, it would have been busy with officers and men on their way to and from Lord Wellington's headquarters at the end of the village or travelling back to their regiments. All active serving men were now up at the lines, having spent an exhausting month chasing Marshal Massena's army up towards the Spanish border. The Allied victory at Sabugal, while not as conclusive as Wellington had hoped, had ensured that the French would not immediately be in a position to make a renewed attack, and Lord Wellington had time to consider his next move and to try to guess Massena's. In the brief respite, he had given Colonel van Daan permission to make a fast journey back to Pero Negro to retrieve his wife's Spanish maid.

Paul was well aware that the indulgence was unlike Wellington and had been granted purely to please his wife. Anne was pregnant with her first child and while Paul could see very little sign of the tears and emotional storms which had always accompanied his first wife's pregnancies, he knew that Anne was very capable of using her delicate condition to get what she wanted. He had not been present when Anne had apparently dissolved into tears before his stricken general at the hospital one afternoon, but he imagined it had been a good performance because Wellington had summoned him within the hour and told him to head back to Pero Negro with a copy of the order sent for Teresa's release.

"I cannot imagine why this has not been carried out and the girl returned," Wellington had said irritably. "It is ridiculous that I should have to be troubled by such trivialities at a time like this, one would think the provost marshal is able to

12

read my instructions. Go and get the girl, she should never have been arrested in the first place and I cannot have your wife upset like this in her condition."

"Yes, sir," Paul said without expression. After a moment, Lord Wellington appeared to realise what he had just said and looked up at Paul with a flash of amusement in the blue eyes.

"I beg your pardon, Colonel. That was a somewhat inappropriate statement."

"That's all right, sir. I know that your abiding affection for my wife is purely avuncular."

"Oh get out of here before I throw something at you. And while you are down in Pero Negro, you may ask if my new ADC has arrived. A Captain Richard Graham, newly returned from the Indies. If he is there, he can travel back with you. At least you know where you are going."

"I ought to, I feel as though we've covered every inch of this ground scuttling after Massena over the last few weeks. Thank you, sir. I really do appreciate this. Both Nan and Sergeant-Major Carter are frantic about her. We may find that it was simply a delay and she is on her way back, but I would like to be sure."

Wellington gave a glimmer of a smile. "Get going, Colonel. And don't hit anybody."

There were two small inns in the village centre, and Paul steered Teresa towards one of them. "Danny is in the tap room, lass," he said. "I wasn't taking him into that courtroom the mood he's in. Go and find him. I've got one or two people to speak to, but we're going to get on the road today if you're up to it."

"Yes, sir." The girl seemed worried, and Paul studied her. He noticed again the bruise on her face and reached out to touch it.

"Where did you get that?"

Teresa seemed to hesitate. Then she said:

"In the prison. The sergeant in charge, Sergeant Lowther."

"He hit you?" Paul said incredulously. "What the bloody hell for, it's not his job to be hitting the prisoners, let alone a woman?"

Teresa did not speak immediately, and Paul suddenly realised from her expression that there was another story here that he knew nothing about. He felt suddenly cold. "Teresa, did that bastard do anything to you?"

"No. At least…he was going to, I think. He thought me a camp follower and was trying to drag me out of the cell. He and the other one, Private Collins. I was so frightened but then one of the prisoners stopped them. He hit the sergeant and kicked him here." She indicated her lower body. "They beat him very badly, sir, and now he has been flogged. I am afraid for him."

Paul swung around. The sounds of the flogging had stopped he realised, and it looked as though the man was being taken down. Paul looked at Teresa. "I am going to bloody kill somebody for this," he said. "Go and find Danny, lass."

Paul strode back up the street. A second man was being strapped to the frame and the portly corporal wielding the lash was refreshing himself from a bottle. At the sight of a ranking colonel bearing down on him he put it away hastily and sprang to attention, saluting. Paul ignored him and pushed through the little crowd to where

13

the previous victim was lying face down on the dirt road, a greasy haired sergeant standing over him.

"All done then, sonny," he said, as Paul drew closer. "Don't seem so free with your fists now, do you? Or your smart German mouth." He prodded the man in the ribs with his foot and the victim groaned a little.

"Sergeant Lowther?" Paul asked pleasantly.

The men turned and saluted smartly. The change in his facial expression was ludicrous, moving from an unpleasant sneer to ingratiating smile within a moment.

"Sir, yes, sir. How can I help you, sir?"

Paul looked down at the man on the ground. He had long fair hair, matted with blood, and his bare back was a bloody mess. His face, turned to one side on the ground, appeared young, but it was difficult to judge his age because of the swollen eyes and black bruising.

Paul looked up at Lowther. "How did he get those bruises?" he asked. "That's not from a flogging."

"Fighting in the gaol, sir. Over some whore. Happens all the time. Collins and me had to go in and break it up, he went for me, sir. Like a mad animal he was, you can see what he did to my face. Took four of them to pull him off me."

"How many did he get?"

"A hundred, sir. Thirty for the original offence, another seventy for what he did to me. I thought it should have been more."

Paul crouched beside the German. His eyes were closed, and he appeared to be unconscious but as Paul moved his hair back to examine the injuries to his face, he opened distinctive blue-grey eyes and said something in German.

"All right, lad, don't try to move, I'll get you looked at." Paul looked up. "Is there a surgeon about?"

"No, sir," Lowther said. "All needed up at the lines. Nearest one is at the general hospital about eight miles off, they're just getting set up for casualties. But this one don't need a hospital, he needs…"

"When I want your medical opinion, Sergeant, I will ask for it, believe me."

"Yes, sir. Sorry, sir."

"No, you're not, but you are going to be. Did you give evidence against this man?"

"Yes, sir."

"That's excellent news, because it's going to be all over the court transcripts which will mean you'll be tried for perjury as well as assault and attempted rape. Did Private Collins give evidence as well?"

Lowther had blanched. "Yes, sir. Was two of us saw it. Not sure what you heard, but it ain't true. I was attacked. Punched. Bleeding, I was…"

Paul got up so fast that the sergeant retreated backwards and almost fell over. He seemed suddenly to recognise from the expression on Paul's face that his over-exaggerated humility was not working as well as it usually did with officers.

"There are a few things I'd like to question about this, Sergeant, including the legality of administering a flogging without a competent surgeon to check if the man is fit for punishment, but I'll take that up in writing with the provost marshal. In the meantime, go and get Private Collins out here, now."

"Yes, sir. But sir, you've got it wrong. She was just a Spanish prostitute, a camp follower, causing trouble. I had to…"

Paul felt his hold on his temper slipping away. He stepped forward, grasped the sergeant by his collar and then wrapped an arm about his neck, holding him in a headlock. Without speaking he marched the squawking man into the centre of the main street where a stone trough stood, filled daily with water for horses and mules to drink. Still in silence, Paul grasped Lowther by the back of his neck and shoved his head under the water. He held it there for a moment and then pulled him up, spluttering and choking.

"If you knew how badly I want to hold you under and put us all out of our misery, Sergeant, you would keep that foul mouth shut. She is not a camp follower, she's my wife's maidservant and she's betrothed to my Sergeant-Major who is going to want to slit your throat when he hears what you tried to do to her. And don't tell me you didn't know that, because she would have told you, she's not bloody stupid. You tried to attack a respectable woman and when that German lad defended her, you had him beaten and flogged to cover your crime. I've no idea what the penalty for all that is going to be, but I hope it fucking hurts. Now get over there, get Collins out here and get to attention while I find Major Courtney. And if you say one more bloody word of excuse, I will fucking drown you. Move."

"Sir."

Paul released Lowther, who scuttled away, dripping stagnant water and coughing and turned. "Yes, Mr O'Reilly, how can I help you?"

Lieutenant Michael O'Reilly saluted. "Teresa has just told us what happened, sir. I wondered if you needed some help."

"No, you didn't, Michael, you came out here to see if you needed to stop me killing somebody. Did you and Manson toss a coin for the job?"

"No, sir, I volunteered. He doesn't know you well enough, yet. Are you…"

"I am going to have a word with Major Courtney. Since you're here, you can make yourself useful and get that German lad into the inn. Get Teresa to have a look at him and clean him up a bit, she's a good nurse. We'll need to find a wagon of some kind; I'm taking him back up for Nan to take care of."

"Which battalion is he from?"

"I don't know, and I don't care, he's not fit to fight anyway, and since most of this happened to him for taking care of a girl I happen to be very fond of, he is staying under my protection until he's well enough. We can work out where he is supposed to be after that."

Paul went back to where the German soldier still lay in the street. He crouched down. "Somebody will be out to help you in a moment," he said. "We'll get you back up to the lines and into my regimental hospital, they'll take care of you properly."

"My battalion. I do not wish to get into more trouble for desertion."

"I'll find out where you should be and write to your commanding officer. That's my problem not yours, lad. Look, my officers are on their way to help you into the inn. We'll speak later."

He rose and moved away, leaving Michael and Carter to carry the boy into the inn. Across the street, next to the makeshift gaol was the house currently being

15

used by the acting provost marshal and Paul walked across to the door. It was firmly closed. As he approached, Lowther emerged from the gaol with a thin private who reminded Paul unaccountably of a weasel. Both men froze and then snapped to attention, saluting. Paul stopped and looked at them.

"Wait there. You move a muscle and I'm going to hit you so hard you'll be needing a surgeon yourselves."

He turned to the door and tried it, but it appeared to be barred. Paul banged on it. There was no response. He banged louder, using his fist.

"Sir. Begging your pardon, sir, but the major might be asleep. He sometimes does during the day. The heat, sir. Doesn't agree with him."

Paul turned to find a stocky sergeant saluting him. "Doesn't it?" he said mildly. "How unfortunate. Name and regiment, Sergeant?"

"Donahue, sir, first battalion 4th infantry, currently on detached duties with the provost marshal's office."

"Christ, Donahue, who the hell did you piss off to get landed with that duty?"

The Irishman gave a splutter of laughter, hastily suppressed. "Wounded, sir. Can't use my arm so well so they put me on light duties."

"Bad luck." Paul thumped the door once more. "Is he definitely in here?"

"Aye, sir."

"Thank you, Sergeant."

Paul took a step back and kicked the door very hard with the flat of his foot, breaking the latch. He stepped into the open doorway. "Courtney!" he bellowed. "Get yourself down here right now, I know you're in there. Don't make me come after you."

There was a sound from the dark interior and then Major Courtney appeared on the narrow wooden staircase, scarlet faced, pulling on his coat over an untucked shirt. What was left of his hair was standing on end. He had clearly just scrambled out of bed. He did not speak. Paul stared at him for a long moment, unable to believe his eyes.

"You are a bloody disgrace, Major. What the hell are you doing taking a nap when there's a court martial in session and you're responsible for half the cases?"

Major Courtney drew himself up to his full height. "My deputy is there," he said. "I am unwell, sir, and…"

"It's clear you are, or you'd have remembered the custom of saluting a senior officer," Paul said. Courtney's flush deepened even further, and he saluted.

"If you will excuse me saying so, Colonel, it is not your place to interfere with the provost marshal…"

"Be quiet, Major, I'm not interested," Paul said, stepping further into the dim room. "You see those two arseholes out there?"

He pointed through the open door at Lowther and Collins, standing motionless in the hot sun. "Last night, in a prison under your charge, they attempted to attack a young woman. A young woman who shouldn't have been there in the first place, I might add. When a private of the KGL stepped in to defend her, they had him beaten bloody and sent for a flogging by giving false testimony against him before a court martial."

16

"I have no idea…"

"Of course you've got no bloody idea, you idle bastard, because you're lying around in bed sleeping off your hangover and leaving your job to other people. But you knew about that girl, Major. You knew bloody well she was my wife's maid and not a camp follower. You put her in that gaol because you're a spiteful bastard and you don't like me, and if they'd got their hands on her she might have been raped. You are so bloody lucky that didn't happen. Before I leave this afternoon, you'll have several written witness statements about what they did and how they just lied about it in court. Arrest them and deal with them. If I have to come back here to make sure you've done your job, I'll hang you from the nearest stairwell without benefit of a trial with one of them each side of you. And in the future, if you come anywhere near any man of my regiment again, especially if they are wounded, I will personally cut off your balls if I am able to locate them and stuff them in your mouth before I display your bloody corpse on the front steps of your office as a warning to any other arsehole who comes after my men. Is that clear?"

Major Courtney made no response. Paul smiled grimly. "I'm going to take that as a yes. This is a copy of Lord Wellington's original letter telling you to release that girl as she'd done nothing wrong. If you lose that one, you'd better sell out. I rather suspect that your career would be over if you lost any more letters pertaining to this case. I don't have time to hang about otherwise I'd go in search of Dr Craddock as well, but when you see him, will you let him know that both Lord Wellington and the Surgeon-General want a chat with him about that little incident, to say nothing of my wife. And I'm putting in a formal complaint about the way that court was conducted today, they made no attempt to investigate the truth of those accusations against that man, they didn't even look for witnesses. I'll also add a word or two about the propriety of giving a man a hundred lashes when there isn't a surgeon present to certify his fitness for punishment."

Paul paused for breath. Major Courtney, who had said very little, finally seemed to find his voice. "Any complaints will be fully addressed," he said in slightly wavering tones. "I should point out, however, sir, that I am currently only acting provost marshal…"

"Well you're not very good at it, I've seen better acting from the Light Division's amateur theatrical group and they're bloody terrible. Now get yourself cleaned up and dressed and do your job. I'm going to find a wagon for that lad and if I don't find those two locked in a cell by the time I get back I'm going to put you in one and throw the keys into the latrines. And I'm damned sure it would be a while before anybody bothered to let you out, you useless gobshite."

Without waiting for a response, Paul went back out and made his way along to the house where the court was sitting. It was clear that the proceedings were over for the day. Major Nairn and Captains Crewe and Cartwright were still seated at the bench. Crewe and Nairn were huddled in conversation and Cartwright sat staring into space. Captain Devlin and the stranger were standing near the door and Paul went to join them.

"All done, Sean?"

"It is, sir, and I'm glad it's over. Hate these things."

"I'm not so fond of them myself," Paul said gravely and Devlin laughed aloud. Paul's own experience of being before a general court martial after the Copenhagen campaign was fairly well known but the other man looked puzzled. Paul studied him. He was probably around Paul's own age with curly dark brown hair and intense brown eyes, his skin very tanned.

"We've not been introduced Captain. Colonel Paul van Daan, 110th infantry."

The other man saluted. "Captain Richard Graham, sir. Just up from Lisbon, I've been…"

"Lord Wellington's new staff member. I know, he asked me to look out for you. I'd like to thank you for trying to do the right thing earlier, I only walked in at the end, but it was clear that both you and Sean here spoke up for the lass."

"I didn't really understand what was going on, sir. "

"Well you deserve an explanation at the least. Why don't you take Captain Graham over to the tavern, Sean, we've commandeered the back room and I've asked Lotta to get us something to eat."

"When did you arrive, sir?"

"About an hour ago."

"And when are you leaving?"

"As soon as I can. But I need feeding and I'd like to catch up. I just need a word here."

"Then we'll see you shortly," Devlin said and guided Graham firmly towards the door. Paul masked a grin and turned to survey the final three members of the court, his eyes coming to rest on Captain David Cartwright.

"I'm surprised at you, Cartwright," he said. "I wouldn't have thought you'd let how you feel about me cause you to send an innocent girl to be flogged. You ought to be ashamed."

He turned, ignoring the other members. As he reached the door, Cartwright said:

"I'd no reason to think she wasn't guilty, sir. We all know the rules don't apply to your regiment. Or its officers."

Paul turned and looked back at him. He wanted to respond, but he was aware of something avid in the other two judges, listening in. Studying Cartwright, he realised that the man did not look well.

"This isn't really the time or place for that conversation, is it, Captain?" he said quietly. "But think about it, will you? And Davy…?"

"Sir?"

"We really need some way of getting that German lad out of here, I don't think he's going to be up to either marching or riding. You're a quartermaster…"

"I can get you a cart if you can drive it yourselves."

"Carter can drive it, he's like a sack of potatoes on a horse anyway. I appreciate it, thank you."

He turned away but Cartwright's voice arrested him. "Sir?"

"What?"

"Is she all right?"

18

Paul turned back to study the other man. "Yes, fortunately. But if that German lad hadn't intervened, she could have been raped by two men. Our own men, Captain, not the French. That thought makes me feel a bit sick. And it ought to make you three feel sick too. Good afternoon."

Chapter Two

Captain Richard Graham emerged from the courtroom blinking in the bright sunlight. He had not eaten since early and the stuffy room had given him a banging headache. He looked around at Devlin. "If this is a friendly reunion I can go back to my billet."

"No, he's expecting you to join us," Devlin said. "Thank God that's over, and with no bloodshed. You all right?"

"I could do with a meal and a drink," Graham admitted. "What a bloody awful introduction to Portugal."

Devlin laughed. "You were unlucky, laddie. Normally these affairs aren't so exciting. Come and be properly introduced."

"I'm not sure I want to be," Graham said.

"Admit, you're curious."

Graham said nothing, although he was. His impression of Colonel van Daan had been of a towering personality with a temper, but he had nothing other than that to go on. He glanced at Devlin.

"What's the story, Captain?" he asked.

"I don't know yet, laddie, although I'm hoping to find out. I like a bit of gossip and Colonel van Daan is usually a good subject."

"Who is he and why the big fuss?"

Devlin grinned. "As he said, he commands the 110th. Haven't you heard of them?"

"No. Don't forget I've just spent three years in the Indies, which is the arsehole of the world, I've not heard of anybody. I don't think they've ever been posted out there. Infantry?"

"Yes. The first battalion is out here and Paul van Daan commands the regiment along with a couple of Portuguese battalions and the first battalion of the 112th. At the moment. Given how he's just distinguished himself in this campaign, look for further promotions. He's on his way up, laddie, and fast. They often fight as part of the Light Division, he's a perfectionist when it comes to training his men and he's got some very odd ideas about discipline and how to behave like an officer and a gentleman."

"Doesn't that get him into trouble?"

"Not as much as it ought to. He started out under Wellington in India and they're as thick as thieves, he's one of the few men Wellington will tolerate arguing with him. He is known in some quarters as Wellington's Mastiff. Hookey likes to keep him close at hand and often gives him the jobs nobody else wants. Which is not a reputation I'd enjoy, but it's certainly a quick route to promotion if you can stay alive."

"And that is why he is so confident that Wellington will support him over this business with the girl?"

"If Paul van Daan is throwing his weight around the provost marshal's department there's a reason. He's not especially dramatic. I'm hoping to find out the real story this afternoon." Devlin grinned. "He doesn't get on well with the provost marshal and there's always a rumpus when it's his turn to serve on the court as he either argues with the verdict or the sentence. He doesn't like flogging."

"Really? Christ, he wouldn't like the Indies then, it happens every five minutes. What's his objection?"

"You can ask him if you like, I did once. He simply said that it doesn't work, and he doesn't need it. And he's right about that, the arrogant bastard. His men are probably the best disciplined in the army. No idea how he does it."

"And what was that about Cartwright?"

"Aha! Now we come to the real scandals, laddie!" Devlin said with relish. "Both officers are married to rather beautiful wives. Second marriage for Paul van Daan. Years ago when he was in Naples with his first wife, he apparently engaged in an affair with Mrs Cartwright. He wasn't the only one, mind, she has a reputation, but that one was well talked of. Cartwright must hate his guts."

"And the second Mrs van Daan?"

"They married just over a year ago. Another impressive scandal. They seem to follow him around. His first wife died in childbirth. Shortly afterwards, Captain Robert Carlyon of the quartermasters' department, tried to murder his very lovely young wife in a jealous rage and was shot dead by one of Paul van Daan's officers."

"So Colonel van Daan was sleeping with another officer's wife again."

"We all assume so. But this one was different, he married her."

"Christ. How does he get away with it?"

"God knows. It helps to have friends in high places. Wellington attended the wedding and the girl travels with the regiment."

"What's she like?"

"I don't know her well. In fact I don't think I've seen her since they married. I remember her when she was Carlyon's wife though. Beautiful girl, very young, very flirtatious. Lord Wellington used to be all over her at every party. I danced with her a few times, and along with the rest of the army spent a fair bit of time imagining what it would be like to go to bed with her. She's that kind of woman. I don't envy Colonel van Daan, having her with him in the middle of a few thousand men, it can't be easy. You'll meet her at headquarters, like I said she's Wellington's favourite flirt."

Graham glanced sideways at his companion. "You seem friendly enough with him."

2

Devlin smiled. "I'm odd," he said. "I like a good gossip, but I think a man's personal life is his own business. And he's a bloody good soldier. I've fought beside him more than once and if I need a man to protect my flank in a tight situation, I want a man with a brain and courage and Paul van Daan has both. Besides, I like him. Come on, let's go and get a drink and find out what's been going on."

***

By the time Paul entered the back room of the small, dark tavern, Devlin and Graham were seated at the table with Paul's own officers. Paul looked around.

"Where are Carter and Teresa?" he asked.

Michael O'Reilly grinned. "Taking care of the German lad," he said. "Carter's been struck by an attack of gratitude. Either that or he's worried she'll run off with him. They'll eat in the kitchen."

Paul shot a glance at Graham and Devlin and managed not to laugh. He wondered if it had been Carter's own idea or if one of the other two had suggested it. On the journey down from Sabugal, Carter had eaten with the officers and Paul knew perfectly well if he had not brought guests, he would have found his new Sergeant-Major seated on the bench drinking ale with the others.

"Fair enough. Sean, how are you?

"Pissed off as ever, sir, and yourself?"

"More so than usual." Paul looked at Graham. "Welcome to Portugal, Captain, I'm sorry it's been a bit of a dramatic introduction. You've been in the Indies, I'm told."

Graham nodded. "Yes, for three years. I obtained this transfer after numerous applications."

Paul regarded him with considerable interest. "You look remarkably well for a man three years in the Indies."

"I seem to be immune to the local fever, sir."

"I have a suspicion my wife would like to talk to you. She thinks she is as well. She's spent several years working on fever wards without a sniff of an illness. She scares the hell out of me, but I've learned to live with it. I've not been to the Indies, but I suspect you'll find it very different here. Have we ordered food?"

"Mutton, sir," Lieutenant Leo Manson said. "There wasn't an extensive menu."

"If it's filling and tastes of something, it will do. Captain Graham, Lord Wellington asked me if I'd escort you up to the lines if you were here. I'm happy to, but I really want to get on the road this afternoon. I need to be back with my regiment, things are still very unsettled, and I promised Lord Wellington I'd be back as quickly as possible. I realise it's short notice…"

"I can be ready in an hour, sir, and I'm billeted just up the street. I'd like to join the staff as soon as possible."

"Good man. Once we've eaten you can go and pack and we'll get our invalid loaded up - I've borrowed a wagon from Captain Cartwright."

"I expect that was an enjoyable conversation," Michael O'Reilly said, and Paul smiled but said nothing. Michael was a former sergeant, awarded a

3

commission without purchase and had known Paul from the beginning of his army career. He was well aware of Paul's history with Cartwright's wife, but Paul did not wish to discuss it publicly.

"How is Teresa?" he asked.

"She's upset, but fine, I think, sir," Manson said. "Carter was getting the story out of her."

"Well once he's heard it, that'll be another reason to get out of here as soon as possible, I don't want my sergeant-major arrested for the murder of Sergeant Lowther and Private Collins. What a bloody mess. I'm going to talk to Lord Wellington about this. He needs to get the provost marshals' department better organised than this, it's like a circus."

"What happened, sir?" Graham said, accepting his drink. "I've only been here five minutes, but there was something off there."

"There really was, Captain. I wanted to thank you for your efforts. Both of you." Paul smiled at Devlin. "But Sean here knows me, knew what to expect. I'm impressed by your impartiality."

"Thank you, sir."

"Ask what you like." Paul said. "You've earned it."

"There were a lot of politics at work there, sir, and I was lost. And I am curious."

Paul grinned. "I like a man who cuts to the point. All right, Captain, although I'd be willing to bet you've already heard a version of this from Captain Devlin. I command the 110th and we're known for being a little unorthodox at times. We were heavily engaged chasing Massena out of Portugal and took some losses and some wounded. We left those here when we went back north to fight at Sabugal. As we were marching out to the battle our wounded arrived in camp, some of them in very poor shape, having been chased out of barracks by Major Courtney who is the acting provost marshal and his brainless deputies. During the course of this, my wife's maid who is also engaged to be married to my sergeant-major, became angry at the deputies' treatment of my wounded men and hit one of them with a jug. Teresa was arrested. When my men got up to the lines, Lord Wellington sent a message back at the request of my wife demanding Teresa's immediate release. It did not happen. After five days of worrying, I decided to come back to see what had happened. Lord Wellington is waiting for intelligence about Massena's next move so we've a short break and he was able to spare me. As a precaution I obtained a copy of Lord Wellington's original order from his military secretary. I've yet to find out what happened to the original, but his Lordship isn't going to be amused, he hates it when one of his orders isn't obeyed to the letter."

"Why was your wife's maid involved, sir?"

"She helps to nurse the wounded. My wife works with the surgeons. Some of them appreciate this, others don't. All I can say is they were lucky my wife wasn't there when they turned up, she'd have taken a scalpel to them. There are other issues here. The provost marshals don't like me much, I try not to get them involved with discipline except in very serious cases."

"Don't they have to be involved if you order a flogging, sir?"

"I don't flog my men, Captain."

4

Paul watched the other man's expression as he thought about it. He was impressed to see that the Scot actually was thinking about it. He was used to a dismissive sneer from officers of equal or senior rank and an attempt to conceal the sneer from more junior officers. Graham looked as though he was considering the matter.

"Do you find that works, sir?"

"It works for me, Captain. You'll be around headquarters, so you'll see a fair bit of my men. I'll leave it to you to judge."

Graham smiled. "It isn't my place to judge, sir."

"That doesn't stop the rest of the army, Captain, but I appreciate your ability to be open-minded. Major Nairn and I don't see eye to eye on this and Captain Crewe dislikes me because he feels I am unduly favoured by the commander-in-chief over longer serving and more respectable officers."

"And Captain Cartwright?"

Paul was sure that Devlin had gossiped. "Personal issues, Captain."

"Cartwright's got troubles of his own at the moment, sir," Devlin said.

Paul reached for the bottle and topped up their glasses. "I thought he didn't look well. What's the matter with him?"

"Have you not heard?" Devlin laughed. "I thought you had, when you asked after his wife in that tone of voice."

"No, I was just picking at him. I don't usually, but I heard what he said about Nan and you know how I am with her. What's the matter with Bella?"

"She's pregnant, sir."

Paul froze with his glass halfway to his lips and set it down on the table again. "Sean, are you telling me she's carrying a child that's not his?"

"Well given what she's like, he'd never have been sure. But there's no doubt in this case. She's been in Lisbon, and he's been up here with no leave granted. I don't know who the lucky man is, but it's not Cartwright."

"Oh shit!" Paul said, feelingly.

"What's the matter, sir?" Michael O'Reilly said, getting up to collect another bottle of wine. He poured for himself and Manson.

"I have just put my foot in it spectacularly with Captain Cartwright."

"Good, he had it coming. Teresa tells me he was all for having her flogged."

"He was. But I thought that was odd, he's normally a fairly gentle soul. If his wife is carrying a child that can't be his, I made a remark calculated to wind him up. If I'd known I'd have kept my mouth shut, he's entitled to a free shot at me. I was bloody angry, but all the same..."

"He's an experienced serving officer, sir, he's not a raw ensign," Manson said quietly. "He ought to have been able to stay professional on that court and see Teresa for what she is. In fact, he must have known she was Mrs van Daan's maid, he will have seen them around in Viseu."

"You can't guarantee that," Paul said with a grin. "The likelihood of my wife taking a respectable escort out and about with her is not that great. He's just as likely to have seen her hobnobbing with Jenson or Carter. I take your point, Leo, but I do feel sorry for him."

5

"Before you have me crying into my wine, you should think about what you're going to tell your wife about this," Lieutenant O'Reilly said shortly. "It's unfortunate timing, sir, because Davy Cartwright has been nowhere near Lisbon in the past year, but we know who has."

Paul stared at him in complete astonishment. "Mr O'Reilly, are you implying...?"

"Don't be daft, sir, no man married to your wife would go near Arabella Cartwright. But old gossip has a way of resurfacing, and you can guarantee somebody is going to make that connection. Best talk to Mrs van Daan about it before she hears it from someone else."

Paul drank his wine. The door opened to admit the proprietor's cheerful wife and her daughter, carrying heavy trays of food. The girl was heavily pregnant, and Paul got up and took the tray from her.

"Ines, what in God's name are you doing carrying that at your time? Lotta, where's that son-in-law of yours, he should be spoiling her at this point."

Carlotta shook her grey head. "He is gone, Señor. He joined the army."

"Oh lord. I'm sorry, lass. Where is he, do you know?"

Ines lifted tired dark eyes. "With General Pack's brigade, sir."

"Well at least he's with a commander who knows what he's doing. But I'm sorry, it must be difficult. Go and put your feet up, we can wait on ourselves."

When the women had gone, Paul sat to eat. The news about Arabella Cartwright had upset him more than he would have expected. His own impulsive and ill-judged affair with Cartwright's wife had been many years ago. He had been twenty-four, newly married and a father for the first time and he had left his wife, who had been very ill after the birth, in the care of her maid on the coast. Cartwright had been married for around the same amount of time and Arabella, a petulant but very beautiful redhead, had made no secret of her boredom with her husband and her attraction to Paul.

Six years later and happier in his second marriage than he could ever have imagined, Paul found it hard to forgive himself for that first stupid and insensitive infidelity. Rowena had known; army gossips would have made sure of it. He knew that Bella, angry when he broke off the affair, had been spiteful to his shy wife on many subsequent occasions. He was equally embarrassed about David Cartwright, a quiet man who seemed bewildered by his wife's frequent and far too public liaisons.

"Are you all right, sir?" Michael said quietly, and Paul glanced over at him and shook his head.

"I bloody hate army gossips, they make me feel I've got a permanent target painted on my back. Poor Cartwright, no wonder he looked so sick. I'd hate to be where he is right now."

"That's not likely, is it, sir?" Manson said.

"No. I'm luckier than I deserve. Captain Graham, I'm sorry, you must be wondering what the hell you've wandered into."

With the meal over, Paul went in search of his sergeant-major. He found him in the big square kitchen with Teresa and the young German. To his surprise, the younger man was sitting up on a bench, having clearly eaten, wearing Sergeant

6

Carter's spare shirt over an impressive collection of bandages. As Paul entered, Carter rose and saluted, and the German did the same.

"At ease, Private," Paul said. "Sit down before you fall down. What are you doing out of bed?"

"I do not like to be sick," Kuhn said. His English was very good, overlaid with the precise German intonation. "Colonel, I owe you thanks. You have all been very kind."

"Don't mention it. I owe you thanks for taking care of Teresa, she's very dear to us. Sit."

Kuhn obeyed, looking faintly surprised as Paul seated himself opposite on the bench. Carter poured a tankard of ale and pushed it towards Paul.

"When are we leaving, sir?"

"A couple of hours. Captain Graham needs to pack his bags and we need to collect this wagon from Captain Cartwright. Are all right to drive it?"

"Yes, sir. Prefer it to riding."

"I know. There's a reason you're in the infantry, Carter."

"I'll go over and see the Captain, sir. Be good to get away from here."

Paul looked at Teresa. They had collected her belongings from the convent where the 110th had been billeted and she had washed and changed and done her hair. She looked much calmer, but he was still conscious of what she had been through.

"Look, Teresa. This isn't going to be easy, I know, but we need to get a written statement from both you and Private Kuhn here. Mr Manson can act as scribe and Captains Graham and Devlin will witness them. Are you all right to do that?"

"I am," Teresa said firmly and met his eyes. "The next woman may not be so lucky. I do not want them to get away with this."

"They won't. I'll send Leo through to you, you'll be more comfortable doing this privately."

He returned to the dining room to find the officers involved in a discussion of Lord Wellington's probable plans. There was a familiarity about the scene which made Paul smile inwardly. During his years in the army he had heard this conversation many times. Paul glanced over at Graham who was listening quietly. Sensing Paul's eyes on him the Scot smiled.

"With your permission, sir, I'll be getting on. I need to pack."

"By all means, Captain. When this is done, we'll stop off briefly to let Courtney have the witness statements from Teresa and Private Kuhn and then get back to the lines as quickly as we can. Wellington is screaming about needing every man back with his regiment. He wants the French out of Almeida, which is why I need to get out of here."

"Did you have permission for this, sir?" Devlin asked with a grin.

"For once, I do, Sean. He's pretty lenient with me, but I think if I'd taken off just now without permission, he'd have shot me. Craufurd is still not back, although he's on his way, and he's shifting Erskine over to the fifth in the hope he'll do less damage. It wouldn't be the best time for one of my madder exploits."

"I'm surprised he let you go, sir."

"He did it for Nan. She's pregnant and she's more emotional than usual; she burst into tears in front of him one evening at the hospital." Paul gave a brief smile. "I'd love to know if she did it on purpose, she's quite capable of it. But she really wants Teresa back; she's been lying awake worrying about her."

"You're going to be a father again, sir?" Devlin said. "How many is that now?"

"My fourth. Nan's first. It should be due around September we think, but she's alarmingly casual about it."

"Are you sending her home?" Devlin asked, and the rest of the room erupted into laughter.

"Sir, you don't send Mrs van Daan places," O'Reilly explained. "You ask her very politely what she would like to do and then run around making that possible."

"You are all extremely rude about my wife," Paul said, still laughing. "Although it's true. No, Sean, we'll send the baby home to Southwinds. My sister-in-law is happily raising my brood which means they'll all be far better brought up than they would be if Nan or I had the rearing of them. I miss them. I barely got to see little Rowena and Nan has never met Grace or Francis, or my family if it comes to that. We lead a very strange life here. But although it's hard letting them go, this war won't last forever, and one day we'll be home with them. She wouldn't leave me, and I wouldn't want her to." He glanced at Graham. "Are you married, Captain?"

"Widowed. Almost four years now. We lost the baby at the same time."

"I'm sorry," Paul said simply. He could sense the pain behind the carefully rehearsed explanation. There was never an easy way to talk about a loss that great. "I lost my first wife that way, but the baby thrived surprisingly. I was with her, it's very hard."

"I was away in Alexandria. I didn't find out about it until I got home, I was a prisoner and they'd destroyed any letters. It was a shock."

"I can't imagine what that must feel like," Paul said quietly. "What was her name?"

"Sarah. I always called her Sally. She was staying with her parents while I was in Africa. She'd apparently had news that I was missing, they suspected it brought the birth on too soon. It's been a long time but I still miss her."

"Of course you do," Paul said gently. "I've been unbelievably lucky to have Nan. She was Rowena's friend and grieved with me. But there are still moments when it hits me."

Devlin drained his glass. "I should be riding back, sir."

"Sean, it's been good to see you. Will you wait a few minutes, I need to get these witness statements taken and written up and I'd like you to witness them. Leo, would you?"

"I'll go and find some writing materials, sir."

"If they've none here, go over to Courtney and tell him what you require. I'm reasonably sure he won't argue with you." Paul watched as Graham left to collect his possessions and turned to Devlin. "I forgot to ask, what the devil are you doing here anyway, Sean? I thought your lot were in Cadiz."

8

"We were, we sailed into Oporto a few weeks ago. Most of them have marched on to join Lord Wellington, I was recovering from an injury, couldn't ride but I should be fit in about a month. Do you think we'll be in action soon?"

"Yes. Almeida is important, it's Massena's last stronghold in Portugal. His career is in the balance after what we've done to him this last year, this'll be his last chance to impress Bonaparte. And Wellington wants to be able to tell London that the French are out of Portugal so that he can argue the case for more money and more men to chase them into Spain."

"I'm looking forward to it, sir." Devlin was looking out of the window. "It looks as though your sergeant has managed to get the wagon."

"I thought he would, Cartwright is feeling guilty about Teresa. I really wish I'd known about Bella, I wonder if I should speak to him?"

"I don't think so, sir," Michael said. "What in God's name could you say anyway?"

Paul nodded silently. He did not think his own brief affair with Arabella Cartwright had been the cause of the subsequent disaster of Captain Cartwright's marriage. During the past few years, rumour had linked her name with a number of men and Paul was surprised that she had not been caught out before. He was bitterly ashamed of his own infidelities during his first marriage. Rowena's gentle forbearance had made it too easy for him and he had been very young when they married but it was no excuse, and he regretted each one. He had learned his lesson, rather late to benefit Rowena, but it appeared that Arabella had not. Paul felt deeply sorry for David Cartwright who would have to run the gauntlet of army gossips.

It was mid-afternoon by the time the small convoy was ready to leave. Paul delivered the signed witness statements to Major Courtney in silence. The major was fully dressed and looked extremely uncomfortable. He took the statements with muttered thanks.

"Are they in gaol?" Paul enquired.

"Yes, sir. It will have to wait for the next court now and I have no idea about witnesses…"

"If necessary, they'll have to be brought up to the lines for trial so that Teresa and Private Kuhn can testify. Make very sure your investigation is thorough, Major, I want the men who witnessed this in the prison block identified and interviewed. I will be following up on this and Lord Wellington will be kept informed."

"Yes. Yes, of course. I will."

"Dismissed."

Riding out of the village, Paul was aware of Michael coming up beside him. "That was very impressive, sir. I don't think you punched anybody from start to finish. Carl will never believe it."

"Very amusing, Mr O'Reilly. I could always make you the first."

The Irishman grinned. "Cheer up, sir, you'll be back with the battalion before you know it."

"I'll be back with my wife before I know it. The battalion doesn't compare." Paul touched his heel to Rufus' side. "Let's speed up a bit. I want to get back."

Chapter Three

After weeks of almost constant daily skirmishing, the men of Paul's battalions were glad of the respite of a week in camp with enough food and no need to be constantly on the alert. Even the early bugle was blown later. Wellington was frantically collecting intelligence about Massena's troop movements and plans, his doctors were treating the wounded and assessing who was fit for duty and who would need to be sent back to Lisbon or Oporto for transport home to England, and his engineers were drawing sketches of the defences of Almeida and talking of ways of taking the city with minimal bloodshed.

Captain Carl Swanson, commander of the 110th light company awoke habitually in time for dawn. With no need to break camp, no prospect of a battle and no early drill, he lay quietly in the grey half-light and listened to the even breathing of the girl beside him.

Turning his head Carl studied her. Her hair, which was a rich very dark brown with hints of red, lay spread across the pillow in a riot of natural curls and long dark lashes lay on a flushed cheek. Her mouth seemed to be curved in a half smile as though her dreams were pleasant. She looked very young and very lovely and Carl marvelled at how quickly he had become used to her being there.

He was thirty and had joined the regiment along with Paul van Daan, his boyhood friend, in time to go to India in 1802. The only son of an impoverished parson whose living was in the gift of the very wealthy Van Daan family, Carl had always known that he would need to earn a living, and when Paul had announced his intention of joining the army it had seemed as good a way as any of supporting himself. He had not realised how much he would come to love it or how good at it he would turn out to be. With no money to purchase a promotion he had reached Captain on merit. He had made friends and seen more of the world than he had ever dreamed he would. But the financial limitations of his profession had made marriage and children impossible.

It had not really troubled Carl. He had watched his childhood friend negotiate two marriages and he knew it had not been easy, especially for Paul's first wife who had been gentle and shy and found army life difficult at times. Independently wealthy, Paul had no need to rely on his army pay to support his wife and the lifestyle within the 110th was not extravagant. Under the advice of Paul's elder brother who ran the family business, Carl had invested his prize money instead of spending it on cards and women and had the satisfaction of seeing it grow significantly. With careful management he might well be able to purchase a Major's commission in a few years, and marriage might not be impossible should he find a woman who was willing to share his wandering lifestyle. In the meantime, he had taken the soldier's usual recourse of bought pleasures and the occasional enjoyable night with a girl in a tavern, anonymous and fleeting. And then, quite unexpectedly, he had met Keren Trenlow.

He had first noticed her marching out of Viseu with the army wives, had appreciated her beauty and had wondered at her choice of the sullen Simpson of the third company but beyond that he had thought nothing of her until Carter had intervened one night to stop her being beaten by her lover and she had been taken under the protection of Anne van Daan. Like many of the women she earned her keep by doing laundry and mending and had taken over some of Teresa's duties with Anne. It threw her more and more into Carl's company and he had watched for several months with amused appreciation as the timid eighteen-year-old grew into her new independence with a confidence nobody could have expected.

The illiterate daughter of a Cornish tin miner, Keren was learning to read and write under Anne's tuition. Wearing cast-off gowns from both Anne and Teresa she had revealed a winsome prettiness which more than one of the officers of the 110th had begun to appreciate. Carl had wondered for a time if she would give in to the determined pursuit of Michael O'Reilly and had hoped that she would not, although he had not been willing to look too closely at his reasons. And then on the day he had returned, battered and exhausted after Sabugal, she had walked into his arms and into his bed as naturally as if they had planned it for months.

It had been only a few weeks and although Carl had tried to be discreet for her sake he knew that many of his fellow officers and some of the men were becoming aware that she was sharing his bed. He had been on his own for so many years that the sense of waking up to find her curled up beside him was a delightful novelty and he reached for her now, enjoying the little murmur of welcoming pleasure she made.

"Morning sleepy," he said softly, leaning over to kiss her.

Keren stretched, reminding him of a cat. "Heavens, is it late? I should be up, I can hear people stirring."

Carl nuzzled her neck. "I don't care. My Colonel will be back in a day or two I imagine, and Wellington will have worked out what he wants to do next and then a lie in bed with you in the morning is going to be something I dream about when I'm dodging musket balls and cannon fire. Which means it is your duty, lass, to stop fussing about getting up and kiss me properly."

Keren laughed and snuggled closer. "Do you truly not mind people knowing, Carl? Because a lot of them do."

"Well I'm not looking forward to Michael O'Reilly working it out, he's going to be as jealous as hell. Other than that, I really don't give a damn. But I

11

don't want you to feel awkward, Keren." Carl kissed her again. "Does Mrs van Daan know?"

"If she does, she's said nothing. I don't know what to say to her. Do you think she will be angry?"

"Not with you, lass. She might well think I've taken advantage of you." Carl regarded her with a rueful smile. "Sometimes I wonder if she might be right."

"I think most other people would think I'm hoping to take advantage of you," Keren said, and Carl heard the edge of bitterness in her voice. He reached up and brushed the dark hair back from her face.

"Lass, I can't control what people say. I only know what I feel. You're not a prostitute, you're a girl I share a bed with because we both want to, but I know it bothers you."

"Carl, it shouldn't." She kissed him gently. "My Methodist upbringing, I suppose. When I ran off with Jimmy Trenwith I was so young, but I thought we'd be wed. And we might have been if he'd not sickened and died."

"How old were you?"

"I was sixteen when I left with him. Seventeen when he died. I was so frightened. Simpson was in the hospital. He offered to take care of me. I didn't know what else to do. Although I knew he didn't intend to marry me. He just wanted..." She broke off and he pulled her closer.

"I know, lass. How long were you with him?"

"Six months. It felt longer. I spent all my time wondering how I could get away from him. I was frightened to tell anybody. I wasn't officially on strength, just a camp follower, and he told me if the officers realised, I'd be thrown out of camp. And where could I go then apart from to the brothel?"

"No wonder you were scared. I wish I'd known, Keren, I'd have dealt with the bastard. Bloody Gerry Edmonds ought to have been aware of it, somebody must have seen it going on. Why didn't the NCOs tell him?"

"They probably felt it wasn't their business. I was shocked that evening when Corporal Carter intervened."

Carl grinned, remembering Carter's fury when he had heard Keren crying and found her drunken lover beating her. "Simpson doesn't know how lucky he was to come out of that evening alive. What's that? Do I hear the sounds of arrival?"

He slid from the bed and went to look, hearing Keren scrambling quickly into her clothes behind him. The sounds from down the lines confirmed his suspicions.

"It looks like the Colonel is back. With Teresa, thank God. I didn't think he'd manage it this quickly, he must have marched since dawn every morning." Carl moved to find a clean shirt and Keren passed one to him while combing out her long hair with the other hand. He dressed, watching her flying about the tent collecting his laundry and several items for mending. When she was ready, he stepped outside the tent and looked down the lines. A group of officers and men had crowded around the new arrivals and he was curious about the small cart they had brought with them. Beside him Keren emerged with her laundry basket. He looked down at her then took the basket from her hands setting it down. Pulling her closer he kissed her, enjoying the sense of her body against his.

12

"See you later, lass," he said, and she smiled and picked up the basket, making her way back up to the tent which she ostensibly shared with Teresa Cortez. Carl watched her go for a moment and then turned at the sound of a soft laugh.

"Captain Swanson, it's very clear you've been making the most of your opportunities," Michael O'Reilly said. "And how long has that been going on?"

"None of your business, Michael. That was a short trip. How's Teresa, did you get there in time?"

"Only just. She was up before the court, just been sentenced to thirty of the best."

Carl lifted his eyebrows. "They were brave, who was on the bench?"

"Major Nairn from the guards, Lieutenant Crewe and Davy bloody Cartwright. Sean Devlin was there and this new lad, on his way to join Wellington's staff. He put up a good fight for her I believe, but the majority went against her. She's not had a good time, it's a bit of a story."

"Tell me over breakfast."

"Breakfast should have been over an hour ago, Captain, you've been having a nice relaxing time while he's been away, haven't you? Not that I can blame you, it's bloody obvious why you're not out of bed early. I am curious, is she as good as she looks? Because…"

"That's enough, Lieutenant!" Carl snapped and then stopped himself and sighed. "Look, Michael. I really don't want to get pissed off with you about this, but I am not going to sit and discuss my love life with you over breakfast. It's none of your damned business."

"I told you, I don't blame you sir, she's a very nice armful. Just let me know when you get tired of her, or the money runs out."

Carl felt a spurt of anger. "She's not a camp follower, Michael!"

The Irishman lifted amused eyebrows. "Carl - she is a camp follower. Very definitely. She's lovely, I've had my eye on her for months and I wish you well, but make the most of it because I'm telling you if some cavalry officer with a title and a full purse makes her a better offer, she'll be off with him. And she should."

Carl was surprised at how angry he was. "Michael, I don't want to keep having this conversation, so can you listen really clearly? She's not a whore, I'm not paying her and she's not available. We're together because it's what we both want. Beyond that, I'm not discussing her with you."

His friend studied him. "Jesus, you're touchy. I understand and I'll keep my hands to myself, she's your property. For now, at least. But a few weeks ago they were laying bets in the mess about who she'd end up in bed with. I'm not sure all the officers are going to be quite so understanding about how sensitive you are. Does Mrs van Daan know?"

Carl stared at him. "How the hell would I know, it's hardly a conversation I'm likely to have with her is it?"

"Oh I've a feeling when she knows you're sleeping with her maid she might have a word or two to say about it, Captain."

"Well why don't you tell her, then, Michael?" Carl walked away not wanting to continue the discussion. His lieutenant had been trying to persuade Keren into his bed for several months without success and Carl had known Michael would be irritated when he found out that she had chosen instead to be with Carl. He hoped that the Irishman would calm down and realise how childish he was being.

His Colonel was talking to Major Wheeler, but he looked up and smiled as Carl approached. "Lazy bastards," he said amiably. "Still, the advantage is I've not missed breakfast."

"We've making the most of the rest," Carl said with a grin. "Is Teresa all right?"

"She will be. She's just gone down to see Nan."

"Before you do?"

"Her need is greater than mine just now," Paul said quietly and Carl did not ask, knowing he would find out in time. He looked at the wagon.

"What's this?"

"We stole it from Davy Cartwright. There's a young lad from the KGL, flogged and a bit of a beating for defending Teresa. I wasn't going to leave him in the hands of the bloody provost, I've never trusted them and after this I wouldn't leave a sick cat in their care. I'm just going to see Nan and then I'm riding up to speak to Wellington, I'll give him my report and I can take Captain Graham with me. Oh, Carl, let me introduce you to Richard Graham, new to Wellington's staff. He's just had the delightful experience of sitting on a court martial jury. I'd like him on my next general court martial board, but after the last one they keep missing my name off."

"Only because you've bribed them, Colonel. Welcome, Captain. Have you had an exciting introduction to Portugal?"

"More than I expected. I'll wait here for you, sir, you'll want to go and see your wife."

"No need," Carl said with a grin, as his commander's wife erupted from their tent and sped along the lines to greet him. He watched Graham's face, enjoying the look of complete astonishment.

Anne van Daan was wearing a loose dark green velvet robe over a white petticoat, attire which would have been suitable for morning wear in a lady's boudoir but which very few women would have worn in an army camp. Her straight black hair was loose about her shoulders and she wore no shawl or pelisse. She reached Paul and he bent to kiss her, catching her close to him and swinging her off her feet.

"Good morning, girl of my heart, have you missed me?"

"Very much. You're back sooner than I expected. But thank God you went. Teresa and Danny have just been telling me the story. When I get hold of that imbecile Craddock, I am going to carve out his liver."

"An admirable intention, love, although you've probably just shocked our guest senseless. Is it too much to request that you manage to dress yourself before inviting my Sergeant-Major into your tent?"

"Don't be silly, Paul. I was perfectly respectable."

"You know that means something different to the rest of polite society don't you? Let me introduce you to Captain Richard Graham, lass, new to Lord Wellington's staff. I'm just about to take him up and give Wellington my report."

14

"Yes, best to get it in before Major Courtney's letter arrives," Anne said sagely. "How do you do, Captain? You must have had a truly shocking introduction to Portugal, but I assure you it is not always this bad."

Her husband laughed. "It is if you're involved, Nan. I think this time Major Courtney might keep quiet about this one. And I didn't hit him."

"What did you threaten to do to him?" Anne asked.

"I don't recall."

"Never mind, Jenson will tell me."

"Or somebody will. You've a better spy network than bloody Bonaparte."

"Almost everybody has a better spy network than Bonaparte," his wife said, and Paul grinned.

"It's good to know we're ahead on something. I'll be back for breakfast. I was hoping it would be ready for me."

"Paul, all normal people in this army are having a rest after the past few months. You are the only one up before dawn to march when you don't need to be."

"I wanted to get back fast, I'm worried about the German lad. He's got a fever, although he won't lie down or stay still. I swear to God, he's got to be the most stubborn..."

"I'll get my bag and go to him now, he won't argue with me for long," Anne said, reaching up to kiss him.

"Well do me a favour and get dressed first. Or at least fasten that garment properly, you'll give the poor boy a heart attack."

His wife grinned and reached for the laces at the front of her petticoat. She took her time about tying them properly and Paul tried not to laugh aloud at Richard Graham's expression as he forced his eyes away from her. "Another husband would beat you, Nan," he said, shaking his head.

"Another husband did," his wife said serenely, and Paul winced as he realised what he had just said.

"Love, I'm sorry. I didn't mean..."

"It's all right," Anne said, laughing. "The fact that we can joke about it now is probably a good sign. Go and see Lord Wellington. And if you happen to see George Scovell up there, ask him if he'll chase up my medical supplies. I've been nagging for weeks, but I trust him to do it properly."

"Is that even his job now?" Paul asked.

"I've no idea, he has so many jobs; he's as bad as you are. But even if he's not, he'll do it for me."

"Don't they all?"

His wife frowned severely. "George is very happily married as you well know, and Mary is a friend of mine."

"Which gives her individual distinction among the officers' wives in this army. I will do as you ask, girl of my heart, and add to poor George's many burdens. We should invite them down to dinner one evening, I've not seen him properly for ages and he hates dining in the headquarters mess, he'd much rather sit around drinking looted wine with my light company. Come on, Captain, let's get you introduced. If he lets you go, you can come back down to breakfast with us. Lord Wellington often forgets to eat."

"I'll ride up with you," Carl said. "Catch up on the gossip."

Paul lifted his eyebrows but agreed. It was a short ride up to the commander's tents and Paul introduced Graham and made a succinct report on the events in Pero Negro. When he had finished, Wellington studied him with hooded blue eyes.

"Is the girl all right?" he asked.

"She is, thanks to the German lad, but it might have been a lot worse. He's been thoroughly beaten. I believe the rest of his regiment is joining the seventh, but with your permission, sir, I'll keep him with us on light duties for a while. I'll find out the name of his commander and write to him." Paul stood up. "I don't know if you'll hear anything more from the provost marshal about this..."

"I had better not," Wellington said grimly. "We have all been put to a great deal of trouble over this nonsense and I don't want to hear any more of it. Captain Graham, thank you for your assistance with this. You must think us all mad."

"No, my Lord, it's been educational," Graham said.

"I am glad you take it that way. Colonel, I am meeting with the Portuguese this morning, and I'd like to introduce the captain to his colleagues and his duties, but I want longer with you to talk over some proposed changes to the Light Division. Will you come up tomorrow afternoon?"

"I will, sir. I'll leave Captain Graham with you. Is George Scovell about? Nan has a request about medical supplies."

"Major Scovell has his head buried in a code book and will make no sense at present. I'll put Murray onto chasing it for her, he'll see it as a personal quest. Is she well?"

"She is. Better now she has Teresa back. Thank you, sir, you've been very generous with my time over this, I appreciate it."

Wellington gave a small smile. "Perhaps it will make up for the many occasions when I have not been," he said. "I'll see you tomorrow."

Paul joined Carl outside and mounted up. "Poor Graham. Breakfast isn't looking likely for him, Hookey has that look on his face. I should have fed him first. I hope he gets a good dinner."

They rode back down the lines and Paul glanced at his friend. "Do we need to take a detour?"

"Yes. Let's go down to the river and ride along. It's nothing serious, don't worry."

They ambled down the grassy track alongside the river and Paul described the events of the past week. Eventually he said:

"What's bothering you, Carl?"

"Michael and I had a bit of a discussion this morning. It's not really anything to do with you, but I've just got a feeling he might try to make something of it, so I'd rather you knew in advance."

"What about?"

"Keren Trenlow."

Paul eyed him. "Well, I know very well that Michael has been trying fairly hard to get her into his bed for a few months. He tried the same with Teresa, it's something of a habit but it's not one I can really take issue with, I used to be just as bad."

"You used to be worse."

"Probably. Is he annoying her? I know you spoke to him straight after Sabugal, I was hoping he'd settled down."

"It's a bit more complicated than that, Paul."

Paul studied him and enlightenment dawned. "Oh."

"Yes."

"It's good to know I can still be surprised, Carl. When did this start?"

"After the battle."

"I didn't see that coming. And yet thinking about it, I ought to have, she was all over you when you were wounded, Nan was laughing about it. I suppose I thought..."

"You thought I'd know better," Carl said, and his friend laughed.

"Christ, Carl, I'm not one to judge when it comes to a pretty girl. It is unlike you, mind." Paul studied his friend. "I'm assuming that the reason you're telling me this is because it's more than a convenient tumble."

"I didn't plan this, sir. And I'm a bit ashamed of myself, to be honest."

"Why?"

"Because she's very young and vulnerable and I'm worried I've put her in a difficult position."

Paul could not help smiling. "I've often thought that you somehow got all the scruples I lacked. Carl, she is already in a difficult position, she's alone in an army camp. Honestly, if it hadn't been for Nan her only option would have been to find a husband or a new lover."

"She did. That's how she ended up being beaten bloody by Simpson. But since she left him she's been on her own. I rather respect that and I was determined not to make her life harder."

"Carl, the girl has been making eyes at you for months. I've admired your restraint to be honest. But I admit she has been choosy, she's not let anyone else near her as far as I know. What changed your mind?"

Carl pulled a face. "They were running a book in the officers mess on who'd be the first to get her into bed. I believe Michael was the runaway favourite."

"Charming. Nobody offered me odds."

Carl grinned. "I'd guessed that, or someone would have had a split lip. They're young idiots, most of them, and the army isn't full of unattached girls as pretty as Keren. But it made me bloody furious. She had an awful time with that bastard Simpson. But Michael and some of the others see her as a prostitute and they'd treat her as such. And she isn't."

"Carl, you don't even treat prostitutes like prostitutes."

"Well I learned that from you." Carl shrugged. "Just before the battle she told me something about how they were treating her. Michael and some of the others."

"I wish she'd spoken to me. Or Nan."

"She didn't want a fuss made. She feels very fortunate to have been offered the chance to work for your wife and she's become very attached to her. I don't think she wanted to jeopardise her job."

"The only thing in jeopardy would have been your Lieutenant's balls, Carl, but I suppose Keren doesn't know my wife that well yet."

"No. Anyway, she told me. I was shocked at how pissed off I was. I knew how attractive I found her. I suppose it suddenly occurred to me that sooner or later somebody was going to talk her round, she's a long way from home and she's lonely. And I didn't want to see her passed around the officers' mess like some trophy until they get bored, and she has to settle for another Simpson. I wanted her to be with me."

"You soft bastard, Swanson, you've got attached to her haven't you?"

"It's not hard."

"No, she's a nice lass. Thank you for telling me, I'll make sure Nan knows. She might already, she doesn't miss much. I imagine Michael is furious. He lost out with Teresa to Carter, but he can hardly make himself awkward over that, they're getting married. You, on the other hand, are fair game."

"I don't give a damn what he says to me, but I don't want her embarrassed. She's less sure of herself than you'd think. She hates the idea of people assuming she's sharing my bed because I pay her and that's the tack he's taking. He's already making jokes about taking over when I've finished with her."

"Jesus, I've taught him nothing over the years. Do you want me to have a word with him?"

"No. If he upsets her, I'll deal with him. I've just got a feeling he might say something to your wife, and I don't want it landed on her without warning."

Paul laughed. "If he says anything to Nan he's likely to regret it," he said. "She knows Michael very well. Carl if this were anybody else I'd be making a speech about how fond she is of Keren and that she wouldn't want her hurt. But I've known you since we were children, and I don't think there is any chance in the world that you'll hurt that girl. I think she's better off under your protection than she would be with another brute like Simpson or being Michael O'Reilly's latest five-minute wonder. I'll let Nan know. If he gives her any trouble, let me know and I'll kick him, it might be easier if I do it." He eyed his friend thoughtfully. "You're keeping it very quiet, but you might want to rethink that. If they see you with your arm around her in public a few times they'll back off and shut up, you're the captain of my light company, they are not going to move in on your girl. I don't know how she feels about it but talk to her."

"I will. Thank you, sir. By the way, we had a visit from Longford yesterday."

Paul pulled an expressive face. Captain Vincent Longford who had previously commanded his seventh company, was currently on detached duties as ADC to General Sir William Erskine, an officer whom Paul considered completely incapable of commanding anything. He and Longford had disliked each other since they had both been captains in barracks eight years earlier. His own career had taken off spectacularly since then and Longford had remained angry and resentful. He seemed glad of his post with Erskine and Paul had no desire to see him rejoin the regiment.

18

"I am sorry I missed that. Is he asking to come back?"

"No," Carl said with a laugh. "He's moving out with Erskine towards Almeida, wants to know if Nan will take care of Caroline for him, there are no wives up there."

"Ah. I'm assuming Nan said yes."

"She did, she'll be joining us tomorrow."

"Good. Although that is one love affair that I really do not want to know any more about."

Paul saw his friend's expression and grinned. He had realised some time ago that Major Johnny Wheeler, his second-in-command was engaged in an affair with the pretty fair-haired wife of Captain Longford, and he had been rather enjoying watching Carl trying to keep the secret.

"I wasn't sure if you knew."

"I knew."

"Paul – back at the convent my room was next to Longford's. Which was not always a good experience, believe me. Once he had his new posting, he didn't even bother to write to her, but he'd turn up once a week or so when he was feeling the urge, haul her off to bed for a few hours and ride out again without even bothering to stay to dine with her."

"Oh Jesus, Carl..."

"Like I said, my room was next to theirs and the walls aren't that thick. I would not share this information with anybody other than you, but he uses that woman like a prostitute, he makes her do things she doesn't want to do and sometimes she's been crying so much in there that I've had to get myself out until it's over or I'll go in there and cut his bloody balls off. So if Caroline Longford is getting some comfort from our Major I'd say she'd earned it."

"Does he hit her?"

"No. If it had got that bad I'd have kicked his door down and you know it. But she's clearly very unhappy with him and he makes no effort to be even civil to her, let alone kind. She was always going to be vulnerable to a man who knows how to behave, and Johnny's got it bad. You must have seen how he looks at her."

"Of course I have. Johnny knows that I understand. But I can't know officially. It's different with you and Keren, you're both single and you're both adults and although in some regiments the commander would make a fuss about an officer keeping his mistress in camp, I don't give a damn as long as it doesn't affect your duty. But if Longford comes to complain to me about Johnny, I'm supposed to take notice."

"He wouldn't dare, Paul."

"I hope so, although Longford is always more stupid than one would imagine possible. It's a shame he's unlikely to be close enough to the action to get his idiotic head blown off."

"You don't mean that, Paul."

Paul shot him a look and then grinned. "I'd like to think I don't mean that. But I've never seen Johnny fall in love before and you need to trust me I am feeling his pain through this. I've been there. Come on, let's get back, I'm starving."

19

Paul had no opportunity to speak to his wife alone until they were settled in bed that night. He lay holding her close, thinking how much he missed her even after a brief separation.

"What is it, Colonel?"

"I had an interesting conversation with Captain Swanson today, girl of my heart."

There was a brief pause. "Did you?" Anne said sweetly. "And is he shaking in his shoes yet?"

Paul broke into laughter. "You knew."

"Of course I knew, is that man an idiot? She is my maid. It has been very entertaining watching her scuttle into her own tent at dawn so that she can saunter out again ten minutes later, but I'm glad we can put an end to it, she must be exhausted."

"He's worried about upsetting you, bonny lass."

"Did he say that? I'm curious as to whether it is you or Captain Swanson who is confused about the difference between upset and angry."

Paul was silent. After a moment, he felt her snuggle in closer to him and he knew that he had done the right thing by not jumping in to defend his friend. "You're all right, Colonel, I'm not angry with you. And I'm not all that angry with Carl, although I will be when it ends, and I have to mop up the remains. Still, I'd rather it was him than Michael."

"For what it's worth, Nan, I don't think Carl intended this. She's been very…"

"She's been falling in love with him before my eyes, Paul. That's why I'm angry, because she's going to get hurt. But I don't really blame, Carl, she must have been hard to resist. Is he about to yield to his high church conscience and end it?"

"I don't think he has any intention of doing anything of the kind," Paul said honestly. "He seems…I think he's very happy at present, Nan."

Anne regarded him in some surprise. "Is he? Well good, then. She clearly is. Perhaps after all we should simply mind our own business and leave them alone."

"I agree. It's not really any of our business, but it appears Michael is being an arse about it, so he wanted us to know."

"Well if Michael mentions it to me I shall slap him, it's none of his damned business and he's been annoying Keren for months." Anne kissed him lightly on his shoulder. "I shall forgive Captain Swanson if he is charming to her. She's very sweet and she deserves it."

Paul laughed aloud, thinking how appalled some of the other ladies of headquarters would be at his wife's attitude. "I think you're right. I thought she might find a husband in the regiment to be honest and I'm sure that one or two of the lads would have obliged. But a few months with you have given Keren a different outlook on life."

"I have that effect," Anne said serenely.

"You actually do. You completely changed my outlook on life."

"Once I'm in your bed, Colonel, your outlook seems fairly consistent," Anne said with a gurgle of laughter. Paul rolled over and kissed her.

20

"You can bloody talk," he said. "Can you tell me, by the way, why we are lying here talking about Carl Swanson's love life?"

"God knows, you started it." Anne shot him a mischievous glance. "I was beginning to think you were losing interest. Whose love life would you rather discuss?"

"I wasn't planning on having a conversation about it, lass," Paul said with a grin. "Why don't you tell me in half an hour if you think I'm losing interest?"

His wife was laughing and Paul leaned over and stopped her mouth with his.

***

Paul found Lord Wellington alone the following afternoon writing letters. He looked up as Paul entered and saluted and waved him to a chair.

"Sit down, Colonel."

"Thank you, sir."

The blue eyes rested on Paul thoughtfully. "Colonel, we talked before Sabugal about a new command for you."

"Yes, sir."

"I've been corresponding with General Craufurd who is on his way back. I intend to establish a third brigade of the Light Division with you in command. It will consist of your current command, with the exception of your guards' company, which I'll detach and send over to the first division. You'll have the first battalion of the 110th and the first battalion of the 112th plus your Portuguese – I'm giving you four more companies of caçadores, which will make up the 14th battalion. In addition I'm giving you half a battalion of the Kings German Legion. I believe your young German casualty is from one of the companies."

"Thank you, sir."

"We are in desperate need of more trained light infantry, and what we all know about you, Colonel, is that is what we will get. Furious but well trained. There will also be two companies of rifles led by Captain Tregallas. They've been at Cadiz and are marching north, they will be with us in a week or so."

"Yes, sir."

"We have already discussed the ongoing problem of the 112th infantry. They have enough officers now, I believe, but Horse Guards do not seem to have been inundated with requests to command them, so I have followed your recommendation. This is their reply."

"Johnny Wheeler?" Paul asked, trying not to sound anxious.

"Yes. He is promoted to lieutenant-colonel, without purchase as the rank is vacant."

"Thank you, sir. I'm going to promote Carl Swanson to Johnny's majority. We'll work something out about the purchase price. There's a majority vacant in the 112th and none of the officers have the required length of service, so…"

"Ha! As if you ever cared about that."

Paul gave him a look. "So I'm going to suggest to Johnny that he speaks to Gervase Clevedon, he's our most senior captain now."

"An excellent idea. Clevedon is a very good officer."

21

Paul grinned. Clevedon was the younger son of an Earl. Wellington's invariable preference for promoting men of his own social standing was well known, but he hated having it pointed out to him so Paul refrained with an effort.

"He is, sir."

"Who is next in line for Swanson's captaincy?"

Paul hesitated and Wellington noticed and pounced eagerly. "You're going to try to give it to O'Reilly aren't you?"

"As a matter of fact, no," Paul said, and enjoyed his chief's look of surprise. "Though I'm going to suggest to Johnny that he offer one of the companies in the 112th to Michael, even if it's a brevet promotion to start with."

"I knew it."

"No you didn't, I just told you. You've repeatedly told me not to come to you about promotions, sir, as they're a matter for the colonel-in-chief and Horse Guards. Though I notice you don't mind endorsing them when it's somebody you like, or any officer with a title. Just the same…"

"That is not true, Colonel van Daan and you are the living proof of it," Wellington said smoothly and Paul laughed out loud.

" Touché, sir, that was definitely a hit. I don't know anything about the colonel-in-chief of the 112th, but Johnny will find a way to get around him, he doesn't need me to interfere. I'm going to offer Carl's captaincy to Lieutenant Manson."

"Your protégé? He's very young, Colonel."

"He's a couple of months younger than I was when I took over the light company."

"Can he afford it?"

"That's between him and me, sir."

"Won't it cause resentment among some of the others?"

"I don't think so. We've still a number of vacancies in the 112th, nobody needs to lose out. The 112th doesn't have a light company, although I've never known why. They probably lost them in the Indies somewhere. I think Johnny should create one and Michael can command it. The rest of the promotions are fairly obvious, they'll be by seniority and purchase, I'm fairly sure they can all afford it. I'm going to move Giles Fenwick over to the 112th with a captaincy. He should have been promoted years ago but Longford had it in for him and blocked it. Have you met Fenwick, sir?"

"If I have, I don't remember him."

"Tall, fair. Nan says he could be related to me and I'm not sure she just means his appearance. I'd not met him until he came out with the seventh. He's seen action in Europe and he's bloody good under fire, no nerves at all that I can see. He's a sarcastic bastard, a junior sprig of the nobility. I think he said he's cousin or nephew or such to the Earl of Rockcliffe."

"What on earth is he doing in the 110th then?"

Paul laughed aloud. "Don't be so rude about my regiment. I'm told the price of commissions is going up all the time."

"The price of commissions is irrelevant in your case, Colonel, since you are so appallingly difficult about which officers you will take on. Why did you ask about Fenwick?"

"I can't believe I'm doing this because he's a really good officer and I like him. He has no money for an expensive regiment, his father was a younger son. But sir - he speaks Spanish better than my wife."

Wellington froze and looked at him. "Really?"

"Yes. I found out quite by accident at a reception in Lisbon. Apparently, he had a Spanish nurse as a child, she taught him, and he's kept it going."

"Intelligent?"

"Very, I'd say. He's a bit full of himself, but I can hardly criticise him for that and it might help for what you have in mind. I'm going to promote him and give him his company because he's earned it and we need good officers. But I know you're always looking…"

"I am. We'll wait until after this next action, but I'd like him to meet George Scovell."

"I'm going to invite George and Mary to dinner anyway, I'll make sure they're introduced."

"Thank you." Wellington gave a little smile. "And if I poach one of your good officers to join my Corps of Guides, Colonel, what do you want in return?"

Paul laughed. "I need more juniors," he said. "And more men. But I've already written to Flanagan from the second battalion about that, he'll find me some good lads and I can train them up the way I want them. I'm going to ask Manson and one or two of the others if they know of anybody good who might want to transfer."

"No wonder you are so popular with the other regimental commanders," Wellington said with heavy irony. "I'm honestly surprised you've not been assassinated."

"It's strange, you're not the first person to say that sir."

"I do not find that strange at all, Colonel."

"I'll need to talk to some of them to make sure they can afford the purchase but I'm fairly sure. When do the rest of the troops arrive?"

"Within a few days. Better get back and draw up your lists, Colonel. Do any of them have any idea?"

"Only Johnny."

"There is one other thing. I've made a request to Horse Guards that the 110th be formally designated as light infantry. If they agree – and I imagine they will – they'll be renamed as the 110th light infantry."

Paul felt a jolt of satisfaction, and his commander gave a little smile. "That is what you've been working towards, isn't it, Colonel?"

"Yes, sir."

"So there is no need for them to have a light company at all."

"There's always need for an elite, sir. It gives all the others something to aim for."

Wellington snorted. "I knew you would say that. We will discuss the detailed organisation of your brigade at a later time. Go and find your wife, Colonel van Daan. And congratulations."

Paul saluted. "Thank you, sir. It's an honour. I'll try to live up to it."

Lord Wellington gave one of his unexpected smiles. "I have faith," he said. "Which would surprise most of my army. Good afternoon, Colonel."

Chapter Four

Paul found his wife reading in a chair outside their tent under an awning. She was wearing a light-coloured muslin gown and her hair was pulled up loosely off her neck for coolness. Paul stood looking at her for a moment and sensing his regard she looked up and smiled.

"You look hot," she said. "Come and have a cool drink."

Paul held out his hand. "I'd love one, but have you the energy to come for a walk first? We could go down to the river."

Anne rose, taking his hand. "I will if you'll leave that coat behind."

Paul laughed and removed his red coat, taking it into the tent. He emerged with her straw hat and Anne pulled a face but tied it on. They walked hand in hand down to the riverbank. It was deserted apart from three young officers with fishing rods who waved a greeting to them as they passed. Once in the shade of the trees it was cooler. Paul glanced at Anne, thinking how peaceful she could be at times.

"You're not too tired, are you?"

"No. I seem to have all my energy back. Maggie Bennett tells me that's common, but I'll tire again close to the birth. I'm starting to show a bit more, though."

Paul reached out and placed a hand on her gently rounded stomach. "Girl or boy?" he asked.

"I think it's a girl, but don't ask me why."

"No, definitely a boy."

Anne laughed. "We'll have to wait and see. Are you nervous?"

"I'm terrified but trying to be sensible. You're nothing like Rowena in pregnancy, no reason to think you won't be just as good at giving birth as you are at being pregnant. Lass, I've something to tell you."

"I thought you had," Anne said tranquilly. "You've been with Lord Wellington. Another posting?"

"No. He needs me here, he wants to get the French out of Almeida and Massena is about to move. You know that Craufurd is on his way back?"

"Yes, thank God. No more Erskine."

"Which is a relief. Nan, Wellington is going to add a third brigade to the light division. The 110th, 112th and half a battalion of the KGL along with my Portuguese battalion and a couple of rifle companies. He wants me to command it."

Anne stared at him silently for a moment. Then she reached up and kissed him. "Congratulations, Colonel," she said. "I'm very proud of you."

"Thank you. I've not told anybody else yet although Johnny knows something is in the wind. There'll be some promotions and some changes, I'll see my senior officers individually later on and they can pass it on down the ranks."

"What's wrong, Paul?"

"Nan – what if I'm not ready for this?"

Anne glanced at him, unable to conceal her surprise. "You are, Paul. Wellington thinks so."

"Wellington put Erskine in charge of the Light Division, Nan. He's not always right."

"No, he didn't, Paul. Horse Guards put Erskine in charge of the light division. Wellington put you in charge of Erskine. That's why he's so sure you're ready for this."

"Every other promotion I've had, I've been so certain. Never a doubt. But now I'm commanding a brigade, and when the army hears about this there is going to be one loud scream. Half the officers are going to be yelling that I'm too young and too arrogant and don't fit in. And they're right about all of those."

"Half the officers and their ladies think you married an adulteress who shouldn't be received in polite society. When did you start caring what they think, love?"

"I don't. I'm just...later on I'm going to go and tell Carl Swanson whom I grew up with that he's promoted to Major in charge of the 110th First Battalion, and when we first joined, we were just boys. Leo Manson's age. I came into this army thinking I could change everything to work the way I wanted it to."

"You didn't do badly at that, Paul. The 110th came about because of you. It was a different regiment after you took it over. And you can be proud of that because they're the best."

"And now I'm supposed to do that with an entire brigade. Or am I supposed to settle down and behave like a normal officer now?"

"Well, if that's what he's hoping, Paul, he's going to be awfully disappointed, isn't he?" Anne said and suddenly Paul felt his heart lift and he began to laugh.

"He really is. Girl of my heart, you are the best thing that has ever happened to me. And you know what? The ladies might well be looking down their noses at you but whatever their opinion about your virtue every officer in this army from Wellington downwards would like to be where I am right now. Kiss me."

Anne complied and he held her for a long time feeling the tension drain out of him and confidence return.

"Feel better now?" she asked, and Paul grinned.

"I am. Time to go and work out how to be a brigade commander. I might need a bit of help with that. You know me and new officers..."

"Don't worry, Colonel, I'll charm them for you."

26

"I know. You are, of course, far too young and beautiful to be the wife of a brigade commander."

"Perhaps I'll become respectable now."

"Don't you dare," Paul said, and she laughed.

They walked back up to the camp arms about each other and found a small cavalcade arrived at their tent. Paul groaned softly. "I'd forgotten about bloody Longford."

"He won't stay, Paul." Anne kissed him and detached herself, going forward as Captain Longford dismounted. "Captain, how are you? Thank you for bringing Caroline to me, it will be good to have her again. How is Sir William Erskine?"

"He's well, ma'am." Longford bowed over Anne's hand, his eyes on her face. As Paul approached, he straightened and saluted. "Sir."

"Captain. Mrs Longford, welcome. Nan is so pleased you'll be with us for a while. They're setting up your tent for you and we'll get Keren to help you unpack."

Anne went to embrace Caroline Longford. During her stay with the 110th the two women had become good friends. Anne did not always find it easy to make female friends, partly because of the scandal of her relationship with Paul and partly because her own somewhat eccentric personality often shocked the ladies who visited headquarters. She had been very close to Paul's first wife, Rowena and Paul thought that Caroline had filled something of the gap left by her death.

Caroline was a slight, fair, pretty woman a couple of years older than Anne. Her marriage to Longford had been the result of an unplanned pregnancy which had ended in miscarriage and had never been happy.

Paul studied his former officer. "Would you like a drink, Captain?"

Longford shook his head. "No thank you, sir, need to get back. I appreciate you taking care of my wife."

"Don't mention it, she'll be company for Nan. You're marching up to Almeida, I hear?"

Longford nodded. "Yes, sir. It might be a few weeks..."

"We'll take care of her, I promise you."

"Thank you, sir. I'll be off then."

Paul watched as Longford mounted his horse and rode away. He made no attempt to speak to his wife and she did not look round at him. She was talking quietly to Anne. Paul went forward. "Lass, I need to speak to Johnny and the others."

"I know. Come and have some tea, Caroline, while they set up your tent. I've told Browning to put it between Captain Swanson and Major Wheeler, you know both of them and you'll feel safe there."

The innocence of her expression almost overset Paul. He nodded and went to find Major Wheeler to inform him of the new arrangements.

He went from there to Carl Swanson's tent and found, to his surprise, that his friend was writing letters while Keren Trenlow sat close by mending shirts. She rose as he entered, going very pink, and dropped a curtsey.

"Excuse me, sir."

She moved to leave, and Paul stopped her. "Keren, Mrs Longford has arrived. They're setting up her tent so she's with my wife, would you mind making some tea for them?"

"Of course, sir."

"Thank you. And Keren?"

"Sir?"

"You don't have to run away every time I walk in here. If I need privacy, I'll let you know."

When she had gone, Paul looked at his friend and lifted his eyebrows. Carl looked back placidly. "Did you need me, sir?"

"Very domestic."

Carl got up and went for the brandy. "Something funny, Paul?"

"I'm assuming she doesn't mind people knowing."

"Yes, she minds, Paul. She's not quite nineteen and very shy and she'd rather not have the whole of the 110th first battalion speculating about what she does in bed with me. But we both know they're going to."

"Carl, I did not mean..."

"I know. You'll be very respectful of her, but some of the others won't. I'm sorry, I feel like a bit of a shit right now, I got her into this situation. Let's talk about something else, you're big with news."

"Yes, I've just come back from Wellington." Paul studied his friend and then put his hand into his pocket and drew out the insignia he had brought from headquarters. He tossed it to Carl. "Job for your lassie."

Carl stared at him and looked up, startled. "Seriously?"

"You'll take over the first battalion of the 110th, Carl. Which will be part of the third brigade of the light division."

Carl stared at him then handed him a glass. "Congratulations," he said quietly. "And thank you, Paul."

"You're very welcome. And who knows, it might stop some of them speculating quite so loudly about your love life. You outrank them by a fair bit now."

Carl laughed aloud and drank. "Tell me the rest," he said.

"We've a lot of work to do and not much time to do it," Paul said. He watched his friend as he explained the details of the new brigade and remembered again the laughing boy who had joined him in training under Sir John Moore at Shorncliffe almost ten years earlier. It still felt slightly unreal, as though a boys' game had gone further than either of them had expected. He answered Carl's questions and poured more brandy.

"Have you told Johnny?"

"Yes. I'm going to see Gervase now, he's moving over to the 112th as a major."

"I'm glad. He should have been promoted a long time ago. What did your wife say about it?"

"She's pleased." Paul gave a rueful smile. "To be honest I had a bit of a shaky moment earlier. I'm awfully young for this."

"You've been awfully young for all of it, Paul, but it's not stopped you."

28

"I know. And it won't stop me now. I want the various battalion commanders to talk to your subordinates about promotions. But I would like to speak to Leo and Michael myself."

Carl laughed. "Be my guest. I'm not sure which of them is going to be more shocked."

Paul got up. "That's why I want to do it myself. Childish, but I want to see their faces." He paused, studying his friend. "Is she all right? Keren, I mean."

"I think so. We've agreed it's easier to be open about this and I'm hoping the others will take their cue from you about how to treat her."

"I'm hoping they do as well, or I'll kick them into the river. She's a pretty little thing and she's definitely put a smile on your face."

"Paul, it's probably hard for you to understand this but I get enjoyment just from having her sit in here with me sewing. Perhaps I was lonelier than I realised."

"Jesus, Carl, of course I understand. I came to that conclusion a lot earlier than you did, lad. I can remember in Italy just after I'd married Rowena. She was pregnant of course and then had a nightmare birth with Francis. And I know I wasn't a model husband through all that. But there was one evening…Francis was with his nurse and she and I went for a walk along the beach. It was warm and there was a fabulous moon on the water - like silver. And I held her hand and I can remember laughing at myself because I'd always told myself I didn't want to be married. But walking with Rowena that night, not even talking much, knowing that she was mine and that she loved me…I don't think I'd ever felt that secure in the whole of my life before. Of course I understand." Paul smiled. "Anyway, how the hell can I judge you given my history with women? I can distinctly remember how pissed off you were after Talavera when you realised that there was something between Nan and I."

"I was furious. Worse because you were at death's door, I couldn't even yell at you. But that was because of Rowena. I stopped worrying about it fairly quickly, neither of you would have hurt her. But it's funny in a way. Both Johnny and I are in a position where most commanding officers would be kicking up a dust. Is that why you're not?"

Paul shook his head. "No. It's because I actually don't think it's any of my business. I will be honest, Carl, I'm more worried about Caroline because if it becomes known that she's sleeping with my new Lieutenant-Colonel, Longford will disown her so fast you won't believe it, he doesn't have it in him to be forgiving. And that leaves her a social leper, she doesn't have the standing to carry it off."

"Nan was once willing to do that to be with you," Carl said.

"She was. I've never forgotten it. But Johnny and Caroline have the potential to make everybody's life difficult. You and Keren are only likely to annoy Michael O'Reilly, and I think you'll treat her better than he would have."

"So do I," Carl said. "Go and find him and cheer him up, sir, your news should give him something to think about other than the state of his love life."

Paul found Michael sitting with Carter and Hammond. Hammond was cleaning his rifle and Paul watched the meticulous procedure approvingly. "Lieutenant, can I have a word?"

O'Reilly got up. "What have I done?" he asked cautiously.

"Guilty conscience, Michael? I've some news for you. Come for a walk."

The Irishman listened in silence. At the end he said:

"Mary mother of God, sir, you still surprise me after all these years! Are you sure?"

"Very."

"Then I'll do my best. Thank you, sir." Michael glanced at Paul. "May I ask a question?"

"Why am I giving you the new light company?"

"Yes."

"Because you're older and you'll carry more authority. Our light company doesn't need you, it's already established. He'll have Carter and Hammond. You have to start from scratch, it's going to be tough. But I'm giving you Rory Stewart on loan."

"Really?" The Irishman's face lit up. "Then I can do it. Thank you, sir."

"You're welcome. I've not told him yet but I'm promoting Danny Carter to Brigade Sergeant Major."

"Is there such a thing?"

"Not officially, he'll still be Sergeant-Major in the 110th. But unofficially, I want it known that he's my senior NCO. I'll need a new light company sergeant…"

"Hammond," Michael said instantly, and Paul nodded.

"I agree. Do you want to tell him, Michael? I'm going to find Manson. Oh, and Michael. The day after tomorrow the light company and selected officers have twenty-four hours furlough. We've a wedding to attend."

"Carter?"

"Yes, Wellington has authorised it providing I can promise we're all ready to march the day after."

"Good time for a party, sir. Congratulations. Better go and give Manson the good news. A few people are going to yell at that one, you know."

"A few people yelled when I took over, Michael. I'll see you at dinner."

He found Manson playing cards with several of the other young officers. He rose and followed Paul to his tent. Paul sat down and waved Manson to a chair then collected a bottle of wine and two cups. Manson accepted with a smile.

"New orders, sir?"

"Yes. You'll hear it all tomorrow, I've called a general meeting for all officers. But part of it affects you, Leo. As of now, I'm commander of the third brigade of the light division. Carl is promoted to major in charge of the first battalion of the 110th which means my light company is without a captain. I'm promoting you to take over."

Of all of them he was the most shocked. Paul watched the young face try to assimilate the news. Eventually, Manson said:

"Michael?"

"He's taking over the newly created light company of the 112th, Leo."

"Is he all right with this?"

"He is. Although if he weren't it wouldn't change my decision."

"Sir, I wasn't expecting this."

30

"That I can see. Drink the wine and breathe. If it's any consolation I had a fit earlier at the thought of taking over a brigade. It suddenly felt like an awful lot of responsibility."

"I'm guessing you got over it, sir."

Paul laughed and drank. "It'll come back from time to time. I won't be sharing it with the rest of the brigade, mind. That's Nan's job."

"Yes, sir. Mind if I borrow her when I have a panic?"

"Be my guest. The rest will be announced tomorrow and then we've twenty-four hours rest before we march. You're invited to Carter's wedding party by the way."

"Yes, he spoke to me." Manson studied him. "Thank you. I'm not sure I quite believe it, but I am not going to give you a reason to regret it, sir."

"I know, Leo. Good luck. Take care of them for me, they'll always be my lads, no matter how high I go."

"I know they will, sir. Just borrowing them."

Paul had been glad of the excuse for a celebration. After an exhausting few months chasing Massena his men were in need of light relief. For the rest of his regiment not attending the celebration he had ordered extra grog and rations and left them discussing their new position in the Light Division while he collected his wife and went to the simple church where Wellington's chaplain, the same man who had conducted his own wedding service the previous year, gave his blessing to the union of a former pickpocket and a girl who had been both a nun and a prostitute. The chaplain knew none of this and smiled benignly on the clearly besotted couple, and Paul reached for his wife's hand and observed that she was determinedly blinking back tears. She was dressed in sprigged muslin, let out slightly as she was beginning to show a little now, pearls around her neck and in her ears and her hair dressed low on her neck. As the chaplain proclaimed the couple man and wife Paul lifted Anne's hand to his lips and she smiled up at him.

"It doesn't seem very long since we were doing this," he said softly, and she laughed.

"On our way to the battlefield. Nothing much changes. It was good of Lord Wellington to come today, Carter is overjoyed."

Paul nodded. "He's off in the morning, riding down to Elvas to assess the situation with Beresford. He's pulling the Light Division back; until Craufurd arrives, I'm not sure he wants too much activity. Of course, that does not apply to me."

They turned hand in hand to follow the bride and groom out of the church.

"Of course not. Where does he want you?"

"We're moving up to Fuentes de Oñoro, we'll await orders there. There's a hospital set up in Villa Formoso, which is where Norris is working from, it's in one of the local mansions, plenty of space. I've spoken to the quartermasters and we've been allocated billets in the village close by, it's about an hour's march from Fuentes de Oñoro. We'll move out the day after tomorrow, get you and the women and baggage train settled there. I've a feeling Wellington expects to engage somewhere in the area."

Anne nodded. Lord Wellington had paused to speak to the bride and groom, and she observed from Teresa's blush that he was being gallant. Then he turned and came over to Anne and Paul.

"A charming ceremony, ma'am."

"Yes, sir, I'm very happy for them."

"I am not always in favour of men having their wives with them, but in this case, it can only be an asset since she is already part of the regiment. And he is a good steady man." Wellington took Anne's hand and raised it to his lips. "You are looking very lovely, ma'am. Are you well?"

"Extremely well, sir. We are to celebrate with the company this evening and then be off to join Dr Norris at the hospital in Villa Formoso."

"I hope you will not tire yourself too much," Wellington said. He was still holding her hand. "I am away myself tomorrow to see how Beresford is doing. Has your husband told you that I am leaving him to keep an eye on Massena for me?"

"Yes, sir."

"I don't expect to be away more than a few days." Lord Wellington glanced at Paul. "Take care of her, Colonel."

"I try to, sir," Paul said, and Wellington kissed her hand again and took his leave. Anne glanced up at Paul and laughed.

"The expression on your face, Paul."

"He has the most nerve of any man I know. I swear to God, Nan, if he thought he could persuade you..."

"He wouldn't, Paul, he's too fond of you."

"Well, he has a bloody funny way of showing it. Come and get a drink, girl of my heart. Do you think you are up to dancing with me?"

"At Teresa and Danny's wedding? Try and stop me love."

***

The hospital at Villa Formoso was situated in what must have been an elegant country house which Anne had learned was called a quinta, with wrought iron gates and a series of courtyards with fountains, shaded with chestnut trees. Whichever wealthy citizen had lived here would probably have been shocked at the use to which his house was being put. Orderlies scuttled about organising wards with blankets and such mattresses as they had available. A series of supply wagons were being unloaded at the front and in one of the inner courts a selection of temporary tables had been created using doors placed across barrels. Anne surveyed the scene with a sang froid which amused Paul.

"Barker, who told you to set these tables up here?"

"Captain Corlett, ma'am."

"I'll speak to him, but you'll need to find somewhere else. All very well in this weather, but if we have a thunderstorm on the day of the battle we'll be operating in a downpour. Find a room inside, will you?"

"There's a covered area at the back, ma'am."

"I'll come and look." Anne turned to her husband who was laughing at her absorption.

"No need to wait, Paul, Gibson and Cregan can help me here and I have Teresa, Caroline and Keren to help me settle in when we find our billet."

"Are you sure, love? I don't mind waiting."

"No, get going, you'll want to set up camp and get the men settled. Adam will know where we're billeted, I'll ask him."

Paul kissed her and watched as she went to find Dr Norris, then went back outside to join his men. Anne located Norris in a sunny courtyard standing beside a covered well.

"Nan, how are you?"

Anne reached up to kiss him on the cheek. "Good thank you, Adam. Do you know where we're billeted? I'd like to unload our gear."

"Edwards has the quartermaster's list over there."

Anne went to find the young doctor and armed with the information went back out to join the other women, her orderlies and servants and Dr Oliver Daniels the regimental surgeon with his assistants. She had been joined by Private Theo Kuhn of the King's German Legion, whose battalion was now fighting as part of the third brigade. Kuhn was not fit for battle but had proved remarkably stubborn in his refusal to remain an invalid, so Anne had suggested he join her orderlies. She had taken a liking to the fair young man with the ready smile and easy manner, and she was curious about his history. Many of the KGL had come into the army when their homes were invaded by the French and were often better educated than the English enlisted men, but Anne had a suspicion that Theo Kuhn was something more.

Browning helped her up onto Bella and turned the ox cart neatly, following the directions further up the lane. The house was set back from the road about a mile from the hospital and its dilapidated state was obvious as they approached. Gibson glanced across at Anne who said nothing. She walked Bella through the rusty gate, which hung off its hinges and waited until Browning climbed down from the box and came to help her down.

It was a fair-sized house, which at some point in recent years had been badly damaged by fire, presumably either by the French or the partisans. Two rooms were habitable, although one of those had an unshuttered window, which would make it cold at night. The place had been used as a refuge for animals. It was filthy and stank.

The women stood looking around. "Oh no," Caroline Longford said softly.

Anne frowned slightly. "Oliver, did Adam say anything about billeting being a problem here?"

"No, ma'am. Most of the medical and non-combat staff are up in the village. I think this is a mistake."

"Who is the quartermaster for this district?"

"I don't know, ma'am, but I'm bloody well going to find out." Daniels looked angry. "You can't stay here, it's filthy."

"We might be better in tents," Anne said, looking around. "Although I suppose there are two rooms we can use. But is there any water nearby?"

"Not that I can see. Why don't you rest here, ma'am? I'll ride back up and find out what's happened."

33

Anne nodded. "Don't make too much fuss, Oliver. I'm well aware that the 110th has a reputation of grabbing the best billets, and some officers think that wives shouldn't be entitled to help at all. Take it gently and let's just find out what's going on."

Anne settled herself under the meagre shade of a small copse of cork oak trees and waited. It was unbearably hot, and she sipped the tepid water from her canteen slowly and swatted at flies, wondering if it might be an idea to start trying to clean out the cottage. They could probably transport water down from the quinta or the village well if necessary.

A horseman was approaching from the direction of the village. Anne rose and shaded her eyes, recognising Adam Norris. He reined in and swung down from his horse.

"Let me see this," he said. He sounded furious, which was unusual for Adam, who was one of the most placid people she knew. Anne led him over to the house and he walked through the rooms in silence. Back outside he turned to her.

"There is plenty of space in the house next to us – as far as I'm aware only one room is currently occupied by the deputy quartermaster. I've sent Daniels to have a conversation with him. Let's get you up there and settled."

Riding back up to the village Anne studied him. "What's going on, Adam?"

Norris glanced at her. "Captain David Cartwright is in charge of billeting and supplies here," he said shortly. "I presume this was aimed at Colonel van Daan."

"Ah." Anne understood. "Well, he isn't going to be all that pleased to have us landing on him then, is he?"

"I sincerely hope not. If he says one word out of place to you, ma'am, I want to know about it."

The house was one of a series of small cottages, which had been built originally to house employees of the quinta. The rooms were clean and dry and many of them at least partially furnished, set around a central courtyard with a well and a balcony to the upper rooms and Anne supervised as her orderlies unloaded the wagon and pack horses and arranged bedrolls and baggage in various rooms. There was no sign of David Cartwright. It was already becoming cooler, and Browning went in search of firewood while Teresa and Keren collected water. Anne went to make sure the horses and pack animals were being fed and watered, and on her way back encountered Cartwright by the front door.

Anne did not know David Cartwright particularly well. He was a compact man with mid-brown hair worn long and tied back from an angular face with a square shaped jaw and wide brown eyes. He was not unattractive, but he wore a habitual air of mild depression. Anne was not surprised; she had met his wife many times and felt that any man married to Arabella had reason to be miserable.

Cartwright looked at her briefly and then looked away. Anne stopped. She was angry enough not to allow him to get away with his piece of unprofessional spite. "Captain Cartwright, I am sorry to impose on you. The dirt and the cold I might have coped with, but the lack of water was a problem. You probably didn't think of that."

"Departmental procedure, ma'am. Best billets go to necessary officers and staff. Women and camp followers get what's left."

"And which category do I come into, Davy?" Anne said quietly, and he flushed and lowered his eyes.

"I didn't mean it like that, ma'am. Only..."

"Don't bother. Is your wife with you?"

Cartwright looked up and Anne realised with surprise that he had gone very pale. Stepping forward he tried to push past her and Anne caught his arm.

"Wait. What's the matter, Captain? That was a very harmless question."

"Sorry, ma'am, I assumed you must know. My wife has returned to England."

"I see. No, I didn't. We often miss the gossip, Paul doesn't spend much time at the headquarters mess, and I socialise more with the enlisted men than the officers' wives."

"Well it's a shame if he didn't hear this one, he'd have enjoyed it," Cartwright said bitterly and something about his tone killed Anne's annoyance.

"Captain, what has happened?" she asked quietly, leaving her hand on his arm. "Truly, I don't know."

Cartwright took a deep breath and looked directly at her. "I might as well tell you if I don't somebody else will. They're having a bloody good laugh about it in the mess. My wife is in an interesting condition, ma'am, just as you are. And who knows, the father might well be the same. What I do know is that it can't be mine. I've been in Pero Negro for eight months. She's been in Lisbon. Weren't you there with your husband six months ago, ma'am? Makes you wonder, doesn't it?"

Anne understood with agonised sympathy. "Oh no," she said softly. "I'm so sorry. Are you sure it can't be yours?"

"Very sure, ma'am. Are you sure it's not the Colonel's?"

"Very sure, Captain. But I am truly sorry, I didn't know."

He studied her and said suddenly:

"You're right, it can't be his. He's not been near her for years. Certainly not since he married you. I believe a young lieutenant of cavalry is the most likely candidate, although they are also speculating about a dashing Portuguese captain. I'm not sure about the German infantryman myself, she's a bit high in the instep, I doubt she'd sleep with an enlisted man. But then again, she might."

Anne shook her head. "Captain come through and have a drink. They'll have unloaded our supplies by now, we've commandeered the back courtyard for cooking and eating and I know Paul left us some wine. Come on, everybody is settled now, you can relax."

Cartwright hesitated and then nodded and followed her through and out through the back door. Her friends were seated in camp chairs under an orange tree. It was very warm and there was a savoury smell from the cooking pot. Teresa got up and came forward, her eyebrows lifted. Not until they were close did Anne remember.

"Oh – things just got even more awkward, didn't they? I'd forgotten. Teresa, I'm sorry. I wanted a private chat with Captain Cartwright, but I'm guessing you'd rather not."

35

The Spanish girl eyed Cartwright indifferently. "There is a bench over there under the almond tree. We were going to move it over here, but..."

"Leave it there, would you? And can Keren bring us a drink?"

Her maid laughed. "Señora, I can bring him a glass of wine without pouring it over him although it is a good thing Danny is not here. Sit down and let me get you a cushion, you look exhausted."

Anne led her guest over to the wooden high-backed bench and sat down. Teresa approached with a pillow for her back and a stool for her feet and she laughed and let her maid fuss over her. Keren brought wine and Anne leaned back and sipped it and sighed.

"Oh, that is much better. I try so hard to pretend this is not affecting me, but by the end of the day I am ready to sink. Heaven only knows how I'll be in four months' time." She glanced at Cartwright who sipped his wine and answered the question she had not asked.

"She will give birth in three months," he said.

"Did she tell you herself?"

He shook his head. "No. It was flying around the army. Captain Scovell heard and thought I should be told before I heard the jokes. I went back to Lisbon to see her and make the arrangements." He sipped again and shook his head. "It was not news to me that she was unfaithful, ma'am. We had only been married a year when we went to Naples. I have no idea if he was the first. He was probably the most obvious but there have been others since."

"Was there nothing you could say to her that would make her change her behaviour?" Anne asked quietly.

"She blamed it on me. I was boring. I was unsuccessful. I was unkind. When we married, she wanted me to transfer into a cavalry regiment, but I hadn't the money. I think she hoped somehow for promotion, and I made Captain on merit but no further."

"But you're still quite young."

"I am approximately the same age as your husband, ma'am."

"You can't compare yourself to him, Captain, he isn't normal."

"Unfortunately, my wife did."

"Well, you wouldn't catch him anywhere near a cavalry regiment, he thinks they're full of idiots. Although looking at some of the things he's been known to do I'm not sure he's a judge. Would you not have done better outside the army?"

"Doing what? I'm not trained for any profession and I've nobody to use influence on my behalf. And despite your husband's opinion, I'm not bad at what I do. But from Arabella's point of view, I suppose it was very dull."

"Somebody should have given Arabella a slap at a young age, it would have done her a great deal of good," Anne said acerbically. "Do you mind me asking if you knew about this when you sat on that court martial?"

He nodded. "Yes. And I am ashamed...I made that decision based on my feelings, not on the evidence."

"You should tell Teresa that, she'd understand."

"Is she...was she all right?"

36

"Yes. As a matter of fact, she got married two days ago. Sergeant-Major Carter wanted to make sure she wouldn't be seen as a camp follower again."

Cartwright's face flushed. "What has happened has made me behave in ways I couldn't have imagined before. Today...I'd forgotten that you were with child. But I should not have done it anyway."

"Well, it serves you right to have us invade your very comfortable billet, Captain. Are you going to eat with us?"

"Ma'am, how can I? There's a mess set up in the village, I'll go down..."

"And is that a comfortable place to be right now?"

"Nowhere is, ma'am. I can see them staring. Sometimes I hear them laughing."

"Eat here. The wine will definitely be better, Paul chose it. Go up to your room, wash, change into comfortable clothes and I'm going to explain to the others. No, don't look at me like that, you'll feel better if they know and they'll understand. Believe me, none of my people will find this even remotely funny. You will spend a comfortable few days with us here before they engage and we're all up to our eyes in blood and gore and you will feel a good deal better for it, trust me."

He stood up and for the first time Anne saw a smile. "Is this how you are with the Colonel, ma'am?"

"If he requires it. It does him good to be ordered around occasionally. Go on, off you go. We'll eat in half an hour."

***

David Cartwright went up to his box of a room. As he washed and changed his shirt, he admitted to himself how much he had been dreading walking into the mess. Somehow the small group downstairs seemed less intimidating, especially under the supervision of the lovely dark eyed girl who had made his confession surprisingly easy for him.

He had met Anne van Daan socially many times since she had arrived in Portugal two years earlier married to Lieutenant Robert Carlyon of the quartermaster's department but his wife's dislike of her and his own difficult relationship with Paul van Daan had meant that they had not really spent much time together. He had heard the gossip and was aware of Arabella's glee when the scandal of Carlyon's death and Anne's hasty marriage to Paul had swept through headquarters and the officers' wives who lived in Lisbon. Arabella had prophesied that Anne van Daan would never be received but instead it was Arabella whose unexpected pregnancy had blown away the facade of her marriage. There could be no doubt that the child was not his and through his misery, Cartwright was aware of a faint sense of relief. They had been laughing at him for years but at least now the laughter was open and would eventually die away.

Going down into the courtyard he saw that the doctor and the medical orderlies were moving the wooden bench over to the fire. Anne van Daan seated herself comfortably again and beckoned but he stood back and waved the Spanish girl to sit down. Steady grey eyes regarded him.

"I am sorry about your wife," she said.

37

"I am sorry that you were treated so badly," Cartwright said. He could think of nothing more to say but it seemed to be enough. He did not really understand the position of this girl who had claimed to be a maidservant but who spoke and acted like an equal.

She sat down and moved up indicating that there was space for him. The one-armed orderly was stirring the pot and a pretty dark girl was handing out bread. The fair-haired officers' wife held a pile of mess tins and held them out one at a time to be filled. One of the orderlies passed him a wine cup.

Cartwright sat quietly, listening. They all talked all the time, he realised, covering a ridiculously wide variety of subjects. They discussed surgery and medicine, the problem of billeting and supplies, a wine supplier in Lisbon who cheated the army on a regular basis, and the possible arrival date of General Craufurd. The women talked just as much as the men and the orderlies and the maids spoke as openly and freely as the Colonel's wife. Cartwright had never seen anything like it in the army before, and he ate the excellent stew and drank the wine and wondered for the first time what it must be like to be part of this peculiar regiment, which was sneered at by many officers who believed it undisciplined and out of control.

He excused himself early, and his hostess, since it was clear she had taken over management of this billet, rose with him. "I'm going to bed too, I'm exhausted," she said. "Captain Cartwright, thank you for sharing your excellent billet with us. Goodnight, everybody."

It was the beginning of the strangest week of David Cartwright's army career. Frantically busy as more and more troops poured into the area he found himself working side by side with the wife of the colonel of the 110th. It became quickly clear that Massena was moving to relieve the blockade of Almeida, and Wellington, back from his flying visit to Beresford outside Ciudad Rodrigo, was gathering his forces and making his depositions in and around the village of Fuentes de Oñoro. The village had been host to the Light Division and the 110th many times during the course of the conflict, to the extent that many of the troops knew each family in the village, and when it became clear that battle was coming, Beckwith's brigade went through the village and evacuated those hardy souls who had remained in their homes out to the surrounding area.

Cartwright received the request for supplies for them with something akin to despair. "Only half the commissariat wagons have arrived," he said. "God knows where the rest are."

"Dawdling on the way while the drivers pilfer the supplies and sell them to the partisans," Anne said scathingly. "Can I give you some advice, Captain?"

He nodded. "Send a message to Lord Wellington asking for a company of the Light Division to head out fast to meet them. You'll be amazed at how the supervision of a company of hungry troops will speed things along. If I weren't pregnant, I'd go myself, that would get them moving."

Cartwright complied and was surprised at how quickly his Lordship responded. As the supply wagons began to roll in and he was able to set up his stores and send food out to the refugees he realised that Anne van Daan was there, supervising the unloading of the medical supply wagons with an eagle eye.

"Does she always do this?" he asked Dr Daniels. The man laughed.

"She's slowing down at the moment. You should have seen what she achieved back in Viseu when I first came out. I thought it was mad, taking orders from an unqualified female, but I don't care anymore, she knows what she's doing. No wonder the 110th runs the way it does. Have you not met her before?"

"Not properly. My wife didn't get on with her."

Daniels eyed him sympathetically. "Have you heard from her?" he asked. Cartwright shook his head.

"I'm not expecting to. She has money, she'd a small allowance from her family, settled on her when we married. That will support her and the child. She went to an aunt in Shrewsbury I believe to have the child."

"Do you think you'll reconcile?"

"No. What would be the point? Neither of us were happy. I can't afford divorce. We'll just live apart. I'm not the first man this has happened to in the army."

"No. Tough, though." Daniels looked up and smiled suddenly. "Now this'll put a smile on her face." He raised his voice. "Ma'am. You've got a visitor."

Anne turned and shaded her eyes looking at the horseman riding along the village main street. A smile broke over her face and Cartwright remembered how lovely he had thought her when she first came to Portugal married to Lieutenant Carlyon. She put down her tablets and pencil and ran forward.

"Paul!"

Her husband slid from his horse and caught her in his arms. "Girl of my heart, what the devil are you doing out in this heat without a hat on."

"Is that any way to greet me?" Anne asked, reaching up to kiss him. He bent and kissed her with obvious enjoyment, apparently completely unembarrassed by the staring bystanders. Then he raised his head.

"I love you. You are my sun and moon and hold my soul in your beautiful hands. Put a bloody hat on, right now."

She was laughing and threw a mock salute. "Yes, Colonel. Teresa, would you...?"

Her maid laughed and went towards their billet. Paul van Daan, his arm still about his wife, looked up and saw Cartwright. He looked at him steadily. Anne said:

"Paul..."

"It's all right, lass, gossip has reached me. Late as usual. As a matter of fact I ought to have told you about it but in the chaos of setting up the brigade I forgot." He released her and came forward. "I wish I'd known it back in Pero Negro, I'd have been just as angry but less personal about it. I'm sorry, Captain."

Cartwright nodded. "You didn't know. And I was drunk, for several weeks."

"I wondered about that. You're not usually that belligerent. Are you all right?"

"No. But I will be."

"Good. I'm aware you don't know it now, but you'll do better without her. Where are you billeted?"

"With us, next door. We're sharing a mess," Anne said.

39

"More convivial than down the hill, I'd imagine." Paul said. "Is Teresa all right?"

"She's been very gracious," Cartwright said. "I apologised. Although I think I'll be elsewhere when her husband gets back."

Paul van Daan laughed. "He'll behave, I promise you. Lass, I don't have long. We're making a stand up at Fuentes de Oñoro, and I'm needed. Massena is on his way. How the hell he's put that army back together so fast I will never know, but he's done it." He glanced across at Cartwright. "Colonel Beckwith tells me you've got the refugees settled and fed, Cartwright. Thank you, it makes our job easier."

"I'm fine here, Paul. We'll be busy soon," Anne said.

"I know. Keep safe and don't exhaust yourself. I'm glad you're billeted so close, my thanks for that as well, Cartwright, I'm guessing that was your doing. I know there's no point in telling you to stay out of the hospital, but take care of yourself and my child, will you, lass? I love you."

"I love you too, Colonel. Take care of our lads for me."

"I will. And I promise I'll try not to get carried in on a stretcher."

"I'd appreciate it, Paul. Come back in one piece we both need you."

Suddenly she laughed, took his hand, and placed it on her belly. Paul stood still, an arrested expression in his eyes then laughed with her. "When did that start?"

"On the journey here. The way he kicks I'm coming round to your view that it's a boy. Just a reminder, love."

"I don't need it."

Cartwright looked away. He was somewhat shocked at the open physical affection between the Van Daans, and he was also bitterly envious of it. During the past week he had told himself that he had got over his resentment of the man who had casually seduced his wife during their time in Naples but the sight of him so happy in his own marriage was unexpectedly difficult to watch. Cartwright had never had that with Arabella and now he never would.

Colonel van Daan looked along the street and saw Teresa approaching. Smiling he took the straw hat from her and tied it onto his wife's smooth head. Then he bent and kissed her again. "I'll be back soon, lass," he said softly and turned back to his horse. Anne stood watching him ride away and Cartwright saw tears bright in the black eyes. The maid stepped forward and put her arm about her mistress and Cartwright remembered that she too had a man in the 110th. He felt a pang of regret that he was here rather than out there, where he had intended to be when he first joined the army. Hesitantly he stepped forward.

"Come inside for a moment, I'll get someone to make some tea, you could do with a break."

Anne turned and smiled, and he felt suddenly good, better, he realised than he had done in a long time. "Thank you, Captain, that would be so kind."

He settled her in the courtyard and Teresa went without being asked to make tea. When it arrived Anne motioned for him to join her. He sat down, no longer so wary in her presence. "He'll be all right, ma'am."

40

Anne smiled, sipping the tea. "He usually is, but I'm a realist, Captain. Every time he goes into battle, I know he could be killed. We just accept it. I'm generally better at it than this, but I suspect I'm more emotional than usual just now."

"Yes." Cartwright gave a painful smile. "He's a very lucky man, ma'am. I always wanted children."

"I'm so sorry, Captain. It must seem so unfair to you."

"Oddly enough I've been feeling better about it this week. I must be getting used to it. You've been a big help, I'm very grateful."

"Heavens, I've done nothing."

"You have, ma'am. And because of that I feel I ought to tell you…it's hard. I suspect the Colonel is trying not to upset you, but I know what the gossips are. That first day when I was so resentful, I implied that…that your husband might have been the father."

"You did."

"I never believed it, ma'am. I know their affair ended years ago, before he even met you. But it's what the gossips are saying. Unlucky coincidence, him being in Lisbon at that time. You know what they're like…"

Anne sighed. "To my cost. Horrible people. It's no surprise to me, Captain. You're right, Paul is probably trying to shield me. But he can't; if this one is going the rounds, I am going to be receiving my fair share of pitying looks. And an even bigger share of concealed sniggers because a good few of them are going to think I had this coming."

"Why?" Cartwright said.

"Because the ladies of the army mostly don't like me, Captain. I don't really fit in. And although the officers will be kinder on the whole, they've all been holding their breaths and waiting for him to slip up, none of them believe he can stay faithful for long."

"I'm sorry, ma'am."

"Captain, it's all right. None of this is your fault any more than mine. I know it isn't true and that's all that matters. It will annoy Paul, which is unfortunate, but he can hardly start throwing punches about it this time. If he hadn't been such an idiot all those years ago when he had a wife as lovely as Rowena, he wouldn't be under suspicion now. The people who matter will know, and the rest aren't important. Come on, let's get back to work."

Chapter Five

Marshal Massena's Army of Portugal had spent the winter prowling before the lines of Torres Vedras, getting more and more desperate for food and supplies. When the French eventually retreated into Spain, harried all the way by Lord Wellington with his Anglo-Portuguese army, they left a garrison in the border fortress of Almeida. It was the last French stronghold in Portugal and its importance was both strategic and symbolic. Paul knew that Wellington needed to clear the French out of the border fortresses before risking an advance into Spain. He also knew that Wellington wanted to be able to inform London that he had liberated Portugal completely from the French. It was what he had set out to do almost three years earlier when London and half the army had bleated that the English would not even be able to hold Lisbon. It was an impressive achievement, and yet Paul knew that the grumblers were still unwilling to give his chief credit. They were also, which was more exasperating to Wellington, unwilling to send him troops, money and supplies as often as he would like.

Wellington had taken up a position that effectively blockaded Almeida and settled down to starve out the garrison, and he had been joined by Don Julian Sanchez with his Spanish guerrillas, who had begun to hope that the austere English general would bring some of his success into their own beleaguered country. Wellington had hoped that Massena would move from Ciudad Rodrigo to relieve Almeida, but Paul knew that once again the French had managed to advance far more quickly than expected. It was a regular blind spot of Wellington's; his enemy seemed able to recover from starvation, privation, and the severe mauling the English had given them on the retreat more quickly than he imagined possible.

The Anglo-Portuguese army were outnumbered in infantry and cavalry although for once had more guns than the French. Paul reflected, surveying the Light Division's preparations for battle in the company of the commanders of the other two brigades, that he was so accustomed to being part of a smaller army that it would seem strange to go into battle as part of a superior force.

"What do you think?" Colonel George Drummond asked, glancing sideways at him.

"I think Massena has the men, but I don't know how ready they are," Paul said in matter-of-fact tones. "They're bloody good at getting back on their feet, it's impressive. But honestly, I wonder how fit and healthy they really are, those men who went through the winter in a scorched land?"

"He's had reinforcements since then," Colonel Sydney Beckwith said.

"He has, but not as many as he hoped. We're not sure what happened, we know he sent to Marshal Bessieres with the Army of the North asking for troops, but all he got was Bessieres himself and a couple of small cavalry brigades. That wasn't really what he wanted."

"How do you know?" Drummond said, and there was a moment's silence as Paul absorbed his tone.

"Wellington told me; he's been getting intelligence through some of the guerrillas who are with Sanchez."

Neither of the other men said anything and Paul did not elaborate. He had told himself that he was ready to accept the resentment which he knew was likely to follow his extraordinary promotion to commander of a brigade at the age of thirty, but the reality was uncomfortable.

Paul had worked alongside both Beckwith and Drummond many times before. Both were older than him by ten years or more and both had commanded men for longer than he had. They were fine soldiers and he liked and respected them both. Under the command of the irascible General Robert Craufurd they had helped turn the Light Division into the finest fighting force in the British army.

During previous campaigns, Paul had often fought under Craufurd, although always as a separate battalion. For several years Wellington had kept the 110th free of divisional loyalties, a specialist battalion under his personal command. It had given Paul a level of responsibility and freedom well ahead of his years and experience and he had never been able to satisfactorily explain why Wellington had lighted on him, a lieutenant of twenty-one on a hillside in India. He was well aware of his privileged position with the commander, and he knew that Wellington tended to share information with him which was not necessarily available to the rest of the army but given his relatively junior position it had been a source of curiosity and some amusement to Wellington's senior officers. He had met with surprisingly little resentment.

It was different now. During the past six months, while Robert Craufurd had been on leave in England, the Light Division had been placed under the command of Major-General Erskine and Wellington had placed Paul with the 110th and 112th to fight alongside the other brigades of the Light Division, responsible directly to Erskine. It had been an appallingly difficult assignment. Erskine had a variety of problems. He was very short-sighted, subject to violent mood swings and inclined to fits of depression and confusion. His management of his officers and men had been chaotic and it had been Paul's task to keep him in check, to intervene when his decisions became dangerous and to keep the two brigade commanders and Lord Wellington informed of what was going on. He had trod the difficult path on tiptoe and taken risks both with the lives of his men and with his own career and reputation, to manage Wellington's impossible problem for him.

43

Paul knew that the third brigade of the Light Division was his reward. He was also aware that for both Drummond and Beckwith, it had changed his status. He had been a respected junior, doing an unpleasant task, and it had caused him at times to take important decisions and impossible risks and they had supported him in a way that he would never forget. But now he was their equal in a situation where there was no commanding officer. Craufurd was apparently expected any day, but he had not arrived, and Wellington had nominated no temporary commander of the Light Division as yet. Paul could sense their suppressed resentment of his knowledge of the commander's plans and intentions along with their fear that if Craufurd did not arrive in time, he would appoint Paul to command the division. Paul did not think Wellington would do anything of the kind; his chief thought well of both Beckwith and Drummond and would not insult them by promoting a much younger and newer brigade commander over their heads no matter how much he liked him.

"Surprised you're down here with us and not up there with him," Drummond said sarcastically. "Mind, it'll be useful having you around, it might mean we get some idea of what's going on now."

Paul thought for a long moment about how to respond. He could sense that his reactions in these early days would set the tone for his working relationship within the Light Division in the future. It was not the first time he had been in this situation and he thought back to his return from India at the age of twenty-three, newly made captain and given wide ranging responsibilities for managing training in barracks which had placed him in effective command of a dozen men equal in rank but older and longer serving than him. He had recognised quickly that he could manage the enlisted men with ease but developing tact with his fellow officers and managing their resentment had taken time and practice and a large number of mistakes. He looked sideways at Colonel Drummond's tight angry face and wondered what the most tactful response would be here. Then he shook his head.

"George, if you keep this up, I swear to God I am going to forget your advanced years and kick you off that horse and straight into the river, I am not in the mood just now. I've got eighteen hundred men, some of whom I've never seen before in my life to get into some sort of battle shape within about twenty-four hours and our commanding officer is taking so long to get back from his holiday I'll have forgotten what he bloody well looks like by the time he gets here. And let us not forget the past few months of enjoying Major General Erskine on a daily basis. I'm here. I've not stolen your job, it's a new command and if Lord Wellington tells me what's going on, it takes nothing away from you, in fact it actually might be a help to you. Get over it."

Paul turned his big roan gelding and cantered away, conscious of the other two men staring at his retreating back. Tact and diplomacy had served him well on occasion, but he had no intention of spending months tiptoeing around these two men. They must both have had time to become accustomed to the vagaries of army politics and he had just made the decision not to apologise for a promotion that he felt he had earned and was more than capable of living up to.

44

As he rode down to his brigade, he heard first Beckwith and then Drummond start to laugh, and he smiled inwardly and thought that on this occasion he had probably got it right.

Wellington had initially taken up a reasonably strong position on the line of the Dos Casas, a tributary of the Agueda River. Although the stream itself was insignificant, the section in front of the Allied left ran through a significant ravine that would effectively prevent any French attack on this part of Wellington's troops. His right was not as strong. As the Dos Casas climbed into the hills the valley was less pronounced and provided less protection. The British position ended at the village of Fuentes de Oñoro, which climbed up from the river to the top of the ridge and was itself a very defensible position. To the south, however the ravine disappeared, and it would not be difficult for the French to outflank the Allies.

With his troops in preliminary positions, Wellington summoned the three Light Division commanders.

"They're on their way," he said without preliminaries. "Marching down from Ciudad Rodrigo. We'll see where he places them and then look at our positions."

"If we get time," Paul said.

His commander eyed him with a forbidding expression. "Have you something useful to say, Colonel van Daan or are you just making sure we all know that your new command is not going to stop you questioning my orders any time you feel like it?"

"Not questioning, sir, more of a comment. You already know we could have done with a bit more time, but we'll manage. Where do you want us?"

Wellington studied him and then gave a small grim smile. "Out on the road initially, to give them a hard time as they approach. I'm sending out four cavalry regiments as well. No major engagements and don't take any risks, I will need your men intact for this battle, we're short enough as it is. Have you heard me, Colonel van Daan?"

"Loud and clear, sir. Getting better at it all the time."

Wellington shook his head. "I must have been mad," he said. "I cannot wait until Craufurd gets back. He approved this promotion but that's because he's forgotten what you're like. You're going to give him a seizure."

"No, he's easily as tough as you, sir, and I haven't given you one yet." Paul glanced at Drummond. "How do you want to do this, George?"

Drummond looked amused. "Was that an attempt at tact, Colonel? Why don't Beckwith and I take the north side and you bring up the south with the cavalry, the ground on that side will suit them better. We'll meet back before Fuentes de Oñoro once they've made camp."

Paul nodded. "Sounds good. Sir, we could do with some fast riders to keep us in touch with each other. I can use some of my ensigns but frankly they'd be more use with their men…"

"I'll get Julian Sanchez to lend you some of his horsemen. They know the countryside." Wellington eyed the three men. "I thought Craufurd would be here in time for this. And he still might make it, he must be very close. Which is why I haven't appointed a temporary commander."

45

There was a brief silence which extended and became difficult. Still, nobody spoke. Finally, Paul took a deep breath.

"I'm glad you shared that, sir, because I've been thinking you'd done that just to make my introduction to commanding a brigade more interesting."

Beckwith gave a splutter of laughter, and Paul glanced at Drummond and saw that he was smiling too. He turned his gaze back to Wellington and for the first time during the briefing there was genuine amusement in the blue grey eyes.

"Colonel there are four of us here and not one of us is in any doubt that if something gets difficult out there you are going to start yelling orders without any thought for rank or protocol. I first saw you do it aged twenty-two at the battle of Assaye when you bullied poor Colonel Maxwell into going into battle ahead of orders and you had been promoted to captain at that point for approximately twenty-four hours. If it happens, I trust Colonel Drummond and Colonel Beckwith to have the experience and common sense to judge for themselves whether to join you, ignore you or punch you, and they have my express permission to do any of those three. Get out of here and keep me informed."

It was the second day of May, Paul's son's birthday. Francis would be seven this year and Paul visualised him as he was riding out at the head of his brigade. It had been just over two years since he had seen the boy and Anne had still not met his two oldest children, but he could picture his son as clearly as the face of some of his men whom he saw every day. He had been tall for his age, a long baby grown into a lanky child with tousled fair hair, more his mother's colour than Paul's, and the deep blue eyes of the Van Daans. Paul wondered how he would spend the day. For the first time, if the postal service had worked as it should, his son would receive a letter from him on his birthday. It had been Anne's suggestion and Paul had been startled and then guilty that it had never occurred to him to do it before. He hoped it arrived in time.

There was a shout from the scouts moving ahead of the brigade and Paul spurred his horse forward to meet them. Lieutenant-Colonel Johnny Wheeler, his second in command, was already there.

"French sighted, sir," he said briefly. "Further up this road, marching in columns. They don't seem to know we're this close."

Paul gave a small grim smile. "Let's get our lads out there and introduce ourselves," he said.

It was the kind of action at which the 110th and 112th excelled, and with the knowledge that they could fall back at any time Paul gave his men their head. They were expert skirmishers; some armed with the Baker rifle which although it was slower to load than the muskets used by other infantry regiments, gave them an advantage of accuracy and distance. The best shots in Paul's brigade were in the two light companies plus the two companies of green jacketed riflemen which had recently been added, and he had given orders that where possible they were to target officers and NCOs. It was harsh but given the French superiority in numbers he was willing to take any advantage he could ahead of the coming battle. He wondered if Drummond and Beckwith would do the same. He knew that many officers would have considered it unsporting to allow his men to pick off their counterparts, but he felt no more kinship to the French officers than he did to their conscripted men.

They fought in open order, in teams of two men, one covering the other's reloading, and took advantage of cover behind trees, bushes and low walls, presenting a poor target for the fire of the advancing columns. When the French looked likely to form line or take a more aggressive approach his officers and NCOs called them back and they melted into the countryside with infuriating thoroughness. Paul remained on the higher ground with his commanders, watching the French advance through his telescope and relaying orders through a series of runners. He was conscious, with rueful self-knowledge, how much he was enjoying himself. For so many years he had managed a smaller force, training and drilling his men to increase their effectiveness, but only occasionally had he been in a position to control a battle personally. Like his men, Paul recognised that he was a natural skirmisher with an excellent eye for terrain and cover, and he let himself admit that despite his concerns about the battle which would follow this, he was currently having the time of his life.

Looking out over the rolling countryside to where his Portuguese caçadores were playing fast and loose with a French line regiment, he glimpsed what he had been expecting, cresting a rise in the distance. "Johnny, call the retreat," he said. "Cavalry. Christ knows why it's taken them this long."

"Maybe they're conserving the horses," Wheeler said, turning to convey orders. They heard the clear call of the bugle and saw the skirmishers turn and begin the retreat back, covering each other with consummate skill. Paul had commanded many of these Portuguese troops since Bussaco last year and they had trained with his men. He had implicit faith in those, but he was aware of the unknown troops of his KGL and the new Portuguese companies. Until he had been given time to get to know them better, he would not risk them panicking and doing anything unpredictable.

"Any minute now," Wheeler said softly, and lifted his own glass to his eye. As he did so, the cavalry began to speed up, a small force, probably no more than two troops. They had the caçadores in their sights and were beginning to charge them down, and the skirmishers were on the run, no longer stopping to fire, apparently in full flight before the deadly sabres of the horsemen. Paul counted in his head, knowing the point at which he expected to hear the first shot and when it came it was almost to the second, so well had Major Swanson and Major Clevedon followed his orders. As he watched, they came out of bushes and trees from all sides and the cavalry troop found itself almost surrounded by skirmishers setting up a wall of rifle and musket fire.

The cavalry was slowing under the steady fire from the sharpshooters of the 110th and 112th and the two companies of the 95th. Paul was too far to see the expressions on the faces of the officers and men as they realised the trap they had been neatly led into, but he could imagine. He lowered the glass and watched as the cavalry swung around to the screamed orders of their officers, galloping at full tilt back the way they had come, men dropping from the saddle as they rode back up over the rise and out of sight. Paul had wondered if they might swing back and try to charge the men down, but he had immense faith in his officers' ability to pull the men into square fast. They did not need to; the cavalry had gone. Paul lifted his arm and the bugle called again. As it did so he saw a rider coming up from the road, one of the Spanish guerrillas who had been extremely effective through the day at keeping him in touch with his officers and with Drummond and Beckwith up to the north. He waved the man forward and took the note he offered with a smile of thanks, his eyes still on the fleeing cavalry. Looking down, he read and then looked up.

"It looks like my fun is over for the day," he said. "They've advanced further up the north road than this, they're almost at Gallegos. We need to pull back now, or we're in danger of being cut off. Beckwith says they're going to bivouac directly before Fuentes de Oñoro and await orders, we'll meet him there. Sound the retreat, Johnny."

Paul rode down to meet his returning men as they straggled in and fell into marching order with the ease of long practice. Paul reined in beside the 110th light company and looked down at Manson, laughing.

"Captain Manson, if that lot see you on the battlefield, they are going to spit you on a bayonet with no quarter given, that was well-nigh perfect. And that goes for you too, Captain O'Reilly. I shall miss both of you, but that's war."

"We'll try to keep out of their sights, sir," O'Reilly said, coming forward. He was laughing as well. "Not that there are as many of them as there were. What do we do about wounded?"

"Do we have any?"

"Not that I know of, sir, I meant theirs."

"We'll have to leave them. Their main army is coming this way, they'll take care of them. We need to get moving now, they're ahead of us on the north road."

"Are they? What the hell have the first and second brigades been doing?" Gervase Clevedon said, coming forward.

"Not as well as your lads, Major, well done. You too Carl. Jenson is bringing your horses down, let's get moving."

Carl looked over at Manson. "Do you know, I did wonder," he said. "But he was right, you're a bloody natural. Did you hear what that French colonel called you when your lads almost cut off his left flank?"

Manson laughed and shook his head. "I heard him yelling, but my French isn't that good."

"Nor is mine, but even I know those words. The Colonel is right, you should keep out of his sights on a battlefield."

Paul sat his horse watching as the remainder of his forces fell in and then gave the signal to Wheeler to lead them off. During the march back, he rode up and down the long snaking column, reining in at each company to exchange words with some of the men, listening to some of their stories of the day and laughing with them. They were in high spirits, giving credit generously to their comrades, many of whom they had not fought beside before. Paul paid particular attention to his new troops, practicing his Portuguese, and making the German troops laugh with his few words of their language. As he rejoined his officers, Carl smiled at him.

"It's going well."

48

"Seems to be. I'm feeling a bit more comfortable to be honest."

Carl glanced back over the marching lines and grinned. He was about to speak when Paul suddenly reined in and turned, looking back. Carl had heard nothing, but he fell silent. It was a standing joke among the 110th that their colonel had the hearing of a bat.

"What is it?" Johnny asked, his eyes on Paul's face.

"Cavalry," Paul said.

"They've followed us?"

"They're ahead of us. Form square – now!"

As the bugles called the order there were answering calls from the advance pickets of the rifles, speeding back to the brigade with the information. Paul watched in the darkening afternoon light as his battalions fell into position with the precision of hundreds of hours' practice on the parade ground. His obsession with perfect drills was notorious throughout the army and when Wellington set up winter parades few men these days would bet against either the 110th or the 112th to put on the most precise display. They were accustomed to their colonel standing watching them with a pocket watch in his hand and now, when it mattered, they moved with speed and accuracy and complete calm.

Paul was using his telescope again. There were more of them this time, at least a battalion, possibly two, riding hard and fast into the attack. He looked over his men and then turned to Johnny.

"Go with our lads. Carl, will you take the Portuguese battalions? I'm going to join the KGL."

"Paul, no, you don't know them well enough," Johnny said. "I'll go…"

"Do you think I'm not up to the job, Colonel?" Paul said with mock indignation.

"I think you're a married man with three children and a fourth on the way," Johnny said shortly.

"That isn't going to count much if we give battle tomorrow, Johnny." Paul surveyed his friend with some amusement. "Besides, I very much doubt Mrs Longford would be all that happy if you got yourself killed either. But you don't need to worry. They're not going to break an infantry square with me in the middle, and they'll be bloody sorry if they try too hard, the men are fine, I just don't know their officers that well yet. This is a good opportunity to learn."

He rode off, hearing Johnny's furious oath with a grin. As he reached the Germans' square it opened smoothly to let him in, and he saw the surprised expressions on the faces of the nearest men.

"Captain Schweiz. Don't look so shocked, I promise I know what I'm doing, I've done it before."

The German captain gave a nervous smile. "Ja. Colonel…"

"It's all right, Captain, I'm not here to check up on you, I just wanted to see my new lads in action. Carry on."

He watched as the officers made the rounds of their men, checking weapons and speaking the odd word here and there. The square was three rows deep, all the men armed with muskets. Most looked reasonably comfortable, and they had formed square confidently although he would have liked them to be faster. But he could see a group on the far side with several younger men, white faced and frightened. Dismounting, he beckoned to a corporal.

"Hold my horse will you, lad? I just want a word. Hang on to him, he doesn't spend too much time in battle so he might get skittish."

Paul walked over to the men. "All right Private? What's your name?"

"Fischer, sir."

"Any of you not fought in a square before?"

Several hands were raised, hesitantly. Paul smiled. "Don't worry, there has to be a first time and this is a good one for you, because we're in no trouble here. It's getting dark. They've come after us because we pissed them off earlier, but they've not worked out who we are yet, or they wouldn't have bloody bothered. They're just circling now, they'll make a few passes, hoping we'll lose our nerve, but they've no artillery and cavalry doesn't break a square, not unless somebody makes a balls-up. Which my men never do."

"Yes, sir."

"Is everybody getting this?"

"Ja, sir. We all speak English."

Paul grinned. "A lot better than my German, I'm guessing. All right, here they come."

He stood with his pistol drawn, eyeing the charging cavalry as they thundered down. Around him men stood, muskets loaded, waiting. He could see the fear, watched one or two men wipe sweating palms on their jackets.

"Fischer."

"Sir?"

"What's the German for shooting?"

"Schiessen, sir."

"Thank you." Paul levelled his pistol at a horseman as the cavalry came into range and fired. Around him muskets crashed, and the horses reared, and screamed, and wheeled away. It was virtually impossible to get a horse to charge into a square, and any who came too close were vulnerable not only to the firepower of the British, but also their bayonets. It was getting dark rapidly and given the shortage of horses among the French cavalry, Paul knew they were not going to charge in the dark on the rutted ground strewn with boulders, rabbit holes and churned up by the troop movements. They only needed to stand until darkness and the French would withdraw back to their main army and his brigade could resume their march to join the rest of the Light Division.

The first volleys had brought down a dozen men and caused the rest to wheel their mounts away. He could see their commanding officer now, a colonel with red hair and an impressive set of moustaches displayed on a thin, angry face. He rode with drawn sword, shouting orders to his men as they galloped in a series of broad circles around Paul's squares. As they turned to come back towards the Germans, Paul saw his men ready, reloaded, and steady in three ranks, officers and NCOs calling encouragement and orders. He reloaded his pistol. Alongside the volleys of his muskets, it was a pointless gesture, but he knew it gave the men a sense of solidarity to see him firing beside them.

Paul glanced around. "What's your name, Private?" he called to a very young dark boy, and the German turned his head, startled.

"Schmidt, sir."

"Schmidt, what's the German for horse? I'm going to impress my wife with this when I get back, she's better at languages than I am, and it pisses me off."

The men were laughing around him. "Pferd, sir."

"Danke, Schmidt." Paul fired and the nearest cavalryman fell. There was a muted cheer from the men around him, and he was conscious that the mood had lifted. They were firing and reloading in ranks, keeping up a steady barrage of rolling fire which drove the cavalry back without them getting anywhere near the squares. Paul clapped one of the men on the shoulder.

"Bloody brilliant," he said. "We'll be back for supper soon and if the first brigade has nabbed all the rations, I'm shooting Colonel Beckwith."

He ran back to Rufus and swung himself into the saddle to give him a view over the field. In the dimming light he could see his five squares, rock solid against the dark plain, hear the musket and rifle fire crashing out, and around were the scattered bodies of fallen cavalrymen, and in one or two cases, their horses. They were almost spent, and he grinned as he surveyed the ground, wondering if the Colonel had been acting on orders or if he had made the sortie of his own accord, realising that the third brigade could potentially be cut off. If so, he was likely to receive a reprimand from on high, he had lost men unnecessarily and had gained nothing.

Paul saw the Colonel pause and realised that he was looking over directly at him. Even through the fading light he gained a strong sense of his opponent's fury and he studied the man for a long moment, then smiled slightly and turned away. As he did so he heard a yell of warning and he wheeled his horse, and then felt the shock run through him as the shot hit and the horse screamed and reared up. Paul hung on grimly, hearing the shouts of the men around him, and a furious volley of fire back at the enemy. Bringing Rufus finally under control he slid from the saddle feeling physically sick and ran his hand down the animal's sweating neck.

"Good lad. Settle down and let's look at you."

"Sir." One of the German captains had reached his side. "Are you hurt?"

"No, but he is, I felt him flinch. Hold him, would you? Christ, he's shaking."

Paul gave the reins to the German and moved around to study Rufus, quickly seeing the dark stain on his right shoulder. Talking soothingly to his horse he moved closer and very gently examined the wound. The horse tried to pull away and Paul held on and put his face against the smooth neck, whispering to Rufus as he checked the wound.

"I don't think it's too deep – a bad graze. He's a bloody bad shot."

"Nein, Colonel. He aimed at the horse, I was watching him," the German said. Paul turned to look at him. Around him he was aware that the sound of firing was dying away, only the shots of the rifles ringing out as they fired after the retreating cavalry.

"It's Captain Steiger, isn't it?"

"Yes, sir. I was looking directly at him. As you turned away, he lifted his pistol and aimed it at you. And then he lowered it and pointed it at the horse."

Paul was holding Rufus' head close to him. He kissed the horse very gently on the nose and smiled as his mount nuzzled him. "Bastard. He probably couldn't see to aim at me in this light, so he went for the bigger target. If I see him on the field this week, I am going to blow his bloody head off. All right, boy, calm down. If you're snuffling for treats, you're not that bad."

He turned to survey the square and found his bugler. "Call them into column," he said. "Let's get back. They're unlikely to come again in this light, unless they're really mad, but get the light companies and rifles out as pickets and flankers just in case. Can't be more than an hour's march now, probably not even that."

As his men fell into line, Paul saw Carl and Johnny riding over to him. "Are you all right?" Carl said. "I saw him rear up, I thought you were hit."

"Not me. He aimed at Rufus. Not too serious, I hope, but I'm not going to chance riding him back, I'll walk with the light company."

"Take mine, sir."

"No, I want to lead him myself, he's as spooked as hell, poor lad." Paul turned and surveyed his German troops. "Fischer!" he yelled.

"Ja, sir?"

"What's German for 'fuck off you French bastards?'" Paul called, and the lines erupted into cheers and laughter around him. He watched, smiling, as they made their way back into line and then led his shivering horse up to join his light company. Carter came forward.

"You all right, sir? Scared the shit out of us for a minute."

"I'm fine, Carter. But if I catch up with that spiteful bastard that took a pot shot at my horse because he made a balls up, I'm going to cut his bloody throat."

Carter fell in beside him, reaching up to stroke Rufus' neck. "Germans did all right, I thought."

"They did. We're ready, Sergeant-Major. I just wish we had Craufurd back."

"Bet he does too. Must be pig-sick at missing Sabugal. All those lovely reports in the newspapers about you and Beckwith and Drummond."

Paul grinned. "I do hope he saw them, they'll put him in just the mood for killing Frenchmen."

They marched in to join the rest of the Light Division in full darkness, and Paul left his men, still laughing at an appallingly vulgar joke told by Private Dawson who had a never-ending selection of them. He handed Rufus over to his orderly.

"Jenson, can you lead him back to Villa Formoso and let my wife take care of him? I don't know if the farrier is there, but she'll be able to clean him up and see if he needs anything more. I'll ride one of my spare horses – Nero is probably best."

"Yes, sir. You sure you're all right?"

"Not a scratch. The day couldn't have gone better until that happened. I need to go and talk to Beckwith and Drummond, find out if we've orders for tomorrow yet. Get him up to safety and have some supper with them. Give her my love, will you, tell her I'm fine and I'm thinking of her?"

"I will, sir. Be back later."

"Thanks, Jenson." Paul ran his hand down the russet neck of his horse. "You get yourself fit," he told Rufus sternly. "I'm not having you out of action, it would be like losing Jenson, I wouldn't know what to do."

His orderly smiled. "Closest I'm going to get to a compliment this year, so I'm taking it. Thank you, sir. See you later."

Paul watched him lead the horse away and then turned and went in search of his fellow brigade commanders and supper.

Chapter Six

The village of Fuentes de Oñoro, on the western bank of the Dos Casas, straggled up the hillside in a jumble of narrow streets and alleys. To garrison the village Wellington had placed the light companies of all the battalions from the first and third divisions plus the 110th and 112th light companies under Captain Leo Manson and Captain Michael O'Reilly, and more than four hundred men from the second battalion of the 83rd. The rest of the Light Division was being held in reserve, but Paul was under no illusion that they would not be needed. Wellington was very conscious of his inferiority of numbers and wanted his fastest troops to be available at a moment's notice.

Fuentes de Oñoro was well known to the men of the Light Division. During the past two years they had spent a good deal of their time on the border, often quartered in the village, and some of the officers and men knew all the villagers personally and were on very friendly terms with them. They had been evacuated to a refugee camp on the edge of Freineda, and Paul knew how unlikely it was that their homes would be intact when they were able to return. He had helped with the evacuation personally and had used his brigade's baggage carts to help them remove as many of their possessions as they could, hoping that if the British were victorious, they would be able to return and rebuild.

In addition to the light companies holding the village, the bulk of Wellington's army was posted on the right. The left was held by the fifth division, now under Sir William Erskine and the sixth division under Campbell, charged with the responsibility of protecting the road to Almeida. On the hills above Fuentes de Oñoro to the right, Wellington had placed the first, third and the newly formed seventh division, keeping the Light Division in reserve.

Mounted on Nero, his second horse, Paul watched the French army come, moving into position in the late morning of the 3rd of May. Beside him Johnny Wheeler and Gervase Clevedon were surveying the ground. Massena was concentrating his forces opposite the village and Paul suspected that was where he would make the first assault. He felt intense frustration that he was up here while two of his companies were down in the village.

Paul was particularly missing Carl Swanson, who was serving down in the village in command of five light companies under Colonel Williams. Paul appreciated the appointment, knowing that Wellington had suggested it for Carl's benefit. Major Swanson had a reputation as a steady and intelligent officer, who had served under Paul from his first promotion in India, but like many of the 110th he had not moved on for promotion. The new brigade had given Paul the opportunity to promote both Carl and Gervase Clevedon to major, but for further promotions they would probably need to move to other regiments. Paul accepted it but he knew he would hate it, particularly with Carl, who had been his friend from childhood.

They had spoken briefly that morning, the unemotional farewells of soldiers, which needed to be contained given how often they were placed in danger. As they stood quietly talking, a horseman approached and Paul recognised Ned Browning, formerly of his second company and now serving as a general orderly. Browning had lost half an arm at the battle of the Coa but had chosen to stay with the regiment along with his Portuguese wife and their young son. He got on well with Anne, and during a battle Paul generally left him with her to assist in the surgery and to run errands as needed. He smiled.

"You got news of my horse, Ned?"

"Yes, sir." Browning put his hand inside his coat and withdrew a letter and Paul felt his heart lift. Anne had established the custom during the painful months of Massena's retreat, and she never failed to send a note to him if she was able while he was on the field or otherwise engaged. He opened it and scanned it quickly, his lips curving into a smile both at the sight of her elegant copperplate hand and the news she sent him.

"Rufus is doing well," he said. "Not deep and he doesn't seem in much pain now, although Nan thinks it will scar. She hasn't bothered with the farrier, she thinks he'll do fine with her. Apparently young Kuhn knows a fair bit about horses, he's helping her."

"He's a useful little bugger," Carl said absently, and Paul looked up and realised in some surprise that Carl was holding a letter that Browning had just handed to him.

"Is everything all right?" he asked.

Carl was opening the note. He read it, and Paul saw a slight smile curve his friend's lips.

"Fine," he said. "Keren just wanted to remind me not to get holes in any more of my clothes until the new uniforms arrive, she's running out of space to mend them."

It was unexpected, and Paul laughed aloud. "Is she worried about you, Major?"

"She doesn't say so," Carl said quietly, and slipped the note into his pocket. Paul found himself wondering, as his friend set off towards the village, what Keren Trenlow had said in the note. It seemed to have pleased Carl enormously and Paul went back to his men thinking about Keren. He did not blame Carl for succumbing to temptation, but he was aware that the liaison had remained surprisingly constant. Carl was showing no signs of tiring of her, and Keren gave every appearance of genuine affection in her dealings with him. She must have realised that Anne was writing to Paul and taken the opportunity to scribble a note to Carl as well. It was the first time Carl had ridden into battle with a girl waiting for him to return and Paul suspected it meant more to his reserved friend than he was willing to admit.

Paul turned back to Johnny Wheeler who gave him a wry smile. "Domestic bliss all around," he said. "I'm jealous."

Paul gave a derisive snort. "And which tent did the lovely Mrs Longford spend the night in before we left, Johnny, because I'm damned sure it wasn't her own."

Wheeler did not look away. "None of your business, sir."

"No, it bloody can't be. Just make the most of it while you can, and for God's sake don't get caught." Paul clapped his friend on the shoulder and moved away.

Major Carl Swanson joined his five companies in the village with a feeling of surprised happiness. Keren had only learned to read and write since she had joined the Van Daan household, so the note had been brief and in an unpractised hand, but Carl was very touched that she had thought to write it.

Carl waited with his men in the village, deserted now apart from the soldiers, its winding cobbled streets, and red roofed houses empty. They waited quietly, listening for the sounds of the approaching French. This waiting was the worst part of any battle, giving men time to think about fear and injury and their own mortality. Glancing around him, Carl could see more than one man's lips moving in prayer and it made him smile inwardly. Many of these men had no time for God during the hardships of their daily life but faced with death they found him again. Carl, the son of a country parson, had retained the steady faith of his boyhood and found it a comfort at times like this.

"Major."

Carl turned to see Colonel Williams approaching. He saluted. "Sir."

"They're coming. About ten battalions from the sixth corps. It looks as though the second is going to attack our left, but they won't get anywhere there."

"No." Carl glanced across to Manson and O'Reilly. "We're ready, sir."

"Your companies will cover the streets to the left of here and we'll take the right, the buglers should sound the alarm if we get into trouble. If need be, fall back up towards the church. Good luck."

The guns fired first, French and then English, smashing into roofs and walls. Around Carl, his men waited, calm and collected. Occasionally, when a shot fell close, one or two of them flinched, but nothing hit them, although Carl heard screams from the right which suggested that some of Williams' men were hit.

They could hear the running footsteps of the approaching French, splashing their way through the stream and then hitting the packed earth of the village streets. Carl heard Michael O'Reilly's calm tones. "Steady now, lads. No need to fuss, we've done this before. Load and ready."

As soon as the French battalions came within range to the east, the English opened fire, but with limited effect. The 110th were armed with rifles and their accurate fire did considerable damage, but the muskets of the other light companies were less effective, and the French pressed on. The Dos Casas Riverbed was almost dry, and easy to cross, and the French quickly took possession of the houses on the lower slope closest to the river. Carl watched them come, assessing their strength.

"In your own time," he called over. "Not really the terrain for a neat line, lads, but keep together and keep aware. Fire when you're ready."

The rifles and muskets crashed around him and Carl levelled his pistol and fired. The French voltigeurs came on, dodging behind walls and hedges, and after them came the sound of the drums as the French columns marched forward. Carl had been through many battles and he knew the effect those drums could have on inexperienced troops especially when coupled with the sight of the solid columns of Frenchmen marching inexorably forward, shouting for their Emperor with the golden eagle standards blazing overhead. But the men of the 110th had been through too many fights to be easily intimidated. The guns up on the ridge began to fire into the columns, and there were cries of agony, spurting blood and smashing bone. Carl heard the clear tones of Captain Manson through the smoke and noise and fear.

"All right lads, fall back when you need, don't take a punishing. Carter, Dawson, Cooper, Hammond – get rid of those bloody eagles, will you? They piss me off, they don't even look like birds."

Carl grinned and fixed his eyes on the eagles. As the men began to fall back steadily before the approaching columns, there was a crack, and one of the eagles fell, its pole snapped. There was a scrabble among the French to retrieve it, and then a scream of pain and the second eagle toppled forward as the man holding it died. Even through the chaos of battle Carl could hear men cheering as each one fell, and he silently applauded Manson's imaginative piece of morale-boosting. It would never have occurred to him, but it was something Paul might have done.

There was no time for it now as the French crashed into the British lines and the fighting became close and personal and bloody. Each man fought for his life, with bayonet and sword, and seeing his men in danger of being overwhelmed, Carl yelled an order and turned to run back, finding new loopholes in three houses further up. His men recovered quickly, reloaded, and turned to fire again.

They fought their way stubbornly up through the narrow streets of the village, in a welter of blood and death. In places, some of the light companies had built makeshift barricades from doors and bed frames, and their officers stood beside them, calling orders in measured tones. When the French overran them, they abandoned firepower once more and through sheer determination forced the French back down the hill at the points of their bayonets, scrambling over the dead and wounded of both sides.

It was impossible, in the tangled streets, to know what was happening elsewhere in the battle. On an open field it was easier to scan the lines and see how other battalions were doing, but Carl was only aware of his own five companies, now somewhat depleted. He found himself alone briefly in a winding lane, closely bordered by white cottages, one of them badly damaged by artillery fire, his men moving into the houses to check for enemy ambush. Carl wiped sweat from his face on his sleeve and it came away black. Keeping a wary eye up and down the lane he reached for his water bottle and gulped down a few swallows.

Ahead of him a smoke-blackened figure emerged from one of the doorways. "Clear in there, sir," Private O'Hara said cheerfully. "Just got to..."

There was an explosion of sound and O'Hara's body jerked violently. He made a strangled gurgling noise and then fell forward, blood spilling onto the baked earth of the street, his back a gaping hole. The Frenchman was only a few feet away and could not have missed, even with the dubious accuracy of a musket. Carl looked down at the dead Irishman and then up at the Frenchman and as he did so there was a babble of French voices and they poured out of the building opposite, a dozen of them, racing towards him with bayonets raised.

Carl dived into the nearest doorway. The house was empty, a bare room, cleared of valuables with only a few pieces of basic wooden furniture. The door was narrow and two of the French infantrymen tried to go through it at the same time and collided, temporarily stuck. Carl could have killed either of them without difficulty, but their comrades were yelling behind them and he had no intention of running towards them. He spun around, looking for an exit, but the only window had wooden shutters firmly closed and he had no time to open them.

There was a narrow wooden staircase and Carl sprinted towards it and scrambled to the upper floor. There were two doors and he dived through the first one, slammed it shut, making plaster fall from above with the force of it, and dragged the big bed in front of it. It was not heavy enough to hold the Frenchmen, but it would buy him some time.

The window here was also shuttered and Carl struggled furiously with the warped wood, showering himself with plaster and splinters as he fought to open it. It gave finally and he flung the shutter open and leaned over the sill, looking down into the lane below. It was a drop of more than ten feet, he guessed and if he jumped, he risked a broken leg. They would bayonet him where he fell and looking along the street, he could see only Frenchmen; the British were further up, fighting their way through the houses at the top of the hill. His stupid pause had allowed him to become cut off from his men and hearing the bed shift behind him, he took a deep breath and swung his leg over the ledge, thinking how furious his commander would have been if he could see his predicament.

Below, under the lower window, three bodies lay immobile, two British and one French. It was impossible to tell if they were alive or dead, but the Frenchman's bayonet lay to one side and he was soaked in blood. Carl eased himself over, trying to lower himself to minimise the fall but a crash behind him told him he had run out of time and he went over in a scramble and dropped deliberately onto the body of the Frenchman.

It broke his fall as he had intended, the feeling of the corpse beneath him making him feel sick. There was no time to think about it; shouts from the window above told him that his pursuers were there and scrambling to load a musket. Carl got to his feet shakily and turned towards the far end of the hill where his companies had been fighting.

"Sir, get down!" a voice bellowed, and Carl recognised it with overwhelming relief, as Private Dawson of the light company. He dropped like a stone, flat to the ground and there was a flurry of rifle shots and an order called in the London accent of Sergeant Hammond. Above him a man screamed and then a body crashed to the ground close to him. More shots were fired and then he heard

58

running feet, hard on the packed earth, and he was suddenly surrounded by red coats. A hand reached to pull him to his feet.

"Sir, are you hurt?" Manson's voice said.

"Just embarrassed. That was a mistake I'd expect from a sixteen-year-old ensign fresh off the boat. You tell the Colonel and I'm coming after you, Leo. And thank you."

He turned and watched as his men surged past him, driving the French back down the hill in a fierce charge. Above, the men at the windows had vanished, driven off by the fire of the rifles although one lay dead in the street beside him and another hung like a broken doll over the window ledge. Carl looked at Manson.

"You all right?"

Manson nodded. His face was black with powder and there was blood on his coat. "Think so, sir. Bastard of a place to defend, mind. Cooper and Blake are hurt, I've told them to get themselves up to the church, it's where we're sending the wounded for now."

"Major Swanson!"

Carl turned to see Colonel Williams coming through the smoke towards him. "They're sending in reinforcements. Ferey's bringing in his second brigade," he gasped.

"Oh shit," Carl looked down the hill over the heads of his men who were engaged in furious hand to hand combat with a French company. He could see a sea of blue coats surging over the Dos Casas into the lower part of the town. "We're going to be overrun, sir."

"We need more men." Williams looked around. "I've lost both my ADCs..."

Carl spun around. "Hammond!" he bellowed. "Get yourself up to the first division, we need help down here. Go!"

Williams watched as the sergeant took off with a loping run. "Is it all right to send an NCO?" he asked.

"Hammond can be trusted," Carl said. "We'll need to fall back, sir."

"We will. Delay them as long as you can."

It was a bitter disappointment after the gruelling fight to push the French back and Carl could sense the fury of the remaining men of his five companies as they retreated; a fighting retreat from house to house, scrambling back over the dead and wounded of both armies. He had lost too many and those remaining were bloody and battered but ready to stand at his word."

"Help is on the way," Carl called. "We just have to hold them until then. We're not yielding this ground, lads."

It was empty defiance, and they knew it as well as Carl did, but the sentiment helped and for the next hour and a half, the light companies fought a furious retreat against the French charge. It was hand to hand combat with bayonets and swords although Manson had sent a dozen of his best shots up to the church tower, and the sharpshooters were a thorn in the French side, taking out individual officers and NCOs when they could with accurate fire. The French slowly and painfully forced the English and Portuguese light companies to withdraw through the village, and by the late afternoon the Allies were putting up a stubborn resistance at the foot of

59

the hill behind the village, and around the small church where the wounded lay, guarded by a dozen Portuguese caçadores.

Colonel Williams was among them. One of his officers came yelling for Carl when he fell and Carl sent men to carry him into the church. Until reinforcements arrived it left Carl in command of the depleted allied forces, but he had no time to worry about it. Time seemed to have stopped as he held the line, yelling encouragement to his officers and men. This kind of close quarter fighting was brutal and exhausting, and Carl could sense his men beginning to tire and possibly to despair. Across the line he could hear Michael O'Reilly bellowing orders and see Manson pulling his 110th behind a low wall, already blown to smithereens in sections, giving them time to load and deliver a shattering volley of fire into the French. Almost, Carl was beginning to wonder if Hammond had not made it with his message then he heard the clear call of a bugle and he realised with a surge of relief that reinforcements had arrived.

It was not over yet, but the tide turned with a vengeance. Carl's exhausted men raised a ragged cheer as the new arrivals, three battalions from the first division under Colonel Cadogan smashed into the tired French, driving them back. Carl called his men into line, running his eyes over them trying to guess how many were missing and Cadogan approached. Carl saluted and the other man gave a grim smile.

"Major Swanson. I am glad you're still standing, he'd have been furious. Where's Colonel Williams?"

"Wounded, sir. He's in the church with the rest of the injured. It is good to see you."

Cadogan, who was a former ADC to Lord Wellington and a good friend of Paul's, gave a grin. "Are you able to follow us in?"

"Yes, sir, I'm not bloody standing down now."

"Good man."

Cadogan moved to join his men and Carl turned to survey his weary light companies.

"We've got a bit of help, lads," he yelled, and there was laughter and a few tired cheers from the men close enough to hear him. "Sergeant-Major Carter, sound the advance. Let's see them off."

They fought with bitter intensity, through houses and lanes and back alleys, climbing back over their fallen comrades, and the French gave ground slowly and agonisingly and then finally on the run, no longer bothering to stop and fight. They fell back across the Dos Casas and onto the eastern bank, and some of the 71st followed them, eager to finish off their work. Both Carl and Colonel Cadogan yelled at the officers and NCOs to get them back. They were too far ahead and at risk of being cut off. As the day drew towards a close, they stood finally on the banks of the river and looked over at the French. Both sides were bloodied and exhausted, but Carl had thought during the advance back down to the river that there were more fallen French than Allied troops in the narrow streets.

It was over for the day. Messengers came and went back to Wellington's command post and as Cadogan stood talking to an ADC, Carl watched the French manoeuvre, bringing up fresh battalions to secure the east bank and sending the walking wounded to the rear.

"Major Swanson."

Carl joined Cadogan and they walked up to the church together. "Do you think they'll come again tonight, sir?" Carl asked.

Cadogan shook his head. "I doubt it, but Lord Wellington is sending in reinforcements just in case. I've a message from Colonel van Daan, he's obtained permission to pull you out, he wants his light companies back with their battalions. The rest of the companies will stay here until tomorrow. It's getting dark. I say, are you all right, Major? I'm told you had a near miss."

Carl pulled a face. "I knew one of them would spill that story," he said. "He's going to give me the biggest bollocking when he hears it. I ache like hell, but I always do after a fight. How's Colonel Williams?"

"I think he'll be all right, they've taken one load of wounded over to Villa Formoso, there's a hospital set up there."

"I know, some of our people are billeted there."

"Are they? Are you worried? It's bloody close to the battle lines."

Carl smiled tiredly. "I think they'll be all right. Do you need me here, sir?"

"No. You can take them back up to the lines."

"Thank you. I want to find my dead and wounded first, I'm hoping they'll send down a wagon for them."

Carl went to find the rest of his two companies. There were some bandsmen and other non-military personnel, including some of the medical staff, beginning to sift through the dead and injured and Carl was pleased to see that Manson and O'Reilly had already got their uninjured men helping. He joined them. It was an agonising task, with men piled up in narrow alleyways. The heat was already causing the bodies to smell, and Carl was beginning to feel sick and lightheaded. As the light continued to fade he straightened his back and glanced over at Sergeant-Major Carter.

"All accounted for, Sergeant-Major?"

"All of ours, sir. Only five dead, four from the 112th one from the 110th. Larkin, sir. We've about ten wounded already gone up from the church – I've told Cooper to make sure they go to Mrs van Daan, Dr Daniels or Dr Norris. About another fifteen wounded here, plus a few minor injuries who can walk."

"All right, let's call it a day. The dead will have to wait until tomorrow. We can't stay down here all night, we might be expected to fight again tomorrow, we need food and rest. Let's get back up to the brigade."

Carter nodded. He looked grey with tiredness and there was a gash across his upper arm from a barely dodged bayonet. Carl put his hand on his shoulder. "Call them in, Sergeant-Major."

"Yes, sir."

They set off to walk up to the ridge where the light division was bivouacked for the night. The sun was no longer visible but there was still the afterglow to light their way and Carl could see the silhouettes of the British infantry on the low hill. There was already a flicker of fires along the lines and the smell of food cooking for those who had rations to cook, and he realised how hungry he was suddenly. It was something he never noticed in the heat of battle when all his senses were full of the sights and sounds and smells around him, but as that wore off, he became aware once again of normal daily sensations, of the smell of woodsmoke and the rubbing of his boot – taken from a French corpse after Sabugal to replace his old worn-out ones. The two companies were quiet, some of them limping. They had formed makeshift stretchers from blankets for the four men who could not walk, and the pace was slow.

Ahead, coming down the winding track towards them was a vehicle, and he peered at it. It was a covered wagon, looking similar to those the quartermasters often used for supplies and ammunition. Carl shaded his eyes from the sinking sun and then smiled as the driver waved to him.

"It's Jenson. And by the look of it, Captain Cartwright."

The wagon came to a halt, and Cartwright swung down, saluting. "Major Swanson. We saw you coming from the ridge, I thought you might like a lift back up. It's empty, we've been delivering rations. I'm going back to Villa Formoso, I can drop you at the top and then take the wounded back to the hospital. Some of your lads have already arrived there, Mrs van Daan has seen to them."

Carl regarded him in some surprise. "Thank you, Captain. Let's get these lads up, and then the worst of the walking wounded can join them."

They loaded the injured men onto the wagon and filled up the spaces with those able to walk but still wounded in some way. Jenson turned the wagon, and Cartwright got down to walk beside Carl, waving to Carter.

"Up you get, Sergeant-Major, you look as though you've earned it today. We were watching from the top, it was bloody."

"It was." Carter saluted. "Thank you, sir."

He joined Jenson on the box, looking down at Cartwright in some puzzlement. As the wagon pulled ahead slightly, he glanced at Paul's orderly.

"What's the matter with him? Not known him to hang around anywhere near the Colonel for more than he has to. He had some kind of vision?"

Jenson grinned. "The colonel's lady," he said succinctly. "They're sharing a billet."

"Are they? I wonder how Teresa likes that?"

"I think he's trying to make up for what he did, Sergeant-Major," Jenson said mildly. "Give him a chance."

"I suppose I can't punch him when he's just given me a lift, can I?" Carter said with a grin.

"You can't punch him anyway, Dan, he's an officer, though I can see why you wanted to."

"Can I smell food? I didn't think there was much."

"Commissariat wagons have been making their way up, but we've had our own delivery, Major Breakspear sent up four wagons. Beef and biscuits, a bit basic but we're not going to starve. It's just over that rise, five minutes at most. You hungry?"

"I'm bloody starving. I…"

Carter stopped suddenly and looked around. "What the bloody hell is that?"

Carl was conscious of the sound faintly at first, a thundering of hooves, and he glanced around without interest, expecting to see a troop of English or Portuguese cavalry redeploying to another part of the field. There were around fifty of them, riding hard and fast, directly towards the two battered light companies, and as they came closer, he realised in appalled horror that they were not Allied troops at all.

"French cavalry!" he yelled and spun around. He had less than two hundred men, not enough to form an effective square, but without making at least an attempt they would be cut to pieces in minutes. He was faintly aware of yells from up on the ridge as the Light Division saw what was happening to their returning men, but any action they could take would be too late.

"Form square!" he bellowed. "It'll be tight, lads, two ranks only."

"Use the wagon." Cartwright shouted. "The wagon can form one side of the square. Move."

It was a desperate idea, but the light companies caught on quickly and formed up in two ranks, a rough rectangle with the wagon as the fourth side. The wounded men in the wagon crouched with loaded weapons aimed at the approaching cavalry and Carl positioned himself and his other officers and NCOs at the corners to reinforce as the cavalry swooped down at them.

Many years ago, Carl could remember standing in a square this small and this vulnerable. He had been twenty-two, in the army less than two years and had never fought in a major pitched battle, and he could still remember the terror and the heat and the screams of the Maratha cavalry as they pounded towards the tiny square. There had been the metallic smell of blood, and his sword had almost slid from his hand with the sweat on his palm and he had thought, for ten horrific minutes, that he was going to die.

Carl was older now and had fought many battles, but he was still conscious of the fear, held down and controlled, as he fought. The men beside him were tough, seasoned veterans, but he knew they could not hold out for long against this. There were not enough of them and they were exhausted and battered from the long day. He would have offered surrender at this point to save their lives, but the ferocity of the French attack told him that he would be dead if he lowered his sword. They had come to kill, not to take prisoners, and he did not understand why they had attacked what was clearly a group of wounded men on their way back to the lines after the day's battle was over. It hardly mattered. He fought, swinging his sword at any blue coat that came close enough to him and thanked God that the cavalry had sabres. If they had been lancers, it would have been over.

There was a yell of pain close by and he turned and saw Manson, hand clutching at an injured arm, his sword on the ground. Carl looked up at the horseman looming above him and was appalled to recognise the red-haired cavalry officer from the previous day's action. He was looking down at Manson and he was smiling.

"I notice you are not laughing so much now, boy," he said, and moved his sword point to Manson's throat. Carl did not dare move; it would break the fragile square and he was not close enough to reach the officer and his heart plummeted as the sword pressed home. The Colonel clearly expected the boy to move, to crash backwards to avoid the blade, breaking the square and letting the cavalry in. Carl thought, with bitter anger, that the Frenchman had chosen the youngest officer and that he could not have chosen worse for his purpose. He saw Manson's whole body go rigid with the effort of remaining steady, saw the golden eyes fixed on the Frenchman's face. There was blood and Carl heard himself shout a horrified denial of what he was watching, and then there was a furious yell.

"Fuck off, you poxy Frenchman."

Sergeant Hammond was on him, stabbing up with his bayonet and the French officer gave a cry of pain. Manson dropped like a stone, snatched up his sword, ignoring the blood pouring from his injured arm, and slashed upwards. The officer swore and fell back, surveying the slopes of the ridge which were turning red and green as every man from the Light Division who had been able to reach his rifle or musket poured yelling down the slope.

The French were beaten, and they knew it. Cavalry should be superior against infantry except in square, but not this many, with so many carrying rifles. Carl stood, watching as the French Colonel assessed his options and then gave the order to retreat. His men followed him as he rode off into the darkness and Carl took a deep breath finally and lowered his sword arm which ached.

"Leo. Leo, are you all right?"

Carl ran forward and caught the boy who was swaying, lowering him to the ground. His arm was bleeding badly and there was blood trickling down his throat. Carl dropped to his knees beside him.

"All right, lad, take a minute. It's over. We've just been relieved by what looks like the entire Light Division. They're not happy either, I bet they were halfway through cooking supper."

Manson gave a shaky smile. "Sorry, sir. Be all right in a minute."

Hammond dropped to the other side of him. "That bloody bastard!" he said furiously. "He did that deliberately. Did you see who it was, sir?"

"It was that Colonel from yesterday. I think he recognised me, I was fairly close to him at one point when we came in behind the Portuguese." Manson took the flask Hammond was holding out to him. "Thank you, Sergeant, I don't think I'd be here if you'd not been so bloody quick. Get me up, I don't want the lads to see me like this."

"Carl."

Carl turned and rose and saw Paul reining in beside him. He slid to the ground and came forward, catching Carl by the shoulders. "Christ, I thought you were all dead," he said softly. "Are you all right?"

"Yes. Thank you. I can't believe you got down here that quickly."

"I didn't give the order, Major. They just came." Paul looked around as men from all three brigades of the Light Division milled about, helping up the wounded and speaking to the shocked men of the two light companies. "What the hell happened?"

"It was the cavalry colonel from yesterday," Manson said, and Paul dropped to his knee beside the boy. Reaching inside his coat he drew out a thin scarf and wrapped it quickly around the wound.

"Hold it hard, it's deep, you'll need that stitched. Are you serious, Leo?"

64

"He's deadly serious," Carl said. "He'd disarmed Leo and was about to slit his throat. It was deliberate, sir, aimed at us. He must have been watching and saw us leave the village. He spoke in English, said something about Leo not laughing now. That has to be a reference to yesterday."

"I suppose so," Paul said. He sounded bewildered. "Come on, let's get you all back up to the lines although I doubt they'll be back. That was a stroke of bloody genius, Carl, closing the square with the wagon."

"It wasn't my idea," Carl said, looking around. He spotted David Cartwright administering first aid to a bleeding private from the 112th. "Captain Cartwright."

Cartwright looked around. "Are you all right, sir?"

Carl moved forward. "Thanks to you," he said quietly. "Honestly, thank you, that was bloody amazing."

Paul had followed him. "Davy, you need to trust me when I say that anything you've done to piss me off this month is forgotten. Thank God you came up."

"How did you come to be here at all?" Carl asked, helping the injured man to his feet. "I thought you were in Villa Formoso."

"Captain Cartwright came up with a wagon of food supplies for the brigade," Paul said. "He brought us some visitors as well, so you need to get your arse up that hill quick time, Sergeant-Major Carter because your wife was up there, waiting to see if you were about to be cut to pieces."

"Oh shit!" Carter began to run. Carl turned to Manson who had got shakily to his feet.

"Up into that wagon, Captain. That's an order."

Around them the men of the Light Division were drifting back up to their bivouacs and the remains of their supper. Paul walked beside Carl, leading Nero. They walked in silence. Carl was tired to the bone, having to concentrate to put one foot in front of the other. After a few minutes his Colonel said:

"Major Swanson, you're going to pass out in a minute. Stop being a hero and get on this horse, why do you think I'm walking?"

Carl laughed. "I thought it was the pleasure of my company, sir."

"You're not much company at the moment. Mount up."

Carl obeyed, walking the horse beside Paul. They made their way slowly up the low ridge and over the crest towards the light division lines. As they approached the bivouac of the 110th there were several supply wagons still there and men were helping some of the wounded up into them. Sergeant-Major Carter stood close by with his wife. She was crying, and he was holding her close, stroking her brown hair soothingly. Carl looked past them and saw the slim figure of his Colonel's wife who must have come up with the supplies from Villa Formoso. Beside her was Keren Trenlow.

Carl had not thought about Keren, presuming her safe in Villa Formoso, but the sight of her reddened eyes and wet cheeks drove everything else from his mind. He swung down from Nero, handing the reins to his Colonel without apology and went forward. She did not move towards him until Anne gave her a very gentle push and then she approached him tentatively as though unsure of her welcome. Carl realised, with a rush of protective tenderness that she was worried about embarrassing him in front of his commanding officer and his battalion and he

65

discovered that he did not give a damn about either. He reached out and cupped the damp face in his hands and bent to kiss her very gently but very decidedly on the lips.

"What the devil are you doing up here?" he said. "Of all the things I thought I'd need to worry about today, I wasn't expecting it to be you. Look at the state of you."

"I'm sorry, sir. I'll go…"

Carl kissed her again. "You'll do nothing of the kind. Stop calling me sir, we've spoken about this. And stop crying, lass, I'm here and I'm safe. Did you see what happened?"

She nodded and Carl realised that she was shivering. He took her hand and enclosed it in both of his. "You're shaking; are you cold?"

"No. I don't think so. I'm sorry, I thought I was watching you die."

There was raw pain in her voice and Carl was moved. He drew her close and held her, warming her against his body. "I'm so sorry," he whispered against her hair. "You shouldn't have had to see that. I'm all right, I promise you."

A hand rested on his shoulder. "Come over to the fire," Anne van Daan said gently. "It's probably the shock, Keren. You'll be all right in a moment. Come and sit down and have some tea."

Keren looked round. "No. No, I'm sorry, ma'am. It was just a shock, but I shouldn't…"

Carl covered Anne's hand with his. "Thank you," he said gratefully. "This must be really awkward for you, ma'am, but…"

"Oh stop it, Carl, for God's sake," Anne said shortly. "I thought you knew me better. None of this is awkward for me. I'm very fond of Keren and she's been breaking her heart. Go and sit by the fire with her, hold her hand and tell her you're sorry for putting her through that. I need to see to Captain Manson."

Carl obeyed, sitting quietly with his arms about Keren. Around him, the exhausted men of the light companies were fed and tended, and he watched as Anne examined Manson's wounds by lamp light.

"What happened, Major?"

Carl turned as his Colonel lowered his tall form to sit beside him. Keren shifted as if to move away and Carl tightened his hold.

"Don't," he said softly. "I just want to hold you."

"Stay where you are, lass," Paul said. "You're keeping him still and he needs the rest. Have you eaten, Carl?"

Carl nodded. "Teresa brought me something. I'm not sure Miss Trenlow managed more than a mouthful, mind."

"Worry will do that to you," Paul said, and Carl blessed his friend silently for his matter-of-fact acceptance of the inappropriate sight of one of his officers embracing his wife's maidservant. At times, Carl wondered if his Colonel lacked any understanding of the rules of polite society or if he simply chose to ignore them, but he was very grateful for it tonight.

"What happened?" Paul asked again.

"I don't know, sir. It was over. Colonel Cadogan said we were to rejoin the brigade, but I wanted to make sure we'd got all our wounded out first. It's hell down

66

there, they're packed in those streets, the dead and wounded piled up on top of each other and I wanted all our men accounted for. We lost…"

"I know, lad, Carter gave me numbers. We'll see to burials in the morning if the French give us time. Tell me about that cavalry colonel."

"It was definitely the same man we were up against out on the road. And he knew it was us; he must have recognised the facings. They came down out of nowhere and we'd barely enough men to form square. Cartwright's mad idea of using the wagon helped, and I swear to God I can't believe how quickly they formed up. You should be very proud."

"I'm proud of you all, Major. And Manson?"

"That ginger-haired bastard rode right up to him. He was trying to break the square. We'd put officers and NCOs at the corners with the wagon – it was the weakest spot. He must have known he didn't have long, we were within sight of the lines, somebody was going to come to help us and there weren't that many of them. So he went for that corner and he went straight for Manson. He slashed his arm badly and Manson dropped his sword. That piece of shit put his sword against Leo's throat and started to push it in very slowly. I swear to God, Paul, it was deliberate. He'd picked out Leo as the youngest officer, and one of the captains from the other day – he made a jibe about him not finding it so funny now. Manson was supposed to run for it, break the square wide open."

Carl could see the fury in his commander's eyes. "Most men would."

"Manson didn't move. I thought I was about to watch him get his throat cut slowly and painfully right in front of me, and he didn't bloody move. I didn't dare go to help him or I'd have let them in myself. It was the weirdest feeling, as if everything slowed down for a moment. The fight was still going on around me, but it felt as though it was happening a long way away. All I could see was that bastard and Manson. But Hammond was on the far side of him and he moved so bloody fast, caught the bastard with his bayonet. Manson dropped, grabbed his sword, and slashed up at him. I don't think he did much damage, but by then the Colonel must have seen he needed to get them out of there, you lot were coming down the slopes like the hosts of hell. I wondered if he'd try to cut Leo down before he left, but with Sergeant Hammond standing in front of him with a bayonet and a bad attitude, he took the wisest course and rode off."

Paul was shaking his head, bewildered. "That is just not normal behaviour in battle," he said. "What the fuck is wrong with him, he could have got his troop slaughtered today? Was that really just because we pissed him off out on the road? I've not forgotten he took a shot at Rufus; he'd absolutely nothing to gain from that, at worst I'd have been thrown. Sheer bloody spite. I wouldn't have an officer like that in my brigade if you paid me, he's going to get his men killed over some imaginary affront to his honour. I wonder who they are? I'm not that good with French cavalry uniforms."

"I could sketch it for you and ask around."

"Would you? Wellington might know. I'm supposed to go up and see him first thing. He's of the opinion we won't see much action early tomorrow, maybe some skirmishing, but they'll want to get their dead and wounded out of the village and we can do the same. I'll report this to him then, he should know that they went

67

after wounded men." Paul glanced around. "They're taking the wagons back to Villa Formoso. I'm sending a bigger escort with them. Given what just happened, I'm not risking my wife. Around twenty men, Major. You'll command it and you can take Sergeant-Major Carter. Stay overnight and get yourselves back here tomorrow morning."

Carl was startled. "Me? What the devil would I be doing commanding an escort party?"

"Obeying orders I hope, Major. Unless your experience of command has made you think you're too senior to do that."

"Don't be an arse, sir," Carl said shortly. "If you're implying that I'm not able to…"

"Carl. Look at me. Tell me if you think I'm joking. I want you to take an escort, get my wife back safely and spend a night recovering. Take Leo so that Nan can see to that wound properly. Find a bed and sleep while you've got a chance." The blue eyes shifted to Keren and suddenly Paul grinned. "And don't stay awake all night. Get moving."

He moved away and Carl got painfully to his feet and went to speak to Sergeant-Major Carter about the escort. Manson was eating, one arm dressed and neatly bandaged and a blanket thrown around him. His Colonel's wife sat close to him, her eyes on the young face, and Carl smiled as he watched them. They were very close in age, Anne and Leo, and looking at the two dark heads in the firelight close together, he thought suddenly that they might almost have been related, sister and slightly younger brother. Their relationship might have been misinterpreted in some quarters, but he knew that Paul valued their bond.

He looked around him at the weary men of the two light companies being fed and tended by their women and their comrades who had seen no action that day and felt immense pride in them. As he thought it, Michael O'Reilly came over and handed him a cup of wine.

"Drink it, it'll help you sleep. And well done, by the way. Your first action in command. It was a bit of a dramatic ending."

"Yes. I'll be happy to hand over to the expert tomorrow," Carl said, his eyes on his commander who was moving among the men, talking and laughing with them.

"Don't sell yourself short, laddie, you did bloody well." Michael was watching Keren who had gone to help get the remainder of the wounded men settled in the wagons. "I was just talking to Colonel Wheeler. He tells me Keren practically ran down the slope when those bastards hit us."

"Yes, I'm sorry she had to see that. It's upset her."

"I'm sorry," his friend said abruptly. "I didn't understand."

Carl looked at him, startled. "What…oh. You mean Keren."

"Yes. I thought she was looking for a comfortable billet and a new dress in return for a few weeks' fun but she's fond of you, isn't she?"

Carl smiled, watching the girl. "I suppose she is. I'm fond of her."

"I'm even more jealous now, of course," the Irishman said with a grin. "All they ever want out of me is the remains of last month's pay."

"That's all you're willing to offer them, Michael. I'd better get going, he wants me to escort his wife back to her billet."

"He wants you to get a decent night's sleep you mean. Lucky bastard. Make the most of it, this quiet isn't going to last and I am not looking forward to another day in those bloody streets. Or wherever else they post us. Our Colonel isn't happy with Wellington's line, he's going up there in the morning to tell him so."

"Oh bloody hell, what's wrong with him now?"

"He says we're too thin on the right."

"Maybe he's right," Carl said. "But Wellington doesn't often make a mistake. And if he does, he doesn't like being told."

"No. Beckwith and Drummond are flatly refusing to go up with him, they're not putting their heads on the block. Someone should tell them it makes no difference if they're there or here; if he gets into it with Wellington, we'll all hear it nice and clear from down here. In fact, Marshal Massena will probably get most of it as well, it'll save him sending out scouts. So you drink up and get yourself over to Villa Formoso for a nice warm night with your lassie because tomorrow promises to be sheer bloody misery with both of them in a foul mood."

Chapter Seven

Carl awoke into a pearly dawn light. He lay quietly for a moment, listening to the sounds around him. Below in the courtyard he heard the sound of Anne's voice and then Paul's, laughing, and he relaxed. If his commander was outside sharing breakfast with his wife it was clear that no action was expected for a while.

"You're awake. How do you feel?"

Carl turned to look at Keren. She was leaning on one elbow looking at him with concerned brown eyes. He thought, inconsequentially, how much he liked her voice, deep for a woman with a slightly husky tone and a mellow west country accent.

"Tired," he admitted.

"You should have gone straight to sleep last night."

"I was never going to go straight to sleep last night," Carl said. "And I'm glad I didn't, it was the best night I've ever had. What's happened, Keren, something's changed with you."

Keren blushed. "Nothing. It's nothing. I came so close to losing you."

"Well if it causes you to make love to me like that, I will willingly risk my life on a daily basis," Carl said and she leaned over him and stopped his mouth with hers.

"Oh no you won't, I'm not having it," she said firmly. "You're to stay at the back and keep safe today, you hear me?"

Carl laughed against her mouth. "I hear, but it's not an order I can obey, lass. So I'm ordering you to stay where you're put in future. You don't need to see something like that again. Promise me. I can't be worrying about you when I'm out there."

"Would you?" Keren asked.

"Yes," Carl said. "More than I realised."

"I'll stay with Mrs van Daan. I can't promise more than that."

"It's a start. Can you ride?"

The question seemed to surprise her. "Ride? I suppose so. I rode farm horses and donkeys back home sometimes. Not proper though, like a lady."

"I'm going to teach you when this is over, and we'll find you a horse."

70

"Sir, you can't. I'm a maid not a lady, I can't be riding like the Colonel's wife."

"Nonsense. Teresa does, has done for years. I'll talk to Mrs van Daan and when we've time I'll find you a mount."

She looked as though she wanted to ask a question but decided against it and kissed him instead. Carl lay holding her, knowing that he needed to get up and ride back to the lines but wanting to prolong the moment. He felt very happy for no particular reason and he wanted to savour it before he found himself back on the battlefield.

There was a sharp rap on the door and they both jumped and then began to laugh.

"Notice that sound, Major?" Paul called in genial tones. "It's called a knock. I thought I'd remind you because you've not always been so good at it when I'm otherwise engaged."

Carl was laughing harder. "It was once," he said. "More than a year ago."

"I've a long memory. Get your arse down to breakfast, we've work to do."

"On my way, sir," Carl said, and Keren slid from the bed and went in search of clothing and hot water.

When they had eaten, they made their way back towards the 110th's bivouac with the escort marching behind. Manson rode alongside Sergeant-Major Carter, talking to him and Paul and Carl drew a little ahead.

"How's Leo?" Carl asked.

"Better for some sleep. Nan's furious with him for coming back with that arm, but he's determined. I made him demonstrate that he could use a sword with it first thing and he almost took my eye out, so I said yes." Paul said. Manson was the only man in the regiment who could come even close to besting him in a fencing bout and he was immensely proud of the boy. "Physically I think he'll be fine, but mentally I think he needs to get back out there and kill a few Frenchmen."

"If I see that red-headed bastard out there, Leo isn't getting close," Carl said grimly. "That's going to stay with me for a while. Does Wellington know what happened?"

Paul nodded. "I went up there this morning early before I came over here. We had a lively exchange of views about the right of our position."

"You mean you yelled at each other."

"For a while, to be honest. Staff officers started coming out of the woodwork to see what the noise was. Poor Gordon was getting very anxious, Richard Graham looked as impassive as he always does and Scovell didn't look up from his code book. Colin Campbell was pulling the most hideous faces at me from the corner behind Wellington trying to get me to shut up. I thought he was having some kind of seizure at first. And I could hear Fitzroy Somerset laughing outside. Erskine was there with Longford, I think they were hoping he'd have me arrested, they got quite excited for a bit."

"I'm honestly surprised that he doesn't at times, Colonel."

"He won't; not over something like this. He'd hate it if I didn't tell him what I think."

"He hates it when you do tell him what you think."

71

"True, but at least he's got the information then. I think he's taken some of it under consideration." Paul grinned at his friend. "He's got his scouts out and they're reporting a lot of French interest on our right flank. They're not ready to move yet, they're down in the village sorting out their wounded and dead. Which is where our lads went first thing, with Captain Cartwright and a few wagons. I think Nan was going to ride down shortly to see if there's anything she can do; Norris has set up an emergency dressing station down there in one of the houses to deal with anything urgent."

"Should she be doing that?" Carl asked.

"Which bit worries you, Captain, the fact that it's a battlefield and the French might attack again at any moment; the fact that she's five months pregnant with her first child or the fact that it's going to be a hellhole which will sicken even me, let alone a well-bred female?"

"All of those really," Carl said.

"Johnny managed to add something about the impropriety of it, but he was laughing even as he said that one. I'm meeting with Beckwith and Drummond and then I'm going down to see if I can help."

"And to keep an eye on her."

"Well don't tell her that, for God's sake, she'll be furious. She doesn't need me for that, anyway, she's got Davy bloody Cartwright on a leash down there, with a grin from ear to ear. If I were a suspicious man, I'd think he was going to attempt to pay me back for making him a cuckold in Naples, but it wouldn't occur to Davy, he's too nice."

"He is," Carl said. Paul looked at him.

"But somebody is going to say it."

"Yes. I rather imagine that's what Johnny was trying to point out."

"If there's anybody out there who thinks Davy Cartwright is brave enough to try it with my lass, especially in a medical tent when she's armed with a scalpel, they're more stupid than I thought. But they can say what they like, I don't give a damn."

"Neither does she," Carl said. "I'm so grateful for how she was with Keren yesterday - and you as well, sir."

His Colonel shot him a sideways glance. "Carl, we all know there are two sets of rules in the 110th; how we behave among ourselves and how we behave when his Lordship comes to dinner. I don't expect Wellington to sit around drinking with my Sergeant-Major although I enjoy doing it myself, and I can't invite your mistress who also happens to be my wife's maidservant to dinner with the other officers' wives on the rare occasion when Nan feels an obligation to entertain them. But in the lines and on campaign she's one of us and she'll be treated that way. And I was actually quite touched at how she was with you yesterday. I think she's genuinely attached to you. Just try not to hurt her, Nan will be furious and none of us wants that."

***

Paul left Carl at the lines and went up to acquaint Beckwith and Drummond with the outcome of his meeting with Lord Wellington. Since his outburst of two days ago both men had relaxed with him and seemed willing to discuss the situation without rancour. Involved in listening to their views it took Paul a few minutes to realise that something was going on out in the lines. He turned his head, listening.

"What the hell is that?"

Beckwith listened. "Sounds like cheering. Is Lord Wellington coming up?"

"I don't know why he'd warrant this much noise." Paul listened. Suddenly he felt his spirits lift and he looked at his fellow brigade commanders. "I know who this is. Who else is going to get a reception like that from the Light Division? Listen to them."

He ran from the tent, peering down the lines at a group of horsemen approaching. At their head was a small stocky dark man with fierce eyes and an expression of grim satisfaction as he surveyed his troops. Paul walked forward. He was aware that he was grinning from ear to ear.

"Welcome back, sir," he said, saluting.

General Robert Craufurd looked down at him. Then he smiled and swung down from his horse, moving forward with his hand outstretched.

"My new brigade commander," he said, taking Paul's hand. "I was just wondering what you'd done to piss me off this week? Bound to be something."

"Very likely, sir," Paul agreed cheerfully. "You have no idea how pleased I am to see you. Do you know he flatly refused to appoint a temporary commander once he moved Erskine on? It's been a bloody nightmare."

Craufurd was laughing. "I bet you've been popular," he said sardonically. "Good to see my lads in such high spirits, although I don't see my officers lining up to cheer me back."

"Cheer up, sir, at least I'm pleased to see you. Look, I was just meeting with George and Sydney, but I want to go down to the village to make sure my lass isn't overdoing it, she's working with Norris in the field surgery, but she shouldn't be on her feet for too long at the moment. Can I...?"

"Why not?" barked Craufurd.

"Because she's expecting a child, sir."

"And she's still working?" Craufurd demanded, his voice rising. "What in God's name is wrong with you, Colonel van Daan? Have you no say in this at all?"

"None at all, sir. She's very well, I promise you. Although if you want to go down there instead of me to tell her to behave..."

His commander gave a snort. "As if I'm that stupid. Half an hour," he said. "Come and get me updated with Beckwith and Drummond and then you may go. I am already beginning to wonder how this is going to work, Colonel van Daan."

"Exactly the same as it's always worked, sir. I am so glad you're back; I'm worried about our line, we're stretched too far and too thin."

Afterwards, Paul rode down to the village. There had been sporadic firing across the Dos Casas earlier in the morning, but it had quickly died out, and he arrived into a state of informal truce as both French and English worked to clear out the dead and wounded which were packed into the narrow streets.

The heat had caused some of the bodies to begin decomposing already, and birds and rodents had also been at work. Paul stood watching in silent horror as men wearing scarves around their faces against the stench lifted bodies onto handcarts which were wheeled out to where mass graves had been dug. He could see the French across the river laying out their own dead ready for burial. Down by the stream a group of guardsmen were exchanging tobacco with several French voltigeurs, communicating through smiles and gestures where there was no common language and he watched for a moment, then turned at the sound of a familiar laugh. In a whitewashed house on the edge of the village which seemed miraculously untouched by the shelling of yesterday, Dr Adam Norris must have set up his emergency field station to deal with wounded men who were still being found alive in the streets, and it was clear that his wife was already there.

Paul walked down and found Adam watching grimly as a dead man was lifted off his makeshift table.

"How's it going, Adam?"

"Not good, they've been out there all night. Some have been stripped, some have been robbed, and I amputated an arm earlier on a man who had also been bayoneted, he swears by one of our own about to rob him."

"Jesus Christ."

Adam studied him. "I've not found any of yours out there."

"I should hope not, if my men had left any of our wounded in those streets last night, I'd have bayoneted them myself. And if every company of every regiment did the same, we'd lose fewer injured men. But don't get me started on that one, Adam. Where is she?"

"She's been helping me for a while, but I sent her outside to sit down for a bit, she shouldn't be on her feet for as long as she is at the moment."

"Is Captain Cartwright with her?"

"No, he's down helping bring out the wounded and the dead. I forbade her to go in there, it's foul and she'll make herself ill."

"So who is she talking to out there?"

Norris grinned. "Some Frenchman."

"Oh lord, I'd better go and see."

Paul walked out of the far door and through the small garden of the house. His wife was perched on the low wall, dressed in her plain dark working gown covered by a once white apron which was stained with blood. Her straw bonnet rested on the wall beside her, and Paul counted to ten in his head, approached her, picked up the hat and placed it firmly onto her shining dark head.

"Have you ever had sunstroke?" he enquired.

Anne looked up at him from under long lashes with unconscious enchantment. "No. Have you?"

"Yes, in India. I don't recommend it, it's very unpleasant. Tie that hat on before I make you eat it."

"I can't see how that would help with sunstroke," Anne said, tying on the hat. "Paul, allow me to introduce you to Major Lucien Delacroix who is from the 32nd ligne, currently seconded to Marshal Massena's staff. Major, this is my husband, Colonel Paul van Daan who commands the third brigade of the Light Division."

Paul was shaking his head, laughing. "Nan, you are outrageous," he said. "This is not a formal truce, for God's sake…."

"Oh stop talking rubbish, they're playing cards and chess down on the bank there," Anne said. "Major Delacroix came down with the ambulance wagons to help with the wounded as he is not otherwise engaged at present."

Paul studied the other man with some interest. He was of medium height and slightly built but with the impression, nevertheless, of steel beneath his slender elegance. He wore his chestnut hair long, tied back with a black ribbon, and he was dressed in shirtsleeves. Shrewd hazel eyes studied Paul with equal curiosity.

"Colonel van Daan, forgive me. Your wife and I were discussing the problems of the wounded," he said. "She is unusually knowledgeable."

"Isn't she? You're very calm about it, I must say, she frightens most strange men into a fit," Paul said in colloquial French, and the Frenchman laughed.

"And you speak my language as well as she does."

"Your English is extraordinarily good."

"I take no credit for that, my mother was Scottish," Delacroix said with a smile. "I have been showing her our ambulance wagons."

Paul pulled a face. "Rather better than our provision, I'm told."

"What provision?" Anne said in tones of disgust. "It's not so bad here, we can get in very close to the battle, but when they have to be transported for miles it's agony for them. They come in on dirty, unsprung farm carts if they're lucky, or they drag themselves off the field, and by the time we treat them it's often too late. I'm going to talk to Lord Wellington about it."

"Girl of my heart, Franck is the surgeon-general and he's asked for better provision so many times Wellington runs every time he sees him. It costs money and time and energy, and Wellington is putting all of those into winning this war."

His wife lifted an eyebrow, a trick he had often wondered whether she had practiced before a mirror. "Is that so?" she asked in a tone he knew well. "I, however, do not have an army to command which gives me more time and energy to devote to the wounded. And I will find a way to get the money, trust me. I love Dr Franck dearly, but he is too soft with his lordship and much too sensitive when he starts shouting."

Anne turned to Major Delacroix who was gazing at her as if he had never seen a woman before. "Major, it has been a pleasure. Thank you for showing me the wagons, you have given me a new project. I need to go back and help Dr Norris. Please take care. I have often thought harsh things about your people in the past few years; it is very nice to meet a Frenchman I like."

Anne gave him her hand and he lifted it to his lips. "Madame, you have lit up a difficult day, thank you."

They watched as she went back into the cottage. From inside the door Anne turned and threw the despised bonnet to her husband, and Paul caught it, laughing, and set it down on the wall.

"What a remarkable woman," Delacroix said.

"Yes, she is, thank you. Most men are dazzled by the way she looks but that is not the most extraordinary thing about my wife."

"By no means. Although she is very lovely. Is it not difficult for her? Forgive me, but I could not help noticing…"

"Yes, it will be her first, we've only been married a year. My first wife found it very difficult to cope by this stage, but Nan just seems to take everything in her stride. I am trying to get her to slow down but it's not easy."

"No, I imagine not. Some men would simply order her home, Colonel, but I can see why you do not. I'm envious of you."

Paul smiled. "So is half the army. At least until she starts ordering them about. Were you engaged yesterday?"

"No. And I do not expect to be immediately."

Paul eyed the other man thoughtfully. There was something about Delacroix that set off a warning bell. "Staff officer?"

The Frenchman's eyes gleamed with amusement. "Of sorts, Colonel. Your wife is astonishingly discreet, you know."

Paul returned the smile. "She would be, she's very intelligent. I'm surprised you're not out riding up and down our lines looking for a weakness, Major, every other intelligence officer in your army is busy doing just that, I waved to one or two as I came down."

Delacroix laughed aloud. "I do not have to ride very far, Colonel."

"I'll just bet you don't. I should go. If something goes wrong tomorrow, Lord Wellington is going to find a way to blame me, and I don't want to give him an excuse by spending too long in conversation with a French spy."

Delacroix studied him with considerable amusement. "I don't think anybody would suspect you of giving away intelligence easily, Colonel. I should go too. But I am very glad to have met you at last. I have seen you before."

"Have you?" Paul said, in some surprise.

"Yes. As I told your wife, I was formerly a Captain in the 32nd. We were engaged at the Coa."

"Oh. I see." Paul grinned. "Yes, there aren't many battles where an individual officer stands out, but I can see why you might have noticed me there."

"Your General Craufurd made a very serious mistake, sir, and we were ready to take advantage of it. We were elated, about to slaughter or imprison the elite troops of the Light Division. And then a Major disobeyed a direct order from his General and took his companies up onto a knoll to cover their retreat. I was very close, I heard him give that order."

"Did you hear what he called me when I ignored it?"

"I did. I did not know the 110th back then, I thought you were just ordinary line troops until your men started shooting. I think we lost every man in our front rank in that first volley, and they did not stop coming. When General Craufurd had his men across the bridge, you executed the fastest retreat I have ever seen and then you lined them up and slaughtered our men as we tried to cross."

"He was so bloody angry with me that day. I'm surprised he forgave me."

"It seems he did, because here you are, commanding one of his brigades."

"Yes, I've been lucky. Major, it's been a genuine pleasure. Whatever you spend your time doing, and I don't for one minute believe it's anything to do with kissing Marshal Massena's arse for him, I'm glad we're not going to meet on that battlefield tomorrow, I'd hate it."

Delacroix shook his outstretched hand, smiling. "So would I," he said. "You seem very sure there is going to be a battle tomorrow, Colonel."

"I might not work in intelligence, Major, but it's not something I'm short of."

"No, I can see that. I would pay a good deal to have a man like you on my staff, Colonel."

"You can't afford me, Major, I've private means. Good luck."

"You also. I hope we have the chance to meet again under better circumstances."

"So do I."

Paul turned to go back into the cottage, and a thought struck him. "Major. I've a question which you might not be willing or able to answer, but it's worth a try. Do you know anything about a cavalry colonel who carried out a surprise attack on a group of wounded men making their way off the field yesterday afternoon?"

Delacroix stopped, his expression arrested. "Were they your men?"

"Yes, two of my light companies."

"Did you lose any?"

"Not in that attack, no. You're probably aware that half the Light Division charged down the slope firing at them and they took off. I understand if you can't tell me."

"No – it's not a secret. I heard about it because the officer is in some trouble over it. There was another incident on the previous day when he took his troop where it shouldn't be as well. His name is Colonel Jean Dupres. Originally from a family of aristocrats, I believe, but they survived the terror and have done well under Bonaparte. I do not know him personally, he came from the army of the north, but he has a reputation for arrogance and cruelty, especially with the locals. I am sorry for what happened, we do not attack wounded men. And I have no idea why he did it."

"It was probably connected to the previous day; he encountered my men out on the road and came off worse, twice. Perhaps he saw their uniform yesterday and couldn't resist. I'm sure he'll be reprimanded, it's never a good idea to forget the courtesies of war in case one's opponent does the same. All the same, I hope for his sake I don't run into him on a battlefield, he has a memorable face. Thank you, Major, and good luck."

He watched Delacroix walk away and then turned to observe Captain Cartwright approaching, leading a procession of four stretchers up towards the hospital. He looked white and sick, and Paul felt a stab of compassion. He came forward.

"How long have you been doing this?" he demanded.

"About three hours, but I think I'm going to take a break, sir. It's not pleasant down there."

"No. Are you still finding them alive?"

77

"Not many now, poor bastards. Any idea how many we lost?"

"About two hundred and fifty, I think, dead and wounded. The French lost a lot more."

Paul reached into his coat and took out his flask, handing it to Cartwright. The man took it with an air of faint surprise and drank.

"Good brandy, sir."

"Yes, my men loot only the best," Paul said gravely, and Cartwright laughed and handed back the flask.

"You don't need them to loot for you, sir."

"I don't, but if they offer, I don't say no. They're very good on the whole, they'd never clean a family out of food or loot churches or money, but they can't resist the odd bottle or two and I turn a blind eye if it's not too bad. Given the conditions they live and march in and the fact that they don't get paid for months at a time, I think they've earned it."

"It's an interesting perspective. Does Lord Wellington share it?"

"We don't have that conversation, Captain."

"I know," Cartwright said. "Which is why the rest of the army says your regiment can get away with anything."

"No it can't, Davy, and if you've not seen that these past weeks, you've missed something."

"I haven't," Cartwright admitted. "It's been an education. But sir…"

"Ask."

"What's changed? You've treated me like a leper for seven years and now we're best friends?"

Paul was startled. He looked at the other man and said:

"Jesus, is that how long it's been, Davy?"

"Yes, sir. It's probably been easier for me to keep track, I've not been as busy as you have."

"No. And you're right, of course. I've avoided you like the plague, probably because my affair with your wife is one of the episodes in my life of which I've been deeply ashamed and embarrassed. I was a lot younger then, but that's no bloody excuse. I hurt you and I hurt Rowena and I spent years trying to pretend it didn't happen. How long had you been married when you came to Naples?"

"About a year."

"Well it was less for me. You'll probably know, since my private business is a source of endless fascination for this bloody army, that I married Rowena because she was with child. My choice, she'd no parents or guardians standing over me. But I was very fond of her and I didn't want to abandon her. It wasn't easy, just because Rowena didn't find pregnancy or childbirth easy. She ended up giving birth in a dark cabin on a ship with only me and some grubby Italian midwife for company, and it almost killed her. She couldn't feed Francis, we had to find a wet nurse and she was exhausted and ill and needed rest. I found her a comfortable billet in a safe area on the coast and left her in the care of her maid while I rejoined the army and I met your wife."

"I'm not sure I want to know this."

"You don't need to. We were both very young and very stupid. I felt guilty as soon as I was back with Rowena. Which did not stop me being unfaithful to her again on a number of occasions. And you and I both know that Arabella took her marriage vows equally lightly. I didn't go near her again after that, although I think she would have if I'd offered. But I'd learned that particular lesson. I never again slept with a fellow officer's wife."

"That's not what your reputation said, sir."

"A fair bit of that is in people's imaginations, Captain. I don't deserve a halo, especially from you, but after that I was a lot more discreet."

"I wish my wife had learned the same lesson. But sir, what about…no, I'm sorry, it's none of my business."

Paul laughed aloud, reading Cartwright's mind. "It actually isn't, but I've a reason for wanting to stay on your good side, Davy, so I'm going to answer the question you're too much of a gentleman to ask. Nan was never my mistress, believe it or not. She was very close to Rowena and neither of us wanted to hurt her. I've always thought it slightly ironic that the scandal people always remember about both Nan and I was actually completely untrue."

"Good," Cartwright said unexpectedly. "I hope they gave you a bloody hard time, sir."

"They did. And after all these years…I am sorry, Captain. It can't help, I know, but I was a bastard to do what I did to you. I've never said it because I didn't think it would help. But as I said, I could do with clearing the air."

"Why?"

"Because I've a proposition for you, and I can't make it to a man who hates my guts. So you need to go away and think about whether you can get over our history and work with me."

Cartwright was staring at him. "You've got a very good quartermaster, sir. Captain Breakspear is one of the best."

"I know, he's invaluable, I've no wish to change him. But Davy – how the hell did you end up in the quartermaster's department?"

Cartwright lifted his eyebrows. "The same way most people do, sir. No other options. I started with an ensign's commission in a line regiment, but I married young, and Arabella was ambitious. I needed the money. I couldn't afford to purchase up in the regiment, but I was offered a lieutenant's commission very cheaply in the quartermaster's department, so I took it."

"Are you happy there?"

"I'm fairly good at it."

"That wasn't what I asked." Paul studied him. "I was standing on that hillside yesterday when that cavalry hit, Captain, and I thought my two companies were going to be slaughtered before we could get to arms and get down to them. The fact that they weren't is due to the courage and quick thinking of my officers, especially Major Swanson, and the training and experience of my men. It's also due to you. You can think on your feet, you've courage and you are bloody cool under fire, I was watching you. So I'm asking again, what the hell are you doing counting stores and arguing with the commissariat? There's a vacant captaincy in the sixth

79

company of the 112th and if you want it, it's yours, Colonel Wheeler will accept my recommendation. Think about it."

Paul could see the sheer astonishment on Cartwright's face. "You want me to serve under you?"

"Yes. But I can see why you might not want to, Captain, given the gossip that's already going round. Don't think I don't know that they're saying I fathered your wife's bastard while I was in Lisbon last year. They all forget how good my hearing is. So if you want to say no, I'll understand it, and I'll ask around to see if anybody else needs a bloody good officer. You should be in combat, it's what you were meant to be doing. Think about it."

Paul gave a brief smile and turned away. He had said what he wanted to say, and he knew that Cartwright would need some time to think about it.

"Yes."

Paul turned back, surprised. "I didn't expect an immediate answer, Captain."

"I know. But I'm giving you one. The answer is yes. It's an amazing opportunity, sir, don't think I don't know it. But it's more than that."

"Go on."

"I like the way your brigade works." Cartwright sounded awkward, but oddly sincere. "I'll be honest with you; I've always felt a bit like a fish out of water in the army. Never really fitted in at the mess. Some of that was because of Bella, but not all of it. These past weeks, working with your wife and the others…it feels very natural not to be on my dignity the whole time. So yes, I'll give it a try."

Paul studied him. He felt suddenly a surprising sense of certainty about this man. "I'll speak to your commanding officer," he said. "If he can release you, you can join us immediately. Welcome to the Light Division, Captain."

Cartwright saluted. Paul thought he looked slightly dazed, and he smiled.

"All right, Captain. First order as your brigade commander. Get out of here, get cleaned up and rest. I'll take over down here for a bit, get them cleared out, and I'll keep an eye on my wife which is a duty I know you've taken on this week. Which in itself marks you out as a brave man. General Craufurd is back, I think we'll be in combat tomorrow and if I can manage it, I'd like you with us."

"Yes, sir. Thank you."

He watched as Cartwright walked away and then turned, taking a deep breath, to make his way down up to the streets of the town where the bodies still lay.

It took several hours for the streets to be cleared. Paul stood eventually beside Adam Norris watching the last of the makeshift hospital wagons rumble off towards the hospital at Villa Formoso. He had sent Anne back an hour earlier, overriding her protests and promising to join her for a meal before going back to his lines. Glancing at Adam he said:

"How are you for supplies and space?"

Norris scowled as they began to walk back towards their horses. "Not enough of either. Are you expecting a fight tomorrow?"

"Yes. So is Wellington. Craufurd came down a while back, he's been meeting with the divisional commanders. Massena has spent the day scouting out our position, he knows how weak our right flank is, the canny bastard. We'd only one battalion posted in Poco Velha, which is only two and a half miles south of here, plus Julian Sanchez with his guerrillas in Nava de Aver, another two and a half miles further on. There's a nice stretch of ground in between those two for cavalry, and Poco Velha is bloody exposed – more so than here."

Norris mounted up. "Wellington must know that."

"He knows. He's marched the 7th Division into Poco Velha, and he's put the cavalry in to guard the line between the two villages. It's not that he's unaware. But honestly, Adam, it's worrying me. They have a lot more cavalry than we do, and the seventh is the weakest division. They're new, there are only four and a half thousand of them and they've not had time to learn to work together. They've only two English battalions and they've got the Brunswick Oels, who desert every five minutes and aren't good under fire. Wellington thinks I'm being over-cautious. And he might be right, but Black Bob Craufurd agrees with me, and his eye for a battlefield is at least as good as Wellington's. We'll see."

He found Anne in her room, supervising the filling of Corporal Bennett's wife's large wooden wash tub with hot water. She closed the door behind her maids and orderlies and latched it firmly.

"Come on, out of those clothes. I know you need to get back, George has food ready and then I'll kiss you goodbye and let you get back up there. But I want an hour or so, I've barely seen you alone for weeks. And I don't know when I'll get to see you again."

Paul turned in the act of taking off his coat, catching her tone. "Oh love – come here."

Anne went into his arms and he held her close, stroking the dark hair. "I take everything about you for granted, don't I?" he said softly.

"No, Paul. You treat me as an equal, which is what I wanted. I'm just tired and worried and missing you."

"Girl of my heart, I miss you every minute I'm not with you, you bloody know that. Help me out of these clothes, I'm not coming near you until I've bathed given what I've spent the past few hours doing. After that I'm all yours, and Wellington can come and find me if he wants me."

Anne laughed and reached up to unbutton his shirt. "And you know he will."

Paul lay beside her over an hour later in the bed, clean and relaxed and enjoying the feel of her body against his, not wanting to move to get food, since he knew it would mean it was time to go. He felt her snuggling in closer to him and he moved to kiss her.

"I cannot describe how little I want to move from here," he whispered.

Anne laughed. "You wouldn't get much sleep, not cuddled up to me like this. Feel."

Paul moved his hand to her rounded abdomen and felt the kicks, strong and hard. "Jesus, lass, is he like that all the time?"

"At the moment, yes."

Paul studied her. "You're not sleeping much are you?"

"No. But I'm well, Paul. Just tired."

"You do too much, Nan."

"So do you, Colonel. I didn't see any of the other brigade commanders in those streets earlier carrying out the dead and wounded."

"I didn't see many other officers' wives on their feet in that surgery either, lass, especially pregnant ones. I'm not going to nag you, Nan, but I love you so much. Please take care of yourself, I couldn't bear it if anything happened to you."

Anne kissed him gently. "I will. You need to go and eat, Paul, before that summons comes."

"That's not what I need right now," Paul said softly, and she laughed and moved her leg so that her thigh pressed against him.

"Colonel, you have no sense of duty."

"I bloody do," he said, laughing, pulling her closer. "Turn over, it's easier that way at the moment. I just want to remind you what my priorities actually are before I leave…"

His wife reached up to kiss him. "I think Lord Wellington and General Craufurd are your priorities just now," she said regretfully. "But I think they can let me have you for another half an hour."

Chapter Eight

The French attack came at daybreak. The Light Division were bivouacked in reserve just behind Spencer's first division. Lying on the hard ground among the men of his brigade, Paul had found himself restless and wakeful. Years of sleeping in impossible conditions had given him the ability to rest anywhere, but he lay on his back in the hour before dawn and admitted to himself how worried he was about the day ahead.

Paul suspected that some of his unusual anxiety stemmed from Anne's pregnancy. He had been into battle before when Rowena had been pregnant. The first time had not really affected him, because he had not realised the difficulties and dangers of childbirth. The second time he had tried hard to ensure that Rowena was safe and away from the fighting, and she had given birth on the journey and died in his arms. Paul's attachment to her had been real and steadfast and he had mourned her death deeply, but he was incurably honest with himself and he knew that his fear for Anne was greater because his feelings for his second wife were very different. Losing Anne would be like losing part of himself and as her pregnancy advanced, he fretted constantly about her well-being and her safety.

Anne had kissed him goodbye the previous evening with her usual smile and told him to take care of his brigade, and he had ridden away from her knowing that she had probably gone back to her room to cry. She would not do it in front of him in the hours before battle because she would not do anything to add to his burdens and Paul appreciated it. He desperately wanted the battle to go well because he needed to survive it and be there for Anne when she gave birth.

Paul was surprised at how badly he longed to hold their child with her. He had not been the first man in Anne's bed, but she had never conceived with her first husband. Paul had never told her how much it meant to him that the first child she bore would be his. It was childish and irrational and possessive in a way that was unusual for him, and he was a little embarrassed by it, but he was still fiercely glad that she had never had Robert Carlyon's child in her womb. This experience would be theirs together and he needed to be there for her.

The long call of a bugle intruded into his thoughts, sounding the alarm.

Paul sprang to his feet, aware around him of men moving, reaching for arms almost before their eyes were fully open. He turned to look for Johnny and found him there as he had expected.

"Get them lined up and ready, I'm going to see Craufurd, find out if he knows what's going on. That's coming from our right. I bloody knew it!"

Paul turned to find Jenson waiting with Nero and swung himself into the saddle with a brief nod of thanks. Jenson mounted his own horse and fell in behind him, and Paul glanced around and motioned for his orderly should move up beside him. He thought inconsequentially how naturally Jenson moved on horseback. His orderly had been unable to ride when he had first joined, but after he had lost half a leg at Assaye, Paul had taken him on as his orderly and valet. Back at Southwinds, his childhood home, recovering from his own injuries, Paul had taught Jenson to ride and discovered to their mutual surprise, that the boy from the slums of Liverpool had a natural affinity for horses. He had added groom to the long list of his duties and Paul could not imagine managing without him on or off the field.

Fuentes de Oñoro was crowned by a rocky hill which swept down to a long plateau to the west and Wellington had concentrated his main force in concealment behind the crest of the hill. He had established his command post at the summit, giving him an excellent view of the winding streets of the village dotted with walled gardens and vegetable patches and white and ochre houses, many of them now in ruins from artillery fire. The tangled lanes of the village eventually converged onto enormous slabs of rock, with the church perched atop one and Wellington's lookout post on another; a good vantage point where he could survey the surrounding countryside and the disposition of his forces. Paul found Craufurd and several other divisional commanders deep in conversation with the commander and his staff.

Craufurd saw Paul and beckoned him forward.

"Are they ready, Van Daan?"

"Yes, sir. Are we moving out?"

"We're in reserve, marching further to the right and awaiting orders. We might need to go in fast, there's a cavalry attack on the Spanish up at Nava de Aver. We're not sure of details yet."

"I'll let Colonel Beckwith and Colonel Drummond know," Paul said.

He turned away and heard the commander-in-chief's voice. "We knew it was a possibility, Colonel."

Paul turned back knowing this was not the time to resume his argument with Wellington about the line. "I know, sir. Wherever you took troops from, they'd have found the weakness, we just don't have as many men as they do. Good luck."

"You too, Colonel."

"Thank you." Paul moved away but Wellington's voice stopped him again.

"I don't like how close the hospital is to the battle," he said abruptly, and Paul turned back again.

"Sir?"

"I'm sending Graham down to Villa Formoso with orders that your wife and her companions join me up here. The medical staff will be all right, but I would prefer your wife to be in my charge until this is settled."

Paul did not speak immediately. Wellington had just told him how uncertain he was about the outcome of this battle. He would never express his doubts openly; his calm demeanour during the heat of battle was legendary and it gave confidence to officers and men in the most difficult of circumstances. But he had never before insisted that Anne join the headquarters party during an engagement."

Under normal circumstances it would have been impossible anyway. Wellington was a commander who liked to move around the battlefield giving orders personally and his staff usually spent a good deal of every battle scrambling to keep up with him or returning from taking a message to find the commander missing. On this occasion the field was too wide, and Wellington had chosen to direct operations from the centre. Villa Formoso was less than two miles from his command post.

"Colonel?"

Paul stirred, realising he had not responded. He wondered if Wellington was asking for his permission. "Yes. Of course. Thank you, sir."

The commander moved away from his staff. "She will have her maid with her, and Mrs Longford, Colonel, there can be no hint of impropriety."

Paul was surprised into a laugh. "Sir, that is not what I was thinking," he said, keeping his voice low. "I was thinking that I hadn't realised how worried about this you were."

He saw a flicker of irritation on his chief's face. Wellington glanced around but the other men were still talking, studying a sketch map of the area.

"I am not worried, Colonel, it is merely a precaution. In her condition, your wife should not be placed in the slightest danger. Should anything go wrong - and I do not for one moment imagine that it will - I will convey her to safety personally."

Paul felt some of his anxiety lift. "Sir, I'm very grateful. If this does go wrong…"

"If it does, Colonel, then I'll get her away. In the unlikely event that I and my staff are captured, she will be better off with me than with the medical staff. They will hardly offer any kind of insult to a member of my household."

Paul wanted to ask what role Wellington envisaged for Anne in his household, but he managed to stop himself. He could see the funny side of his commander's enduring devotion to his wife, but he was also passionately grateful that Wellington was prepared to go to so much trouble even in his current danger, to ensure her safety.

"I know. Thank you, sir," he said simply. "I'll be all right. But if I'm not, take care of her."

"You have my word. Get moving, Colonel. General Craufurd has my orders."

***

Anne received Captain Graham's arrival at the hospital with a warm smile. "Captain Graham, how are you? Are you looking for Dr Norris or Dr Franck?"

"No, ma'am, I'm here with a message for you." Graham bowed. "From Lord Wellington. His lordship sends his compliments and requests that you join him on the hill with the other ladies in your party. To ensure your safety."

"Safety?" Anne looked around blankly. "Captain, I have worked in a lot of army hospitals and always been perfectly safe."

"This is very close to the battlefield, ma'am and the lines are very stretched. It is hard to predict where the fighting may spread to."

"Well I may not be a military strategist, Captain, but I think it might be expected to spread to Lord Wellington's command post before it reaches here, don't you?"

The Scot flushed slightly. "I'm sorry, ma'am. Lord Wellington's orders."

Anne frowned. "Is my husband aware of Lord Wellington's orders?"

Graham relaxed a little. "He is ma'am. I was there when Lord Wellington spoke to him about it."

Anne took a deep breath and managed not to say any of the things she wanted to say. It was not Graham's fault. "Is Colonel van Daan still with Lord Wellington?"

"No, ma'am. The colonel has marched out, there's fighting out to the right."

Anne hesitated then capitulated grudgingly. "I'm not sure how happy I am about it, Captain, but we'll come. Let me tell the others. Come and have some tea while we get the horses ready."

Anne rode up beside Graham with Caroline, Keren and Teresa and found Wellington on the high ground looking out over the battlefield with his telescope. He lowered the glass at the sight of her and moved his horse forward to meet her.

"Ma'am. Thank you for coming."

"I wasn't aware I had a choice, sir," Anne said shortly and saw, to her satisfaction, that he had flinched slightly at her tone.

"My apologies, ma'am," he said stiffly. "As I informed your husband, I was concerned for your safety. Should the French attacks succeed, the battle might well fall back onto Villa Formoso and although I have no fear for the medical staff and the wounded, I could not contemplate putting you in such a perilous situation."

Anne studied him for a moment and her irritation melted in the face of his obvious concern and his even more obvious discomfort. She gave him a warm smile.

"Thank you, it was very good of you to think of Caroline and me. I am sorry for snapping your nose off, sir, you know how much I dislike taking orders. But I do appreciate your concern. Where should we go, to be out of your way?"

Wellington gave her the smile his staff rarely saw. "You could never be in my way, ma'am."

He swung down from his horse, handing it to his groom, and moved to lift Anne out of the saddle. Taking her hand he placed it on his arm, indicating to Graham to assist the other women. "Your husband has marched out with the rest of the light division," he said. "Until he returns, he has commended you to my care. Mr Beaumaris ask them to make some tea for the ladies. Come, my dear, you will have a better view from up here."

Anne accompanied him, quelling her desire to laugh at the expression on the face of Lord Fitzroy Somerset, Wellington's young acting military secretary, who was staring at his chief with a look of frozen horror. Wellington helped her up onto a low pile of rock and pointed.

"Look. Over there, what do you see?"

Anne looked out over the rolling countryside. She was surprised at how clearly from up here she was able to see what was happening. "Cavalry."

"Yes. There are two villages over there. The far one is Nava de Aver, the closer is Poco Velho. Your husband came up yesterday morning to shout at me about the weakness of our line on the right."

Anne glanced up at him. "I'm sorry, sir."

"Don't be, ma'am. Colonel van Daan and I have been shouting at one another for many years. Between you and I, we rather enjoy it. I was aware of the weakness, but I still expected the main attack to come from the centre, through the village. And I think it might; this could be a feint out on the right. But reports are coming in that Sanchez has pulled back his Spanish irregulars to avoid a slaughter and the seventh division is too isolated out there. I've sent Dryden and Gordon out with a small group of hussars to assess the situation, but it looks as though they're pushing our skirmishers back through those woods. I don't want the seventh cut off, so I'm…"

"Lord Wellington. I'm sorry to disturb you, sir."

The voice was that of Colonel Campbell, Wellington's long-time ADC and commandant. Both Anne and Lord Wellington turned. Campbell saluted.

"Runners on their way up, sir, looks like Major Dryden and Major Gordon."

"Excellent. Let us see what they have to say," Wellington said. Anne stepped back slightly. She was aware of the tension of the men around her and her own heart was beating faster. Usually during a battle she was away from the fighting, busy in the surgeons' tents or at the district hospital and she had never been this close to the centre of the action. Wellington's staff members all looked anxious. Only the commander himself appeared unmoved and Anne silently approved his remarkable calm in the face of what was clearly a dangerous situation. She had heard Paul speak of it many times as one of Wellington's greatest assets as a general.

"Yes, sir," Campbell said, his tone carefully neutral. "The servants have made some tea, sir. Perhaps Mrs van Daan…?"

Wellington looked at Anne and she met the blue eyes in a moment of shared amusement. "Colonel Campbell is concerned," Wellington said mildly, not looking at his commandant. "He appears to believe that the presence of a beautiful woman is likely to cause me to forget my duty, ma'am. I am surprised, however, that he is making his opinion quite so obvious. It seems to suggest a lack of faith in me and a lack of respect for you, which I cannot think he intended."

It was a spectacularly crushing reproof, uttered in a tone of gentle astonishment and Anne was not surprised when Campbell coloured to the roots of his hair.

"My Lord, Ma'am, my apologies. No disrespect intended. I just…"

His embarrassment was painful, and Anne took pity on him. "Of course there was not, Colonel, Lord Wellington is just funning. He has a similar sense of humour to my husband, but I am sure you must be accustomed to it, you've known him a long time. I would, however, very much like some tea. Thank you."

Campbell bowed. "Ma'am. Allow me to..."

"Are you trying to cut me out, Campbell?" Wellington enquired with mock indignation. "We will speak about that when this battle is won. Ensign Beaumaris."

"Sir."

"Take care of Mrs van Daan for me, please."

"Yes, sir."

Anne did not recognise the young man who came forward, a very young dark-haired ensign in the uniform of the guards.

"Allow me, ma'am."

He offered his arm and Anne smiled at him. "Thank you, Ensign. I'm not sure we've met."

"We won't have, ma'am, I've only just arrived.   Ensign Sebastian Beaumaris."

"Staff officer?" Anne asked, smiling.

"ADC, ma'am. Unofficially. I'm new to the service and Lord Wellington kindly offered me this opportunity; he knows my parents. Fetching and carrying mostly." The warm brown eyes shifted to the battlefield. "I'd rather be out there."

"You will be at some point, Mr Beaumaris. Don't rush it." Anne held out her hand. "Anne van Daan. My husband commands the 110th and..."

"I know who he is, ma'am," the boy said, and Anne repressed a smile at the tone. "I've been hearing stories about him for years. Army family, you know."

"Well thank you for your help, Mr Beaumaris."

Anne moved to where one of the staff orderlies had lit a small fire and was distributing tin cups of tea. It was warming and she stood holding the cup in her gloved hands, listening to the talk around her. Her mind was not present, was reaching out over the ground to where Paul marched with his brigade. She watched as Wellington's two ADCs rode over the crest and dismounted, saluting the general. Wellington was speaking to them, firing questions and although Anne could not hear all that was being said, she was watching Campbell's expressive face and she could see that he was worried.

Eventually Wellington turned and went back to the vantage point, his glass to his eye. His staff waited around him, fidgeting. Anne looked over at Caroline and saw her friend's blue eyes fixed on her, wide with anxiety. The atmosphere was tense and strained.

"Well then, gentlemen," Wellington said abruptly, snapping his glass closed. "It seems we've a fight of it over on the right."

He turned to face them. "We need to shift the line," he said decisively. "It was a gamble, stretching it so far out. If it had worked it would have protected our retreat back to Sabugal, but it seems the attack is too strong. We'll pull them round to form a new line running west from Fuentes de Oñoro to Freineda."

There was a long and difficult silence. Eventually, General Alava, one of Wellington's Spanish liaison officers, said:

"How, my Lord?"

"The seventh need to pull back. They've two battalions in Poco Velho but their outposts are already getting badly mauled. Sanchez has already pulled his men out of Nava de Aver and back to Freineda, it seems." Wellington met Alava's dark eyes and seemed to read something in them because he gave a faint smile. "He had no choice, General, they'd have been slaughtered. He became confused in the fog and mistook advancing French troops for his own pickets. Brotherton was up there with the 14th dragoons, it seems by the time Sanchez realised his mistake, they were on top of him. The 14th are putting up a good fight but they're taking heavy losses and the voltigeurs are going through the woods to the east clearing out our skirmishers. Dryden, I'll need more runners."

Wellington had taken a small notebook from his pocket and was scribbling fast. Anne moved away, her eyes back on the battlefield. Somewhere out there, people she cared about were marching and fighting and possibly dying and she felt suddenly very sick. Somewhere out there was Paul.

"Nan, are you all right?" Caroline asked.

"I'm fine, Caro. Worried. But we all are."

Caroline nodded and Anne reached out and took her friend's hand, squeezing it. She understood more than Caroline realised, what the other woman was feeling. Caroline had two men in the army. Her husband, currently acting as ADC to Major-General Sir William Erskine, was in no immediate danger with the fifth division guarding Almeida but Anne had so far seen no sign that Caroline cared much about her bad-tempered husband. Her anxiety was focused on the light division and Lieutenant-Colonel Johnny Wheeler.

Caroline had never told Anne that she and Wheeler had become lovers and Anne had never asked. Wheeler was a very private man and although Anne had known him for almost three years and considered him a friend, she knew nothing of his personal life although she guessed that like so many impecunious officers, Wheeler had not married because he could not afford to support a wife. Until Caroline had arrived, Anne had never known Johnny to show any signs of an attachment. Remembering her own unhappiness during her first marriage when she had fallen in love with Paul, Anne felt a painful sympathy for Caroline, who could not openly talk about her feelings for Johnny.

Another rider was coming in, a plainly clad Spanish irregular. Wellington conferred quickly with the Spaniard and then turned to his staff who were waiting expectantly.

"As we expected, gentlemen," he said calmly. "Marchand and Mermet's divisions are attacking the 85th and 2nd Caçadores. I'm sending orders to the seventh to get out of there and I'm sending in the light division. Between them and the cavalry they'll protect the retreat."

Runners came and went as Wellington issued a stream of orders to messengers and staff members. The level of activity ought to have been frenetic but was not, due to the commander-in-chief's monumental calm. Anne could sense the underlying anxiety of Campbell and Wellington's other staff members, but the chief himself showed no sign of panic.

"We'll need the cavalry to keep them busy," he said.

"We don't have any more cavalry to send in, sir," Stewart said, and Wellington shook his head.

"No. But I think the light division should be able to handle it, they're on their way."

"Sir." Grant had come forward, saluting. "They're moving on the village again. It looks like a full attack, sir."

Wellington looked out over the crumbling walls of Fuentes de Oñoro. "Excellent," he said mildly. "At least we seem to have read that part of their plan correctly. Let them come, Grant, but be prepared to reinforce if necessary. Take that away, Samson."

An orderly had approached with a tin mug of tea. Wellington waved it away irritably and the orderly turned looking unsurprised. Anne reached out a hand.

"Give it here, Samson."

The orderly handed Anne the tea, and Anne walked over to Lord Wellington.

"Drink it or I'm going to throw it over you," she said very quietly to avoid being overheard by the younger staff members. "I'm well aware that half the time you forget to eat or drink all day, but it's not a virtue and you're not doing it while I'm here. And next time, remember to thank the man. You'd be angry enough if one of your sons forgot his manners so badly."

She had spoken on impulse and was not sure how the commander would take her reproof. Wellington disliked being criticised, but he tended to be more tolerant of his few friends and Anne knew that she was one of them.

After a long moment, Wellington gave a reluctant smile. His eyes on her face he took the mug and sipped the tea then raised his voice. "Thank you, Samson. It's very good." He glanced at Lord Fitzroy who was trying hard not to laugh. "I wonder if Colonel van Daan would be prepared to lend me his wife every time I am directing a battle. It is a very educational experience."

Beckoning to Captain Graham, Wellington handed him a note. "Take that one yourself, Captain. And take Mr Beaumaris with you. He could do with the exercise, and besides, I have realised I should not allow my new junior ADC to see me being ordered about by a slip of a girl in a straw bonnet. Why don't you take a seat, ma'am? It is likely to be a long day."

***

Wellington's new line ran west across the ridge behind Fuentes de Oñoro. It was formed by the first and third divisions under Spencer and Picton along with Ashworth's independent Portuguese brigade, with its left flank in the village itself. He had left his fifth and sixth in their original position on what had been the Allied left, and Craufurd's light division marched out towards the beleaguered seventh which looked in danger of being cut off and destroyed. The two battalions who had retreated back from Poco Velho had already suffered over a hundred casualties and the French were marching in columns to attack. Paul could hear the drums echoing across the plain. Answering a summons from Craufurd he rode up to join his chief with Drummond and Beckwith.

90

"We need to get the seventh out of there," Craufurd said. "Lord Wellington wants them back on his right. The cavalry are doing a good job of shielding them up there, but there aren't enough of them."

"How are we going to do that, sir?" Drummond asked, studying Craufurd. The Scot lifted bushy dark brows.

"Take their place," he said. He was looking at Paul and there was a gleam of amusement in the dark eyes. "Colonel van Daan is particularly good at controlled retreats. I once saw him do it at the Coa. At the time, I seem to remember I was thinking about asking one of my riflemen to shoot him and put us all out of our misery, but I realise now that he has his uses. Get them moving, gentlemen. Fast."

Paul saluted and wheeled his horse, trotting back to his brigade. He could sense the genuine excitement in his chief, and he did not blame him. Craufurd's light division had shone at Bussaco, but his extended period of leave had robbed him of his part in Massena's retreat and he had been obliged to read reports in the newspapers of the honours heaped upon his division, in particular Colonel Beckwith and Colonel van Daan, after the battle of Sabugal, knowing that he had not been present. There was the added frustration of knowing that if he had been there in command instead of the incompetent Erskine, the light division might have stopped Massena in his tracks. Craufurd was looking for the opportunity to remind his division and the commander-in-chief who had been responsible for turning the light division into the elite troops of Wellington's army, and Paul could sense that his irascible commander could hardly wait.

The Allied cavalry had been conducting a skilful running retreat which allowed the seventh division to take up a slightly stronger position, and the initial French cavalry attack was successfully fought off as the light division marched south. It was an easy march of slightly less than two miles, mostly over open countryside which made it possible to watch the progress of the battle. Behind them, to the north, the sound of fighting in Fuentes de Oñoro made it clear that the French had resumed their attack on the village, now defended by the Highlanders. Ahead of them, Paul could see both French and Allied cavalry sweeping across the plain and hear the crack of musketry and the crash of artillery as the Allies tried desperately to hold off the French attack.

They found that French troopers had swept everything before them as they pursued the 85th and the Portuguese out of the village. They had been slowed down by the light cavalry of Slade's and Arentschild's brigades and Bull's battery of the Royal Horse Artillery which stood in their way in a gallant holding action. They were faced with hugely superior numbers of Frenchmen and Paul watched from a distance, advancing with his brigade as fast as they could, as the British troopers fell back, one squadron fighting while the other retreated, and then swapping over. It was a spirited defence with both sides reluctant to give way but eventually the British troopers were spent and retreated behind the infantrymen of the seventh division leaving dead and wounded scattered around the field.

Craufurd must have seen it at the same time as Paul did and gave the order to speed up. Sergeant-Major Carter uttered an impressively vulgar oath.

"Always been glad we weren't with the light division on the way back to Corunna," he muttered.

91

"Cheer up, Sergeant-Major, we don't have far to go here. Imagine what it was like on the way to Talavera – what was it, forty-two miles in twenty-six hours?"

"So they say. Still missed the bloody battle though, didn't they? Can't believe their march was worse than our fight."

Paul grinned and turned to check that his brigade was keeping up. Craufurd was notorious for his strict discipline and his willingness to push his men to their limits. In the past he and Paul had occasionally clashed over disciplinary methods, but a mutual respect had kept them on good terms despite their differences. Privately, Paul knew that his general allowed the 110th and 112th considerable latitude which he would never have given to the rest of the light division because he admitted that although Paul's methods were unconventional, they resulted in well-disciplined troops. Craufurd was a firm advocate for the practice of flogging and used it frequently and brutally. Paul refused to flog his men but made very sure that his officers understood the need to keep them strictly in line when Craufurd was about. He had no desire to find himself up against Craufurd over disciplinary methods because of some piece of stupidity on the part of one of his men.

General Houston had deployed his seventh division at the foot of a slope and some of his battalions had taken cover behind low stone walls. Montbrun's cavalry was unable to maintain its orderly formation, but the French troopers were doing a fine job of intimidating Houston's centre while another brigade was sent to try to outflank the British on the west side. Paul and his officers were watching with some concern at the new attack but from behind a wall, a tremendous volley opened up at close range and the dragoons fell back.

"Bloody hell, who's behind that wall?" Paul enquired. Johnny Wheeler had his glass out and was studying the approaching battle.

"The Chasseurs Britannique," he said. "And the 51st, by the look of things."

"Impressive. If they could stand and fight like that instead of deserting every five minutes, they'd be a real asset."

Wheeler grinned. The Chasseurs Britannique consisted mainly of French emigres who opposed Napoleon, many of them deserters from the French armies. Their tendency to melt away at the first sign of battle was legendary and they could never be used as pickets or given any unsupervised duty.

The French cavalry had fallen back to regroup as the light division made its way through the woods to emerge at the rear of the seventh. There had been no serious encounters with the French other than a few skirmishes with remaining tirailleurs in the woods and Paul could sense the relief as the two divisions met. The seventh was very new and had a fair number of inexperienced troops; it had not been the best division to leave so far out on the flank.

Paul watched as the two divisional commanders conferred. "Must be nice for Craufurd to feel so welcome," he said dispassionately. "Mostly, he's not that popular."

"I'd say Houston would have welcomed the devil himself to get him out of this mess," Carl said, drinking from his water bottle. "I bet the seventh will be happy to get moving. They've held well, mind, for a new division."

"They have. That looks like orders, Major, get them ready."

General Houston was giving orders to his senior officers and there was the sound of a bugle. The battered battalions of the seventh division began to form up. Paul kept a wary eye on the French, ready for a concentrated attack, but the cavalry had pulled back a little, making the occasional sweep on the artillery but not attempting to charge the infantry divisions. Paul suspected that they were waiting for further orders given the new situation. Looking back towards the north he could see movement in Wellington's lines and guessed that his commander was pulling his divisions into a new and more defensible line around the village. Paul would have made that decision yesterday, but he knew that Wellington had hoped to protect his line of retreat towards Sabugal with this extended line.

Houston began the march north-west, wary of any possible flanking manoeuvre, his retreat covered by the British dragoons and light cavalry. Paul watched the horsemen wheeling about.

"Even Wellington can't find anything rude to say about the cavalry today," he said to Carl. "If we get out of this mess in one piece, I owe this lot a drink or two. Bloody maniacs the lot of them, but Christ they're cool under fire." He looked over at Carter. "Sergeant-Major, get the light companies out and the rifles, fire at will, let's draw some of their attention off the seventh while they get out of here."

Surveying the ground with an experienced eye, Craufurd yelled out his orders and the green jackets of the rifles began to spread out in skirmish formation, covering the retreat of the seventh division. As Houston's men made their way northwards in fairly good order, Craufurd turned to his brigade commanders.

"At the ready gentlemen. We're forming square and making a controlled retreat out of here. Every single one of your lads knows what he's doing. Wellington has ordered the cavalry to support us, they'll keep the French artillery off us. Get them formed up, battalion squares. Take it steady and listen for my orders. We'll go in brigade order, Beckwith take the lead, Van Daan, you'll form the rear guard." General Craufurd turned back for a brief conversation with Wellington's messengers. The bugles called, high and clear over the drums and chants of the French, and under the watchful eye of their commanders, the light division formed into squares, with the cavalry and a few field guns in between. Paul watched as the French infantry and artillery were brought into place ready for the attack, coming under steady fire from the rifles and light companies.

"Oh this should be fun," Johnny Wheeler breathed. "I would so like to get out of this alive."

"You will," Paul said, looking over his squares. He had placed the 110th in one, the 112th in a second and his Portuguese and KGL in a third. "Lt-Colonel Wheeler, take the 112th. Major Clevedon, you and Captain Peso will command the third square. Major Swanson, with me."

Johnny saluted. "Good luck, sir."

"I won't need it," Paul said, and he heard Wheeler and Clevedon laughing as he moved towards the square which opened to let him through. He was aware that at times, his confidence sounded like arrogance, but he also knew that his certainty was loved by the bulk of his men who took him at his word when he told them they could do anything. In a situation as perilous as this he preferred not to dwell on any doubts. His men had spent endless hours on the training field perfecting every aspect of these manoeuvres and when the time came they would perform them as second nature. Paul had seen it many times and he had faith.

Beyond the squares, Paul's two companies of rifles and the two light companies were providing cover as the light division organised itself with Bull's guns in between and the cavalry riding nearby, ready to protect the squares from an artillery attack. Paul kept his eyes on his skirmishers conscious of a furious impatience for the rest of the division to move faster so that he could call them in. Both Manson and O'Reilly were excellent at this, but their position was becoming increasingly dangerous as the sheer numbers of the French began to drive them from the cover of trees, bushes, and rocks.

Eventually Paul heard Manson yell an order. He turned to Carl. "Open up," he shouted. "Let them in."

They came at a run, alongside the rest of the riflemen, scrambling into the squares as the cavalry bore down on them. The last of the rifles made it into the square formed by the 52nd with moments to spare and shots were fired as the square closed, driving the cavalry back. Paul ran to his horse and swung into the saddle, looking over at Craufurd. His commander, also on horseback, looked back and nodded.

"Call it, Sergeant-Major," Paul said, and Carter shouted orders to the buglers.

The light division began their retreat slowly across the plain. By now the French had brought up artillery, but the British cavalry wheeled about the field, repeatedly charging the guns preventing them from being used effectively against Craufurd's men. The pursuing French cavalry swung around time and again to make passes against the light division but maintained their distance. It was hopeless for cavalry to throw itself against an infantry square, especially squares as impenetrable as those of the light division. The men of the 43rd, the 52nd, the 95th, the 110th and 112th along with their associated battalions of German and Portuguese troops were the best in the world at this and every time the cavalry threatened they stopped the square immediately, bayonets, muskets, and rifles ready to fight them off. Paul, at the centre of his square, felt a huge pride in his men. He glanced over at Sergeant -Major Carter and Sergeant Hammond and saw Carter grinning, knew he was feeling the same thing.

"You got that bloody pocket watch anywhere, sir?"

"I'm not timing it today, Carter. Just get us there alive and I'm happy."

"All the same we'll speed it up if we can for you, sir. Don't want your wife getting herself into a state just at the moment."

The thought had occurred to Paul, knowing that Anne was probably up on the high ground with Wellington's staff, watching the battle unfold from a distance. It would be impossible for her to see exactly what was going on, but she would certainly see if one of the squares was badly hit. It was not happening at present. The English, German, and Portuguese cavalry, hugely outnumbered by their French equivalents had come into their own and were fearlessly charging down the guns, giving the French no chance to stop long enough to set up. On the few occasions the French managed to get artillery into position, the Allied cavalry were there to break up the gun batteries with repeated charges.

"What the hell is going on over there?" Carl said, and Paul followed his gaze to where there was a sudden burst of activity among the French cavalry. As he watched, they swung about, and the commotion resolved itself, as a troop of the Royal Horse Artillery burst from their ranks, two guns bouncing behind."

"Oh Jesus, it's Ramsey's men, they've got themselves cut off." Carl said. They watched in horror as Captain Ramsey's troop galloped frantically towards the British lines, the gunners fighting off the cavalry with sabres.

"Carter, get that cavalry off them," Paul bellowed, and the sharpshooters of the 110th dropped into position, firing at the French to break up their attack as the gunners thundered forward. It looked as though Ramsey was certain to be either killed or captured then Paul heard a thundering of hooves to his right and saw Captain Brotherton with his squadron of the 14th light dragoons galloping at full tilt towards the French. More cavalry galloped up on the left of the squares, a squadron of the Royals, and they hit the pursuing French hard, driving them back. The French turned to fight as Ramsey approached, pulling up between the squares. Paul called an order and the 112th moved to protect him. Many of the light division were yelling cheers, and they grew louder as some of the cavalry came in. Paul recognised Charles Stewart, the Adjutant-General leading them, grinning from ear to ear as he shepherded a small group of French prisoners one of whom appeared to be a colonel. Paul wondered what on earth Stewart was doing there and whether Wellington even knew where he was.

Paul looked over at Ramsey who had come to a halt, his horse sweating with the effort, his gunners breathless.

"Norman, you bloody idiot, you nearly got yourself gutted there."

Ramsey was laughing. "Didn't though, sir."

"What the hell happened?"

"We stopped to get off a few shots and misjudged it."

"Well don't bloody do it again, we've got enough to do," Paul said. He knew as he said it that he was wasting his breath. Ramsey and his men were completely elated by their escape and Paul would have put money on him taking another suicidal risk before the end of the day. Ramsey did not argue with Paul though, he merely saluted, still grinning broadly. Paul pantomimed shooting him then turned to check his square.

With the gun team safe, Craufurd gave the order to move on, closely followed by the French cavalry, ready to swoop down on any square that showed the slightest sign of disruption. Paul was grimly aware that the French must know how difficult it was to march in square. The outer lines on all sides needed to keep in perfect formation. Any gaps would allow to cavalry to ride in and break the square, cutting the men to pieces. Paul was confident in the men of the 110th and 112th and the Portuguese who had been with him for a while, but he admitted that he was nervous about his new troops. He wished he had elected to go with them as he had done several days earlier, but he needed to display confidence in them, and they had performed very well so far.

Craufurd had positioned the squares to flank and protect each other and despite the frequent passes of the cavalry there were no breaks. Cavalry did not break a well-formed infantry square, but artillery could, and the French had fifteen guns. It was a delicately balanced operation. The French cavalry vastly outnumbered the British and milled about the squares, shouting, and jeering at Craufurd's men. When the light division paused in square to fight off the cavalry charges, Montbrun ordered up his guns quickly to fire on the squares.

They were given little chance to do so. The Allied cavalry were magnificent, swooping down the moment the French tried to get off a shot, forcing the gunners to pull back or be slaughtered. There was no possibility of a pitched cavalry battle; the Allies were too outnumbered, but they played an infuriating game of cat and mouse with the French and it was working.

"We're going to make it," Carl said. Paul was on horseback surveying the other battalions through his telescope.

"We are. With very few casualties; they're not getting close. Although the cavalry are losing a few. They've been bloody brilliant today, it would only take one artillery barrage to break a square and it would all be over, but they've not given them a chance. Not long now, thank God, I can see the first division ahead. We'll let the others go through and protect the rear if we need to, but I think the French will pull up at that point. They're not going to charge the first, they don't have the numbers."

"I do hope not. How is Gervase getting on?"

Paul looked over at his third square. "They're holding very well. I'm bloody impressed with them, they're good lads. Sergeant-Major Carter."

"Sir?"

"Ease them back a bit, into position behind the 112th. The front squares are getting close. I..."

Paul broke off suddenly. His square was passing a series of rocky outcrops to the left, interspersed with trees and shrubs and there was a body of French cavalry, around half a squadron, milling about between two small hills covered in trees. They looked as though they were preparing for a charge and as Paul thought it, his major gave the order. The 110th dropped into a defensive square and waited.

Chapter Nine

As the French cavalry lined up for the charge, Paul put his telescope to his eye. There was something very deliberate about the movements of the French officer and also something very familiar. Paul studied him and felt an odd twist of concern in his gut.

"Carl, it's that red-headed bastard Dupres. He's seen us and he's going to try to cut us off."

He was watching the colonel who was yelling orders over to the French gunners. Carl swore.

"Bloody hell, I was hoping we'd seen the last of him. Do we need to speed them up?"

"No, that's what they're hoping. He's going to pull those guns as close as he can while there's no space for our cavalry." Paul slid from his horse. "Jenson take him. Carter, Hammond, pull them up, we're going to stand. Let the rest of them get through and then they can give us covering fire – it'll give space for our cavalry to come through…"

He broke off as Carter began calling orders. The square halted and fell into firing position, and Paul looked around him. He had a strong feeling that he was missing something, although he could not imagine what. The squares of the first and second brigade had almost reached the safety of the line held by the first division, and his other two squares were not far behind. Only his own square, bringing up the rear, was in danger of being cut off, but there were still plenty of Allied cavalry wheeling around to take another pass at the French gunners. There was no reason for concern, yet all of Paul's senses were screaming danger. He looked over to the corners of the square, well-reinforced. Every man was on his feet, every man alert and ready.

"What is it, Paul?" Carl asked quietly.

"I don't know. I honestly don't know. I just don't like being anywhere on a battlefield with this bastard."

Carl glanced over at the French. "He's ugly, I know…"

Paul laughed, but his eyes were still on the small troop of cavalry which was circling. Ahead of him the squares were beginning to break up, marching through the lines of the first division, but he could see Craufurd looking back, concerned. Paul looked over at Dupres.

"Where are the rest of them?"

"Who?" Carl said.

"His men. There are less than half of them there. Where…?"

Paul swung around with an oath, suddenly understanding. The squadron of the 14th which had been protecting his square had already been decimated earlier in the battle but there were still around fifty of them, led by a young captain by the name of Thatcher. He was around twenty-five, a bright eyed, optimistic young man who adored Anne and had spent winter quarters inventing excuses to visit the 110th's billet in the hope of scrounging a dinner invitation. Earlier on, Paul had reflected that given the work he had done today against such appalling odds, he intended to speak to Wellington about the younger man.

Thatcher had wheeled his horsemen again and was bringing them round to take a pass back at the guns which Dupres had ordered up against the 110th. Even at a distance, Paul could hear him calling his cavalrymen into line and he felt a surge of sheer horror as he realised.

"Jesus Christ, he's going to cut them off. The rest of his men are behind that outcrop."

Paul ran towards Nero and swung himself into the saddle yelling, but the Allied cavalry had already begun to gallop towards the guns, sabres ready. The gunners were limbering up and preparing to move, and Paul saw Dupres swing around and give a signal. To the rear of Thatcher's small troop, a mass of French cavalry appeared, and Dupres galloped his men forward, trapping Thatcher's men neatly between the rocky ridge and the solid lines of the 110th. They were vastly outnumbered, and half of Dupres men were armed with lances. Paul felt his guts twist in horror. The only possible help he could give would involve opening his square and once it was broken, the French would be in and his men would be slaughtered.

Paul swung around. "Carter, four ranks. Hold square, but back three ranks loaded and ready. Take out every one of them you can."

Thatcher had realised his danger, but there was no option but to carry on. He raised his sword and pulled out at the head of his men, thundering down towards Dupres and his cavalry. Paul slid from Nero's back and ran to the side of his square nearest to the approaching cavalry. He placed a hand on the shoulders of the nearest men.

"On my word," he said softly. "Open up."

Paul saw Carl swing round to stare at him, appalled, but Paul ignored him. Around him the light company rifles had opened fire, and Dupres' cavalry were beginning to fall. Paul stood waiting, watching the Allied cavalry approach.

"Now," he said, and his square parted.

Thatcher saw the move and Paul saw him haul back on the reins with a yell. His horse reared up and he was shouting orders. His troopers wheeled sharply right and rode into the centre of the square, pulling up quickly and shuffling close together to make space. Paul found that he was counting them in, as his muskets continued to pound in three ranks into the approaching French cavalry. The centre of the square was becoming crowded, but the horses and men were highly trained and stood very still, leaving space for more. Paul watched, his heart in his mouth as Dupres' men moved in towards the gap. There were fewer of them, but he knew he had only moments left before they broke into the square. Looking up he saw Thatcher watching, and then the boy looked over at him. There were twenty cavalrymen still outside the square. Thatcher lifted his hand and then wheeled and shouted to his men. Paul watched in sick horror as the men thundered away, galloping on towards Dupres.

"Close it!" he yelled.

The gap closed smoothly, and the rifles continued to fire. Paul looked over to where Dupres waited and saw the Colonel looking directly back at him. The Frenchman's face was flushed. He stared at Paul, and Paul looked back. Dupres' lips curved into a smile and he lifted his sabre and yelled an order, then Thatcher's men crashed into him, with the other half of the Frenchmen hitting them from behind.

It was short and brutal. Paul's rifles continued to fire where they could, but it was impossible to aim at the French without risking hitting the English. It was quickly over, and the English cavalrymen were cut down. Around him, Paul could sense the distress of his men and of the rest of the troop. They had all seen deaths in battle many times, but there was something deliberately cruel about the massacre of twenty men within a few feet of them and there was no attempt to take prisoners. Paul could no longer see the young Captain, but Thatcher's horse was loose and galloping off and he stood watching, feeling the prickle of tears in his eyes. The French cavalry massed around the English troopers who were on the ground, then there was a thunderous volley of fire, and Paul looked up and saw that Craufurd was up on the ridge and the Light Division was lined up, rifles at the front, firing volleys down on the French.

Dupres wheeled his horse with a shouted order and the French were on the run, some of them falling as they galloped away, their Colonel at their head. The guns of the 110th crashed out and another two of the cavalry fell from their horses as Dupres men rode out of reach. Paul watched, feeling sick and grief-stricken. For a moment, unusually, he felt unable to move or speak. Around him the guns still fired, and he moved his eyes to the bodies on the ground.

He felt a hand on his shoulder. "We need to get moving, sir," Carl said quietly, and Paul stirred and looked over to the lines.

"Open up," he said to Carter. "Let the cavalry out first."

He stood watching as the men filed out, trotting briskly, then called to his square to move on. With the rifles now in position and ready to defend their rear guard, no French cavalry came close, and the guns did not return as Paul's officers led their men up onto the ridge to join the rest of the Light Division who had formed up beyond the first division. Further away, Paul could see the French infantry advancing in column, but they were too far away to be an immediate concern. As his men marched ahead, Paul broke away and ran to where the bodies of the English cavalry lay.

Captain Thatcher lay on his back and his body had been slashed over and over. Across his throat was a gaping wound, which reminded Paul of what had almost happened to Manson. Thatcher's eyes were open, staring at the sky. Paul reached out and closed his eyes very gently.

"Colonel van Daan!"

Paul recognised the bellow of General Craufurd from the ridge above. Ignoring it, Paul stooped and lifted the long form of the young Captain. He moved forward towards the lines and saw several of his men break away and come back, ignoring the yells of the General. Carter, Hammond and Dawson came to assist him, and they carried Captain Thatcher's body up the ridge and behind the lines.

At the top Paul stepped back and let his men carry Thatcher to the back. Craufurd came forward.

"Colonel van Daan. That has to have been one of the…"

Paul swung around. "Don't, sir," he said savagely and Craufurd stopped. He studied Paul for a long moment and then grunted.

"Well, you got away with it," he said. "Well done."

Paul shook his head.

"No it wasn't. I couldn't save him. I stood there and watched that bastard cut him down and I couldn't do anything to help him. And he came in to save our arses."

Craufurd put his hand on Paul's shoulder, a rare gesture of sympathy from his irascible General.

"He did his duty, Colonel. A good officer. Did you know him personally?"

Paul nodded. "He had a tendre for my wife, he was constantly hanging around hoping she'd invite him to dinner. A nice lad."

"I'm sorry. It was a trap, nothing you could have done. I suppose they wanted one last crack at us. But it was nasty. Back to your men, there's nothing more you can do for him now. We've orders to move to the west to hold the rocky part of the ridge and extend the line."

Paul nodded and turned away, making his way over to his lines. He gave the order and watched as his men marched out after the second brigade. The Light Division formed up behind a series of rock formations, a natural fortress at the edge of the ridge. Paul saw them into position, feeling curiously numb. Mechanically he checked their lines and approved the rocky outcrops behind which they were stationed. He was conscious of his immense pride in them. Their retreat across the plains had been a textbook piece of infantry work and at some point he wanted to tell them so, but his eyes and ears were still full of the tragedy of Thatcher's pointless death.

Craufurd had moved away and was speaking to one of the Spanish runners, giving him a message to take to Lord Wellington. Paul watched, still feeling oddly detached. Craufurd came back towards him.

"They're fighting in Fuentes de Oñoro again," he said briefly. "The Highlanders are holding their own. We're to hold up here, wait and see what those infantry columns do. They might attack, although we're in a strong position up here."

"Yes, sir," Paul said. Craufurd nodded and moved away up towards the first and second brigade to speak to Beckwith and Drummond. Paul turned and looked out over the French columns, three infantry divisions moving into place to threaten

100

the British lines. Silently Paul assessed the distance and the situation and then he turned and yelled an order.

Shock rippled through the first division and Light Division as the 110th fired. Their first tremendous volley ripped into the first line of French infantry and blew them apart. Craufurd moved forward with an oath.

"What the bloody hell is he doing?" he said furiously.

There was another enormous blast of gunfire and the second French rank exploded. It had taken them that long to realise, incredulously, that the British were not waiting for them to attack. Under shouted orders from their commanders, they fell back quickly, dragging some of their wounded with them. Paul stood watching their frantic movements, his face expressionless.

"Major Swanson, Major Clevedon, Colonel Wheeler. You've got the range. If any one of them steps within it, I want him dead. See to it."

"Yes, sir," Johnny said. Paul walked away towards where Craufurd waited with Beckwith and Drummond. Behind him he heard the voices of his officers.

"This could be interesting," Clevedon said mildly.

"I bet poor Craufurd is wishing he was still on furlough," Carl replied. "All right, Sergeant-Major, you heard what the Colonel said. Keep them loaded and if there's a Frenchman you can hit, he's dead. The Colonel is seriously vexed with them and I don't want him annoyed with us as well, it's never pleasant."

Paul approached Craufurd, saluted silently and waited.

"I did not give the order for your men to open fire, Colonel," Craufurd said furiously.

"No, sir. I did that."

"Without orders. What in God's name is wrong with you, Van Daan? You've been in charge of a brigade for five minutes and you already think you don't have to follow my commands."

"Sorry, sir."

"Sorry? What do you mean, sorry? You're not fucking sorry at all!"

"No, sir. Not at all. Just being polite."

"Polite?" Craufurd looked as though he might explode. Paul glanced at Beckwith and Drummond then back at his chief.

"Permission to go back to my men, sir?"

"Van Daan, you are an arrogant young bastard without any respect for authority or…"

"Yes, I have, sir. Immense respect for authority, especially your authority. I could point out that you didn't tell me not to fire those volleys, but you and I both know that would be nit-picking. I fired them because I'm fucking angry, and I felt like letting them know that if they cut down our men like that I'm going to fucking slaughter them any chance I get. And you know what? I think they got the fucking point. Let's see how quickly they come forward against my lads again today, shall we? And if Lord Wellington is looking for volunteers to march down to Fuentes de Oñoro and kill a few more of them, you just let me know because I'm in the mood. Permission to go back to my men, sir?"

Craufurd studied him for a moment. Unexpectedly he said quietly:

"Dismissed, Colonel."

101

"Thank you, sir."

Paul turned away. Robert Craufurd's voice stopped him. "Colonel, I'm sorry, I was watching. It was bloody awful, and that boy was a hero, he let his men go through ahead of him and then he rode off so that you would close the square and save your men. You were rash, but you pulled it off and you probably saved the lives of thirty cavalrymen. But you can't save everybody."

Paul turned to look at him. "No, sir. But that's not much consolation just now."

Paul had expected more action, but Massena's three divisions kept their distance, cautiously awaiting orders and careful not to come within range of the Light Division again. Instead, the French Marshal threw his strength against the village, putting off further action until it was in his hands. The fighting went backwards and forwards through the streets with the 71st and 79th driven out of the lower and middle village, and then joined by the 24th driving the French back to the river.

Drouet's division joined the attack with his elite grenadier companies and forced the British back to the highest ground in the village, but they could push no further. There was a ferocious struggle through the streets with no side gaining ground. Wellington ordered in the remains of the light companies, many of whom had fought over the same ground two days earlier, along with the Portuguese 6th caçadores. A deadlock ensued with the streets piling with dead and wounded once again from both sides.

Drouet sent in another 6,000 men to assist the grenadiers, and the British were swept back by sheer force of numbers. The French even made it beyond the church, but at that point Wellington sent in Mackinnon's Brigade from the third division who charged into the choked lanes with bayonets and fought a street battle of fierce intensity. Eventually the French began to give way, and once broken, retreated back up the streets, fleeing before the cold steel of the English bayonets. As had happened two days earlier, the British and Portuguese, bloodied and exhausted, were in possession of the village with the French retreating over the river to the eastern bank.

Paul had watched what he could of the fight from the shelter of his rocky fortress. Part of him wanted Wellington to call on the Light Division to go into the village and sweep the French back. He was still tense and angry and unsettled. The other part, the sensible part, knew that he had been incredibly lucky to survive the difficult retreat with his brigade intact and that he should not ask for trouble. He needed time to calm down and deal with his anger at Simon Thatcher's death. Paul could not help feeling that the French colonel had used the young cavalry officer and his men to settle some imaginary personal score against him. He could not shake off the sense that he was in some way responsible although he knew it was silly.

As the afternoon drew on, the sounds of battle began to die down. It was frustrating not to be sure what was happening, but Paul, studying what he could see of the village through his telescope, thought that the Allies had the best of the encounter and there was no further sign of a French advance. He waited, restless and miserable, with his brigade, for further orders.

***

Anne and her companions remained on the hill with Wellington's staff officers. By mid-afternoon, all fighting below had ceased. The commander-in-chief was deep in conference with his officers and an endless stream of messengers rode up and down. Still Anne waited, tense and afraid until she saw Lord Wellington look over towards her.

"Help me up, Caroline."

Her friend did so, and Anne walked to where Wellington was waiting for her.

"He's safe," he said. "I've no details of casualties but they seem to have been very light among Craufurd's men although others haven't been so lucky. You should be proud of him, ma'am, the Light Division saved our right flank from what might have been annihilation."

"I am, sir. Thank you for finding out for me, I know you've so much to do."

"It doesn't matter how busy I am, ma'am, I always ask for news of my friends."

"I'm grateful, sir. And thank you for taking such good care of me today. With your leave, I'll go down to the hospital now, they'll need me."

"As you wish. I'll provide an escort. They seem to be done for today, but we don't yet know if they've retired to regroup and will attack again tomorrow. Should there be the least danger, I will send Graham down to bring you back up."

Anne smiled and gave him her hand. "You're as bad as Paul, you both fuss too much," she said. "But I do appreciate it. May I ask where my husband is now? I'd like to send him a note."

"They're holding the ridge over to the west, ma'am, but I intend to send them down into the village shortly."

"Thank you, sir."

The ride back to Villa Formoso was completed mostly in silence. Wellington sent the young ensign with half a dozen cavalry troopers to escort the women. Most of the action seemed to have ceased although Anne could still hear desultory shooting over to the south between French and Allied skirmishers. She was suddenly exhausted, as if she had spent the day on her feet in the hospital rather than sitting on a hillside watching the battle unfold and she supposed it must be the emotional strain that had drained her energy.

The quinta was chaotic, with wagonloads of wounded being brought in and Anne summoned her reserves and went to put on her apron. She arrived to find lines of men waiting for treatment and she joined Norris in the surgery.

"Nan, thank God you're here, we're swamped."

"I knew you would be, I'm sorry, Adam, Lord Wellington insisted. He seems to have thought the fighting might spread this way."

Norris grinned. "I'm not sure I'd have noticed I've been up to my eyes in it. Here, take this table, it's lower. You look tired, are you all right to work?"

"I can manage an hour, I think."

She managed three in the end, stopping only when Norris intervened.

103

"Go and rest, Nan, you look exhausted. You're as white as a ghost. It's getting dark, it must be late. Get out of here, eat something and go to bed. I think George Kelly has food ready next door."

Anne untied her bloodied apron. "I'm not sure I can eat," she confessed. "I'm feeling a bit sick. Perhaps a rest will help."

Anne made her way through the courtyards, stepping around injured men on the ground, and out towards the main door of the quinta. Outside the wrought iron gates another wagon was unloading injured men and two bandsmen were carrying a big wooden bucket between them towards the side of the house. Protruding from the top was a blood-soaked arm, its fingers drooping over the side of the bucket. Beside it, was what looked like a severed leg. Anne stared for a moment and then turned and ran to the side of the house, her stomach churning. She was sick briefly and violently, supporting herself with one hand on the wall.

"Here, ma'am, are you all right?" a voice said. Anne straightened, feeling shaky and a little dizzy, to see a Corporal of the 74th sporting a dirty bandage around his head, peering at her anxiously.

"Yes. I'm sorry, Corporal. It doesn't usually bother me. Silly."

"Silly, is it?" the Scot said, turning to glare at the bandsmen who had set down their grisly burden to refresh themselves from a bottle. "Silly is the word that comes to mind when I see a pair of scabby bampots, waving around a bucket of bloody arms and legs in front of a lady in a delicate condition like their Ma never taught them better. You rest here a minute, ma'am, while I go and shove their heads in that bucket and then I'll see you back to your billet."

One of the bandsmen shoved the bottle hastily into his coat. "Didn't know there was a lady about," he said defensively.

"Not sure that a woman alone in a place like this is likely to be a lady, Corporal," the other said, with a hint of insolence. "Not sure any lady would be hanging about an army camp…"

He broke off with a yelp as a hand smacked him hard across the back of his head, knocking off his forage cap. Recovering, he turned belligerently, then froze and snapped to attention, saluting smartly. Anne felt her heart leap.

"Not sure you've enough brain in that thick skull to know a lady from a lamp post, but you speak like that about my wife again and I'm going to rip your arms and legs off and shove them in that bucket you stinking piece of goat shit. Apologise and get on with your job. And before you go, I'll take that bottle, you can't afford to addle the few wits you've got left."

Anne came forward as the two bandsmen gabbled an unintelligible apology and staggered off with their revolting cargo. Paul turned to the Highland Corporal who was saluting.

"Name, Corporal?"

"Mackenzie, sir. Third company, 74th."

"Jesus, you've had a day of it down there. Head wound?"

"Bayonet, sir. Took half my ear off."

"Seen the surgeon yet?"

"No, sir. Might not wait, there's a lot worse than me and the bleeding's almost stopped."

104

"Well whatever you do, thank you for taking care of my wife. Here, you might find a use for this, it's almost full."

He handed the bottle to Mackenzie whose face brightened. "Thank you, sir."

Anne looked at her husband. His face was still black with powder and streaked with sweat but beneath it she could see that he looked tired and depressed. She wanted to run into his arms but the grubby cloth around Mackenzie's head bothered her.

"I'm so glad to see you," she said, looking at Paul. "Can you wait five more minutes?"

The blue eyes regarded her gravely through the fading light. "For you, girl of my heart, I will wait an eternity. Get on with it or I'll never get you out of here."

Anne led the protesting Corporal back into the hospital where she cleaned and dressed the wound. Outside she found Paul waiting by the door, talking to one of the surgeons. He came forward and took her hand.

"Are you all right, love, you look exhausted? I thought you were up with Wellington."

"I was," Anne said. "When the worst was over I came back down. I didn't mean to do too much but poor Adam and Oliver were drowning in wounded men."

Inside the house they found Kelly presiding over a cooking fire in the courtyard. "Glad you're back, ma'am. I was just going to send Teresa to find you. Good to see you, sir. I think Jenson just took some hot water up to your room."

"Thank you, Sergeant. Teresa, Danny is safe and well. Not a scratch on him."

"Thank you, Colonel."

Paul looked around. "Where's Keren?"

"She went to help Mrs Longford, I think."

"Will you find her and tell her that Major Swanson is alive and unhurt, Teresa. She'll be fretting."

The Spanish girl gave a broad grin. "I will, sir. Thank you."

Upstairs in the big, bare room, Paul lowered himself tiredly into a camp chair. Anne knelt before him and reached for his boot and he shook his head.

"Nan, one of these days, you'll get down there and won't be able to get up. It's not your job to wait on me, I'll get Jenson."

Anne rose easily and stood looking down at him, her hands on her hips. "I am perfectly capable of doing that again if you need another demonstration, Colonel," she said shortly. "I don't want Jenson, and my job is whatever I say it is. What I do want, is to see you clean and changed and then you can tell me what's wrong. Did we lose somebody? What aren't you telling me that's causing you to snap like a terrier caught in a rat trap?"

Paul looked up at her with a startled expression then to her relief, broke into laughter. "Oh no, did I? I'm sorry love. What did you just compare me to?"

Anne laughed. "It's what the head groom used to say at home," she said.

"I didn't think you'd picked it up from your stepmother. It's all right, Nan, our lads are all fine. It's just…we lost Simon Thatcher."

"Oh." Anne felt her heart sink. "Oh, no. I liked him so much."

"So did I. But I've lost a lot of friends in battle, Nan. This was worse somehow."

Anne knelt down again and reached for his boot. "Stop talking. You look like a demon, I can't have a conversation with you until you're clean. When you are, you can tell me."

His boots removed, Anne eased off Paul's stained, dirty coat and went for brandy. He sat at the small table and drank, seeming unusually to be too tired to speak and Anne took the opportunity to find Jenson. He was downstairs with Keren and Teresa, giving them an account of the day and reassuring them, but he broke off at Anne's approach.

"Freddie, is he hurt? I can't see anything, but…"

"No, ma'am, but he's bloody upset. Those poor lads. Did he tell you?"

"Not yet. He's getting washed and changed, I'm going back up to hear the story now. Poor Simon Thatcher, I'll miss him."

"Was he married, ma'am?"

"No, but he'd an informal understanding with an Irish girl he met in Dublin. I'll find out and write to her, she might not get an official letter if his commanding officer doesn't know about her. Thank you, Freddie."

She found Paul washing the dirt and blood of the battle away and went to help him. He stood unresisting and when finally he was clean, she wrapped a towel around his waist, sat him back on the chair and began to massage his shoulders. He sat back, closing his eyes. After a moment he let out a little sigh and then he opened his eyes and twisted his head to look at her.

"Kiss me, would you?"

Anne leaned forward. He kissed her gently at first and then harder, pulling her onto his lap, his hands reaching around to the buttons at the back of her dress.

"You're in a hurry, Colonel."

"I've had a bad day," Paul said. He stood up, lifting her into his arms. "I don't want to talk just now, Nan. I just want you."

Paul carried her to the bed and Anne lay back and he stretched out beside her, the long length of his body against hers. The tensions of the day faded in the fierce intensity of his need. There were no words and none of the laughter that usually accompanied their lovemaking and when his climax came she heard him gasp her name.

Paul was quiet in her arms afterwards and Anne held his head on her breast, stroking the still damp fair hair, running her fingers through it, smoothing the skin of his temples, and feeling his face wet with tears.

"I swear to God I don't ever want to move from here," he said finally. Anne gave a soft laugh.

"You will once you smell food."

"How well you know me, girl of my heart. Are you all right? I'm not sure I was as gentle there as I ought to be with you just now."

"I'm not that fragile, Paul, in case you hadn't noticed."

He twisted his head to look up at her, smiling through his tears. "You're not fragile at all, it's an illusion. You look almost delicate you know? That beautiful bone structure."

Paul turned and placed a kiss on her collar bone, very delicately, tracing its line up to her neck, his hand sliding lower down her body. Anne gasped as his fingers found what they had been seeking and arched her body against him as he began to stroke her again. She felt his mouth biting at the skin of her neck, and she was dizzy with pleasure, running her hands over his chest and back.

"But you're not delicate are you?" he whispered, laughing at the desire building in her dark eyes, at the movement of her hips as he continued to rub his hand over and into her. "You don't have a ladylike bone in that very lovely body when it comes to this."

"No," Anne admitted, her voice husky with desire, and he laughed.

"Prove it," he said, and she moved, pushing him onto his back and moving her mouth over his body and downwards.

"You're very full of it this evening, Colonel," she said, laughing, and he gave a little groan as her mouth teased at him. "Been ordering them about out there all day, haven't you? Let's just see how bossy you can be when I'm doing this."

"Nan…" His voice came out something between a laugh and a groan as she lowered her mouth to him. "Oh Christ, bonny lass. Don't stop doing that."

Anne gave a gurgle of laughter, her mouth hovering above him, feeling the tension of his body under her hands as he waited for her. "Is that an order, Colonel?"

"Yes," Paul said, and Anne bent her head to him.

They lay finally, entwined in a tangle of sheets in the darkness. Outside there was the smell of cooking and then sounds of arrival and Anne stirred. Paul tightened his arm about her.

"Don't move."

Anne gave a gurgle of laughter. "You can't possibly, Colonel."

"No, I'd kill myself. I just don't want you to move, I think I might have died and gone to heaven." Paul gave a sudden laugh.

"What?"

"I was about to say something very unsuitable."

Anne bit his shoulder. "Given what we've just been doing, I doubt you're going to shock me, Paul."

Paul twisted his head to look at her and Anne was overjoyed to see the laughter back in his eyes and the taut misery gone from his face. "I might. I was going to say that I spent too many hours of my youth in a series of very expensive brothels, but I have never met a woman as good at that as you are."

"Paul!"

Paul was laughing uncontrollably. "It's true, bonny lass, it must be natural talent because it's not as though you had a whole stable full of lovers before you married me."

"It would serve you right if I told you I had," Anne said indignantly. "What a thing to say to your wife, who is carrying your child."

"I did say it was very unsuitable. I particularly love it when you try to sound shocked and look prim, especially after you've just done what you did."

Anne was beginning to laugh. "Paul, you just compared me to a prostitute."

"I really did, didn't I?" Paul shifted so that he was leaning over her and kissed her. "But a very, very expensive one, girl of my heart. Worth every penny, I promise you."

Anne smacked him hard, and he fell back, shaking with laughter. She was laughing too, looking down at him. Like this he looked like a boy and she wished it could always be like this that there would be no more death and war and sorrow. His eyes met hers and the laughter died although he was still smiling.

"I need to tell you about today, bonny lass. I can't stay the night, we're stationed in the village in case the French come again tomorrow. Wellington thinks they may well give it another crack. So I need to eat and get back up there."

Anne nodded. She held out her arms and he moved back into them, settling beside her, and pulling up the blankets to cover them both. After a moment of silence he began to talk.

Chapter Ten

It was late when Paul finally moved. They remained quiet and still after he had told his story but he knew Anne was crying for a while because he could feel her cheek damp against his shoulder. He felt curiously peaceful, as though telling her the story had somehow washed away the worst of his fury and all he felt was sorrow at the loss of a man he had known and liked.

Kissing her gently Paul slid from the bed and turned up the oil lamp, lighting two candles from it. He went to find clean clothing and heard Anne move behind him. Buttoning his shirt he felt her arms go about his waist and her cheek laid against his back.

"You seem better, Colonel."

Paul turned into her arms. "Much better. I wonder how thick this door is, I'm fairly sure I heard Carl's voice a while back. He's probably come back to give me my orders.

Anne took a robe from the chest and picked up her chemise from the floor, pulling a face. "This is going to need mending."

"I'm sorry, lass. Once we're in winter quarters I'll take you shopping, your clothes are a disgrace."

"Not much fits at the moment anyway," Anne said, searching for a shift. Paul took it from her and helped her on with it. She reached for her blue velvet robe and Paul finished dressing, easing his tired feet into his boots, and reaching for his coat with a grimace of distaste.

"Do you want me to try to clean that a bit for you?" Anne asked.

"Not much point if I'm fighting again in the morning." Paul surveyed her, smiled and went to the chest she was using as a dressing table. He picked up her hairbrush.

"Come here. You look as if you've just spent a day in a high wind."

Anne came forward, letting him run the brush through her long dark hair. It was a ritual he had carried over from his first wife who had been as fair as Anne was dark, and he loved doing it. When her hair lay smooth and shining over the dark blue velvet he put down the brush and surveyed the room, beginning to laugh. The wooden floorboards were splashed with water and there were clothes and shoes and towels scattered about the room. The simple wooden bed frame was piled with a tangle of bedsheets and covers.

"It doesn't take us long to wreck a room," he said.

"I wouldn't worry, Colonel, neither of us is going to be spending much time in it for a few days."

"No," Paul said soberly. He had been conscious for a while of the rising noise in the street as more of the wounded were brought into the hospital. "I know you may not want to hear this, lass, but you might be better with a different billet, it's going to stink to high heaven here with the dead and wounded, and you'll get no sleep."

"I'll be all right, Paul."

"Nan, normally I wouldn't interfere, but I don't want you billeted next to the charnel house that place is about to turn into. Bad enough that you'll be working in it."

"They need me, Paul."

"I know they do, bonny lass, but that doesn't mean I have to like it. Come on, let's go and eat, it must be almost midnight and I need to get going."

They found Carl Swanson below, eating mutton stew. Beside him, Keren was curled up like a sleepy puppy. She made to get up and Anne put a hand on her shoulder. "Stay there," she said, and Keren smiled and settled back.

Carl greeted Paul with a weary smile. "We've moved into the village along with Beckwith's brigade. Cartwright has found some sheep to roast from somewhere so they're being fed. Michael and Leo have got them building barricades and doing emergency repairs to some of the buildings and walls to provide some cover tomorrow. At least this time they're going to run up against experienced skirmishers."

"Brilliant idea. Somebody should have mentioned it to Wellington. Although it would be difficult right now for me to decide if I prefer retreating over three miles of difficult countryside with artillery and cavalry trying to slaughter me or being blown to pieces in a crumbling village with no cover left. I'll sleep on that one and let you know. Thanks George. How you manage it, I'll never know."

George Kelly pulled a face as he handed a bowl to Anne. "Not so keen on staying here, sir. Can already smell the poor bastards coming in, and I'm told they're digging a grave pit next door."

"Oh tell me you're joking. Can't the idle bastards do it out in the countryside, people have to come back and live here?"

"There's no time to transport the bodies," Anne said. "I suppose that's where they were taking the amputated limbs earlier. But you're right, if they're turning this into a graveyard, and in this heat, my stomach is not going to stand it, it's very delicate at the moment. Let alone the vultures. Perhaps we should move into tents on the edge…"

"I've got a better idea than that, ma'am. Captain Cartwright and I got talking to the woman we bought the sheep from."

"Bought?" Paul enquired genially.

"Bought, sir," Kelly said firmly. "My Colonel won't let us rob the locals, he's a right mean bastard. Anyway, she's from an estate just to the north of

Freineda. Only about three miles away, big place, must have been worth a lot of money once although it's fallen on hard times. They grow grapes, grain and fruit trees and run sheep and goats, a few cattle. Just her and her daughter now, her husband was killed fighting for the partisans."

"Christ, that's hard."

"I think they were well off from what she says, but it's run down now. They've a couple of old fellows working for them but the young men have all gone to war – or died in it. I wondered…"

"It might be ideal," Paul said, glancing over at Anne. He was surprised when she nodded.

"I'll talk to Breakspear and he and I can go out to have a look, Paul. Don't look so shocked, I am occasionally reasonable, and even I don't want to live next door to an army hospital. I know what it will be like. I can ride over during the day." Anne smiled. "To be honest, I'm thinking ahead. I'm going to need somewhere to have this baby when the time comes, I'd rather not give birth in a tent in the middle of an army camp. Although I expect I could if I needed to."

"Very likely, girl of my heart, but I'm glad you're planning. In fact, I'm delighted, since this is possibly the first time I've heard you acknowledge that you are in fact going to give birth to this baby."

"You do exaggerate, Paul. Just because I'm not sitting here on a cushion with my feet up…"

"Do we own a cushion?"

"Teresa has one. She won't let me take charge of it in case I give it to the wounded."

"Thank God for Teresa," Paul said, smiling over at the Spanish girl who had just emerged from the house. "Go with her to inspect this place, will you, lass? You look more respectable than she does, you should be able to convince them…"

"If you keep this up, Colonel, you're not going to make it back to Fuentes de Oñoro," Anne said.

***

Anne was happy, watching Paul, that he had relaxed enough to laugh again. Up in their room he had fallen asleep for an hour and she lay holding him, studying him through the darkness. Every time he left to go into battle she knew that he might not come back, or that he might do so maimed or crippled. Anne never told him how difficult it was, or how often she lay awake trying to imagine what it would be like to live without Paul.

They had been married just over a year but had fallen in love three years ago when Anne had met him in Yorkshire. She had been seventeen, resisting the attempts of her wealthy family to marry her to a suitable man. He had been twenty-six and a major already, married with a young family whom he had left in Leicestershire, second son of a wealthy businessman and a man on his way up in the army. They had found themselves thrown together in a snowbound shepherd's hut on a moorland road and she had fallen in love with him almost from the first

111

time he smiled at her. Their love had survived her own first brutal marriage to another officer as well as her friendship with his sweet, diffident wife, Rowena.

Their relationship had scandalised Wellington's army, conducted as it was under the critical eyes of the other officers and sometimes their wives. Anne had not fitted in well with the other wives. She was too different, too unconventional, and she had always suspected, too beautiful to be liked. When Rowena died in childbirth and her own husband had been killed, she and Paul had married quickly and braved the scandal.

Anne had not met his older children or his family and had not seen any of her own family since she had sailed for Portugal with Robert Carlyon. Instead, she had been absorbed into the life of his regiment and they had become her family and her friends. She could not imagine, now, bearing their first child without him beside her or sailing back to England leaving him buried beside some battlefield, and yet her reality was that it could happen at any time.

Anne's way of coping was to live each day in the moment. She threw herself into her work at the hospital and immersed herself in the technicalities of supplies and transport for the the brigade, taking on burdens which were not rightfully hers in order to give Paul time to do what he did so spectacularly well with his men. She snatched every hour she could with him and went into his arms each time as if it might be the last. It brought an intensity to their time together which she found, at times, exhausting, but it was worth it to be with him.

When Paul had eaten he got up wearily. Anne could feel the prickle of tears in her eyes, and she fought them back determinedly. Jenson was ready with the horses and out of the corner of her eye she saw Carl taking Keren into his arms for a long kiss. She was faintly amused. Something had shifted in that extraordinary relationship and her husband's oldest friend was suddenly quite open in his affection for his mistress. Anne thought that at some point she was probably going to have to look for another maidservant. Teresa needed to be able to concentrate on her husband and whatever the outcome of Keren's liaison with Major Swanson, it was going to become difficult to give orders to the girl when Carl clearly wanted her with him.

At the gate, Paul drew Anne into his arms and kissed her very tenderly. "Nan, will you do something for me?"

"Anything, Colonel."

Paul laughed. "You should be more careful what you agree to before you've asked what it is," he said. "I could ask you all kinds of things you don't want to do."

Anne wound her arms about his neck for a long kiss. "Paul, when you get me in your bed you could probably get me to do pretty much anything," she said.

"It's mutual, girl of my heart. Sadly, we've no time. But this is nothing that complicated or that surprising. Before you go into that hospital and start sewing people up, get yourself out to the estate and find another billet. I want you safe and secure and away from this charnel house. I'm not telling you not to work. But…"

"I'll go in the morning," Anne said softly. "I promise."

"Good girl. You were right, you need somewhere secure to have this child and unless the French win tomorrow and we have to make a hasty retreat, this sounds like a good place. It's possible this baby may come sooner than we think."

"What makes you say that, Paul?"

"Just an educated guess. I've been through it twice with Rowena and I've talked to the women about it as well. I can't be exact any more than you can, but you're getting much too tired now for a lass in her fifth month. We're all fooled by how well you cope and how slight you are – Rowena was twice your size. But it might be a small baby, or it might just be how you carry. I think you've two months to go – three at best. But we'll wait and see. Let's just get you settled. Wellington is going to establish his headquarters in Freineda and if we can find good billets close by you won't have to keep moving about just before the birth."

"I'll go tomorrow."

"Thank you. I need to get back to my brigade. Au revoir, love of my life. Keep well and take care of my child until I come back to you both."

"Make sure you do, Colonel," Anne said, and released him, pulling herself up straight and keeping the smile on her face. She saw Carl move away from Keren and join Paul at the horses. Glancing over, she saw Keren forcing a smile and felt a sudden fierce kinship with the girl. She moved over and put her arm about Keren's waist. Keren turned to look at her in surprise and then suddenly she smiled properly, and Anne felt her arm go about her in turn. It felt good to stand there with another woman who understood.

Anne slept restlessly, missing Paul beside her. She woke early, dressed and went over to the hospital. Already it was crowded with patients. They had dug a large pit at the back and the smell was overpowering, making Anne want to gag. She pushed her nausea down and went to find Dr Daniels.

"How are you, ma'am?"

"I'm all right, Oliver. Feeling guilty that I'm not in here working."

Daniels laughed. "The only person who thinks you should be in your condition, ma'am, is you. They're going to start going through the town again at first light. We're just trying to get ready. We're almost full on the wards here, God knows where we'll put them."

"Possibly next door," Anne said. "I'm going out to look at an alternative billet this morning, Oliver – Paul's worrying about me being so close to this and having seen what they've dug at the back here I think he might have a point."

Daniels pulled a face. "I know. We didn't get a say in it, but it's a bloody stupid idea, it'll make the men sick until it's filled in. And those poor villagers…"

"Don't get me started. If this place is suitable, we're going to move our gear out there today, and I'll move yours as well, you could do with somewhere clean to come back to. It'll leave the cottage empty and you can fill it up with wounded."

"Thank you, ma'am. What about Cartwright?

Anne laughed. "I can tell you've been busy. Captain Cartwright is no longer in charge of billeting for this area. Or indeed working for the quartermasters. He's up with the brigade commanding the eighth company of the 112th."

"He's serving under the Colonel? Jesus, ma'am, the gossips are going to make hay with that one during winter quarters. Are you aware…?"

113

He stopped suddenly, and Anne laughed and reached up to kiss him. "Yes, Oliver, I'm well aware that they're saying that my husband fathered Arabella Cartwright's bastard. I don't care and if Paul and Davy don't, what does it matter? I need to get going. I'll be in as soon as I've settled this."

Anne rode out towards the small village of Freineda, accompanied by Sergeant George Kelly, Private Ned Browning, Teresa, Keren, and Caroline Longford. Their route took them very close to the battlefield. The French lines were still visible, with Massena and Wellington playing a waiting game as their troops dealt with dead and wounded. Sooner or later the battle would either start up again or one or other of the parties would need to withdraw. Despite his concerns, Wellington had not lost his line of retreat back to Lisbon, but Anne knew he had no intention of going. He wanted to set his new line at the Spanish border, and to do that he would need to hold Almeida plus the two Spanish border fortresses of Badajoz and Ciudad Rodrigo. Anne had already accepted that Paul might be in action again today and had said everything that she needed to say to him before he left. It was not enough, could never be enough, but it was all she could do to ease his way.

Anne was not dressed in the blue riding habit which she usually wore. Since marrying Paul and joining the regiment she kept her luggage as simple as possible. She wore her riding clothes by day and had two plain dark gowns for use when she worked in the hospital, with a series of aprons over them. In addition, she carried an evening gown and a couple of muslin day dresses should she be expected to attend some kind of headquarters function, and around camp and in the evenings she had two soft velvet robes which were almost medieval in design, fitted over her breasts and falling in gentle folds to her feet. They had originally been designed for morning wear at home and she was aware that strangers looked askance at seeing her so casually attired around the camp, but Anne found them practical and comfortable, warm in the cold evenings, and easy to pack and transport. She was amusedly aware that Paul did not care at all about the conventions of feminine costume and he particularly liked the velvet robes on her. During the past few weeks most of her clothing had become too tight and the robes were invaluable. Today she wore one of her hospital gowns which were looser and easier to let out than the fitted riding habit.

Señora Mata was a tall spare woman who was probably no more than forty but lined and exhausted-looking. Her home was a substantial stone built quinta, which despite its peeling paint and shabby air had clearly been a residence of some importance before the war. It was surrounded by a selection of gardens which were overgrown and tangled but still beautiful. Beyond them stretched acres of fields, pastures, vineyards and orchards. Many of them were badly neglected or lay fallow.

There was a selection of tenants' cottages and outbuildings in various stages of disrepair. Anne accepted Señora Mata's invitation to drink wine and listened with sadness to her story. She had lost her husband and two sons to war and a younger daughter to illness. During the French invasion her estate had been used as a base by French troops out of Almeida. The woman was reticent on the subject, except to say that they had taken all without payment and then left her with few

114

beasts, struggling to grow grain and harvest her land with the help of one or two elderly tenants and her nineteen-year-old surviving daughter. The girl brought bread and cold meat to the table and kept her eyes lowered, flinching when George Kelly spoke to her, complimenting her on the bread. As she turned to leave there was the wail of a young child. Anne touched her arm.

"Is that your child, Renata?"

The girl looked down at Anne's obvious pregnancy then up into her eyes. "Yes, Senora. He is three months old. Excuse me, I must go."

There had been no mention of a husband, and Anne suspected there never had been. Renata Mata's child almost certainly had a French father and Anne wondered if it had been a love affair brought abruptly to an end or if the girl had been raped.

Anne toured the house and inspected the outbuildings and then entered into negotiations with the woman who seemed puzzled at the outset that either payment or permission were being sought at all. Some of the barns and outbuildings could be repaired and used for winter barracks for the men and one would do for stabling the horses. Señora Mata seemed astonished when Anne informed her that they would buy her grain and any other food she could produce and grew suddenly animated when asked of other farms or producers who had managed to keep going in the area. They were pitifully few. War had devastated the region and whole swathes of agricultural and grazing land lay fallow and desolate, ruined by marching armies and plundered by hungry soldiers. The Matas were not unique or even slightly unusual. They probably did not realise, Anne thought as she set off back to Villa Formoso to collect their possessions, that their fortunes were about to improve with the arrival of Paul's brigade. His men were well disciplined and although they were not above looting a wine cellar or two, they would behave themselves far better than the French had.

She was slightly concerned about Renata, a thin sad looking girl with a wealth of red-brown hair bundled untidily into a net. She was still young, and Anne suspected that she was going to find it difficult with eighteen hundred men of the Light Division billeted on her lands. Paul's own regiments could be trusted to behave around the girl, but Anne knew nothing of the KGL and Portuguese troops. Señora Mata seemed impatient with the girl's obvious fear around men and Anne supposed that in these times survival was more important than sensibility, but that was no consolation to a girl who had already been brutalised by war.

Back in Villa Formoso Anne set the others to packing up the wagons and wrote a quick note to Paul to tell him of the new arrangements, and another to Lord Wellington, thanking him for his courtesy of the previous day and telling him where she could be found at need. It was not incumbent upon her to keep the commander-in-chief informed of her whereabouts, but she knew that the news of the potential winter quarters of the third brigade was likely to set off the usual howling about the 110th and 112th taking the best available billets leaving other officers and men to struggle in ruined buildings and open camps. There was some truth in the accusation, but it was purely because Paul refused to leave it to the quartermaster-general to find billets for his men for anything more than a few nights. His own quartermasters had become experts in scouring the district to find dry quarters for his men and Anne usually helped in the search. Lord Wellington would not care where they were billeted as long as Paul was reasonably close and now that she had apprised him of the arrangement he was likely to lift a supercilious eyebrow to anybody who questioned it.

With that in mind Anne wrote an equally charming letter to General Craufurd inviting him to dinner as soon as he should be free of his military obligations. She adored the bad-tempered, black eyed commander of the light division, who was seldom invited to socialise with his officers since most of them heartily disliked him. Anne understood why. He was a strict disciplinarian who gave no quarter to either officers or men, but while his men seemed to accept this and saw also his genuine concern for their welfare, his officers resented his sarcastic outbursts and his refusal to treat them with the respect they felt they deserved. He was harsh on any failures and tended to reserve any warmth in his personality for those few people he considered friends.

Anne knew that his early relations with Paul had not always been good, but over the year or more working closely together out on the borders away from the main army they had developed a mutual respect and liking. Many officers were irritated by her husband's complete unconcern about protocol and considerations of rank. He would be as rude to a fellow officer who had infuriated him as he would to a pickpocket newly dumped in the army from the courts, and he showed little respect for army traditions. He also had an astonishing ability not to take offence which was useful when dealing with Robert Craufurd who was likely to call his officers names which actually shocked some of them. Craufurd had developed an exasperated fondness for his unconventional junior which had not been harmed when he had married Anne. She had first encountered Craufurd before she married Paul while she worked in the Viseu military hospital. He had been genuinely interested in the work she did and had supported her ruthlessly when some of the older surgeons had tried to prevent her doing anything more than basic nursing care. Craufurd liked her unorthodox behaviour and enjoyed her light-hearted flirting and she knew that he loved being invited to her table.

Sealing her letters, she gave them to Ned Browning to deliver and then went back to her room. Teresa and Keren were packing and as Anne began to reach for a folded apron her Spanish maid stood up, hands on hips.

"Señora, no."

"Teresa, you don't need me out at the farmhouse to set up. George will go with you and Ned can come back here to wait for me. There are injured men piling up in the street outside…"

"What did the Colonel say to you?"

"He told me to take care. And I will. But even just a few hours of my time might make a big difference here, Teresa. It might save some lives. And at least I can kick those orderlies into line and make sure they're washing the patients and giving them food and drink."

Keren was laughing. "Nothing we say is going to make any difference to her, Teresa. Ma'am, just don't do too much."

"I'll be sensible." Anne smoothed down her apron. It was made of white cotton, much washed with stains which would never come out but it hardly mattered. She looked around and found the white scarf which she always wore to keep her long hair out of her way when she was working, then located her black medical bag. It had once belonged to a junior surgeon in Lisbon who had died soon after coming out to Portugal and Adam Norris had given it to Anne in the run up to the battle of Oporto when he had first begun to realise that she was capable of far more than simple nursing tasks.

"I'll see you later," she said. "Look after Caroline for me, I'm a bit worried about her, she's very quiet at the moment."

There was a silence. Anne stopped by the door, realising that something about the silence bothered her.

"What's going on?"

"Nothing," Keren said quickly. "We'll take care of her…"

"Teresa?" Anne snapped.

Her friend met her gaze steadily. "I don't know for sure, Señora, but I think she may be pregnant."

"Oh dear God," Anne said. She was not sure when Caroline Longford's love affair with her husband's second-in-command had begun, but she was very sure that the child, if there were one, could belong to either man. "How sure are you?"

"She's not said anything," Keren said. "But she's been sick a fair bit. And as you say, she's very quiet. We thought it might be that she was worried about Colonel Wheeler in the battle, but I think it's a bit more than that."

Anne looked from one to the other and gave a faint smile. "Is there anything that happens around here that you two don't know?" she asked.

"Very little," Teresa said drily. "People talk in front of the maids, Señora."

"Around here people talk in front of everybody." Anne said crisply. "It would be a miracle to have a secret in this place. Right, I'm going. Take care of her and I'll think about it when I don't have a queue of men developing gangrene in the street outside my door."

Men had been carried out of Fuentes de Oñoro since the previous evening. The dead and wounded lay piled in the streets and houses. Many had been injured by shot and cannon fire, but a surprising number had suffered bayonet injuries. It was the first time Anne had treated this many bayonet wounds from one battle.

"Found a whole pile of them trapped in a dead end," a private from the 85th told her laying another injured man on Anne's makeshift table. "Found some of them, French and English, their blades still stuck in each other's bodies. Horrible it was." He watched Anne for a moment as she lifted the head of the injured man to let him drink from a bottle. "That rum you got there, ma'am?"

"Yes," Anne said. She set the bottle down and began to peel back the injured man's shirt.

"Do I get a shot for my trouble, then?"

"Are you injured, Private?" Anne asked cordially.

"No, ma'am. Just thirsty."

"Go away and drink water then."

Anne felt him move closer. "Just a tot," he said. He reached for the bottle, and to Anne's astonishment she felt his other hand on her waist, sliding down intimately over her hip. "Very nice," he said, close to her ear. "The rum's good as well."

Anne spun around, lifting her scalpel as she did so and placed the blade against the man's neck. "Do you know anything about anatomy, Private?" she said in tones of ice. "That's the jugular vein. Messy if it gets cut. Put that bottle down and take two steps back."

The man obeyed, eyes wide in shock, widening further as they slid down Anne's body and realised her condition. "Fuck! What's a pregnant woman doing in this hellhole?" he demanded. "Your man should get you out of here and keep you where you belong."

"My man commands the third brigade of the Light Division, Private, so he's a little busy right now, but if you run into him in the village today, make sure you tell him what you think, won't you?" Anne lifted an imperious hand and Gibson, one of the hospital mates, came running towards her.

"Want me to kick him into the river, ma'am?"

"There isn't enough water in it to make it worth your while, Gibson. Which regiment, Private?"

"85th, ma'am." The man's face was white.

"New out here, aren't you? Seventh division?"

"Yes, ma'am."

"Just remember I'm married to the man who saved your backsides out there yesterday. Now get on with your job and don't ever touch me again."

"No, ma'am."

Gibson was grinning as he escorted the man to the door. "You got off lightly, Private," he said cheerfully. "If Colonel van Daan saw you put your bloody hands on his wife he'd cut them off for you."

"She likely to tell him?"

"Not as long as you behave yourself, she knows you're new out here and she's a very good lass. Go on, get out of here."

Anne worked steadily. There were horrific sabre and sword injuries from the cavalry fighting out on the plain and she treated wounds from splintered stone where the houses in the village had been struck by artillery fire. Many men lost limbs from round shot and there was soon another pile of severed arms and legs outside the house, waiting to be carried to the burial pits. Outside, men laboured over the mass grave, lowering in bodies ten at a time and shovelling earth over them before throwing in more. Twice Anne went outside for air and then returned inside quickly as the stench reached her. Vultures were wheeling overhead, and Anne saw three young drummer boys with sticks who had been set to chasing them off.

It was late afternoon when she was aware of a stir outside. The private from the 85th was back, lifting a boy of fifteen or sixteen onto the table dressed in the uniform of a bugler of the 95th. He had been savagely slashed across his chest and upper body and Anne shook her head.

"Oh no," she said softly.

"I know," the soldier said. "French bastards, he's only a lad."

Anne reached for the boy's coat, pulling it away from the wounds. He had been out in the sun for hours and the material had stuck badly. "I need some water for this," she said.

"I'll get it, ma'am."

Anne looked up with a quick smile. "Thank you," she said, and he smiled back tentatively, went for water and stood beside her holding the bowl as she swabbed at the wounds and peeled away cloth and leather to reveal the horrible gashes.

"He likely to make it, ma'am?"

"I doubt it," Anne said. "The bleeding's stopped but he must have lost so much blood already and the heat and thirst…I'll clean it up and dress it and we'll try and get some water into him. After that we'll just have to wait and see. Poor lad."

She looked around. "Gibson, I need a dressing."

"Run out, ma'am. No bandages left either."

"Oh not again." Anne looked around. There was a pile of dead men outside, reeking in the late afternoon sun. She took a deep breath. "Are you feeling brave, Private? I need you to help me to lift some of these, I can rip up the shirts for bandages."

The man's face was appalled. "No! No, ma'am. You stay right there with the lad. I'll do it. Do not move."

Anne smiled tiredly. "Private, by the end of this you might have earned that tot of rum."

"He's earned a damned sight more than that if he's ordering you around, bonny lass," a voice said, and Anne turned, her heart lifting.

"Afternoon, Colonel. I've run out of bandages and dressings again."

"The joys of the army medical board. All right Private….sorry, what's your name?"

"Edwards, sir. Third company, 85th." The man was saluting. His eyes were on Anne's face and he looked terrified. Anne smiled reassuringly.

"Private Edwards has been a godsend today, Paul."

"The 85th did bloody well yesterday as well," Paul said. "Come and help me get some shirts off these poor buggers, lad, I'm never going to get her out of here until she's dealt with this boy."

Anne watched them through the doorway, heard Paul talking easily to the man. They returned with an armful of dirty shirts. Anne wrinkled her nose and chose one, using a surgical knife to rip it into strips. She had carefully cleaned the wounds and she bound them and instructed Paul and Edwards to take the boy next door where her old billet had been taken over by the hospital. While they were gone she washed her hands and as Paul and his assistant returned she handed the rum bottle to Edwards.

"There's not much left in it, Private, but take it. And thank you, you've been a great help."

Edwards took the bottle uncertainly. "Thank you, ma'am. I'm sorry about earlier. What you've done for these lads…"

119

"Forget it, Private, it was harmless. I already have. I think my working day might be over here, but I'll be back tomorrow to see how those lads are doing."

"We'll see how you are, you're going to be tired," Paul said. "We're burying Captain Thatcher and his lads over on the far side of the village, I was hoping you'd come up with me."

"I will. Private Edwards, go back to your company and get some food, you've not stopped today."

"I will. Thank you, ma'am. Sir."

Anne and Paul went out to where Jenson and Browning waited with their horses.

"I see you have a new admirer, love." Paul sounded amused. "What was he apologising for?"

Anne considered, then decided against telling him the full story. "He questioned my medical credentials and I told him off," she said lightly. "Nothing serious. Any movement from the French?"

"No. Not even scouting. I'm beginning to think they're going to run without a fight, but we're being cautious," Paul said, lifting her into the saddle.

"I hope they do," Anne said tiredly, and he studied her.

"Bad, isn't it?"

"Yes. Have you been in the village all day?"

Paul nodded. "Yes, I've had them grave digging and burying. I hate this duty, especially the mass graves. I hope to God I never end up in one."

Anne studied his face, thinking how weary he looked. "You won't, Colonel. Your men would dig a grave with their bare hands to prevent it. But don't you dare, I need you."

Paul's serious expression broke into a smile.

"What a topic for an evening ride. Come on, girl of my heart, let's get this over with and then I shall escort you back so that you can show me our new billet. The first and second brigades are yelling already, but something tells me that once again we will have nabbed the best winter quarters on the lines, long before winter, for which I am profoundly grateful. After this almighty cock up I am looking forward to a few months with enough to eat and drink, a bed to sleep in and making the acquaintance of my new child."

120

Chapter Eleven

For five days after the battle the French remained outside Fuentes de Oñoro and the Light Division settled down in the ruined houses of the village and waited for a renewed attack. It did not come. Commissariat wagons arrived with rations and the men lit fires and cooked food, sampled wine found miraculously undamaged in some of the houses, and played cards and dice. There was a summer storm one night and the rain washed blood from the streets while the men huddled inside broken buildings, watched the lightening brightening the sky over the massed army of Marshal Massena and wondered what was going on.

On May 10th Massena drew his ravaged forces together and marched out, moving east across the Spanish border towards the fortress of Ciudad Rodrigo. Wellington summoned his army and began a cautious pursuit, more to establish that the retreat was genuine and not a feint by the wily Marshal who had caused Wellington to lose too many hours sleep over the past few years. The English did not have the guns or the cavalry to risk another major engagement with Massena and once Wellington was sure that the retreat was genuine, he called a halt to his army ready to take stock and plan his next move.

That evening there were the muffled sounds of heavy explosions from the direction of Almeida.

Paul heard them from his tent. He was writing to his brother Joshua about coming to Lisbon to collect Anne's child and take it back to England. Already the knowledge that he was sending another of his children away to be raised by his family weighed heavily on him. He had talked with Anne, sitting late into the night during the long months of her pregnancy, holding her hand and dreading her decision, whatever it might turn out to be.

This would be her first child and Paul admitted that no matter how hard he tried he could not imagine how Anne would be as a mother. There had always been something maternal about his pretty, domesticated first wife and Rowena had hated her separations from the children. She had been fortunate to be able to spend most of their babyhood with them, and during his spells in barracks and in Ireland with the regiment, Paul had loved having Grace and Francis with him, seeing them grow and develop. His duty in Portugal had put a stop to that and his third child had been

121

only a few months old when he had sent her back to England for Josh and Patience to raise, her mother dead at her birth and his marriage to Anne new and full of joy.

Anne had never conceived with her first husband and he had no idea if that had bothered her or not. She had treated this pregnancy with a down to earth practicality which was typical of her, but Paul did not know how she felt about motherhood. He had gently reminded her that she had the choice of going back to England with Josh and Patience to raise her child in comfort and safety, or even of remaining in Lisbon at the villa he rented there, close enough to see him sometimes, but still safe with her child. He had not been surprised when Anne shook her head.

"No, Paul. I'm not leaving you. Perhaps that makes me a bad mother, I don't know. I'll keep the baby with me for a few months if I can, but I won't put it at risk. If your brother and sister-in-law are willing to take another of your offspring then I'll go to Lisbon if I may, to meet them and to let them take our child. I'm surprised at how much I hate that idea already, but I can't have this both ways. I'm not risking my child in an army camp – disease alone carries off more than half the children born here to the men's wives. But I'm not leaving you. Not unless you tell me I have to."

Paul felt guilty at his treacherous joy at her decision. "You can change your mind about that when the time comes, bonny lass. And at any time in the future. You know how I feel about you, I'm always going to want you here with me. It won't be forever. One day we can go home to them."

Anne tried to smile but there were tears in her dark eyes. "It's fortunate that I'm good at letter writing until then."

They had not discussed it after that. Paul had discovered that both he and Anne were able to avoid going over the same topics repeatedly, which made for a surprisingly harmonious married life. When the child was born they would talk again, based on how Anne felt with the baby in her arms. Paul sat trying to relay this in a letter to Joshua and realised that his conventional brother was never going to be able to understand anything about his marriage to the extraordinary young woman he had chosen to be his second wife.

In the distance, the fortress of Almeida exploded.

Paul rose and went to the tent flap. He was not close enough to the fortress to see anything and it was not the responsibility of the Light Division. Wellington had moved his headquarters temporarily to Villa Formoso and had instructed Craufurd to halt his pursuit of the French and await further instructions. Privately Paul was aware that his chief was expecting to be told to move back into quarters around Fuentes de Oñoro again. Some of the refugees were beginning to cautiously return to their ruined village, and Paul had released several dozen of his men up to the Quinta do Santo Antonio to begin repairs on the barns and outbuildings ready to receive the third brigade. With the fifth and sixth divisions blockading Almeida, Wellington would wait now for news from Beresford who was down at Badajoz, besieging the town.

"What the bloody hell is that?" Johnny Wheeler said, emerging from his tent. He had clearly risen from his bed and stood beside Paul, tucking in his shirt, and pulling on his coat, staring around him. The men of the third brigade were all stirring and getting to their feet. Some were reaching cautiously for arms, but there was nothing from sentries or pickets and no sign of attack.

"No idea. An explosion, but it's a way off."

"Not back at Fuentes de Oñoro?" Johnny said. Paul shook his head.

"Calm down, lad, if I thought it was, would I be standing here digesting my supper? They're miles from the nearest French; we're in between Massena and them even if he should turn back. I don't know…but I think that came from west of here. Almeida?"

"Also Freineda," Wheeler said uneasily. Paul shook his head.

"There's nothing there, Johnny. No powder store, no fortifications, no guns. Nothing to make that kind of racket. Look, I can see you're on edge about your girl. Take young Morse and ride back there, see if you can find out what's going on. If we've sudden orders I can send Jenson out after you, but I'm telling you, this isn't our business, it's Erskine's."

"Well Erskine isn't there," Carl said approaching from his tent. "I was in Villa Formoso earlier today, saw him with Longford, he's dining with Sir Brent Spencer."

"It's hard to know if that's a good thing or a bad, at least he can't get anybody slaughtered there," Paul said. "Although it's an interesting point as to why he's dining in comfort when he has an actual job he should be doing, while I'm out here missing my wife in a tent when I am doing nothing useful whatsoever. I often don't understand army life."

A hand descended onto his shoulder and Paul jumped and swore. His chief was one of the few people able to walk silently enough to creep up on Paul, who had very good hearing, and he was aware that Craufurd enjoyed doing so at any opportunity.

"That's a point we'd all like information on," Craufurd said. "Sorry, Colonel, did I make you jump?"

"Yes, you bloody did," Paul said. "Bet you didn't get invited to dinner either, sir."

"Only by your wife, but we have to get back for me to enjoy that particular piece of hospitality. Mind, I'd rather dine with her than with Spencer, he's a bloody old woman and his cook's terrible. Man could poison half a division."

"I wish he'd poison Erskine and Longford then, it would be a good day's work. Any idea what that was, sir?"

"I'm not sure, boy, but I'm rather afraid it's Almeida. I had orders from Lord Wellington about two hours ago. Wasn't urgent so I thought I'd wait until the morning. But perhaps we should talk now. You – what's your name, I can never remember."

"Hammond, sir."

"Yes, that's right. Sergeant Hammond, will you run over to the first and get Colonel Beckwith to join us up in my tent. And get one of your lads to find Colonel Drummond as well."

"Colonel Drummond's not well, sir," Sergeant-Major Carter said coming forward and saluting.

"Not well?" Craufurd said, his voice rising. "What the devil does that mean? Stubbed his toe? Got a cold? Not well enough to obey an order from me?"

Carter shook his head. Paul was amused at his complete unconcern at Craufurd's belligerence.

"Bit more serious than that, I'm afraid, sir. I was talking to his orderly about half an hour ago. He was out inspecting his pickets this afternoon, got off his horse and collapsed. Bad fever, they've carried him to his tent."

"Why the devil did nobody come and tell me about this?" Craufurd demanded furiously. "Aren't there any other officers in the second brigade? What's wrong with them?"

Carter said nothing. Sergeant Hammond saluted. "I'll get Colonel Beckwith, sir, and I'll ask Corporal Dunnett to tell Lieutenant-Colonel Grey to come up shall I, he'll take command while Colonel Drummond is ill?"

Craufurd snorted. "I find it interesting, Colonel van Daan, that the sergeant of your light company seems to have more initiative than the entire officers' mess of the second brigade. Perhaps I should promote him to colonel-in-charge."

Hammond grinned and saluted. "That mean I get fed any better, sir?"

"Nobody gets fed any better than the 110th, Sergeant, because you are all a bunch of unprincipled looting scoundrels who would have been shot years ago if I'd had the commanding of you."

"Wonder what you'd have done at Poco de Velha then, sir?" Hammond said placidly.

Get out of here before I put you on a charge!"

"Yes, sir." Hammond saluted and moved away and Craufurd looked back at Paul, a reluctant grin curving his lips.

"I don't know where you find them from, Colonel."

"You actually don't want to know where I found Hammond, sir," Paul said gravely, and saw Carl and Wheeler both look away, trying not to laugh. Hammond had been a deserter from the 87th when Paul had picked him up after the battle of the Coa and he had joined the light company under a new name.

"I'm sure I don't. Colonel Wheeler, you can come up as well. And if you've a bottle of brandy between you, bring it, I've run out."

"I can do better than that," Paul said with a grin. He nodded to Jenson who went into his tent and emerged with three bottles of wine. Craufurd looked at them and then at Paul.

"Looted?" he enquired with heavy sarcasm.

"Not unless Nan has been plundering the neighbourhood, she sent a case over this morning She seems to have found a house with a very well hidden wine cellar locally, but I think she paid."

"How the devil did she do that if it's well hidden enough to escape the notice of the French and the English armies?" Craufurd demanded, taking a bottle, and turning back towards his camp. Paul laughed, falling into step beside him.

"According to Browning who rode over with a wagon of supplies for us, the man's wife was in labour and in a very bad way. Nan was able to help her deliver successfully, it was a boy. Celebrations all round, she mentioned casually that she was in charge of supplies for our new billets and that she'd money to pay. The rest was inevitable."

"Well I'm very grateful to her, but she ought to be shopping for a cradle for that baby, not supplying my division. Don't we have a commissariat any more?" Craufurd snapped.

"We do, sir, but they're not as effective as my wife."

Craufurd led the way into his large tent which doubled as a command centre. An orderly was there, cleaning a pair of boots. He got up and saluted, and moved to light more lamps, then went to bring several more camp chairs. Paul noticed that the man, who wore the green jacket of the 95th, had a black patch over one eye. Craufurd grunted at him.

"Thank you, Bennett. Find some wine cups as well, will you, Colonel van Daan has saved my life."

"Yes, sir." Bennett went for cups and set them on the folding table just as Colonel Beckwith and Lieutenant-Colonel Grey entered and saluted. Paul uncorked a wine bottle, smiling at the orderly.

"You're new, aren't you?"

"Yes, sir. Rifleman Bennett, sir, third company, first battalion. Can't shoot now so the General asked if I'd help him out."

"I'm not surprised, he can't keep an orderly for five minutes, he's such a bugger to work for," Paul said with a grin.

"He's not, sir," Bennett said firmly, and Paul laughed.

"I'll never convince a rifleman of that, will I, Bennett? What happened to your eye?"

"Stonework went into it, sir, in Fuentes de Oñoro. Bloody painful. Not much use now."

"Still hurt?"

"No, sir. It was awful at first, but then Dr Norris had a go at it and got all the pieces out. Much better now." Bennett saluted and left, and Paul reached for his glass and caught an expression of pained disapproval on Lieutenant-Colonel Grey's face. He grinned.

"All right, Grey?"

"Yes, sir. Good to see you on such good terms with the men."

Craufurd gave an explosive snort. "Is that a complaint, Colonel Grey?"

Grey looked wary. "No, sir. Not my place."

"No, it isn't. Your place was to get your arse up here earlier to tell me that one of my brigade commanders was out of action, but you bloody didn't, did you? You've command of the second brigade until Drummond is on his feet or until I find somebody with a brain to take over."

Paul sipped his wine to mask a grin. "You said you'd orders from Lord Wellington, sir."

"Yes, came a couple of hours ago. Not urgent, I was going to wait until morning, but given that we've all been rousted from our beds by that bloody racket..."

"What racket, sir?" Grey asked. Paul buried his face in his wine cup again and waited for the explosion.

125

"What racket? Jesus Christ, did you sleep through that? The whole third brigade was on its feet, and half of them were at arms and you didn't even notice there was an explosion? God help us if the French have any surprises for us, you're likely…"

"It sounded like a powder magazine going up," Paul interrupted, taking pity on the hapless Grey. "I'm not sure but it seemed to come from the west somewhere."

"It could have been some idiot with a cigar near an ammunition depot, but I doubt it," Craufurd said, abandoning his prey. "Lord Wellington thinks the Almeida garrison is going to try for a break out. In the past couple of days, the pickets have intercepted two messengers trying to make their way through with ciphered letters to Brennier."

"Decoded?" Paul asked.

"Scovell is working on them now, we'll have them in a day or two. The couriers gave up nothing and they've been shot as spies; they were out of uniform. But his Lordship has sent orders out to the fifth and sixth to watch for trouble. And I'm wondering if that explosion has something to do with that."

"Very likely," Paul said. "Is Denis Pack still in charge of the blockade?"

"No," Craufurd said briefly. "Campbell and the sixth have taken over with the fifth nearby. In the meantime, we've orders to pull back and establish ourselves in local villages. After that we spend our time up and down the border depending on where we're needed, rather as we did last year. Each brigade will establish a base for supplies and kit etc. Beckwith, you can take Gallegos, you know it well enough from last year. Grey, the second will take Espeja. The third has already found a base just this side of Freineda…"

"I'll just bet they have," Beckwith said bitterly. "Nice and comfortable is it, Paul?"

"I've not managed to spend much time there so far, but I do hope so, Sydney given that my wife needs to be able to give birth there shortly," Paul said affably. "But if you like we'll do a swap. We can manage just as well in Gallegos, you know. Give my quartermaster twenty-four hours talking to the locals and we'll still be set up better than you are."

"Would that be Captain Breakspear, Colonel? Or Captain Cartwright? I understand he's become very friendly with your wife of late."

There was a shocked silence in the tent at Grey's tone. Paul turned his head very slowly to look at the man. Craufurd said harshly:

"Have you gone mad, Grey? Have you completely lost what few wits you were born with? Have you genuinely forgotten that Colonel van Daan is a senior officer and one of my brigade commanders?"

"I don't know about that, but I suspect he's forgotten my well-known tendency to throw any man who says the wrong thing about my wife into the Agueda River," Paul said in conversational tones. "Do you need him this week, sir? Given his performance so far, I can't think he'll be much use to you, but I'll be guided by you. I can delay punching his face in until it's more convenient to you, I don't mind waiting."

126

Beckwith sighed and looked at Grey. "Apologise, you bloody imbecile," he said briefly. "He actually means it, you know, he isn't joking."

"Sir. I apologise. Just joking, sir." Grey's voice was slightly unsteady. Paul looked over at the man's empty wine glass and then up into his eyes.

"You've been drinking," he said abruptly.

"We've all been drinking, Paul," Beckwith said genially. "It's bloody good wine, you can thank your wife…"

Paul got up. "That's not what I mean. He was drunk when he got here. That's why he slept through that noise earlier and that's why he didn't think to send up a message about George being ill."

He saw Craufurd's eyes narrow. Paul met his gaze steadily. After a moment Craufurd said:

"I'll look into it, Colonel. Now's probably not the time. Hopefully Colonel Drummond will be back on his feet quickly. Lord Wellington wants us to break camp tomorrow and get ourselves established to await further orders. I am going back to Fuentes de Oñoro with my staff, we'll find billets there."

"You'll be lucky to find a house with four walls and a roof there, but it's your lookout," Paul said. "We'll march back to Freineda first thing and get billets and supplies sorted out and we'll await your orders there. Sir…"

"Yes, Colonel?"

"Do you think we should send somebody over to headquarters for news? Just in case we're needed?"

Craufurd studied him. "Send one of your officers," he said abruptly. "It's not currently our problem but if Lord Wellington decides to make it so, it might be nice to know in good time."

"Yes, sir." Paul saluted. "Good night."

"Do you want to take the wine…"

"Keep it, sir," Paul said. He gave a provocative grin at Colonel Beckwith who was getting up. "Let Sydney here have a bottle. Plenty more where that comes from."

"Bastard," Beckwith said, laughing. "I hope I get a good dinner when I come calling."

"When do you not, Sydney? I'll see you tomorrow. Get some sleep, Grey. Come on, Johnny, I'm going to haul Captain Manson from his bed, the fresh air will do him good."

They stepped outside the tent followed by Beckwith and Grey. Paul was amused to see that Beckwith was holding an unopened wine bottle. He lifted it in salute to Paul with a grin and turned to walk back up to his brigade.

"Ill-mannered old fool," Grey said clearly. "Rudest man I've ever met. Shouldn't put a man like that in command of officers and gentlemen, he's got a foul mouth and…"

Paul turned, stepped forward and punched Grey hard in the midriff. Grey doubled up with a whooshing sound and stood clutching his stomach, apparently unable to speak. Paul took hold of his hair and hauled him upright.

"Get to attention and salute when you speak to me, you drunken feckless piece of shit, I'm a senior officer."

Grey pulled himself up with an effort and raised a hand in salute. Paul surveyed him without sympathy.

"In the past twenty minutes you've insulted my wife and my commanding officer, and you don't get to do either unless you've earned the right which you haven't. I don't know which shady market stall sold you your commission in the 52nd but it's one of the finest regiments in this army and you do not get to wear that uniform and disgrace it as you have tonight. I don't know what Colonel Drummond makes of you, but I'm telling you you're in my sights, boy, and if you don't shape up and start acting like an officer and a soldier of the Light Division you won't need to worry about the French because you're going to have me coming after you and that is very much worse. Now piss off to bed, sober up, and if you let me catch you drunk on duty again you are going to be so very much beyond sorry that you can't imagine. Get moving!"

He turned away, hearing Grey vomiting distressingly in the grass. Paul glanced at Johnny. "I bet that sobers him up."

He had taken three steps when Grey's voice stopped him, querulous in the darkness. "You, sir, are a cad and a dirty dish. You are not a gentleman."

Paul turned and studied him thoughtfully. "No," he admitted finally. "But I'm a brigade commander which is all you need to remember. Get to bed. Come on, Johnny, I want to get Manson out, I'm dying to know what's going on."

His friend shot him an amused glance as they walked back up to the lines of the third brigade. "I suppose it is pointless to tell you that it is not acceptable to punch a lieutenant-colonel who is also a temporary brigade commander in the guts, sir?"

"You show up drunk on duty one night, Johnny, and trust me, I'll punch you in the guts. But what are the chances?" Paul raised his voice and bellowed. "Captain Manson! You awake in there?"

There was a brief indignant pause. Then Manson's voice responded tiredly.

"I am now, sir. Good to hear your voice as always."

Paul grinned. "Get some clothes on and get your arse out here, Captain. I've got a job for you."

By the time the third brigade marched into their new headquarters the following day, Lord Wellington's army had been rocked by the news that the French had managed to escape from Almeida after blowing up part of the fortress and having eluded all pursuit until they reached the bridge at Barba del Puerco early that morning, had escaped into Spain with the loss of their baggage train and around a hundred and fifty men killed and two hundred taken prisoner.

Captain Manson returned to camp in the early hours with the news of the escape but with no information about where the French might be heading and no orders for the Light Division. Seething with frustration Paul went back to bed and collected news on his way back the following day.

He found his wife uncharacteristically resting on her bed. The room was a comfortable one at the back of the big rambling quinta with a solid wooden bed frame, blissfully long enough for Paul's tall frame, and a mismatched collection of furniture including a massive oak tallboy. Anne had allocated rooms in the house for as many of Paul's officers as it could accommodate with the rest scattered around the selection of small tenant cottages around the home farm. There was space in the barns and outbuildings for the men of the 110th and 112th and she had found billets for the Portuguese, the KGL and Paul's two rifle companies in a dilapidated and deserted selection of stone buildings approximately a mile and a half further down the road towards the Spanish border. She had been told by Señora Mata that the adjoining farm had been a successful wine producer and there was still a faintly sour smell about the buildings which testified to their original use. Paul's two regiments boasted three or four skilled carpenters and he had sent these over immediately to start constructing roofs and making repairs which would render the various buildings weatherproof for the winter. Long weeks of the summer would be spent on patrol, sleeping on the ground, and living off their rations, but Paul knew the value of a secure base for his men to return to and he was pleased with his new headquarters.

He was less pleased with the condition of his wife. Going into the room he dropped his pack and tossed his hat onto a chair then went to sit on the bed beside her. "Don't get up," he said. "What the devil have you been doing to yourself? Keren tells me they brought you back here this morning in an ambulance wagon."

"They did, but it was a huge fuss about nothing. I fainted at the hospital, that's all. You know how Adam and Oliver fuss."

"Adam and Oliver are doctors. It's their job to fuss."

"They're surgeons. Not much use to a pregnant woman in my opinion."

"Stop evading the subject and tell me what happened."

Anne sighed. "To tell you the truth, I was at the hospital all night. I probably overdid it. I am sorry, Paul…"

"You bloody will be. What have I told you?"

"I was there because I was invited to dinner," Anne said regally, ignoring him. "Sir Brent Spencer had invited General Erskine and Captain Longford, and Caroline and I were asked as well. I couldn't let her go alone, Paul, it would have been so awkward for her. So I went. We'd finished dinner and were getting ready to ride back when some wounded were brought in. You've heard about Almeida?"

"I have. Skirmishes all night and they still got away. Somebody is going to be in serious trouble for this one, bonny lass, and I am very glad that I was a long way away from it. After losing so many men to maintain the blockade, Wellington wanted it captured or to surrender, not bloody blown up with most of the garrison back with the French army. And he doesn't like Brenier."

"Why?"

"Apparently Brenier owes him £500. Long story. I…"

"It can't be that long."

Paul took a deep breath and counted to ten in his head. "There is a story that after Brenier was taken prisoner at Vimeiro, Wellesley as he was then, lent him some money. Brenier later managed to escape and returned to France, defaulting on the debt. I've no idea if it's true, it's army gossip. And you've neatly distracted me. Where were the other surgeons?"

"Adam was over at one of the other hospitals, all their doctors are ill – some kind of food poisoning. Oliver was out at some officer's billet – the poor man's wound had become infected, and he had to amputate. I called in to see a patient and there was no surgeon anywhere around, so I stayed. But I must have been more tired than I realised."

Paul reached for her hand. "Nan, I really want to yell at you just now, but I know how pointless that would be. Please, girl of my heart, stop worrying the life out of me. I know we were joking the other day about when you might be due…"

"All right."

"I beg your pardon?"

Anne laughed. "Don't look so shocked, I'm agreeing with you. I think I need to stop going to the hospital every day now. I would like to call in, just to keep an eye on one or two patients. But if you want the truth, I frightened myself."

He studied her soberly. "Did you?"

She smiled wryly. "I had pains. Fairly bad ones, I was doubled up, then I woke up on the floor with Private Edwards kneeling beside me."

"Are you all right now?"

"Yes. Oliver checked me over when he got back and then I had a long talk with Maggie Bennett when I got back here. She assures me that a lot of women get this a month or two before the birth, nothing to worry about. And I feel fine now. But I am very tired and my back aches all the time. I might be stubborn, but I'm not stupid. It might be time to stop and pretend to be a lady." Anne laughed. "All these months I've been telling myself that the men's wives have to put up with a lot worse than this. And that if they can do it, I can do it. I admitted that to Keren yesterday. She laughed and laughed. And then she pointed out that they only do it because they have to, and I don't. I felt silly, to be honest."

Paul silently blessed Keren Trenlow. "I do understand," he said. "I feel the same sometimes. Like this week, we've been up on the border. Officers had tents but my men didn't. No point to be honest, the weather is good, and I didn't want to haul the pack animals out and spend time setting up camp each night…but I feel bloody guilty settling into bed in my nice warm tent when Carter and Hammond and Cooper are sleeping on the open ground."

"Most of the army don't even have tents," Anne said.

"No. I know our lads have it better than most. But I still feel it, so I do understand, Nan. I've seen you on the march walking through the mud, leading your horse with some pregnant or nursing lassie on her back." Paul lifted her hand to his lips, his eyes on her lovely face. "It makes me so proud of you. Like no other woman in this army. But I want you safe and well to have my child, bonny lass."

"Sir."

Paul rolled his eyes and counted to ten silently. "Yes, Jenson. It's only been a week since I saw my wife, and…"

"It's been four days, sir, and you've moaned for at least three of them solid. Sorry, ma'am, but Lord Wellington has sent a message, wants him over at headquarters."

Anne smiled at Paul's expression. "Go on. I'm going to try to catch up on some sleep. At least you can be reassured that I'm here doing the right thing."

Paul kissed her, resting his hand very gently on her abdomen. "Good girl. I love you, bonny lass. See you later."

130

Paul rode into Villa Formoso and dismounted outside the house which Wellington was using as his temporary headquarters. Jenson took his horse and Paul walked through into the wood panelled hallway.

"Colonel van Daan."

"Morning, Richard. I've received a summons. I thought he'd been quiet for a while."

Captain Graham pulled a face. "Well he's not been quiet this morning, trust me."

"Did they all get away?"

"Pack and a few others caught up with them at the bridge, they lost about a quarter of their force dead and taken prisoner, but more than a thousand men are currently marching off to join the army in Spain."

Paul pulled a face. "Clever bastards," he said with reluctant admiration. "Brilliant. But there was a cock-up on our part, no question."

"I bet Erskine was at the centre of it," Paul said.

"Quite probably. But sir, can I make a suggestion?"

"What?"

"Don't go out of your way to antagonise him today. I've been with him for a couple of months now and I've seen him crusty, but I've never seen him as angry as this. And Dryden has been with him for years and he says this is the worst he's ever seen him."

Paul studied Graham thoughtfully. "Is it? Well it shouldn't be, Richard, he knows what Erskine is like and it's not the first time he's screwed up this badly. But thanks for the warning. May I go in?"

Graham nodded and Paul walked through and knocked at Wellington's door.

"Come in."

Paul entered and saluted. His commander-in-chief was writing a letter and he did not immediately look up. Paul had seen him employ this technique many times over the years and knew its impact on officers who had displeased Wellington, but he had seldom known his commander to use it on him. He stood in silence, studying the austere face. The silence lengthened and became uncomfortable. Paul wanted to either pull up a chair and sit down or to turn and leave the room, but he did neither. He stood with an assumption of patience and waited. Eventually Wellington looked up and Paul knew that he had surprised his chief.

"Colonel van Daan."

"Still here, sir."

"Indeed. I am surprised."

"I thought about leaving," Paul said in matter of fact tones. "But I'm making allowances today, you've a right to be furious. I'm not sure what I've done to make it worse, but clearly it's something."

"Don't choose today to be insolent to me, Colonel, you're likely to find yourself short of a brigade to command," Wellington snapped.

Paul, who had been priding himself on keeping his temper, lost it unexpectedly. "Good idea, sir. Why don't you give it to Sir William Erskine instead?"

131

Wellington got up from the desk. His face was completely white, and his blue eyes were blazing with anger. "How dare you walk in here and speak to me like that?" he said. "I have put up with your complete lack of respect for me for ten years, Colonel. I have overlooked your manners, your morals and your refusal to comply with army regulations because I have told myself that your undoubted talent as an officer has compensated for that, but I am beginning to believe that I have made a gross error in promoting you to a command for which you are very obviously not ready."

"That's completely fine by me, sir, you just go right ahead and demote me. In fact, why don't you go the whole way and cashier me as well? Don't worry about the money, I can afford to take the loss and we'll call it a donation to your army fund, shall we, I know you're always short of ready cash. Although if you're going to do it, let's skip the whole court martial circus, I've done that already and it wasn't much fun. Just do it out of hand because I'd like to get my wife back to Lisbon to have my child in comfort, instead of lying back with her feet up because she collapsed at your army hospital yesterday treating your wounded men because you can't get the army medical board to send you enough actual surgeons to take care of the men you throw into harm's way on a weekly basis. Just say the word and I'm on my way."

There was a painful silence in the room. For a moment Paul thought that his commander-in-chief was going to hit him. Finally Wellington said:

"Get out of here. Come back when you're ready to apologise. Otherwise I've no wish to speak to you again."

Paul saluted and turned on his heel. He had his hand on the doorknob before he felt his anger subside as quickly as it had flared up and he was appalled at what he had just said. Wellington was clearly furious, but he had good reason and Paul knew that he had not even bothered to wait to find out what his chief wanted to say to him. He thought of his wife and remembered her words after his spectacular falling out with General Craufurd after the Coa.

"Apologise, Paul. He's a senior officer, he can't, so you need to."

Paul stopped and turned.

"Jesus Christ, what the hell am I doing?" he said. "I am sorry, sir. That was completely out of order. I don't even know what you wanted me for and I'm yelling at you on a day when you could probably do without it. There is something about Sir William Erskine that has a very peculiar effect on me, but I'm old enough to know better. I'll get out of your way. But I am sorry."

He turned the doorknob and his chief said:

"Oh for God's sake come in and sit down you infuriating young whelp. I should hit you."

Paul turned quickly. "You can if you like, sir, I'm not going to hit you back, you're a senior officer."

"As if that would make any difference to you," Wellington snapped. "Go and get me a brandy. And have one yourself."

Paul obeyed, feeling relieved. Wellington still sounded furious, but he had a sense that it was no longer directed at him and he wondered if it ever had been. He poured two drinks and placed them on the desk, sitting down facing his chief.

132

"What the hell happened?" he asked quietly, and Wellington picked up the cup and drank deeply.

"I have absolutely no idea," he said bitterly.

Paul studied him in silence, waiting for him to speak. He realised that he should have listened to Richard Graham's attempt to tell him how angry Wellington was. He had never in the ten years he had served under him known Wellington to lose his temper so quickly with him. In fact, he had often remained calm under far greater provocation.

Eventually, Wellington said:

"I have received a complaint about you."

"Have you?" Paul said in some surprise. "I thought I'd been fairly good recently. Apart from shooting the French when I wasn't told to, but that's rather my job. Anyway, Black Bob dealt with that. What have I done now?"

"Lieutenant-Colonel Philip Grey," Wellington said.

Paul studied him for a moment. "And just why am I hearing this from you rather than my divisional commander, sir?"

"Because the complaint came to me through the commander of another division, Colonel. Are you aware that Grey is related to Sir Brent Spencer?"

"No. Should I care?"

"He tells me that you punched his cousin in the stomach. And insulted him."

"Yes, sir."

"Nothing to say in your defence?"

"Do I need to mount a defence, sir?"

"You need to tell me what happened. I'm furious that Craufurd didn't come to me with this."

"Craufurd doesn't know. I'm furious too, but not for the same reasons you are. If Grey wanted to complain about me he should have gone to General Craufurd. Chain of command, sir. You're usually fairly wedded to that. More so than I am."

"There is literally no aspect of army discipline that you are wedded to, Colonel."

"Oh yes there is, sir. Being drunk on duty. One of my particular dislikes. I was at Ahmednaggur when the captain of the third company of the 110th infantry went over that wall as drunk as a lord and got fifteen of his men indiscriminately slaughtered because he took them the wrong way. I stood there and watched it and I screamed myself blue for them to come back but they ignored me and followed him because he was the senior officer and I saw them cut to pieces. He survived it. Got promoted to major soon afterwards, went to Cape Town, I believe. I hope he had trouble sleeping, but he probably didn't because he was too bloody drunk to realise what he'd done."

Wellington studied him for a long time. "Was he? Grey, I mean."

"Yes, sir. I didn't realise it immediately, and we'd just opened a bottle in the General's tent so he could put the smell down to that. But he slept through Almeida blowing up, which woke up every other man in camp and he failed to report to Craufurd that his brigade commander had collapsed with fever earlier in the day, even though it meant he was now in command."

"How did you realise it?"

"He sat there and insulted my wife in front of us all. That makes him either very brave, very stupid, or very drunk. And he was slurring his words. He didn't do that on half a glass of Spanish red."

"Is that why you hit him?"

"No. I let that one go but when we stepped outside he was appallingly rude about General Craufurd. I could have put him on a charge. I chose to punch him in the stomach and warn him what was coming if he didn't shape up. And yes, I was bloody insulting. As he had just been."

Wellington sighed. "I presumed there must have been a reason. But Colonel, you need to stop doing this. You're too high up now, you need to make more of an effort to fit in with other officers."

Paul studied him then smiled. "I'll try not to lose my temper and punch people," he said. "But if you wanted a brigade commander who would fit in you chose the wrong man, sir. Do you want me to resign?"

"Resign?" Wellington looked startled. "Do you want to?"

"No. I want to command a division one day. But if I'm making your life difficult, I will. I can tell people it's too much, with Nan about to give birth, go back to commanding the 110th. Just so long as you don't put me under Erskine again."

"You'd kill him, he's getting worse," Wellington said. "I don't want your resignation, Colonel. And if he insulted your wife, I feel very comfortable telling Spencer that this was a personal quarrel not a military matter and that he asked for it. But there is a potential problem."

"Sir?"

"The 112th. They've been under your command now for how long?"

"Seven months. It feels like longer to be honest, they've come on amazingly. Hard to believe they arrived with just Manson and Will Grey and now we're almost up to strength with officers."

"Colonel, what you've done with those men defies belief. They were the worst regiment in the army. and you've turned them into one of the best. But they still have no commanding officer."

Paul studied him. "They do, sir. Lieutenant-Colonel Wheeler and Major Clevedon are commanding the battalion and doing it very well."

"In the field, I agree. They have, however, no colonel-in-chief, as of last month. Colonel Caldwell has taken full retirement. He is very unwell, and I understand he is not expected to live much longer."

"I see." Paul studied his chief, suddenly uneasy. "Sir, that isn't generally a problem. Usually they'll appoint a new colonel-in-chief and leave the commander in the field alone."

"Not in your case."

"I'm the exception to the rule and let us be honest, I paid through the nose for it. Is that what they're expecting again with the 112th?"

Wellington acknowledged the hit with a flicker of a smile. "There has been a suggestion that a serving lieutenant-colonel be appointed to the post, who will also command in the field. I don't think the 112th quite merits a senior political appointment just yet, Colonel."

"Have they a man in mind?"

"I have been asked to make a recommendation and it has been intimated that Horse Guards will accept it."

"At a price?"

"A rather generous one. Far too generous for a regiment with the recent reputation of the 112th."

"And I'll just bet they told you who to recommend."

"Lieutenant-Colonel Philip Grey."

"Over my fucking dead body."

Wellington gave a deep sigh. "I was expecting you to start swearing."

"Sir, given how I was always going to react, was this a good day to have this conversation?"

"Unfortunately, there is some urgency about it, Colonel. Grey is very well-connected and he can pay for it."

"You can't buy a regiment, sir."

"Don't be naïve, Colonel, of course you can. As a matter of fact, I think I did, back in the day. I don't know much about Grey, but although he's new out here he has seen service in Europe. However, if he has a drinking problem…"

"I don't care if he never touches another drop, he is not coming in and taking over the 112th. He'll never be able to serve under me anyway, I'll kill him stone dead. If it's time to find a colonel for the 112th and it probably is, to be honest, there's only one possible candidate and you know it."

"That is going to be difficult, Colonel. Wheeler is a provincial nobody and he probably cannot afford the premium they are going to expect for this."

"He probably can, but it will wipe out his savings and I'm not having that." Paul studied Wellington for a long thoughtful moment. "But you think there's a way around this, don't you?"

"Yes. If I recommend somebody other than Grey, and he can pay the price, it is going to be difficult for Horse Guards to actually refuse to accept without a good reason. I am not popular in some quarters, but I think on this occasion, providing I can offer justification, I will have my way."

"And can you?"

"I don't really want somebody brought in over Wheeler's head. It would disrupt the success of this brigade."

"I'll buy it," Paul said quietly. His chief studied him.

"He's a proud man, Colonel. He isn't going to like that."

"I know. I'll talk him round. Can we do this?"

"Yes, if I make a stand over it. I have some leverage at present."

"With what?"

"It is probably best if you don't know, Colonel, politics is not your forte. For the time being I'm going to spike their guns. If you can persuade Wheeler to overcome his pride and accept your offer, I will write to Horse Guards explaining that I cannot recommend Grey because of his unfortunate habit of being drunk on duty. I will suggest that until his problem is brought under control, it might prove embarrassing for his family if such a promotion brought it into the public eye."

Paul gave a splutter of laughter. "Did you know? About Grey's drinking?"

"Of course not, and neither do you. It might well have been a single incident; you are assuming far too much. But it is very useful at present. I will recommend Wheeler in terms that will be difficult to refute. He's older than Grey with years of excellent service and not a single blot on his record, and he has done much to improve the performance and retrieve the reputation of the 112th. I will also quietly suggest that to promote Grey over such a man might cause people to wonder if we are about to return to the shocking days of the illegal sale of military commissions to the highest bidder."

"Isn't that exactly what you're suggesting I do, sir?"

Wellington rolled his eyes. "Of course I am, Colonel. But very discreetly. While I appeal to their sense of honour and their reputations, you will wave your purse in front of Colonel Caldwell, through the offices of the regimental agent. Caldwell has a son with a hopeful family and his own promotions to purchase. I think he will take your hand off."

Paul was silent, studying him. "No wonder you were so furious with me when I came in here and started being mouthy with you if you had this tucked away for me," he said. "But sir…"

"Don't start asking difficult questions, Colonel."

"I have to. Because if you don't tell me the truth you know perfectly well that at some point something is going to happen that I don't like, and I'll probably blow up about it when I ought to keep my mouth shut."

Wellington sighed. "I would rather be dealing with your wife at this point," he said.

"Well you can't. I know she's a better politician than I am, sir, but she's not well. You're far too sure that this is going to work. What are you giving them that I'm not going to like?"

Wellington studied him for a long time. Then he rose and went to the decanter. He brought it to the table, poured two more drinks and sat down. "I am writing to London concerning this disgraceful affair of the Almeida garrison," he said. "In it, I am listing the reasons I believe it to have gone wrong. What I will not be doing is hanging Sir William Erskine out to dry. Privately I intend to convey to Horse Guards that I could do so at any moment if I am asked to place yet another officer of dubious competence over a man of honour and ability. I am then going to request the appointment of Lieutenant-Colonel John Wheeler to full colonel of the 112th light infantry."

"Light infantry?"

"May as well make it worth my while."

"All right, sir. And who, may I ask, is the chosen scapegoat?"

"Not a scapegoat, Colonel. Not in the sense you mean. A lot of mistakes were made but the biggest was the bridge at Barba del Puerco. I sent out an order the previous day to Sir William Erskine to send the 4th under Colonel Bevan out to the bridge. For reasons which nobody seems to be able to explain to me, Colonel Bevan did not go there. The result was that Brennier had free passage over the river."

"I thought I'd heard that Bevan was there," Paul said.

136

"He arrived in order to join in the attack on the retreating French troops. If his men had held the bridge as they should have…"

"Have you had this properly investigated?" Paul asked quietly.

"Is Colonel Bevan a friend of yours, Colonel?" Wellington asked.

"Have you met Colonel Bevan, sir? He is a charmingly naïve gentleman with his head stuffed full of notions of honour and gallantry which make my hair stand on end and a tendency to sink into black despair on a regular basis. No, he's not a friend. He disapproves of me. I frequently want to shake him. But he's a good man and not a bad officer. And he has a reputation for being highly conscientious. If he's actually being blamed here for something he didn't do…"

"He isn't. I'm not lying about anything, Colonel. I'm just not stressing the obvious, which is that both Campbell and Erskine, who command divisions, ought to have been able to work out between them how to prevent the French from breaking out of Almeida and managing a night march on little known paths to cross into Spain. If you and Craufurd had been guarding Almeida for me he wouldn't have got beyond the first line of your pickets."

"No, he wouldn't," Paul admitted. "So you let the commanders off the hook and blame poor Bevan for getting lost in the dark and quietly point out to Horse Guards how embarrassing it would be for them if their appointment – namely Erskine – should later turn out to have been grossly negligent. And then you bring up Colonel Johnny Wheeler and the 112th. Don't you have any other favours you're asking at the same time?"

"A more regular pay chest might be nice, Colonel, but I'm not optimistic."

Paul drank. "You were right. I bloody hate it and I wish I didn't know anything about it. But I want Johnny Wheeler commanding the 112th. What will happen to Bevan?"

"Nothing. God in heaven, Colonel, I'm not going to court-martial the man, he won't be the first to make a mistake in this war. I would hate to be hauled over the coals for some of my recent choices at Fuentes de Oñoro. I'm not even going to give him a dressing-down in person. There will be a report in the London Gazette which might be embarrassing for him, but he'll survive it. At some point he will do something gallant with his regiment and I'll issue a commendation which will also be mentioned in the London Gazette and it will all be forgotten." Wellington studied Paul. "There is another name which is going to suffer the same fate by the way, but I doubt this one will distress you as much. General Erskine is placing some of the blame for the delay in my orders being sent onto Captain Longford."

"Is he? What is Longford supposed to have done?"

"He was at a dinner in Villa Formoso with the General when my orders were delivered. According to Erskine he told Captain Longford to deliver them to Colonel Bevan and the captain failed to do so for several hours."

"Bollocks," Paul said shortly. "Longford's not that stupid. He's trying to build himself a career out of this posting, if he'd been handed your orders, he'd have taken them on the spot. What happened, did Erskine put them in his pocket and forget about them?"

"We will never truly know, Colonel."

137

"I'll know, sir. Well it might put a brake on Vincent's ambitions, but he's used to that. He'll smile and say the right things and keep kissing arses until it's all forgotten. It will do him good after what he did at Sabugal. Although it is bloody unfair that Erskine gets off scot free."

"Colonel – you cannot tell anybody about any of this. Not even your wife."

"If I told Nan about this she'd crucify me," Paul said bluntly. "We share a passion for justice which I'm setting aside for Johnny and the 112th. Do I need to do anything about Grey?"

"No. Try not to hit him again. But he insulted your wife, another officer would have called him out. What did he say, by the way?"

"It involved Captain Cartwright."

"Ah. Yes, that has caused some gossip, Colonel. People are saying you are about to become the father of two children."

"Is that what you meant about my morals earlier? If I'd fathered a bastard on Arabella Cartwright last year, sir, we wouldn't be sitting here having this conversation because my bloody corpse would have been found castrated in a ditch outside the nearest military hospital. And if she finds out what you and I have just done to Charles Bevan you might be right there next to me, so you'd better be able to carry this off."

Wellington laughed and for the first time it sounded unforced. "Go and see how she is, Colonel. Is she all right, I should have asked before?"

"I think so, but she's going to discontinue her hospital work now. Honestly, sir, we don't have a clue when this baby is going to arrive, but I've a suspicion it will be sooner than we think. She needs to stop taking care of my brigade and start looking after herself for a bit."

"I agree. All the same, do you think she can spare you for a week or two?"

"If I'm needed."

"Is there ever going to be a time when you tell me to get lost, Colonel?"

"When you questioned my competence to command a brigade earlier it was close, sir."

"I lost my temper," the commander admitted. "There are many things about you that I find difficult, Colonel, but I hope you know…"

"It's all right, sir. Neither of us covered ourselves with glory today, let's forget it. What do you need?"

"I'm riding south to see Beresford and assess the situation at Badajoz. Moving fast, just a small escort. I was hoping you could accompany me."

"Gladly, sir, providing I can come back if I'm needed."

"Any time, Colonel." Wellington smiled suddenly. "I don't need you. I'm indulging myself. It's been a while since you and I spent much time together and I find I'm missing it. It's been a difficult few months."

"It has."

"Bring your light company captain. I'd like to get to know the boy better; I'm always looking for promising youngsters for my staff."

Paul grinned. "You're just trying to bait me," he said. "He'd say no anyway, he'd be worse than I am at headquarters politics. Do you want to speak to Johnny yourself?"

138

"Yes. Providing he agrees to accept the loan from you, I am happy to tell him that I will be recommending him and that I expect them to accept. Off you go. Oh by the way – I saw Major Swanson in the village yesterday."

"I believe so, sir."

"And who was the charming young person he was buying clothes for?"

"Sir?" Paul said in wary surprise.

Wellington grinned. "One of the pedlars has made it out from Viseu and was selling his wares in the inn," he said. "A number of the army wives were in there, but Major Swanson seemed in the process of buying up half the man's stock. I was there visiting Armstrong, he's billeted in one of the rooms."

"Is he? I should go up, I like Sym. How's he doing?"

"Better. They're going to fit him with a wooden leg. He tells me your wife has some ideas about it, she's been corresponding with some fellow in London."

"Very probably, sir."

"Stop trying to distract me; I require the gossip. Who is Carl Swanson's female companion?"

Paul laughed. "Her name is Keren Trenlow, she's a Cornish lass. Came out with her childhood sweetheart who was in the 95th but he died of fever in Viseu. She was picked up by one of the men from the fourth who was a drunken brute and used to hit her."

"I see. And Major Swanson saved her? How chivalrous."

"Nan saved her. She didn't want to dump her on a transport back to England, the chances were that another Simpson would have got hold of her and to be honest for all her adventurous life she was an innocent little thing, very shy, very sweet. Nan took her in, she helps out with laundry and mending, generally made herself very useful."

"Especially to Major Swanson."

"I suspect more than a few of my officers fancied their chances. She's very bright and learns very fast. She's been learning to read and write and she's a capital nurse, Nan tells me, willing to turn her hand to anything. I know you and I disagree about the value of women in camp, sir. With one notable exception. But Keren's made herself part of the regiment. As for Carl, it's none of my business, as I said."

"He can't marry her, it would be very unsuitable."

"I don't suppose he's considered marrying her. But like most of my officers, he hasn't married because he has neither the time nor the money. I think he's become attached to Keren and I think she's good for him."

"Indeed. I must say from the glimpse I had of them, and I took care he didn't see me noticing, it looked more like a romance than a business transaction. As long as it doesn't get in the way of his duty."

"Seriously, sir?"

Wellington gave a grim smile. "Colonel, I hate men having their womenfolk with them, it brings all kinds of complications. Why I tolerate your regiment, which travels in my army like a biblical plague of locusts, I have no idea. I make a point when we're on the move, never to ride back as far as the 110th because I am well aware that I am likely to find you walking with your Sergeant-Major, your Lieutenant-Colonel making eyes at the wife of General Sir William Erskine's ADC and your own wife back with the camp followers up to her knees in mud carrying their brats on her very expensive thoroughbred mare."

"Very likely, sir," Paul said placidly. "I must say we all appreciate your tact in staying away. Let me know when you want me, won't you?"

"It will be a few days. We'll need a small escort, cavalry I suppose. Perhaps I could ask a few of Thatcher's men from the 14th."

"I'd like that, sir. I can guarantee they're useful if we get into trouble. Who has taken over his troop?"

"Captain O'Malley, he's purchased up. He was there that day."

"I know him. I'm glad it's someone Simon would have approved of. Thank you, sir."

Wellington returned Paul's salute. "Go and talk to the new Colonel of the 112th."

Chapter Twelve

Paul went in search of Johnny Wheeler. He found him with a group of officers in the field at the back of the farm. Caroline Longford and Anne were seated in two camp chairs with Keren Trenlow perched on a fallen tree stump beside them. Paul studied her as he approached. She was dressed in the plain muslin gown that Anne had given her months ago, faded and stained at the hem now, but her shabbiness was no worse than either of the other two women who travelled with the army. Anne's velvet robe was threadbare in places and Caroline's hem was ragged. Keren was laughing up at something Anne had said, and it occurred to him that had he not known where she had started life, he would have seen no difference in status between her and the other two women. His wife's eccentric attitude to social standing meant that she tended to treat the wives and camp followers with exactly the same bracing directness that she employed with the officers' wives and he realised that she was beginning to treat Keren, as she treated Teresa Carter, as a friend.

"What in God's name is going on?" Paul demanded coming forward, and Carl turned, laughing.

"Cricket, sir. We've been challenged to a cricket match by the second brigade. Johnny is sorting out the team."

"Cricket?" Paul groaned and pantomimed putting a gun to his head. "Dear God, somebody shoot me now. Why in the name of all that's holy, with Marmont taking over from Massena and Soult probably on his way, are we spending our time on cricket?"

"Because the officers like it, you miserable bastard and it's good for morale," Wheeler said laughing. "There is also, I am reliably informed, a fancy dress ball being held by the Portuguese brigades in Villa Formoso on Tuesday."

"That's good," Anne said happily. "I shall go as a whale. No costume needed."

Paul laughed and bent to kiss her. "I'm going to miss that one, Lord Wellington wants to borrow me to go to Badajoz with him for a few days. Which is just as well because none of this is good for my morale."

"You're not normal, sir, your morale boosters include punching other officers and shouting at the commander-in-chief."

"Jesus, how did you know? I've only just come from there."

"I wasn't referring to any particular episode, although from what I hear, Lord Wellington probably needed a good fight this morning."

"He got one," Paul admitted. "Details are not for discussion, however. Can your team manage without you for a while, Johnny, I need you?"

"Carl can take over. Unless you want to, sir. Can you even play cricket?"

"I was, believe it or not, a child once, Colonel Wheeler. Although not for very long, I'll admit. I played cricket at Eton. It was an experience for everybody involved. The master said that I had good natural athleticism and an excellent eye, but that I wielded both bat and ball as though they were weapons rather than sporting equipment."

"He must have had the second sight," Anne said. "Do you know, I don't think I even knew you went to Eton. The things we've yet to learn about one another."

Paul grinned. "Due to the slightly unorthodox start to our love story, girl of my heart, there are probably a few things we forgot to share. It's how I first met George Brummel although he was a few years older than me. Other than that it wasn't particularly memorable. I was expelled for throwing the Greek master into a fountain. I think it may have been that which convinced my father that a career at sea was a good idea."

"I'm beginning to have more sympathy for him than I had before," Anne said. "I wonder if our son will manage anything that impressive?"

"Certainly I am looking forward to landing them with Francis for a year or two, it will be a fitting revenge for the times they used that cane on me. Good training for the navy though, I must say."

Paul kissed her again and left, walking beside Johnny up towards the house. Inside they found the dining room, where George Kelly had set up the officers' mess, deserted. Paul sat down and waved Johnny to a chair.

"What were you fighting with Wellington about?" Wheeler asked.

"Charles Bevan and Vincent Longford, believe it or not. He is going to land them with the blame for this Almeida fiasco. I disapproved. A pointless exercise, but it gave him somebody to shout at. Also Lieutenant-Colonel Grey complained about me punching him and it turns out he is related to the apology for a divisional commander that is Sir Brent Spencer."

"I'd a feeling that one would come back to bite you. Are you going to have to apologise?"

"No. I told Wellington he insulted Nan which probably means Grey will have to apologise."

Johnny laughed aloud. "You lying bastard, that is not why you hit him."

"No. But he did do it, so who will ever be sure of my real motives? Sometimes I meet a man who just needs hitting, Johnny. But once he miscalled my wife, he's at risk of Wellington punching him."

"So what's this about?"

"You won't have heard yet, Johnny, but they're going to appoint a new colonel-in-chief for the 112th, Johnny."

"I see. What about Colonel Caldwell."

142

"He's retiring. He's very ill, Wellington thinks he may be dying. To be honest, Johnny, when the 112th first joined us, I thought that eventually they'd merge them with our lads. And I think that was the original intention. But we've made them more of a success than anybody expected. They've got an identity now and they're building a reputation."

"I'm glad to hear that," Johnny said ironically. "So who is it going to be?"

"There are two possibilities. One of them is that excrescence Philip Grey, who is getting into my brigade carried in a coffin or not at all. The other is you."

Wheeler stared at him. "Paul – I don't know what to say. But truthfully – there is a catch, isn't there?"

"Not for me, Johnny. In a minute you're going up to Wellington and he's going to give you the good news. But Grey has influence and it's already been discussed at Horse Guards. Wellington is going to overrule them, but to do that he needs a sweetener."

"Money?"

"I'm going to buy it for you. Either that or Grey will and then I will be cashiered and possibly hanged when he gets one of his companies slaughtered because he's too drunk to take an order and I rip his head off. I've more money than he does, and I've got Wellington's backing. So I'll win this particularly unseemly bidding war. But I need you to take a deep breath, put your pride to one side and say yes."

Wheeler studied him. "I'm not as broke as I was ten years ago, Paul."

"You don't have the money Grey has. He'll push up the price if he knows you're involved, and Caldwell will let him, he wants the money. If they know I'm funding it, they'll shut up and give in. I can outbid anybody else in this army."

Wheeler laughed aloud. "Sometimes I completely forget you come from a wealthy family, Paul. I've never seen you in that setting and it just doesn't feel right somehow."

"That's because, as Grey so directly put it, I am not a gentleman. But I was raised as one. God knows what went wrong. I was once told that an ancestor of mine was a pirate. Made a fortune robbing the Spanish at sea and then settled down to be respectable in Antwerp and made another fortune. It could be true. My father does very well at pretending but he's a ruthless bastard. My mother was a genuine English lady, a viscount's daughter. I think Joshua is like her."

"And you got the pirate."

"Yes. Not sure where my lass gets it from."

"There's gypsy in her somewhere, I swear it," Johnny said laughing. "I thought it the day I met her, she's half wild."

"She is. I swear to God, Johnny, if I live to be a hundred I am never going to forget my first proper sight of Nan. She'd picked me up in the snow after I'd been thrown from my horse and helped me up to a shepherd's hut. Worst blizzard I've ever seen to this day, you couldn't see a hand in front of your face. I think I might have died out there trying to walk to barracks, I'd hurt my knee. I hobbled up there with her and she walked in, shut the door, and pushed her hood back and I saw her face. She was so beautiful, but it was more than that. I thought at the time that she'd no idea how much trouble she was in, but actually it was the other way around. She broke my heart in about two hours."

Wheeler gave a faint smile. "I know. I had my doubts about this marriage, you know I did, but they've long gone. You couldn't have done better."

"And what's my answer, Johnny?"

"I'm going to say yes."

Paul was both relieved and surprised. "Thank God for that, I thought you'd kick up a dust about this."

"I'd like to," Johnny admitted. "But I'm not going to. Paul, when you handed me my captain's bars in Dublin, my first thought was that you'd somehow paid for them without me knowing. And I'm still suspicious about that one, although I don't know how you did it. But you know what? I don't care any more. I fought out there a week ago with those lads and they're very good soldiers. Michael O'Reilly, who was an obstreperous young private with an attitude when I first knew him, commands a company in that regiment now. I'm not letting my pride get in the way of commanding the regiment he serves in. And I'll be part of your brigade, serving under you, which is what I want. I think I'd find it difficult to go back to the old ways now, with another regiment. If you can pull this off I'm not going to be stupid about it, providing you allow me to pay you back one day if I can."

"Ten years ago you would have been a lot more difficult."

"Ten years ago you wouldn't have apologised to Wellington this morning."

Paul laughed aloud. "How do you know I did?"

"You always do, because you know he can't."

"I suppose we've both grown up," Paul said. "Congratulations, Colonel Wheeler. Go and get the news officially."

***

Wellington left to move south on May 16th, taking some of his staff members, a small cavalry escort, Captain Leo Manson, and the commander of the third brigade of the Light Division who found it unexpectedly difficult to leave his wife.

Anne seemed well again and was obeying her doctors finally, resting for part of each day and when she needed to travel, using a neat barouche which Paul had managed to hire from a householder of Villa Formoso. She accepted the news of his departure with a rueful smile.

"I'm beginning to understand how Rowena felt in the run up to the invasion," she said.

Paul felt himself flinch internally and knew that she had seen it and understood. "Oh Lord, that has to be the worst attempt at a joke I have ever made. Love, look at me, I'm very well. Nothing like poor Rowena was. I am surrounded by my friends and they will look after me very well. If there is the least hint of a problem I will send a message, I promise you."

"He doesn't really need me, Nan. He's admitted as much."

"He wants you. And after the past couple of months, he's probably entitled to be capricious."

"I thought it was the pregnant woman who was entitled to be capricious, not the Commander-in-Chief."

Anne laughed. "Go. Take care of him. I'll send a message if anything happens. Chances are, it will just be one of his flying visits and you'll be back before I know it."

"If it's more than that, bonny lass, I will leave him and ride back to you. I love you."

"I love you too, Colonel."

They rode fast and light, as Wellington often did when travelling. They slept in the open, finding shelter only when it rained. Paul was amusedly conscious of how much Leo Manson was enjoying himself. Lord Wellington knew that Manson was Paul's favourite junior officer and had taken some trouble to know him. But this was the first time Manson had spent extended periods of time in the company of the commander-in-chief and Paul watched with interest to see how it would go.

He was not disappointed. Wellington did not easily inspire affection in his officers and did not relate particularly well at all to the enlisted men. He could be distant and cold, and his abrupt and often sarcastic manner tended to freeze enthusiasm. He was a poor fit with the more sensitive souls in his army as he had no tolerance for what he saw as incompetence or laziness and no hesitation in raking down an officer he believed deserved it, in front of an entire regiment. He found it hard to delegate and held the belief that he could rely on nobody to manage any situation unless he was personally there to direct it. He could be pleasant enough to new juniors joining him, but he did not easily incorporate them into his very small circle of intimates.

Paul knew that some of Wellington's staff members, particularly the younger ones, were a little jealous of the completely unnecessary presence of he and Manson on this journey. Paul's friendship with the commander-in-chief had always puzzled other officers. They found it hard to understand how Wellington, who abhorred initiative and originality in most of his officers and complained at the least sign of variation from orders, could be on such excellent terms with the colonel of the 110th who had the reputation of being the most unpredictable officer in the British army. Paul knew that recent arrivals tended to put their friendship down to Wellington's tendre for Anne, but the old hands knew that Wellington had favoured Paul and sought out his company from their first meeting when he was a twenty-one year old lieutenant, new to the light company in India.

Although they were very different in many ways, Leo Manson reminded Paul of his younger self. He watched with considerable enjoyment as some of the staffers glowered at Manson who seemed to be monopolising a good deal of Lord Wellington's attention without being even slightly aware of it. He rode on his chief's other side and listened to Wellington asking Manson questions about himself and sharing in return, reminiscences of his own early days in the army, of Europe and India. He told several stories about Paul which Manson had not heard and Paul smiled at the younger man's genuine enjoyment of them.

"I can see what you mean about him," Wellington said one evening as they sat around the fire. Manson was with the horses, checking on a possible loose shoe,

145

talking and laughing with the cavalry escort. "He reminds me a little of you. I don't think he's as arrogant as you were, but that can only be a good thing."

"And there, speaks the man who is so arrogant he thinks the army can't function without his constant presence," Paul said, passing his flask to Wellington. His chief took it and drank.

"It can't," he said.

"Some of us manage tolerably well."

"You and Craufurd. And even then...."

"The Coa, sir. One incident. You left him to his own devices to patrol the border while you built the Lisbon defences, and he didn't put a foot wrong."

"No, I know, he did a splendid job. I do trust Robert." Wellington passed the flask back. "And you. Hill is very good and thank God he's on his way back from sick leave. Picton...I don't like him, but he's mostly reliable. But some of the others..."

"You're not wrong, sir. I'm not sure that this trip is making many friends on your staff for Captain Manson."

"Ha! It will do them good. They gossip like a gaggle of silly debutantes."

"Not all of them, sir."

"No. All the same it is good to have new blood. I could probably find a place for him, you know, if he was interested."

"Don't you dare," Paul said laughing. "He wouldn't anyway. He's too good at what he does, and he knows it."

"You mean he wouldn't leave you," Wellington said caustically. "Hero worship."

"Nonsense."

"He's no worse than most of the others. It's not a criticism, Colonel. I don't have that ability, to inspire affection in my officers or men. I'm not much of a showman."

"You don't need to be, sir. To be honest I've not always done so well with my officers although it's got better. Never had any trouble with the men. Nan's helped a lot, she often steps in to tell me when I'm getting it wrong and putting up someone's back."

Wellington gave one of his barking laughs. "I find that very ironic, Colonel, given that is often what I expect you to do for me."

They arrived in the pretty border town of Elvas on Sunday and found rooms in a large house which Wellington had used before. His chaplain, the Reverend Briscall held a short service in one of the parlours and their host, a local wine merchant and his wife, bustled about arranging dinner. Paul watched with interest as Wellington's quartermaster allocated rooms and billets.

"Jenson," he called softly, and his orderly came forward.

"Sir?"

"Do me a favour will you? Go over to the inn on the corner and speak to Señora Corella about rooms for the three of us. And stabling for the horses, tell her it's for me, she'll find us space, I stayed there last year, she'll remember me."

Manson glanced at him. "Sir?"

"We are about to find ourselves without rooms for the night, Leo, the penalty of offending some of the staff by getting on too well with the commander-in-chief. I could speak to Murray and get him to sort it out for us, but I'd rather be there, she's a nice woman and we'll get fed properly which is never guaranteed at headquarters."

Manson gave a splutter of laughter. "I don't know why you think you're not a good politician, sir."

"I'm not that bad, I just can't be arsed most of the time. But I'm used to this. His staff aren't always that fond of him and I can't say I blame them. He doesn't even try to be pleasant to them for most of the time, and if they make a mistake he hauls them over the coals as if they were scrubby schoolboys. He's sarcastic, rude, and intolerant of any weakness. And I think he's getting worse."

Manson was studying him with interest. "So why do you like him so much, sir?"

"He's not like it with me. Or if he is, I don't care. We share a slightly odd sense of humour, and I've got such a thick skin that he can yell at me as much as he likes and I don't get upset. I think he appreciates that. He doesn't cope well with the sensitive types."

Manson grinned. "I would think they'd be grateful to you, you're very good at drawing his fire."

"On a good day they know that, but they're puzzled by me. One or two of them see me as a jumped-up middle class upstart who bought his way to success and gets on the right side of the Commander-in-Chief because he'd like to go to bed with my wife."

Paul could see that he had shocked the younger man. After a long moment, Manson said:

"If that's what they think, they don't say it within my hearing. Which is probably a good thing. I didn't realise it was that bad with the staff, they seem friendly enough."

"They are. I get on very well with some of them, particularly Campbell and Fitzroy Somerset. And I think Murray is getting used to me but there's still some resentment. It happens when you're successful very young."

Manson studied him. "Are you giving me a warning here, sir?"

"It's worth remembering," Paul said. "I don't blame Murray to be honest. He's brilliant at his job and Wellington doesn't appreciate him at all. Anyway, wherever we sleep, we should get a good dinner this afternoon. This fellow is impressed by hosting a lord, I can tell."

The meal was enormous and the wine plentiful although Wellington partook sparingly of both. They were almost at the end of the second course when sounds of arrival made Wellington look up. Paul turned to follow his gaze and found Jenson entering the room.

"Sorry to disturb you, sir, but Colonel Arbuthnot is here with news from Marshal Beresford, and I think his Lordship will want to hear it."

Every man turned to stare at Paul's orderly. Lord Wellington set down his glass.

"Send him in, Jenson."

"Yes, my Lord."

Arbuthnot came into the room. At the sight of him both Paul and Lord Wellington rose. Arbuthnot saluted. He was a dark man in his mid-thirties, his face still black with smoke and blood darkening the sleeve of his coat. What could be seen of his white shirt was filthy and his shoes and trousers were splattered with mud.

"My Lord, I've dispatches from Marshal Beresford."

"A battle?"

"Yes, sir?"

"In whose favour?"

"Ours, sir, I suppose since they withdrew. Three days ago. But the losses – the losses are huge."

Paul moved forward, pulling out a chair. "Sit," he said, putting his hand on Arbuthnot's shoulder. "Have some food – Jenson..."

"On my way, sir."

There was virtual silence around the table as Wellington read the letters and Paul supplied the exhausted Colonel with food and drink. Eventually his chief looked up.

"Was it a victory or not?"

"It was sir. But..."

"No buts. I'll see Beresford as soon as I can. What's wrong with him?"

"He's distraught, sir. So many dead. The issue was in doubt for much of the battle. We can't calculate our losses yet, but Colborne's brigade is almost gone."

"Gone?"

"Dead, sir. The Polish lancers. The weather – there was a hailstorm, and they could see nothing. And then the lancers hit them, it was over in minutes, I've never seen anything so bad. We were going to retreat but then the fourth came in under Cole and it turned the tide. But we're still trying to collect all the dead. I can't tell you..."

"Don't try," Paul said quietly. "Have another drink, Robert and breathe. It's over now."

He glanced at Wellington who had been about to speak and was relieved to see his chief close his mouth on whatever scathing remark he had been about to make. They waited until Arbuthnot had finished his meal and then Wellington rose and came around the table to him.

"Thank you, Colonel. I'll need to consult with my staff and then I'll write to the Marshal. Once I have had the opportunity to assess the situation, I will send for more troops. Will you be fit, do you think, to ride back..."

"Captain Manson can take them, sir," Paul said. "You might want to keep Robert here in case you've questions for him. Leo, why don't you take Colonel Arbuthnot over to our billet, give him a chance to clean up and rest a bit?"

"Of course. A very good idea." Wellington said absently, scanning the letters again. "Thank you, Colonel."

When Arbuthnot had gone the chief looked at his staff. "This won't do," he said, dropping the dispatches on the table. "Beresford is in pieces. I can't tell from this if we won or lost. Bad enough that we lost the Almeida garrison and struggled

148

so badly at Fuentes de Oñoro. Another despondent report to London and they'll start whining about pulling us out again or at least replacing me in command."

"We wouldn't want that, sir," Paul said.

"It would serve you right if they replaced me with General Erskine, Colonel." Wellington said waspishly. "I need you all to get to work on these. No falsehoods, mind, nothing that can be brought up against us. But write me down a victory, no matter what happened. In the meantime I shall look at our troop dispositions and decide where we can best deploy them. Colonel van Daan, did you say you were not billeted in this house?"

"Just at the end of the road, sir, in the tavern. A few minutes away only."

"A few minutes of wasted time if I should require you. I am fairly certain I have a quartermaster with me with limited occupation at the moment and if I have more staff with me than rooms in this house I would be very surprised. Perhaps..."

Murray got up quickly. "An oversight, sir, the Colonel not being a member of your regular staff. I will..."

"Colonel van Daan commands a brigade, sir, and has more active fighting experience than most of the men in this room. Make arrangements and don't let this happen again. The rest of you apply yourselves to improving the tone of this letter. I need to take the air and then I shall return to give you your orders."

Wellington's tone was arctic. His staff were on their feet saluting. Wellington stalked from the room and Paul regarded the others, trying hard not to laugh.

"I'm not sure if I'm supposed to be there or here," he said. "I'm sorry, Murray, but can I suggest you find space for Arbuthnot and Manson as well, I wouldn't like to predict what might piss him off next today."

"Of course." Colonel Murray gave a wry smile. "Sorry. I should have..."

"Don't worry about it, I've the hide of an elephant. I..."

"Colonel van Daan, where the devil are you?" Wellington yelled, and Paul's heart sank.

"That answers my question. Would anybody else like to take my place out there?"

There were grins around the table and Paul, who felt he had made his point, left to follow Wellington.

The field of Albuera was still strewn with bodies when Paul finally visited with his chief. He stood beside Wellington watching as men, wearing makeshift masks to try to limit the smell, carried bodies to the mass graves which were already beset by birds of prey. Many of the corpses were already naked, stripped and looted by men of both sides, by the camp followers or by the local population.

"Colborne's brigade," Wellington said quietly. "There weren't even enough of them left to go back and search through their dead and wounded. They started with 1600 and have 300 left still able to fight."

"Like the 74th at Assaye," Paul said, watching the men lifting another dead man. He felt sick. "These poor bastards couldn't have stood a chance here. They couldn't fire their muskets because of the rain and hail and didn't see the lancers approaching."

"They were caught in line which made it worse." Wellington glanced over at Paul and gave a slight smile. "I know what you are thinking, Colonel."

"I'm not going to say it, sir, given what just happened to these poor lads."

Wellington glanced over at Captain Manson who was watching the field with sombre eyes and Paul saw his lips quirk. "What is Colonel van Daan not saying, Captain?"

"This feels like an examination in Latin, my Lord," Manson said unexpectedly. "I did my homework, though. Colonel van Daan is not asking why they didn't get into square the moment that rainstorm hit, their officers must have known instantly they were blinded, they can't have known what was coming. It might not have helped much, they still had no firepower and lances are longer than bayonets. Still, I think fewer would have died."

"I believe they tried," Wellington said quietly. "But they couldn't see."

Manson turned his gaze to them, and Paul read an echo of his own impotent fury in the golden hazel eyes. "Then they weren't bloody fast enough my Lord, which is why our Colonel walks through training with a pocket watch in his hand until we get it right. And our men can do it in the dark."

He turned and walked away, and Paul watched as he summoned an uninjured guardsman to pick up the feet of a dead soldier. Beside him Wellington watched as Manson helped carry the corpse across the field.

"He'll do," he said quietly.

"He will, sir. How's Beresford?"

Wellington shook his head, his expression sombre. "He isn't well. He seems to have taken this incredibly badly. I've tried talking to him, but I swear he's lost all his confidence."

"It can be hard, sir. Both you and I know that."

"Remembering Assaye?"

Paul nodded without speaking. Assaye had been his first major battle, fought on the baked earth of India when Wellington had been a relatively young and inexperienced general with his way to make in the world and Paul had been twenty-two, promoted to captain only twenty-four hours earlier on the death of Captain Mason. It had been a brilliant victory but bloody, and Paul had been injured and lost too many of his company.

He could remember sitting outside the crumbling clay farm building which Carl had found to house them for the night at the end of the battle, leaning back against the wall, aware of the pain of his wounds, and feeling tears sliding down his cheeks at the loss of men he had come to care about in the past year of service. He had not immediately noticed the other man who lowered himself to sit beside him until his General said:

"Are you all right, Captain?"

Paul glanced over at him, startled, and realised that Wellesley too had been crying.

"Not really, sir. Thinking about my lads."

"So am I," Wellesley said quietly. "So many dead. I am sitting here wondering if it was worth it."

150

Paul could remember his surprise at the unexpectedly candid admission. "It's what we do, sir. I was just thinking maybe I need to get better at it than this. I don't like losing them."

The general turned his head and studied Paul with something like amusement in the hooded eyes. "You're already very good for your age, Captain. I've heard nothing but praise for you out there today. I'll be mentioning your name in despatches home."

"That's good of you, sir, but would you be offended if I told you that doesn't help at all just now?"

Wellesley laughed aloud. "No, boy, nothing offensive in that. I think I see your Sergeant hovering waiting to help you inside."

Paul looked over at Sergeant O'Reilly. "Yes, he's been like a hen with one chick over me today but I'm grateful. It turns out this was worse than I thought it was, I'm not sure I'll be much use to you for a while."

"You'll recover. Give it time. I'll be up to see you when we're settled in camp, Captain. If you need to take time out for this, keep in touch with me, will you? I will be honest with you, I do not meet very many young officers who impress me as much as you do, despite your inability to wait for a simple order."

"Sorry about that, sir."

"Would it offend you if I called you a liar, Captain?"

"No, sir, nothing offensive in that."

Paul studied Wellington now. It had been nine years ago, but the short encounter had stayed with him. He was aware that something had shifted in those few minutes which had changed the nature of his relationship with his Commander in Chief. They had kept in touch ever since, writing regularly when they were not serving together, and despite their frequent arguments over the years, Paul knew that he was one of the few officers in his army whom Wellington considered a friend.

"What now?" he asked.

"Back to the siege. We need Badajoz. Fletcher seems to think it can be done."

"We don't have the equipment, sir."

"I need to trust what my engineers tell me, Colonel. Although I can see by the expression on your face that you don't agree."

"I'm not an engineer, sir. What do you want me to do?"

"I'd like you to stay for a week or two if you can, Colonel. If she needs you, she'll send. Beresford needs a rest, I'm sending him back to Lisbon to be a diplomat with the Portuguese for a while, he's good at that. Hill will be here any day, he can take over. I want the Light Division along the border keeping an eye on the French for me. Can you…"

"I can, sir, as long as you're not expecting me to lead the Forlorn Hope. If you get me killed just now she'll be after you with a bone saw."

"An advisory capacity only, Colonel, I promise you. I am seconding you and young Manson temporarily onto my staff."

"Well good luck with that one, you couldn't have picked two officers worse suited to the job; between us we'll piss off every one of them. I'll write to Nan today, let her know I'll be a little longer."

"Give her my apologies, Paul, and my best wishes. I'm aware I'm being selfish here…"

"She'll forgive you. She's got a soft spot for you."

"It is entirely mutual," his commander said.

Paul knew that he was likely to find the weeks of the siege difficult. His temperament was not suited to the patient waiting required as trenches were dug and plans studied although he liked Colonel Richard Fletcher with whom he had worked during the construction of Wellington's defences in Portugal, and he was happy to spend time with the man. Privately Paul doubted the wisdom of Wellington's decision to lay siege to Badajoz at this time. The French were going to send reinforcements and given the huge losses of Albuera added to those of Fuentes de Oñoro Wellington was short of men fit to fight, as well as a proper siege train.

Paul was obliged to endure the tedium without the presence of the captain of his light company. They had been in Elvas for two weeks when Manson sought him out in his room where he was writing a letter to his wife.

"Can I help you, Captain?"

"Sir, I've just had a letter from home, from my mother. Apparently my father is very ill. A seizure of some kind."

Paul put down his pen. "Leo, I'm sorry. Come and sit down and have a drink. You're going to need to go home, aren't you?"

Manson seated himself. He looked depressed. "I suppose I am," he said. "Read it for yourself."

Paul poured brandy and passed Manson the cup then took the letter, smiling inwardly at his junior's automatic inclusion of him in his family's private correspondence. The letter was short and emotional, and Paul put it down when he had finished and looked up.

"I know you don't want to, lad, but you're going to have to. It sounds serious."

"Yes. I've not heard from them for a long time. To be honest we had a bit of a falling out, sir. He told me I was disowned since I wouldn't follow his orders and instructed my mother and my cousins not to write to me either. So I've had no news for a few months."

Paul gave a slight smile. "You have my sympathy, Captain, I've had a difficult relationship with my own father over the years. It did get better, although he isn't impressed by my somewhat precipitate second marriage."

"Does that bother you, sir?"

"No. When he meets her he'll understand, but to be honest, what I do is none of his business. Are you financially dependent on him?"

Manson shook his head. "No, there's never been much money, sir and he's never made me an allowance. I suppose at some point what he had would have been mine but it's not that much and I'm better without it."

"I agree. You'll make your own way, Leo, and do very well out of it trust me."

"You've not asked me what it was about, sir. The quarrel."

"I know what it was about, Leo, he wrote to me."

Manson's eyes widened. "He did what?"

"You told him very clearly that you'd no intention of transferring to his old regiment and that you'd accepted a captaincy in the 110th and he wrote to me complaining of it and telling me that I should withdraw my offer and tell you to comply with his wishes. He was somewhat unflattering about my regiment I must say."

Manson's face was scarlet. "Sir, I am sorry, I'd no idea he would do that. I..."

"It's all right, Captain, I understand. It had nothing to do with you. He is an overbearing rude old man and I replied very briefly to say that I wanted you in my regiment, that you were a very promising young officer whom I was proud to have serving under me and that your career choices were your own. I was polite and to the point."

"You should have told me."

"It would have embarrassed you, Leo. I've only told you now in case he mentions it. Other than that forget it. But for all his faults he is your father, lad, and if you don't make a push to see him before he dies you're likely to regret it. Get going, take a few weeks and get back to your company as soon as you can. It's not bad timing actually, you don't need to be here dancing attendance on Wellington just because he's bored."

Manson managed a smile. "No, I know, sir. But I was quite enjoying it to tell you the truth."

"So is he, he's taken a liking to you. But he'll understand, I promise you. Get your kit packed and get yourself off to Lisbon, you'll get passage on one of the packets, I'll give you all the necessary papers. Do what you need to do and if it's taking longer than a couple of weeks write to me and I'll extend your leave for as long as you need me to."

"Thank you, sir. I feel terrible about going..."

"Don't, Leo, it's family and you've three women who will need you there. Plus there might be business matters for you to deal with. In case there are and you need help with any of it, I'll give you a letter of introduction to my man of business, he'll do whatever you need."

Manson left to pack and Paul went back to his letter to Anne, telling her of Manson's departure. He went on to write the various letters Manson would need for his journey and then wrote to Carl Swanson to inform him that he would need to manage the light company for a little longer without its captain. With Manson gone Paul sat back and waited with limited patience either for success in the siege or for his chief's permission to abandon it and return to his brigade and his wife.

The siege was not going well. While the two armies decimated one another on the field at Albuera, General Philippon, the wily governor of Badajoz had ordered his troops to fill in the Allied trenches and battery positions and remove much of the topsoil around San Cristobal. Hamilton's Portuguese troops resumed the siege immediately after the battle but there was little activity until Wellington and his staff arrived and began to direct operations.

Wellington had sent for the third and seventh divisions of his northern army under the overall command of General Picton, leaving General Spencer in command in the north. With the new troops in place and setting up camp around the city, Soult retreated slowly southeast to Llerena with his large convoys of wounded soldiers, followed by Beresford and Blake. They met with little resistance apart from a clash at Usagre on May 25th when Soult sent a force of dragoons to push back the Allied cavalry and ran them into a trap which resulted in 250 killed and 78 captured to a mere 20 dead and injured among the allies.

As Paul had expected, Beresford was officially replaced in command of the southern front by General Hill who took over command of the second and fourth divisions along with Alten's brigade and Lumley's cavalry, an army of some ten thousand men. Paul liked Rowland Hill whom he had known since Rolica and Vimeiro back in 1809. He was a gentle man with a placid demeanour which hid a remarkable ability to manage his officers and men and a fierce courage in battle. His kindness and consideration for his troops had led him to be nicknamed 'Daddy' Hill. Paul sometimes wondered what his own men called him behind his back, although he suspected it might be better not to know.

Wellington had decided to personally take charge of the siege corps, which consisted of the third and seventh divisions and Hamilton's division, a total of 14,000 men including 700 gunners. There was the usual lack of trained engineers, with only 25 on Fletcher's staff, and watching them patiently trying to teach the enlisted men the skills needed, Paul wondered when Horse Guards would wake up to the dangers of conducting siege warfare with inadequate resources. There was also a shortage of artillery and the guns they had were ancient relics from the ramparts of Elvas.

Wellington's engineers were urging him to attack the San Cristobal fort and to make a major attack on the Castle on the south side of the Guadiana. With Houston's seventh Division investing the north side and Picton's third along with Hamilton's Portuguese on the south, Paul settled down and tried to summon his patience. He understood that Wellington wanted him for his advice rather than his fighting skills, but he fretted away from Anne and the rest of his brigade. As the days went by he watched in growing frustration as siege works were started and then wiped out again and again by French artillery fire. The battery set up against San Cristobal was ineffective due to the distance involved and the guns battering the city were either annihilated by the French cannon or failed due to their age and defects. The castle walls were strong and proved hard to damage, although the San Cristobal fort had taken a considerable pounding.

Paul was shocked when Wellington told him of his decision to try an assault on the San Cristobal. He had received a letter from Anne which reassured him considerably. She was well and in good spirits, busy sourcing supplies for the winter and chasing up orders of uniforms and medical supplies from England. Paul could visualise her seated at her table, paper and ink neatly set out around her and his regimental and brigade ledgers piled nearby. Captain Breakspear his competent young quartermaster had been working with Anne even before she and Paul were married, and they made an excellent team.

Paul went to find Wellington who had been making enquiries about Anne with monotonous regularity and found him deep in conference with General Houston.

"I'm glad you're here," he said, when Paul tried to excuse himself. "Look over these orders with me, will you? We're going to make an assault on the San Cristobal."

Paul shook his head, his eyes on Houston. "I don't need to look at anything, sir, it's mad. We've no viable breaches and they're too well prepared, our men will get slaughtered."

"I knew you would say that" Wellington said. "General Houston here agrees with you and I think you both have a point. But we need to work out if this siege has a chance of succeeding or if I need to withdraw into winter quarters. Sooner or later they'll reinforce."

"Sir – you know what I think," Paul said. "But if you're determined, give it here and let me look, I'll give you my opinion of the least worst option. Personally I'd send a small force to test the waters first."

"Where?" Wellington said briefly and the three men bent over the plan of the town.

They chose midnight for the assault led by 180 volunteers from Houston's division. The 25-man forlorn hope managed to reach the ditch with only minor casualties only to discover that the ditch had been cleared of debris and the breach had been blocked up by carts and chevaux de frise. The rest of the storming party poured into the ditch and made an attempt to mount the wall only to discover that their ladders were too short by around five feet. The defenders directed heavy musket fire down onto them and Paul was relieved when Houston called them back with losses of around 12 dead and 80 wounded.

Three more days of bombardment followed and although more than half the original siege guns were out of action they had been reinforced by six iron ship guns from Lisbon which proved effective. Paul had suggested trying to maintain progress by firing grape shot through the night to keep the French from undoing the work that had been done during the day, but its effect was limited and progress remained painfully slow. As the days passed and Wellington's frustration mounted, Paul found himself longing to be away from headquarters. He waited daily for letters and news from his officers and men and treasured each communication from Anne, privately resolving that if nothing changed within another week he would approach Wellington and ask leave to rejoin his brigade.

Chapter Thirteen

Colonel Johnny Wheeler spent the final days of May coming to terms with his new responsibilities as colonel-in-charge of the 112th. He was becoming aware that his position as Paul's second-in-command, which he had held informally for many years, had shielded him to some extent from the vast amount of correspondence and paperwork which was an essential part of administering a regiment. For a man so clearly at home in the field, his commanding officer had a surprisingly good grasp of administrative matters and was ably assisted by his young wife who had helped to manage his battalion since before she was even married to him. Walking back up to where his horse was stabled after a long and frustrating meeting with an officer of the commissariat about winter rations and horse feed, Johnny reflected that he was looking forward to the day when his colonel's wife was back on her feet after the birth and ready to take up her completely unofficial duties again. He was beginning to sympathise with Paul's frequently expressed desire to punch the commissariat.

A voice hailed him, and Johnny paused, recognising it with a pang of discomfort. He had very little to do with Captain Vincent Longford these days, but his ongoing relationship with the man's wife made him reluctant to spend any time with Longford. He was aware of the difficulties Longford was experiencing in the wake of the Almeida fiasco and he felt, despite his instinctive dislike of the man, a pang of sympathy. There were many reasons why Johnny believed that Vincent Longford should not be an officer of the 110th but he genuinely believed that on this occasion Longford had been unfairly scapegoated.

"Colonel Wheeler. Do you have a moment?"

Johnny paused. "Captain Longford. I've not seen you for a while."

"I don't tend to feel very welcome up with the 110th, Colonel. Although that's not your regiment any more is it? Congratulations."

"Thank you," Johnny said studying the man. "Can I help you?"

"I need to speak to you privately. You got a minute?"

Johnny felt a weight settle about his heart. For months he had tried to block out the reality of his situation with Caroline Longford, but he had always known that at some point he would have to face up to it and he had a strong premonition that the moment had arrived. "Yes. Walk up to the orange groves with me, there won't be anybody about, it's too hot for a stroll."

They walked in silence until they were past the last straggling buildings of the village. Longford spoke first. "Is Colonel van Daan still away?"

"Yes. It's taking longer than we thought, he's helping Wellington with the siege, although he doesn't sound optimistic about it. I think he'll be back fairly soon."

"He should be. That poor woman."

"She's fairly well looked after, Captain."

"I know. Still, he ought to be with her."

"Vincent, if you're criticising Paul's treatment of his wife…"

"I'm not. Even if I thought he was beating the shit out of her there wouldn't be any point in saying it to you, would there? He can't do anything wrong."

"He can and often does, but I don't have any concerns about his behaviour towards his wife. You didn't walk up here with me to talk about your problems with Colonel van Daan, did you?"

"No. I rode up this morning to speak to my wife, Colonel. We had a very long conversation. She'll tell you about it when you get back, I expect."

Johnny felt the lead weight of sorrow settle in his chest. "Have you upset her?"

"She is upset, certainly. But she was always going to be, wasn't she, some day? And it's come. I'm going back to England. Erskine wants rid of me. Having blamed me for the Almeida fiasco, which was entirely his bloody fault, he now doesn't want to be associated with me any further. So I'm on half-pay until something comes up."

Johnny stared at him. "I'm sorry Vincent."

"Which is odd because I thought you'd all be laughing yourselves silly over it."

"None of us are. We all know what Erskine is like. Paul has said from the first that he doesn't think you got that message, or you'd have delivered it on the spot. He told Wellington so."

"Did he? I'm surprised. Good of him although it wasn't any use. But I suppose it wouldn't be. Anyway, I'm being sent home, pretty much in disgrace."

"And Caroline will have to go with you."

Longford studied him. "You know something, Colonel? It's up to her. But for what it's worth, I think she will. And although this is going to surprise you, I want her to."

"It doesn't surprise me at all. You're going to be broke, you'll need a woman who'll give it to you for nothing, won't you?"

"That's nasty, Colonel. It's also not true. Look, none of this should be your business, but it is. You've been her lover now for almost a year. I knew it very early on. I was furious at first, just because it was bloody humiliating having every one of Paul van Daan's men watching you make a cuckold of me. But then I thought why the hell not? I didn't want her and she didn't want me. It was easier not having to manage her in camp, find billets for her. I knew Mrs van Daan would take good care of her and I knew she was happier there. So I shut my eyes and ears and I pretended I didn't know that she spent every night she could in your bed."

"Not all of them, Vincent."

"No. I came back from time to time, and I went to bed with her. I felt I was entitled to something. I was angry that I'd had to marry her at all. We were bloody idiots to put ourselves into that situation, what was I going to do with a wife? I'd no money and no prospects and you ought to know how that feels."

"I do."

"I never bothered to try to get to know her. And then this happened. These last weeks, since Almeida…she's been really good to me. Supportive. Somebody to talk to when I'd nobody else. I know she doesn't like me. She's doing it just because she's a good person. But I was very grateful. And I felt like a bit of a shit, to be honest. I never gave her a chance. I pushed her into your arms because I couldn't be bothered."

"And now you're telling me you want her back."

"She's pregnant," Longford said quietly. "She just told me. I think she's been working herself up to telling both of us. Because although it's very likely your child, it could be mine, no question."

"Oh Jesus Christ," Johnny said. He stood very still. The thought of Caroline bearing his child brought a stab of joy, and a rush of pure horror. He thought of Anne, struggling through the heat and the long marches and the stress of watching Paul ride out to battle as their child grew within her and he wondered with agony if he could bear to watch Caroline do the same. And the child would not be born, as Anne's would, into the security of a happy marriage. He looked at Longford and finally understood.

"I don't have much. But I can give them a home and some security. I can be a father. I can learn to be a husband. And if she comes back with me she'll have a place in the world, we're married. If she stays out here with you, we can't pretend any more that she's still my wife, just staying with the regiment for convenience. She'll be your mistress, bearing your bastard. An adulteress. They'll call her a whore. No more walking in with her to headquarters parties. She'll have the same status as Carl Swanson's pretty little mistress. Less actually since neither of them have broken any marriage vows. And no matter how much you love her, you can't give her her good name back once it's gone. People whisper behind their hands about you and my wife, but while she goes to the odd dinner party with me and I don't call you out, they're obliged to pretend they don't know. Once I'm gone – and I have to go, Colonel – there's nothing more I can do to cover this up."

Johnny stopped in the shade of an oak tree and turned. "Is that what you've been doing?"

"Yes." Longford gave a humourless smile. "I am the new David Cartwright. They feel sorry for me. But when I'm gone, they'll fall on her like vultures and there is nothing you or I can do to protect her."

Johnny knew with agonising certainty that he was right. "Vincent – I've always known I was likely to lose her one day. You'd get another posting…we've talked about it. But if I let her go, I need to know she'll be all right."

158

"She will. Look, I'm not denying I was a shit to her. But the shittiest thing I could do would be to get on that transport without her and leave her to mop up her own mess. I'm not going to do that unless that's what she wants. I'll take her home and look for another posting. If I can't find one, I'll sell out and find employment. The child will have a name and a father and even if I see your eyes looking out at me, I'll never make it suffer for that. I give you my word."

Johnny felt sadness overwhelm him. At the same time he felt an odd sense of gratitude to this man whom he had never liked. He nodded. "I need to get back and talk to her. But you're right, of course. Longford, I would not have expected you to behave this well over this."

"No, well, your opinion of me was fairly fixed. We're not alike, Colonel. Not at all. But if you look back, to the days in India and then back in barracks before Paul van Daan walked through that door, did you really hate my guts? You might have thought I was too hard on the men, and I probably was at times. I know you first transferred O'Reilly to the light company to get him out of my way. But you've changed too. I've seen you order a flogging or two, it's the army, it's what we did. And you didn't sit drinking wine with your enlisted men for the first ten years of your career, you did what we all did, stuck with your own kind, and dined in the mess like a gentleman. We weren't best friends, but we got on all right back then."

Johnny thought back a long way to his younger self and smiled suddenly. "We did," he admitted. "But I discovered a different way of doing it, Vincent. And I liked it better."

"I know. I don't understand it, but then I don't need to now, I'm out. But if you think of it from my point of view, my career was effectively over when he came back from Assaye and took over. I remember him as a cocky young bastard when he set sail for India, and I can remember thinking that a year in the army would knock that out of him. But it didn't, he just found a way to make it work for him, and I couldn't stand it. Couldn't stand him. But they all loved him – Johnstone, Dixon, and Wellesley – and they spent years dumping me wherever he wasn't. When the battalion was first sent out here, they sent me to Ireland to be a policeman and then to fucking Walcheren just because of him. I was the joke of the army – the man they couldn't put in barracks with Paul van Daan in case he killed me."

"And that's eaten you up, hasn't it?"

"Yes. But no need to worry any more, it's got about as bad as it's going to get. That's almost a relief." Longford shrugged. "I'm travelling to Lisbon with a convoy of wounded in about a week. It's not much notice, I know…"

"It's probably as long as I could stand," Johnny said. His throat and chest felt tight and constricted. "I need to go and see her, Vincent. You seem fairly sure she'll go with you."

"I am."

"I can remember when Rowena van Daan died in childbirth," Johnny said quietly. It felt odd to be talking to Longford like this, but he felt, in spite of everything, a sense of gratitude to the man. "Carlyon was still alive, but he'd just hit Nan in the middle of the square outside headquarters in Viseu and accused her of sleeping with Paul. Which surprisingly, I don't think she was. Gervase Clevedon got her out of it and brought her up to us and I know that Paul offered her the choice to go home to her family or to stay here with him. She chose to stay. To brave the scandal and the social ruin of being a married woman living under another man's protection."

"Her husband was killed soon afterwards wasn't he? In fact, rumour says…"

"I killed him," Johnny said quietly. "He came back for her, was about to shoot her and I put him down. But in those weeks before he did, we were off at the Coa fighting with Craufurd and I can remember just feeling angry with Paul. Because I knew he shouldn't let her do it. Shouldn't let her ruin herself because she loved him. But I knew that he would."

"Colonel, I know he's your friend. And I'll admit – just this once – there are many things about him which are admirable. He's talented and he's good to his men. And he does love her, any fool can see that. But she shouldn't be out here in her condition. Caroline isn't like her, you know. She's surprisingly brave but she wouldn't cope with what Mrs van Daan copes with."

"I know. I feel terrible, and it's about to get a whole lot worse. But I can't watch her struggle with pregnancy and childbirth in a bloody army camp. I'm not Paul van Daan. I don't know if he just doesn't see it or if he deliberately ignores it because they need to be together so badly, but…"

"Maybe you're just less selfish than he is," Longford said quietly. "And surprisingly, maybe I am too. Wouldn't that be a laugh? Talk to her and one of you send me a note telling me what she's going to do. If she's coming with me I'll let her know the arrangements. I don't need to see her until then, she's yours for the next week."

"I will. Vincent - thank you."

Johnny stood watching as Longford walked away, then made his way slowly back to where he had stabled his horse.

He found Caroline waiting for him in his room. She had been crying, but she seemed composed now. As he closed the door and turned to her she said:

"Has he told you?"

Johnny nodded. "How did you know?"

"I watched you walk across the yard just now."

Despite the ache in his heart, Johnny smiled. "Jesus, lass, if it's as obvious as that, my men are going to be crying into their grog rations watching me for a while."

"Johnny, I'm sorry I didn't tell you first. About the baby. I've been trying to work up the courage, but then Vincent approached me about leaving, and I couldn't not tell him."

"Love, it's all right. Somebody had to be told first, and he has as much right as I do. Most people would say he has more. I didn't realise he'd known from the first."

"Nor did I. There's a good deal I didn't realise."

"Caroline, I want you to go."

She nodded, and he could see that she was crying again. "I know. I think I have to, Johnny. We've always known this could happen. I feel as though my heart is completely broken – as if I could never be happy again. I love you so much, I

160

can't stand it. But there's a child, and there's your career. And there's also Vincent Longford. I've hated him at times, but just at the moment I don't. I stood in a church over a year ago and promised to be faithful to him, and I wasn't. I didn't even try. I met you and I walked into your arms without any hesitation. I'll never be sorry I did that, but…"

"Was he faithful to you?"

Caroline laughed through her tears. "Do you know something, Johnny – I think he might have been. Not because he cared about me. I just don't think Vincent is much of a womaniser. Before he married me I expect he went to the brothel occasionally – most men do. But he doesn't really understand women and never bothered to think about it until he came here."

"And got to know you better?" Johnny said, doubtfully. Caroline laughed.

"Johnny, Vincent has literally no romantic feelings for me whatsoever. Surely you must realise…"

Johnny thought about it and suddenly understood. "Nan."

"Of course. It was so obvious from the moment he set eyes on her."

"Him and the rest of the bloody army."

"I used to think so, but I'm not so sure now. He genuinely likes and respects her. She once told me that although she has often wanted to hit him for some of the horrible things he has said and done to other people, she had never once found him less that courteous and pleasant to her. And she's right. But I honestly think it's more than how lovely she is."

"Really?"

"Don't sound so sceptical. I think he envies what she has with Paul. I don't think Vincent ever saw that in his own family, or anywhere else, but somewhere inside him I think he wants children and a home and security. And a wife who cares about him."

"You don't, Caro."

"No. But I can try to learn. So can he."

"I wanted those things too."

Caroline smiled. "I'm not going to patronise you, Johnny, and tell you that you can still have them. But you can. You're Colonel-in-Charge of the 112th light infantry now, you've a career and money in the bank and you don't have to behave like that young lieutenant who couldn't afford much more than his uniform and a horse."

"It's ironic. Now I have those things, but I can't have you. I wish to God I'd met you before he did, Caro, but I didn't. We can't go back. I'm just afraid he can't keep this up."

"If he doesn't – if I'm truly unhappy or something goes badly wrong – I'll write to Nan. I promise you, Johnny. I can't have what I want with you and he certainly can't have what he would like with Nan. But at least we both have some idea now what we would have liked. I wonder if we can learn to give some of it to one another."

Johnny could feel tears in his eyes, and he blinked. "That sounds very grown-up," he said.

"I have to be, Johnny, I'm going to have a child. Probably our child."

161

"I hope it is. I shouldn't say that, but I do. I want the first child you bear to be mine. I want there to be a child somewhere in the world with my blood. And that is very selfish."

"No it's not, I want that too. At least I'll have that much of you."

Her voice broke on the word and then she was in his arms. Johnny kissed her, feeling already the pain of losing her. "He's leaving in a week. He said you should write to him to let him know and he'll tell you the arrangements."

"I know. Oh God, Johnny, how am I going to carry on without you?"

He was crying too, burying his face in the mass of fair hair. "The same way I will without you, darling girl. I know you're doing this for me as much as for you."

"Honestly, Johnny? Mostly I'm doing it for the baby. But I'll miss you every day for the rest of my life."

In response, he kissed her hard. "Pack a bag. I'm going to speak to Carl and Gervase. We're going away for a few days – I'm taking you to Viseu. We are going to stay in my favourite tavern and eat paella outside in the sunlight and drink wine together, and I'm going to make love to you every day to give us both something to remember through the years."

"Can we? With Paul away…?"

"Yes, we bloody can. Pack a bag, we're leaving in an hour."

She was laughing through her tears. "Johnny, people will talk!"

"Let them. As my commanding officer would say, they'll get over it."

***

Paul van Daan received letters from both his wife and Colonel Wheeler on the same day and he read them both with a sense of sadness. He had always known that Johnny's relationship with Caroline Longford was likely to end painfully for both of them and he knew from his own experience how it felt to watch the woman he loved walk away with another man. He had known Anne for two years before the death of both his wife and her husband had allowed them to be together and he had accustomed himself to the idea that she could never belong to him no matter how much he loved her. He felt deeply for Johnny and wished he could be there for him when Caroline left with her husband.

The siege dragged on. The engineers had decided that an assault on the Castle would be hopeless as it would have to cross at least 600 yards of open ground and wade the Rivillas stream. The San Cristobal fort was badly damaged, with two breaches in its walls but its garrison had been doubled and the French had managed to clear the ditches and block up the breaches every night. Paul was deeply unhappy about the idea of an assault although he admitted that his hatred of siege warfare might well be colouring his judgement.

On 9th June at nine in the evening Houston launched his second assault on San Cristobal. The storming party consisted of 400 soldiers and was supported by 100 sharpshooters who were ordered to shoot at any Frenchman who appeared at the breaches. The French opened a heavy fire as soon as the attackers appeared. The major commanding the column and the ranking engineer lieutenant were both killed at once. The attackers put up their 16 ladders but most of the men were shot down and the few who managed to reach the top were bayonetted by groups of Frenchmen who charged down the breach. After almost an hour most of the ladders were smashed and the Allied survivors fled back to their trenches to the loss of fifty four killed and over eighty wounded and on the following day Phillippon agreed a truce for the Allies to go in and recover their wounded. Paul observed cynically that it was also an opportunity for the defenders of San Cristobal to repair their defences.

Paul was called up to Wellington's headquarters the following morning. His chief looked tired and depressed.

"I am raising the siege," he said briefly. "I've sent orders out to the various commanders. Marmont is on his way, I had intelligence last night and I think it's reliable. Once he joins Soult we will be vulnerable, and I am not going to risk everything we've won this year. We'll hold the border and see out the winter and we'll try again next year."

Paul felt a lift of his heart. "Yes, sir."

"We'll be here for another week or two. I'm sorry, Paul, I know I've kept you from your wife and you should be with her. I had hoped…"

"Sir, it's all right. She's fine, I had a letter this morning. I'll be back with her soon."

"You will."

Paul hesitated. "I also had a letter from Johnny Wheeler. I gather Captain Longford has been relieved of his duties as ADC to General Erskine."

Wellington gave a snort. "I cannot imagine that is a source of distress to you, Colonel."

"I won't be sorry to see him go, sir, but I wish it was over something that he deserved."

Wellington's lips twitched into something that was almost a smile. "Sometimes you surprise me, Colonel. And what is happening to his wife?"

"She's going with him," Paul said briefly.

Wellington was silent for a moment. Then he said quietly:

"She is doing the right thing, Colonel."

"Very likely, sir. But not much consolation to Johnny Wheeler who is very much in love with her. And I am concerned about how they'll manage. With this hanging over his head he might find it difficult to find another posting."

Wellington got up. "I need to write these orders, Colonel. Go and write to your wife, tell her you'll be back soon. And stop trying to solve everybody else's problems. You wanted rid of Longford and now he's gone. He is not one of your officers anymore."

Paul looked at him thoughtfully. "Yes, sir," he said.

***

Captain Leo Manson made the journey back to England in an unquiet dream. It had been a year since he had set off on his voyage to Portugal after a few weeks basic training, but he felt as though he had left his younger self behind in a way that it would be difficult to explain. His first month with the 110th in Lisbon had been a nightmare, with everything he had believed and learned blown apart by his new commanding officer's explosive temper and complete disregard for all that Manson had been taught by his father to be important in an officer.

His rock throughout those first difficult weeks had been his commander's young wife, a girl close in age to himself but who had seemed at the start much older. He still did not know why Anne van Daan had chosen to fly in the face of general opinion and offer him her help and support, but it had given him something to cling to as he went through the painful process of readjusting to life in the 110th.

Going back to his father's house felt like entering a world he had very much left behind and had no desire to revisit. He recognised with new understanding that throughout his childhood and youth he had been trying to play the part that his father had written for him, a part with which he had never been even slightly comfortable. He had bitten his tongue and curbed his temper and followed as well as he could every rule and dictum in an effort to please the angry, critical old man who had fathered a son late in life and seemed unhappy with everything about him.

It had led to a parade ground in Lisbon and a flogging which had caused a man's death. Looking back on it, Manson flinched internally every time he remembered the bloody stripes on Private Barker's back, and the fever which had killed him a week later. It had taken Manson less than that week to realise that under his new commander none of the rules and beliefs he had been taught by his father would help him at all and he had set himself painfully to unlearn everything and to learn a new way of being an officer. He had found to his own astonishment and to the considerable surprise of his new fellow officers that he enjoyed it very much and was extremely good at it.

As the hired post-chaise pulled up outside his family home Leo saw his mother coming out onto the drive to greet him. Left to himself he would have travelled on the stage, but when he had arrived in Southampton he had found that his Colonel had been ahead of him and his travel arrangements were already in place and paid for. Manson was not sure if he should have been insulted by Paul's high-handedness, but he was not. He did not want to spend a day longer than he needed to in England and travelling post made considerable sense although he could not have afforded the extravagance himself. He knew that Paul could and made the decision to accept the gift gracefully.

Manson's family home was not a large house, a solid pile of weathered stone, and even in the bright summer sunlight it made him feel faintly depressed although he knew that was more to do with the occupant than the house. He stepped down from the carriage, his eyes on his mother's face. She looked older than he remembered her, thinner and more tired, and he supposed that the burden of nursing his father must have worn her out. He moved forward and embraced her.

"Mother, it's good to see you. How are you? And how is he? You look exhausted, has it been bad?"

She looked confused. "Yes. No. Well, it's been difficult, Leo. And you. You look…"

She paused and studied him for a long time. Quietly she said:

"You look older."

"I rather imagine I do," Manson said with a wry smile. "It hasn't been that long but so much has happened. I should go up and see him, I suppose. Is he conscious? What have the doctors said?"

His mother lowered her eyes. "They…they were very concerned about him, Leo. He is not a young man, and the strain…the stress…"

"I should think so; not many men of his age could survive a heart attack for this long. I am glad I made it in time."

"Yes. But Leo - travelling post? So extravagant."

Manson laughed. "It was a gift from Colonel van Daan," he said. "He wants me back in good time, I think. Will you get them some refreshment in the kitchen, Mother, before they leave?" He glanced over at the postillion and smiled. "Arrangements are in place for the return journey, I think…"

"That's right, sir. Just let Mr Hawkins at the Black Horse know when you're travelling, and he'll make all the arrangements."

"Thank you. Get yourselves round to the kitchen and have some ale before you go."

He dropped a coin into the man's hand and turned, aware of another figure coming out of the door. "Elinor. Cousin, it's so good to see you. Come here."

He swept her into an embrace, aware of his mother's faint protests. She had been telling him for some years that he was too familiar with his young cousins and he had privately thought it nonsense although he had never said so. He and Elinor were only two years apart, and her sister was two years younger again. They had been raised for many years as brother and sister and he had never been able to understand his mother's objections. He realised ruefully, as he put Elinor at arm's length and studied her, that he was going to find it very difficult to readjust to the rules and conventions of his parents' home.

"You've grown up," he said. She would be almost nineteen now and had blossomed during the year he had been gone, a quiet studious girl with soft brown hair and his own hazel eyes, a sharp contrast to her lively sister Juliet who was without doubt the beauty of the two.

His cousin was studying him with some interest. "Not as much as you have, Leo. You seem so different."

"I've had an interesting year, cousin. But you're almost as pale as my mother, are you sharing the nursing? You shouldn't do too much, you need to get somebody in to help. If it's money I expect I can help a little…"

His cousin flushed a deep red and lowered her eyes and Manson stopped speaking. He was suddenly aware of a sense of unease, as if there was something he did not understand, a feeling he had not known since his first weeks with the regiment. He studied Elinor's face.

"Elinor, I'd like to see my father. Will you come up with me? Is he in his old room or have you moved him…"

"He's in his study."

Manson looked past her and saw Juliet, a vision of golden curls and wide blue eyes, regarding him steadily. Releasing Elinor he went forward, and she ran into his arms. At just seventeen she had blossomed more obviously than her reserved elder sister and she was a beauty by any standards. And then the sense of her words reached him.

"In his study?"

Juliet stepped back and looked up at him. "I am sorry, Leo. I tried to write to you, but he found out and I was locked in my room. And beaten, of course, but you'll know how that feels. But if I could have found a way to get a letter to you in time I would have."

Manson looked at Elinor and then at his mother, who had taken refuge behind a handkerchief and he understood very suddenly what his younger cousin was saying. He looked back at Juliet.

"He isn't dying is he?" he said quietly. "Was he even ill at all?"

"Yes – oh yes, Leo!" his mother said quickly. "My son, you cannot think we would have deceived you. The shock, the distress of your letters, your quarrel…indeed I feared that he had suffered a seizure, and I told the doctor so. He was in bed for several days and…"

"Jesus Christ, he's been taking to his bed every time something upset him for as long as I can remember, that's no reason to take me away from my duty!" Manson bellowed. "By this time the new campaign might well have started, they could be out there without me and you've brought me home on a wild goose chase because my father wants the opportunity to berate me in person. I thought he'd gone his length when he wrote to my commanding officer, but…"

"But Leo, you must understand, he received the curtest of replies from that man," his mother said, sobbing. "And in truth we have heard such things about him. I cannot believe him fit to be your commanding officer – or to be in command of men at all…"

"Oh for God's sake mother, cut line. You know about as much of military matters as I did when I first started, which makes you impressively ignorant. Suffice it to say I'm happy with my regiment and its commander, and I won't be changing. I'm going to speak to him. It's probably best you don't come with me if you're feeling fragile."

He looked over at his cousins. "Thank you for trying to get word to me, Juliet. Did he beat you badly?"

"He beat both of us," Juliet said quietly. "You can't think my sister didn't try either?"

"No, I'm very sure she did. I'll speak to you afterwards. Best get this over with. Will you make sure the coachmen get some refreshment?"

"I will," Elinor said.

Manson walked into the house and through into the study, thinking how often over the years he had made the same journey, sick with fear even when he had no idea what he might have been supposed to have done wrong. His father had been an elderly parent with no patience with his son or his nieces and had used physical punishment for the least infraction. Manson wondered suddenly if his years in the army, where flogging was used for the most minor offence, had affected Colonel Manson's sensitivity to corporal punishment. He was aware this time not of fear but of anger, and a sense of distaste. He wanted it over with quickly, since he was very aware that this was the end.

166

Manson opened the door without knocking, and his father looked up from his writing, startled. Nobody ever entered his sanctum without knocking, and he usually took his time about giving permission to enter. Manson walked in and closed the door.

"Father. I have to say you're looking remarkably well for a man on his death bed."

Colonel Manson's face darkened to a deep purple with anger. "How dare you walk in here and speak to me like that?" he demanded. "By God you've caused me enough trouble and embarrassment. Get out and..."

"When I walk out of here, father, I am not going to be coming back, so if you've something to say you'd better get it over with quickly," Manson said evenly. "You've dragged me back here with a lie, but I've somewhere better to be and better things to do, so say your piece and I'll leave."

"You'll leave when I tell you to." his father snapped, getting up. "I can see the regiment you think so highly of hasn't improved your manners, boy."

"It really hasn't," Manson said. "In fact, I think it's made them worse. Get on with it."

"You've brought shame on me and upset your mother. You're making a complete fool of yourself in that uniform and its time you realised it and came to heel. You're lucky, I've still friends at Horse Guards, who..."

"That doesn't surprise me in the least given their level of incompetence for most of the time. I'm not sure what it has to do with me, mind. Let me cut through twenty minutes of bluster and rhetoric, I'm not in the mood. I am not transferring to any other regiment. I was made captain on merit in a regiment that I love and to which I feel immense loyalty. I like and admire my Colonel and I don't want to serve in the cavalry under some badly trained lunatic who is likely to get his men killed because he has no idea what he is doing. And father – since I live off my pay and take no money from you – I intend to make my own choices about my future career, which I confidently expect to be rather more long-lasting and distinguished than yours. So if that is all you have to say to me, we can get this over with now. I will accept that you see me as an undutiful son and that you never want me to darken your doorstep again. In return, I would like to inform you that as a father, you were a brute and a bully and taught me nothing useful apart from a level of physical courage which probably developed from being thrashed on a weekly basis from early childhood. So let us part company cheered by the knowledge that we never have to see each other again. Good afternoon."

He turned on his heel. His father made a sound which was remarkably like a growl.

"You little bastard!" he said softly. "What in God's name has happened to you?"

Manson turned. "I grew up," he said. "It brings clarity of vision. Goodbye father."

His hand was on the doorknob when his father said, as he had known he would:

"And what about your mother?"

Manson felt it like a blow hard in the gut, and he stood very still absorbing it, giving himself time. He could never remember a time when his father had not used his mother to blackmail him into falling into line. Manson thought about Paul and Anne for a moment, remembering the moment he had stepped off the packet to be met with a quiet unobtrusive man with details of inns, travel arrangements and a purse of money which Manson had no intention of using if he could possibly help it. He was aware that his Colonel was wealthy enough for the money not to matter to him, but it was the fact that he had taken the trouble to do it at all, for a junior officer he had known for barely a year, which mattered. He had never felt that level of concern or caring from his father in his entire life.

Manson opened the door. In the hallway stood his mother, white faced, looking at him. He turned to look at his father.

"If my mother wants to leave you, she can come outside and get in that carriage and come with me today," he said softly. "And so can my cousins."

The colonel gave a snort. "And just how would you support them, boy? If you walk out of here, you don't get a penny from me. Once you realise that your wonderful career is going to take you nowhere once that regiment is disbanded and…"

Manson laughed aloud. "That regiment and the rest of the Light Division is winning this war. You are living so far in the past that I don't have a word for it," he said contemptuously. "As I said, it's up to my mother."

His mother gave a sob. "Leo, no! Don't go, please don't go. He doesn't mean it; he'll accept your apology…"

"I don't have anything to apologise for, mother. I'm sorry because I know this is going to distress you. And that he'll bully you because of it. But you refuse to help yourself and I am not going to stay here and knuckle down to him because of you. You can come with me."

"I can't, Leo. He needs me."

"Fair enough. I love you and I will miss you. And if you want to write to me at any time I'll happily reply."

"Over my dead body!" his father said. Manson looked at him.

"One of these days that will actually be true. And the sad thing is that you've treated her appallingly all your life together, but she'll still be the only person who will mourn you."

Abruptly his father stepped forward, reaching into his desk drawer and Manson knew what he was going to see. Colonel Manson moved around the desk, the riding crop in his hand.

"I've had enough of this," he spat. "You think I'm too old to thrash you, boy?"

Manson studied him. "I think I'm a little old to be thrashed, father. I can take that off you in five seconds and you won't even know how it happened, but don't be afraid, I won't use it on you. I'm rather off the idea of whipping people since I ordered a flogging during my first week with the 110th and ended up killing a man."

There was a brief, shocked silence. Into it, his father said:

"I hadn't heard that."

"You won't, my commanding officer decided to overlook it and give me a second chance. I took it. I won't be flogging anybody else, even a spiteful old bastard like you."

"Namby pamby modern ideas. Can't keep discipline without flogging, ..."

"Yes you can. I can. I do. And I'm bloody good at it, father. Put that thing away unless you intend to use it on my mother or my cousins, but I don't recommend you do it while I'm here. Now if you'll excuse me, I need to go and make sure the post-chaise has waited for me."

Manson turned and walked back out to the carriage. As he was speaking to the driver his cousins approached.

"I'm sorry, Elinor. I know this is going to be hell for all of you. But I..."

"Hush, Leo, don't. I'm glad you've done it although I still can't believe you spoke to him like that."

"My mother..."

"She will never leave him, Leo. Her choice."

"And what about you and Juliet?"

"Leo, there hasn't been time to tell you, but I am to be married."

He was startled. "Are you?"

"I am. To a Major of light dragoons."

Manson lifted his eyebrows. "I'm glad to hear you've found yourself a cavalry officer, cousin, my father must be very pleased."

Elinor smiled. "Leo, you must know he arranged it."

"I rather imagined so. Elinor – do you want this? Because if you don't..."

"Leo, I need to be married. I cannot stay here forever, and I have no dowry as you know. At some point I suppose I could search for a post as companion or governess although I am poorly qualified for either, but what of Juliet?"

"Which means you don't like him," Manson said flatly.

"I hardly know him. I know nothing bad of him, he is older than I am but that is quite usual. He has some money of his own, a house in town and a small estate, I believe, and he wants an heir. I hope I can provide him with that."

"Where is he stationed? Or is he on half pay?"

"He has been acting as an adjutant at Horse Guards but has now accepted an overseas posting with his regiment and I believe he wants me with him, at first anyway. And he will take Juliet as well. I think both he and my uncle hope that she will find herself a husband in the regiment."

Manson looked at his younger cousin and laughed in spite of himself. "Well there won't be a shortage of offers, lass, I can tell you that for nothing," he said. "But she doesn't look keen."

"I have told her not to do it," Juliet said. "She does not know him at all well and has no way of knowing if they should suit. But she does not listen to me. And no offence to you, Leo, but living with my uncle doesn't suggest that an officer would make the best husband."

"That would probably depend on the officer. Elinor, I really wish you didn't have to do this," Manson said. "What I would like is to say come with me and don't take this chance. But the only way I could do that would be to offer for you myself. And I couldn't, you've been my sister most of my life."

"I couldn't either, Leo, but bless you for the thought. I love you so much. And once I'm away from here, I'll write to you, I promise."

Manson bent to kiss her. "Please do, cousin, I'll be worrying about you. Juliet, come here."

She moved into his arms and hugged him hard. "I'm glad you did it!" she said fiercely. "And I'm glad you ended up where you did. I don't know what changed for you, Leo, but it's for the good. Stay safe."

"I'll do my best, cousin. Is there any point in my asking that you'll write as well when you can?"

"I will," she said laughing. "In fact, I'll do my best to work out a way to do it before we leave."

"Don't get yourself into trouble, cousin, I know you." Manson looked up to see his father approaching. Behind him came his mother, still crying. She looked as though she would have liked to have come forward to embrace him, but she did not and he was glad. He knew his father would have stopped her and it would have hurt more to see her held back by him.

"Don't come back here," Colonel Manson said harshly. "I disown you as my son. You won't inherit a penny."

"That's all right, sir, I don't think I could come back and live here anyway. Too many unpleasant memories. Divide what there is between my cousins, I'd be happier with that." Manson turned to the carriage.

"Where will you spend the night?" Elinor said. Manson smiled at her.

"I've a standing invitation to go to the Colonel's family, he wrote to them. It's only twenty miles north of here, near Melton, I'll get there before dark. I can stay a day or two and then head back to Southampton and get the first packet I can, back to where I belong."

"Oh Leo..." Elinor was smiling through her tears. "You found a home, didn't you?"

"I did. I hope you're as lucky, Elinor."

His father snorted. "I asked around at Horse Guards about your colonel, boy. Picked up some interesting information. You're keeping very poor company."

Manson ignored his father. He kissed both his cousins and put his foot on the carriage step. Behind him his father snorted again, more loudly. He was unaccustomed to being ignored and Manson wondered if it was going to bring on the promised seizure after all. He was scarlet with rage.

"Good riddance, you get back to him. The man's a mountebank already survived one court martial and he's sure to trip himself up at some point; then you'll see what it's like to serve under a real officer. As for that woman he married, rumour says she's made herself notorious across half Europe, little better than..."

Manson felt the anger he had been keeping down explode without any warning. He turned and moved towards his father, and Elinor sprang forward and stopped him by the simple expedient of wrapping her arms about him and holding on.

"No. You can't, he's an old man."

Manson could not move forward without potentially hurting his cousin. He met his father's eyes. "If you say one more word on the subject of Mrs van Daan,"

170

he said, very quietly, "I am going to forget your advanced age and considerable infirmities and throw you straight through the parlour window. I'm leaving. Stay here and rot, you vicious, mean-spirited old bastard."

He put his cousin from him very gently and kissed her on the forehead. "Write to me," he said. "I love you both."

He looked over finally at his mother who was crying. "I love you too, mother. And I am sorry for you. But it's not my problem any more. If he has another seizure, real or imaginary, don't bother to tell me about it. I'm not interested."

Chapter Fourteen

Paul was writing letters in the small parlour when Jenson appeared on the afternoon before his departure. On the previous day Paul had found Wellington and asked permission to ride ahead of him back to his wife and his brigade. Wellington was beginning to dismantle his siege apparatus and would probably only be a few days behind him, but Paul could not bear to wait any longer.

He looked up as Jenson came in.

"Jenson. Any news on that farrier? If he delays me because he can't be arsed to shoe a horse properly…"

"It's done, sir, I've checked it. But there's somebody here to see you."

"Anybody I want to see?"

"I think so, sir. Mrs Longford."

"Oh – yes send her in, would you, Jenson?"

Paul rose as Caroline entered. She was dressed in the grey riding habit which she had worn the first time he had seen her in Lisbon, and he came forward and embraced her.

"Caroline, come and sit down. How are you? Are you on your way south?"

Caroline nodded. "Yes, we're travelling with a convoy of wounded men. We've stopped to pick up supplies and let the surgeon look at one or two of them and I thought I would take the opportunity to see you, to say goodbye. And to thank you so much for all your kindness this past year."

"It's been a joy having you with us, Caroline. I'm sorry you have to go. How is Nan?"

"Very well, but very tired now. Are you going back soon?"

"Yes. I'm doing nothing useful here, I'm going in the morning, so I'm glad you caught me." Paul studied her. "Are you all right, lass?"

"Yes, I'll be all right. I'm glad I had the chance to see you. To say goodbye."

"We'll miss you, Caroline. If it helps at all, you're doing the right thing."

"I know. It just hurts so much."

"I know how it feels, lass. I can remember driving away leaving Nan standing outside the barracks in Thorndale to go back to my wife and children and I thought I was never going to see her again. Nothing has ever hurt that much.

172

Which is why I have such huge respect for what you're doing and why you're doing it. I'll take care of him, make sure he's all right. I wish there were somebody who could do the same for you."

"There is."

Paul looked up, surprised as Longford walked into the room and saluted. "I'm sorry to interrupt, sir. But if you want to ask me any questions about who is responsible for my wife, why don't you ask me?"

Paul studied him for a long moment. "I did that, the week you arrived in Portugal, Vincent, and you told me to mind my own business."

"And would you please stop calling me Vincent. We're not friends and it's bloody patronising."

Paul was startled. He looked at Caroline and then back at Longford.

"I'm sorry. You're right, it is. Sit down, Captain."

Longford complied and Paul was amused and slightly surprised at how deliberately he sat beside Caroline. "I was in the process of writing to you, Captain. I thought it might catch up with you before you sailed. But I am glad you stopped by."

"It's good of you, sir. I know you care about Caroline. I am tempted to tell you to mind your own business all over again, but I'm not going to. I've already spoken to Colonel Wheeler about this, but I will tell you the same thing. This is a new start for both of us. If I don't manage to make her happy she will write to your wife and she can come back here. I won't stand in her way. But I'm not stupid, I know that if I tried to stop her you'd send somebody to come and get her."

"I wouldn't need to, Captain. Nan would."

Longford gave a wry smile. "She already told me that, sir."

"How is she?"

"She seems well, but very tired. Sir – shouldn't you get back there?"

Caroline touched his arm. "Vincent, no…"

Paul found himself laughing. "It's all right, Caroline. Captain Longford, on this occasion, has the right to interfere in my business since I have just made myself very free with his. Lord Wellington has given me leave to go, I'm going to set off tomorrow. I want to be with her in time."

"I know you do, sir. She is all right, I promise you. I think the news about Colonel Bevan upset her, but I think it upset all of us. Very sobering."

Paul regarded him blankly. Caroline put her hand on her husband's arm, and he thought how odd it seemed to see them behaving, for the first time ever, as a married couple. But his thoughts focused on what Longford had just said.

"What's happened to Bevan? I don't even know where the 4th is at the moment, did they run into the French?"

Longford coloured slightly. "I'm sorry, sir. I thought you would have heard by now. Colonel Bevan is dead. He shot himself a week ago in Portalegre. He was buried a few days ago."

Paul stared at him. He felt as though he had been punched hard in the stomach. "Shot himself?" he said, and even to his own ears his voice sounded wrong.

173

Longford nodded. "Yes. He left a note – something about his lost honour and the honour of the regiment."

"Honour?" Paul said. He was aware that he was behaving in a way which he would never normally have done in front of Vincent Longford, but the shock had hit him hard.

"Sir, you might not know all the details. I know you take very little notice of gossip. He'd been pushing for an enquiry, even for a court martial to try to clear his name. Lord Wellington refused to countenance it, refused even to see him. He…"

"Clear his name of what, making a mistake? Jesus Christ, it would have been forgotten in a year." Paul got up. His stomach was churning. "Will you excuse me?" he said and moved towards the door without explanation. Outside he moved over to the hedgerow out of sight of the windows, reaching it just in time. He was sick violently, leaning over with one hand on a tree trunk to steady himself.

When it was over, he straightened, breathing the cool evening air.

"Sir. Sir, are you all right?"

He turned in some surprise to see Longford studying him with what looked like genuine concern. Paul forced a smile.

"Yes. I'm sorry, Captain, must be something I ate, I've been feeling off it all afternoon."

"No you haven't, sir, you were fine just now."

"Don't worry about it, Captain. You can't leave Caroline…"

"She's gone back to our billet, sir, she's all right. She wanted me to stay, just to check. Look, I'm sorry. I didn't realise you were that friendly with Bevan."

Paul looked at him. Suddenly he was sickened in a different way. "I wasn't. Come inside, Captain, will you? We can't have this conversation out here."

He led the way back into the house and waved Longford to a seat. "I'm sorry. I don't often do that these days." Paul poured brandy into two cups and picked one up. "It used to be a regular feature after a fight in the early days."

"I find that hard to believe, sir."

"I know, wouldn't you? I go into every battle fearlessly and breathing fire. The legends of the army."

Longford drank from his brandy cup. His eyes met Paul's steadily. They were brown. It occurred to Paul with complete irrelevance that he had never before noticed the eye colour of this man whom he had disliked and despised for eight years. "I wouldn't know. I've never been into battle with you, sir."

The irony of it struck Paul abruptly and he gave a short laugh. "No, isn't that the truth? Look, Captain – I told you earlier I was in the middle of writing to you. Now that you're here, I might as well tell you in person. I've found you a posting. If you want it."

"A posting?" Longford looked astonished. "Where?"

"Dublin. You may or may not know what's been going on with the second battalion since you came out here. They were in Europe for a while, got badly decimated by illness after Walcheren. Since then, we've been recruiting and using them to replenish our numbers out here, so they've not been posted abroad. In fact, I've just written asking for another two hundred men. We've a lot on the sick list.

They've recently been posted to Dublin. There's a new overall commander there, General Sir James Wolverton. Jerry Flanagan – you must remember him – has purchased up to Major and is taking command of the second battalion for me with leave to carry on recruiting. But the general has no staff and wants to appoint an ADC from each of the regiments currently under his command in Ireland. I've been asked to nominate somebody and I'm nominating you. It comes with a free promotion to major and there'll be an increase in pay, plus a house in the city. Property rents are very cheap in Ireland so the army can afford to be generous."

"A promotion?" Longford said blankly. "I thought I was going home in disgrace."

"You were. You're not now. You're still going to have to live down Almeida, and that's bloody unfair because I don't think you did a single thing wrong. But when you start feeling hard done by over that, you think about Lieutenant William Grey and take it as your penalty for doing something dangerously stupid that day because you acted out of spite without thinking it through. I don't think that's the first time you've done that, Captain, but it needs to be the last."

Longford's face was pale. "I don't understand. Is this because of Caroline?"

"No. I'm very fond of your wife, Captain, but even my wife doesn't get to influence the appointments I make. This is because I feel bloody guilty about a number of things. I probably shouldn't be telling you any of this, but I'm going to take a big chance that you'll keep your mouth shut for the same reasons I did."

"Almeida?"

"Almeida. Vincent, we both know Erskine screwed up. I've been certain from the start that you didn't. I'm still not sure what happened with Bevan to be honest He might have made a poor judgement call, but it shouldn't all have been on him and the 4th – Campbell and Erskine shouldn't have let that garrison get beyond sight of the walls, they should have been sitting on Brennier so hard that he couldn't sneeze without them noticing, and he managed to spike his guns, blow up the fortress and do a night march to the border without either of them apparently noticing."

Longford gave a sardonic smile. "It wouldn't have happened if the Light Division had been guarding the place."

"No. That's what Wellington said. I blew up at him over this, as one might have expected. I thought he should have told the truth and used it to get rid of Erskine once and for all and risked the political fallout. He wanted me to back off and keep quiet, and he offered me Johnny Wheeler's promotion to colonel in charge of the 112th to do it. And I took the bribe."

There was a long shocked silence in the room. Longford drained his brandy cup and poured another. His expression almost made Paul laugh in spite of himself. "You look genuinely horrified, Captain."

"I…sir, it's something most of the army establishment would have done. And Wheeler deserves that promotion."

"He does."

"But I'm still shocked. It just doesn't sound like you."

175

"Thank you, I'm going to take that as a compliment. I was trying to be a pragmatist, Captain. There was nothing much I could have done to change the outcome of this. But I'll be honest with you, Wellington would probably have done something about Bevan if I'd been on his back yelling at him. At the very least he ought to have seen him in person and reassured him privately that this wouldn't have been counted against him in the future. I don't know why the hell Bevan did what he did and actually it pisses me off. He's got a wife and children and a family who cares about him, he'd no right to put some bloody mad idea of honour ahead of them. If he really couldn't live with it, he should have resigned his commission, telling Lord bloody Wellington where to shove it along the way, and gone into the navy instead."

"Is that what you'd have done, sir?"

"No. Although I have frequently told Wellington where to stick his army, but that's just arrogance because I know I don't need the money. No, I'd have stayed and stuck it out and proved every bastard of them wrong. Which is what Bevan should have done. And what you should have done eight years ago, Captain, when your career stalled because you and I fell out."

Longford nodded, his eyes on Paul's face. Paul set his glass down and leaned forward. "It's over, Vincent," he said gently. "You and I. Let's not go down the list any more. Neither of us come out of it that well. You're going to be a major in the 110th on detached duties and if you get this right, you're going to get that comfortable administrative post at Horse Guards that you wanted. Look after your wife and family and don't screw this up. Your new commanding officer is General Sir James Wolverton, whom I am told is a very nice old gentleman who will like you because he wanted a serving officer on his staff. And Caroline will charm him, get her some new clothes, take her to parties and flirt with her, you're going to find it pays off both professionally and personally."

"Are you giving me advice about my love life, sir?"

"Yes," Paul said with a grin. "And you need to believe me, Vincent, that is one area in which I am very well qualified. I am going to tell you something about your lassie. She likes to take care of her man. She fell head over heels for my reserved Major because he looked like he needed it, he was lonely. Just at the moment, what's happened to you makes you appear very vulnerable. She loves Johnny; that might never change. But it doesn't mean you can't get her to care about you, and I suspect you'll enjoy the experience. Let her look after you, Vincent, somebody needs to."

Longford laughed. It occurred to Paul it was possibly the first time he had ever genuinely shared a joke with the man.

"Yes, sir. But before I go, I'm going to return the favour. Go and tell Lord Wellington you're needed at home, will you? She's missing you."

Paul studied him. "I've already told him. Thank you, Captain. I feel somewhat better. Get back to your wife and tell her the good news."

He found Wellington inspecting his horse, which appeared to have strained a fetlock. At Paul's approach he spoke a final word to the groom and moved away.

"Colonel. I understand you had a visit from Captain and Mrs Longford?"

"I did, sir. They're on their way to Lisbon."

"Did you give them the good news?"

"Yes. Just out of interest, when were you going to give me the good news about Colonel Bevan?"

Wellington sighed. "Ah. Better come back to my office, Paul."

"That's all right, sir, I'm not staying long. And just at the moment I don't feel like sitting drinking brandy with you."

Wellington studied him. "I am not responsible for how Colonel Bevan chose to manage his difficulties, Colonel."

"I know you're not, sir. Neither am I. The difference is you'll stand there and pretend you don't give a damn whereas I'll admit that it made me sick. Just for future reference, don't ever again put me in a position where I hear something like that from Captain Longford."

"I'm sorry, Colonel, I should have told you immediately. To tell you the truth I was putting it off. I knew how you'd be."

"Yes, you've known me a few years now."

"And you blame me."

"Not for what you did. We all make decisions we don't like sometimes in this war and I'm learning that the higher you get, the worse they get. I'm equally responsible for this. And I admit when I heard he'd started yelling for an inquiry, my overwhelming feeling was exasperation that anybody could get to where he had and still be that naïve. But you should have called him in and told him it was going to be all right. And when you didn't, I should have."

"He wasn't your responsibility, Colonel. If there was a mistake it was mine. Not necessarily for blaming him in the first place – whatever Erskine did or didn't do, I still say if you'd been where Bevan was you'd have got to that bridge in time to do some good. But I couldn't possibly have known how upset he was or what he would do. I don't understand any man taking his own life."

"Nor do I, sir. I'm off early tomorrow, unless you need me..."

"Go," Wellington said briefly. "Be with your wife."

"Thank you, sir. If you have a crisis, let me know. But..."

"Colonel, just for once I think we can let somebody else manage any crisis. Stay with her now. And send to me as soon as there's news. We'll have that drink when my godchild is born."

"Thank you, sir. I'll tell her."

"Do. Get going."

Paul approached the farm in the late afternoon after several days of steady riding, sleeping on the ground rather than taking time to find lodgings. The weather was still very warm, and he slept well and awoke surprisingly rested. He was glad of the time with just Jenson for company, away from orders and bugles and the restless demands of his command. The long ride during the day cleared his head and put the tragedy of Charles Bevan into some perspective for him. Like Wellington he would never understand what had driven the man to such an extreme, and although he felt some guilt about not realising how desperate Bevan might become, he was not the only one. The man must have had friends in the 4th, and nobody appeared to have realised.

The tragedy had taught him an important lesson about himself, and Paul was somewhat surprised that it had taken him this long to know it. He had thought, so many times through his career that he needed to learn to adapt to army politics, to be more pragmatic about accepting the injustices that he saw. He realised he had been wrong. He might never reach the very heights of his profession with his current attitude although it would not stop him trying, but he remembered very clearly laughing with Michael O'Reilly years ago beside a campfire in India about his ambitions. Michael had accused him of wanting to be in command and he had admitted it with the carefree arrogance of a twenty-two year old, and declared his intention to do it without needing to compromise his integrity. He had come a long way without doing so and after this, he did not intend to do it again. It had gained him the reputation of being the most difficult man in the army, but it had also gained him the reputation of being the most incorruptible and he was happier that way.

Paul reined in, glancing round at Jenson. "Will you take Rufus for me, Jenson?" he said. "I want to go and find my wife. I sincerely hope George has supper on because I am bloody starving."

There was a shout from the field behind the house and he turned to see Carl coming towards him.

"Afternoon, Colonel. Good to see you, it's been quiet around here."

"I'm glad to hear it, Major. I thought I'd better get back to see my wife. I'm just going up..."

"You're a bit bloody late, lad," Carl said with a grin. Paul froze and looked at him.

"Carl...?"

"You might want to head up to your room, Colonel."

Paul slid from Rufus' back, tossed the reins to Jenson, and began to run. He went through the door to the house and up the stairs. At the top he saw Corporal Bennett's plump wife Maggie coming towards him with a basket of laundry. She stopped at the sight of him and gave a broad smile.

"Welcome back, sir. Something tells me you've heard the news."

"Only that there is news. Is she all right?"

"Why don't you go in and ask her?" Maggie said.

Paul went to the room at the end of the passage and opened the door very quietly. Anne was in bed, propped up with pillows and cushions, her hair loose around her shoulders. She looked pale and tired, but very lovely, and she was looking down at the child, which was feeding greedily at her breast. As he came forward, she looked up and her face broke into a smile.

"Paul."

Paul sat on the bed beside her, leaned over and kissed her very gently. "Nan. I just rode in. I observe we weren't wrong about an early birth. Earlier than I thought."

"You'd think so, but when you see the size of him I rather suspect he's full term. I told you I was clueless about the dates." Anne met his eyes. "Is Leo all right?"

"Yes, I sent him off to Lisbon as soon as we heard. I'm sorry I wasn't here, love. How are you?"

178

"Well it was definitely sore," Anne said pulling a face. "But honestly not as bad as I thought it would be. Maggie was very surprised at the size of him. She was convinced that I'd give birth to something akin to a rabbit, because I wasn't that big. But here he is, very hungry, and surprisingly nice I think." She reached to detach her son's mouth from her breast and lifted him over to Paul with an air of confidence which surprised him. He took the swaddled bundle and looked down into the face of his son. Blue eyes regarded him sleepily, and Paul grinned.

"I wonder if his hair will stay dark?" he said. "Francis and Rowena are both so fair. As is Grace. And it's much too soon to tell about his eyes."

"No, they'll be blue. I think he's very like you."

"Sleepy and self-satisfied?"

Anne laughed. "That rather sums up how I'm feeling just at the moment. I don't know why I thought I'd be a disaster at this. Probably because I am a disaster at most feminine pursuits. But it feels surprisingly natural."

Paul was staring at her, laughing, shaking his head. He was not going to tell her so but he realised he had shared her doubts, to the extent that he had quietly organised for a wet nurse to be on hand along with the Portuguese girl whom Anne had taken on to act as the child's nurse. At this point his vision of his wife lying weak and tearful, unable even to hold the baby after the ordeal of the birth felt slightly ridiculous. She looked so delicate that at times, he forgot her extraordinary toughness.

"Well it's new to me as well," he said. "My poor Rowena was so ill after she had Francis. We had to find a wet nurse and it was weeks before she was up and around. You look as though you're considering joining us for supper."

"I probably could, actually, but they'd all die of shock if I went down there with him tucked under my arm, demanding dinner. Although I do seem to be very hungry."

"When did he arrive?"

"Yesterday morning. I'd been feeling strange for the whole of the previous day. Not really in pain, just restless – I couldn't settle to anything. I made Teresa come for a walk with me in the evening and halfway back up the hill I suddenly couldn't move."

"My poor love, I should have been here."

"Teresa ran up to the 112th's barracks to get help and two of Michael's lads carried me up here."

"Did Adam come over?"

"I didn't need him. Maggie, Keren, and Teresa were with me. And I was fine. I thought I'd be terrified, but once it started, I wasn't. If you'd been here you'd probably have been worse than I was, you can't stand to see me in pain." Anne laughed. "Although I was very fidgety according to Maggie. She kept trying to make me lie down. But it went well."

Paul reached out and smoothed the dark hair back from her face. "I can't believe how well you seem." He looked down at the child, who had closed his eyes. "He's perfect, Nan. Thank you, love. I don't seem to be able to find the right words..."

"I love you, Colonel," Anne said quietly, and he met her eyes.

179

"I love you too, lass." Gently, Paul stroked his son's face. "So soft. What are we going to call him?"

"I don't know. I'm not sure I want the traditional naming after grandparents, do you?"

"I already did that. Francis is the English version of my father's name. We could go for Matthew?"

"Not for his first name. My brother's eldest is Matthew." Anne glanced at him. "If we're going to name him after anybody...how would you feel about William? For Will Grey?"

Paul felt his throat constrict and he looked up at her quickly. "Yes," he said. "That feels right. William Matthew. To be known as Will, I think."

Anne smiled. "I'm glad you're back. I really wanted you to see him. He is lovely, isn't he?"

Paul nodded, realising suddenly that he could not speak. He could remember the birth of Francis, the cramped cabin and his frantic anxiety for Rowena who had seemed close to death. She had not survived the birth of her second child, and he could admit to himself now how afraid he had been that something would happen to Anne.

He bent to kiss his son again and then looked up into her dark eyes. They were smiling at him. "You can breathe again now," she said gently, and he laughed.

"Girl of my heart, if I'd known you were going through this without me I'd have ridden all night. But you didn't need me, did you?"

"I always need you, Paul, but I know you can't always be here. Although I'm glad you are now. I know this is not the first time you've done this..."

"Yes it is. Like this, anyway. I didn't meet Grace until she was over a year old and with Rowena, she was always so ill, all I can remember is how frantic I was about her. I barely looked at either Francis or Rowena as babies. But you... you seem so sure of yourself."

Anne reached out and took her son. "I never thought I was going to be able to do this," she said, sounding unusually serious. "You've given me so much, Paul. And now you've given me him. I don't think I've ever felt quite so complete."

He met her eyes steadily. "Nor have I," he said, hearing a slight break in his voice. "Sorry, I'm having trouble speaking just now."

Anne smiled and shifted over. "Come and sit with me until he's finished feeding. Tell me about everything – did you see Caroline? How is Lord Wellington? Love, it's been a long month without you."

"It's been endless without you," Paul said, settling himself on the bed beside her, watching as she opened her shift and propped a pillow under her arm, easing her son onto her other breast. "You seem very good at that."

Anne laughed. "I am so smug about it. Maggie had asked Renata to act as wet nurse. Did you ask her to do that?"

Paul smiled. "Just in case," he admitted. "Rowena was too ill to feed Francis and I remember the panic of trying to find somebody."

"I guessed it was that. Maggie was absolutely convinced I wouldn't feed easily, she thinks I'm too skinny. But I think I'll be all right, it isn't as difficult as I thought it would be. And I'd like to, for as long as I can. Eventually I'll need to find

180

somebody, especially if he needs to go home before he's weaned. But as long as you're happy with this…"

Paul gave a choke of laughter. "Me? Oh Nan…just sitting watching you two is a joy. I'm guessing I'm ousted from my bed for a while…"

"No…not unless you want to be. We've a rather lovely cradle, feel free to go and admire it. Private Gage made it for me, he brought it up a week ago. And some of the women have been working on the linen. I actually cried, it's so beautiful – Keren's embroidery is exquisite, I'd no idea she was so talented. If he keeps you awake too much you might want to bunk in with Johnny for the odd night to catch up, but other than that I'd rather you were here with us."

"You might find it hard to get rid of me," Paul said.

"Then talk to me. How was Caroline? And Captain Longford."

"How is Johnny?" Paul said soberly, and Anne smiled sadly and shook her head.

"The same as ever," she said. "Busy, steady, pleasant. And in so much pain it hurts me to look at him. I wish she'd been here for the birth. And for hers."

"I know. But she looks well, although she's clearly heartbroken. It took me back a long time to a morning in Yorkshire when I thought I'd seen you for the last time."

"I can't be sad just now, Paul. I feel so sorry for them both, and for poor Leo with his father. But we have each other, and now we've got Will. I don't have space for sadness."

When William fell asleep Anne settled him into his new cradle and Paul tucked her in tenderly to rest and then went out into the darkness to where Sergeant Kelly presided over the cooking fires. As he passed through the lines his men called out good wishes and Paul lifted a hand in acknowledgement, his heart full. Carl came to meet him.

"How is she?"

"She's…" Paul laughed. "She's amazing. She seems so well."

"Congratulations, sir." Sergeant-Major Carter came forward. "She all right?"

Paul nodded. "Very well. Teresa, thank you for taking care of her. I should have been here, but it's typical of Nan to cope perfectly well without me."

"What are you calling him?" Michael asked, coming forward with a cup of wine.

Paul hesitated. "Will," he said quietly. "After Will Grey."

"Captain Manson will appreciate that," Carl said. "William van Daan. Sounds like a future major -general to me."

"Is she sleeping?" Michael said.

"Yes. I'm going to eat with you and I'll take her up something when she wakes. I could do with filling you all in on what's been going on."

"Did you hear about Bevan?"

Paul nodded. "Poor bastard."

"Stupid bastard," Michael said shortly. "Leaving a wife and children that way. His family are going to try and cover it up. Let the poor lass think he died of fever."

"They can't do that forever," Paul said. "But it's up to them. Come on, let's get a drink before dinner. I'm starving. I'll tell you about the mess Beresford got himself into, it'll make you glad we were up here with Wellington, let me tell you. I thought Fuentes de Oñoro was bad, but that was a bloody slaughterhouse. Where's Johnny?"

"He went riding," Carl said briefly. "Said he was going to check on the pickets. He'll be back for dinner."

"And then he'll disappear into his room on his own again," Michael said.

"I don't suppose he's feeling social, Michael."

"No. I feel so bloody sorry for him. She should have stayed."

"She couldn't, Michael. With a child on the way…Johnny doesn't have family who would take the baby, nor does she. And he didn't want her to be shunned for bearing his bastard."

"How did Longford take the news of his little windfall?" Michael said. Paul had written to Carl about the posting he had found for Longford.

"He was surprised. And pleased."

"Gracious of him."

Carl was studying his friend. "You shocked the hell out of me with that, Paul. Promotion and an ADC post? Normally you'd have offered that to one of our lads who'd had to go home ill or injured."

"Yes, I would."

"I'm guessing you've been patching up old wounds."

"Trying to. I don't think Vincent Longford and I are ever going to be friends, Carl. But surprisingly I find myself hoping he finds what he's been looking for finally. He's out of my shadow now, and she's a good lass, I'm fond of her. I hope they make it work."

"Well I hope he gets some nasty Dublin fever and goes to join Lieutenant William Grey and the rest of our lads that he fucking murdered," Michael said tightly.

"He didn't kill them, Michael, the French did. And he didn't order them into battle, Erskine did. Vincent was doing what he does, sucking up to a senior officer looking for promotion. I don't believe he thought for one minute they'd get slaughtered out there."

"So what did he think, Paul?"

"He didn't. He often doesn't, it's why he's not a good officer. Some of us lose our temper and it sharpens our wits, but it causes Vincent to lose his. He sent out the 112th that day because Manson was effectively in command and he wanted him to fail badly. And I can tell you're pissed off that Vincent Longford walks off with a plum posting when you think he's responsible for the death of a young officer you liked. I'm sorry. I didn't do it for Longford."

"So who did you do it for? Caroline?"

"No," Paul said flatly. "I did it for Johnny so that he knew his child was going to be born into security with a mother who feels safe and a surrogate father who is grateful because he's getting a new start. Because he's just lost the girl he loves and his child all at the same time and I couldn't think of anything else I could

182

do for him. So say whatever the hell you like to me and get it over with, but you say one word in front of Johnny, and I will punch you on the spot."

There was a long silence. Then Michael's gaze dropped. He pulled an expressive face. "Welcome back, sir. Have you any idea how much it pisses me off when you do something like this, and I end up thinking that you're probably right?"

"Yes," Paul said.

There was a silence and then Michael started to laugh. "You arrogant bastard, sir. Is any of this going to help Johnny?"

"It will, Michael. Knowing that she's all right, it will help. And at least he knows that if she's not, she's got Nan to write to and we'll get her out of there if I have to go myself to do it." Paul shook his head. "Caroline is a lovely woman. But she shouldn't be out here bearing a bastard child in army conditions and being snubbed by the officers' mess. She wouldn't cope and nor would Johnny watching her struggle."

"Unlike your wife," Carl said quietly. "Who would have been very willing to stay with you when her husband deserted and didn't seem to give a damn about the officers' mess."

"Don't compare other women to my lass, Carl. She's not normal, thank God. I'm going to find Johnny, go and dig out some wine, will you? I've just become a father again, this is supposed to be a celebration."

"I will." Michael hesitated. "Look, I'm sorry, sir. It's just…"

"Michael, forget it. Ten years ago he bullied Private Venables into waylaying me one dark night and trying to cut my throat. I don't like him either and he doesn't deserve that job. But that's why he'll make a success of it because he'll want to prove me wrong. And that's good for Caroline which means it's good for Johnny. I'll be back soon."

He met Johnny coming up the road towards the quinta and turned his horse to ride back with him. Johnny smiled at him. "Congratulations, Paul."

"Thank you."

"Is your wife all right?"

"She's very well. Treating motherhood with her usual competence, I don't know why I expected anything else. I'm not going to ask how you are, lad."

"Thank you because I can't tell you. I'm glad you're back, you can do me a favour and keep my well-meaning friends off my back. I can't have a conversation about it, and they can't help. I just need to pretend that everything is normal, although I'm not sure I'll ever get over this. But I need to just carry on and I'm tired of avoiding them."

"I'll deal with them. Look, about Michael…"

"He's angry. He blames Caroline and he blames Longford."

"It's how he always reacts to people he cares about being hurt. He'd got very attached to Will Grey and he holds Longford responsible for his death. He'll never forgive him for that."

"I'm not sure any of us will. But I need to believe he means what he says – that he'll take care of her. I don't even know what strings you had to pull to get that posting for them, but thank you, Paul. I know you did it for me."

"I did. And your child. Like you, I think it's almost certainly yours. Caroline needs a clean break, but I've told Jerry Flanagan I want regular reports on them. If he's got any reason to be concerned, I'll be on to it like a hawk. I wish I could do more."

"You've done plenty. And honestly you're the easiest person to be around just now, because you're the only man here who has any idea how I feel."

"It's tough, Johnny. I don't know when it gets easier. My life ended up more complicated than most given than I ran into Nan and her bloody husband a year later coming out here, with everything that entailed. But for what it's worth, and I swear to God I can't believe I'm saying this about Vincent Longford, I think he has every intention of turning over a new leaf with Caroline. Something about the child...I wonder if that first baby of theirs had lived, they'd have done better."

"Mrs van Daan seems convinced, and I've a remarkable amount of faith in your wife. Let me get changed, Paul, and I'll be in for dinner. I'm waiting to hear what's been going on at Badajoz."

"Sheer sodding chaos, and a complete waste of time," Paul said with a grin.

He went up to Anne and found both her and the child sleeping peacefully. Smiling, he retrieved his clothing and changed in Manson's room before going down. In the hallway he met Keren Trenlow.

"Keren, I need to thank you for taking care of Nan so well. You're a very good lass."

Keren smiled. "Isn't he lovely?"

"He really is. She's asleep." Paul eyed Keren with some appreciation, remembering suddenly what Wellington had told him two months ago. He could see the results of it. She wore a simple sprigged muslin gown which was clearly new and nothing he recognised as being passed on from his wife or Teresa. Her hair was dressed to emphasise the natural curls which fell about her face and there were a pair of neat pearl earrings and a simple gold chain with a cross on it about her neck. She had always been a pretty girl, but he was aware of a new maturity in her, as if something had changed over these past two difficult months and he suspected that his friend was the cause of it.

"I'll take some food up to her when he wakes, she'll be hungry."

He smiled. "Thank you, Keren. Will you do something else for me?"

"Of course, sir."

"Come in to dinner with me. Without either Nan or Caroline there, we'll be pining for female company; we're not used to this masculine atmosphere in the 110th."

The brown eyes widened in horror. "I can't," she said quickly. "It wouldn't be right."

"Why not?"

"Sir, you know why not. I'm not a lady and I'm not married to an officer. You can't take a camp follower into an officer's mess, they'd be horrified."

Paul looked at her and thought about the past months. He remembered her crying on the ridge above Fuentes de Oñoro and then shaking with reaction in Carl's arms. He remembered her cheerful patience on the long marches and the way she had struggled to learn to read and write. He remembered all the times he had walked

184

in to Carl's tent or room and found her sitting with her sewing, happy simply to be with him. He thought about Johnny's taut misery and Caroline's gallant determination to make her marriage work and thought about Anne and how much he loved her. He was suddenly irrationally furious that convention dictated that Carl could not sit beside this girl at dinner because of an accident of birth and circumstances.

"Do you know what, Keren, just at the moment I don't give a damn. I never bothered to ask how many of them were laying bets on who would get you into bed with them because I didn't want to know. But if they were willing to sleep with you, they can sit down to dinner with you and right now if any one of them says one word or even looks at you the wrong way, I will throw him through a fucking window. And if my wife were here, she would agree. Take my arm and walk into that dining room and make him smile. The girl who had the nerve to get on a ship and follow her lad into the unknown at the age of seventeen has the nerve to do that."

Keren looked at him for a long time without speaking. Suddenly she lifted her chin slightly and he saw a spark in the brown eyes. She looked down at herself.

"Is this gown respectable enough?"

"A lot more so than some of the garments my wife owns. You look very pretty. Take my arm."

There was a shocked silence as they entered the room. Several men put down their glasses and every one of them stared openly at Keren. Paul put his hand over hers on his arm and gave a reassuring squeeze, but she did not pause or panic. She walked quietly beside him past the goggling officers to where Carl had been about to take his seat.

Carl was staring as well, his eyes on Keren as if he could not believe it. Paul stopped before him.

"Major Swanson, close your mouth," he said pleasantly. "I've invited Miss Trenlow to dine with us, will you take care of her for me, please? We've no guests tonight, it's a family occasion and I want her with us since she's become part of my family with her care for my wife."

Carl moved finally. He came around the table and took Keren's hand and his expression told Paul what he had needed to know. He lifted the work roughened hand to his lips as if she had been a duchess.

"Thank you, sir," he said pleasantly. "Come and sit down, lass. Colonel Wheeler, would you mind sitting on the other side of her? Just because his wife is indisposed it doesn't mean he can spend the evening flirting with her, I know what he's like. You, I trust."

"He doesn't trust me, that's for sure," Michael said mournfully. "I'm glad you decided to join us though, Keren, at least we've one pretty girl to gaze at through dinner, it'll be like a monastery in here otherwise."

"Fat chance of that with you around," Johnny said. "How long have you been here – about ten minutes isn't it – and don't tell me that wasn't a female voice I heard when you were in the stables yesterday. Is it the dairy maid?"

"I was discussing my laundry with Private Clegue's wife, Colonel, and she is not the type of beauty I admire."

185

The conversation had begun again around the table and looking around, Paul observed that most of his officers had got the point. The two lieutenants of the fifth company were still staring openly and Paul raised his voice.

"Mr Crispin, Mr Steele. Are you not hungry? Because if you're not, I can find you something more useful to be doing than goggling like a pair of trout on a line."

"Sir. Sorry, sir."

Beside him he heard Carl laugh and turned. Keren was talking shyly to Johnny and it occurred to Paul that the effort of making her feel comfortable was taking Johnny's mind off his own misery. Carl was looking at him.

"You are the bloody limit, Colonel," he said very softly.

"I didn't think you'd mind, Major."

"You know I don't. Thank you."

Paul sat, listening to the banter and the rising noise around the table, and thought about Charles Bevan who would never again sit at a mess table laughing with his friends. He wondered if anything he could have done would have made any difference to Bevan. None of them knew what the man had been thinking. Perhaps, in the end, he believed that his mistake genuinely had led to the escape of the Almeida garrison, but Paul would never understand how that could have led to a man taking his own life. He knew that he was a natural survivor and that he might well have that much, if nothing else, in common with Vincent Longford.

"Paul! Wake up, I've spoken to you three times."

Paul looked round at Johnny, startled, and laughed. "I'm sorry, Colonel, miles away. What did you say?"

"I was asking about Badajoz. He's lifting the siege, I gather."

"Yes, he'll be marching back up to winter in Freineda. We're not ready for a lengthy siege, especially after Beresford's bloodbath at Albuera. But we'll have a siege or two to look forward to next year I imagine, since we'll need to take Ciudad Rodrigo and Badajoz before he can move on into Spain. And you can all look forward to that, by the way, because you know how much I hate sieges. I will be in such a charming mood."

"We do, sir. Never forgot the fuss you kicked up at Ahmednaggur all those years ago," Michael said mournfully, and there was laughter again and the talk rose, discussing the next campaign and reminiscing about former years.

Paul excused himself early and went up to find that Anne was trying to feed her son in one arm while eating from a tray with the other. Paul laughed and scooped up the baby.

"Let your mother eat, you greedy little monster. If she's not fed, you won't be. Finish your supper, lass, I'm going to take him outside for a minute."

He had been anticipating a shriek of protest, knowing that Rowena would have made one, but his wife leaned back and smiled.

"Thank you, love. He'll be good with you, he only yells when he sees me, Maggie says he can smell the milk. Which sounds objectionable, but I'm trying to be philosophical about it. There's a shawl on the side in case he's cold."

Paul grinned, picked up the shawl and swaddled William and went downstairs and out into the yard with him. Something told him that while his son remained with them he was likely to have a different level of involvement in his daily care than Rowena had ever allowed, and he wondered why that should have come as a surprise. With Will supported gently against his body he wandered over towards the first of the big barns which housed half the men of the 110th, including his light company.

"Welcome to the army, William," he said softly. Outside the barn, several fires had been lit. Supper was over but many of the men and their wives lingered around the fire drinking and talking. Sergeant-Major Carter looked up as Paul approached and rose with a broad grin.

"You brought us a visitor, sir?"

"I have. Come and meet the new recruit."

He handed the baby to Carter, and several of the men and their wives approached to inspect him. Paul watched, amused, as Carter passed William to his wife and came forward with a cup of wine.

"How's she doing?"

"Very well as far as I can see. She's going to be tired if she insists on feeding him herself, but we'll see how it goes. But she's very relaxed about the whole thing."

Carter was watching William's progress with a grin. "So are you, if you don't mind me saying so, sir. Wonder how many other officers' new-borns are being passed around barracks like this one."

"He might as well get used to it, Danny. You seem surprisingly competent with him, I must say."

"Need to get in practice, sir."

Paul shot him a glance. "Really?"

"Pretty sure, but it's early days so we're not shouting about it yet. You can tell your wife, though, Teresa will anyway."

"Good luck with it, Danny. Christ, funny to think our lads will grow up together. Who'd have thought that back in India?"

"Not me, sir. Of course it might be a girl."

"That could be even funnier," Paul said, and Carter laughed and choked on his wine.

"Don't let Lord Wellington hear you say that about his godson," he said.

"I'll behave until after the christening. Has he gone back to sleep? Give him here, then, and top up my cup will you? Might as well let Nan sleep while he's happy, get Hammond and the others over and I'll fill you all in with what happened at Albuera."

Paul sat late into the night and returned only when William stirred and began to fuss, wanting food. Anne was soundly asleep, and he woke her gently and settled the baby with her then went down to the kitchen and brought up some warm milk for her. Anne watched him undress and slide into bed beside her.

"Are you always going to be this good or is this a special effort at the start?" she asked, and Paul laughed, leaning over to kiss her.

"No idea. I'm enjoying myself at the moment, but if the novelty wears off we'll hire help, I'm very rich."

Anne laughed aloud. "You're incorrigible, Paul."

187

"I am. I'm also a man very much in love with his beautiful wife who has just given him a son. Also I've survived two unpleasant battles recently, and completely dodged a third, so I am going to lie back here watching you do the work and feel smug about how unbelievably lucky I am."

Anne smiled and they lay quietly for a while. Eventually she shifted William to the other breast, and Paul moved her pillow to support her other elbow.

"I thought you were asleep."

"Not yet. Just thinking."

"So was I. How long can we keep him here, Paul?"

"That's going to be up to you and the war, bonny lass. While he's with you, you're going to have to stay away from the fever wards."

"I know. And once we're on the move it's going to be difficult. But we should get a few months."

"You're still sure?"

Anne nodded, looking down at her son. "Yes. Even more so. I didn't realise. I mean, I knew I'd love him. But I didn't know it would feel like this."

"Nor did I."

She looked up, smiling quickly. "You've done this before."

"I know I have, but not with you. And Rowena was just not like you, Nan. I love all my children equally, always will, but Will is ours. I wish I'd been here to see him born but seeing you with him...I can't really describe what I mean. I don't want him to go. But like you, I'm not willing to risk him. We'll get you to Lisbon in the new year and Josh and Patience can come out to collect him. The rest will be up to you."

Anne lifted dark eyes to his face. "I'm not leaving you, Paul. No matter how much I love him. I'm not leaving you."

Paul studied her, thinking about the enormity of what she was prepared to give up for him. "Christ, Nan, I'm lucky," he said softly.

Anne lifted her son away from her breast. "He's asleep. Will you settle him for me?"

He obeyed and then came back to the bed and drew her into his arms for a long, gentle kiss. She lay relaxed and warm against him, her head on his shoulder.

"I love you, Colonel."

"I love you too, girl of my heart. Settle down and go to sleep, you need it at the moment."

Anne obeyed and Paul lay holding her, hearing the faint sounds of the camp settling for the night. He thought about Bevan and the wife and children he had left, and about Johnny and Caroline and the sacrifice they had just made for their child. He thought of Carter and Teresa and wondered how they would manage life in the army with a child. He knew that many of the women used such forms of birth control as they could manage to minimise the risk of pregnancy in this difficult life, and he was aware that his wife quietly helped with that. He wondered with some curiosity what Carl Swanson would do when Keren found herself with child, which was entirely likely sometime soon.

Somewhere in the distance a voice was lifted, singing, as somebody made his way late to bed, and he heard with silent laughter a barrage of abuse telling the

188

reveller to quieten down. An owl hooted softly close by and he was lulled by the sounds of the cicada in the grass outside. Paul moved his head slightly to study the girl in his arms, her breathing deep and even. He had talked earlier of the battles he had survived but she had survived her own battle with her usual panache, and Paul drifted into sleep thinking about how much he loved her.

Author's Thanks

Many thanks for reading this book and I hope you enjoyed it. If you did, I would be very grateful if you would consider leaving a short review on Amazon or Goodreads or both. One or two lines is all that's needed. Good reviews help get books in front of new readers, which in turn, encourages authors to carry on writing the books. They also make me very, very happy.

Thank you.

Lynn

Author's Note - may contain spoilers.

An Uncommon Campaign is a work of fiction. My imaginary characters rub shoulders freely with those who really existed, and I try to stay close to the known facts but Paul van Daan and the 110th are not real and nor are any of his officers and men. Lord Wellington did not create a third brigade of the Light Division although at times he probably wished he had.

The various other commanders of the divisions and brigades really existed, and where I have been able to find out information about them I have tried to portray them as their contemporaries wrote about them. A lot of letters, diaries and autobiographies exist from this period and as with current public figures, very different opinions exist about them. For example, many of General Robert Craufurd's officers genuinely disliked him, while his enlisted men seemed devoted to him.

In my books, I have given a slightly more human aspect to the cold, distant figure of Lord Wellington. Wellington's officers often found him very difficult. He could be thoughtless, sarcastic and was inclined to pay very little heed to the sensibilities of his fellow man. There are various stories about his poor treatment of his officers with sometimes dramatic consequences. But there is no doubt that he had his favourites and to them he could show a less austere side to his character. Captain Harry Smith of the 95th wrote very warmly of both Craufurd and Wellington in his memoirs and there were others. Colonel Paul van Daan of the 110th was very close to him despite their frequent disagreements but this is possibly because Paul is so thick-skinned.

The tragedy of Colonel Charles Bevan and his suicide is a true story and definitely not Wellington's finest moment. Nobody really knows exactly what went wrong at Almeida and Bevan was certainly not the only officer to be criticised by his commander in chief, who went completely off the deep end about the escape of the garrison. Bevan was known to suffer from black moods and in reality probably lived with what we would now call clinical depression. Many other officers endured Wellington's displeasure at times without ill effects, but Bevan was unable to live with what he saw as the disgrace.

There is a memorial to Bevan in the English cemetery in Elvas, Portugal, and I visited it during my research trip. It is a lovely spot, an oasis of peace in the town and well maintained. Bevan's family, as mentioned in my novel, took the decision not to tell his wife that he committed suicide and although his children later knew, as far as anybody is aware she continued to believe that he died of fever until the end of her days.

Bevan's friends and family were highly critical of Wellington's behaviour over the Bevan matter. Wellington, in typical high handed fashion, refused to admit that he had done anything wrong. If there is a softer side to the Iron Duke it doesn't appear in this particular episode.

I try to take as few liberties as possible with history but if I did not take some, I wouldn't be able to write my novels. The 110th is always in the thick of the fighting and occasionally I give them credit for exploits which rightfully belong to other regiments for which I hope they would forgive me if they knew.

For readers who want to know more about my sources and research, please visit my website at www.lynnbryant.co.uk where there are various blog posts and a book list.

I'm including one of my short stories in each of the new editions of my books. All these stories are freely available on my website, but I've been conscious for a while that not all my readers spend their lives online. In some cases, the story included is directly relevant to the action in the book. In others, the connection is more tenuous, but still fun.

A Winter in Cadiz was written for Valentine's Day in 2021. It takes place during Lord Wellington's brief trip to Cadiz and Lisbon during winter quarters 1812-13 which is later than this book, but the reason I've included it here, is because it follows a later adventure of Captain Richard Graham, who is introduced for the first time in *An Uncommon Campaign*. I hope you enjoy it.

A Winter in Cadiz

"I have been three days longer on my journey than I intended, owing to the the fall of rain, which has swelled all the torrents, and I am now detained here by the swelling of the Gevora. I hope, however, to get to Badajoz this evening."
(Wellington to Beresford, 18 Dec 1812)

"The weather is foul and the roads are impassable, we are held up every day by floods and even Lord Fitzroy Somerset is low in spirits. His Lordship's temper is so bad that the men of our escort invent excuses to scout the area to avoid him and Lord Fitzroy and I are counting the days until we reach Cadiz so that he will at least have somebody else to shout at. I wish he had chosen someone other for the honour of accompanying him so that I could have joined you for Christmas.
(Captain Richard Graham to Major-General Paul van Daan, 18 Dec 1812)

Cadiz, Spain, 1812

Captain Richard Graham had almost forgotten about Christmas. During his army career he had spent the season in a variety of places, some of them extremely uncomfortable. During their long, wet, miserable journey from Freineda to Cadiz he had fully expected to spend the day huddled in a draughty farmhouse listening to Lord Wellington complaining. They arrived in Cadiz at midday on the 24th and Richard was swept from drenched, muddy misery into surprising luxury in a matter of minutes. Lord Wellington and his two aides were conducted to an elegant house in a side-street just off the Plaza San Antonio and Richard found himself in a comfortable bedchamber with a maid bringing hot water and wine and the information that a light meal would be served before his Lordship joined the parade through the city.

Wellington was in the salon and Richard drank wine and listened to his commander being charming to his host and hostess as though the irritability of the past weeks had not existed. Colonel Lord Fitzroy Somerset, Wellington's young military secretary, appeared at Richard's side eating a chicken leg.

"Grab some food, Captain, while you can. We'll be off shortly and I've attended these things before, it could be hours before we see food again."

Richard headed for the silver platters laid out on a sideboard. Filling a plate, he said: "Should I take some to his Lordship?"

"I just tried," Fitzroy said. "He looked at me as though I'd offered him a dead rat then waved me away like the under-kitchen maid. Feel free to see if you do any better."

"Does he even need food?" Richard said, spearing a slice of cheese.

"Yes. He just doesn't remember that he does. I'm not too worried, there'll be some kind of ball or banquet this evening, he'll be hungry enough to eat by then."

"Well if he's not, I definitely will be," Richard said philosophically and Fitzroy laughed and clapped him on the shoulder.

"I'm very glad he chose you for this journey, Captain, you are so blissfully even-tempered. Most of the others would have been worn down on the way but it doesn't matter what he says, you don't flinch."

Richard felt absurdly flattered. "I've no idea why he chose me, sir. I'm by no means his favourite ADC."

Fitzroy gave a little smile. "You're mine," he said. "The others are all very good fellows, but when I need something done without a discussion about whose job it is, you are my absolute favourite, Captain Graham. And although he hasn't the least notion how to express his appreciation, I suspect he feels the same way."

The thought cheered Richard. He had arrived in Portugal eighteen months earlier with a position on Lord Wellington's staff after a miserable few years in the Indies. His appointment had been the result of a good deal of hard work by a cousin at Horse Guards and Richard had arrived with the strong sense that he was here on sufferance. His discomfort had initially increased when he realised that Lord Wellington's staff consisted almost entirely of young sprigs of the English aristocracy plus the twenty-one year old Dutch Prince of Orange. Richard's fellow ADCs had been polite but puzzled and Wellington had been coolly civil. Richard, who was not particularly sensitive and knew how fortunate he was in this appointment, gritted his teeth and smiled a good deal.

His breakthrough into acceptance had not come from within the commander-in-chief's household, but from an early meeting with a young colonel, recently promoted to command a brigade of the Light Division. Richard had instinctively liked Paul van Daan, who came from a very wealthy Anglo-Dutch trade family. Paul was not of the aristocratic background of Wellington's inner circle although his mother had been a viscount's daughter, but he seemed to have the ability to effortlessly bridge the gap. Wellington was rigidly wedded to the existing social order and enjoyed the company of his young ADCs, but he was at his most relaxed and informal in the company of Colonel van Daan and his attractive, intelligent wife.

Richard quickly became friends with Paul van Daan. Such friendships happened in the erratic shifts of army life. Sometimes they proved as fleeting as a short posting and at other times they stood the test of sudden parting and long absences. Richard suspected that Van Daan's early friendship with Wellington had been the subject of some jealousy and backbiting at headquarters although by now he was recognised as a valuable asset in managing the Commander-in-Chief. Van Daan he appeared to understand why Richard felt like an outsider, and he invited him frequently to dine and to socialise with the officers of the 110th. Richard was grateful initially for the company, then unexpectedly for the opportunity it gave him to see his difficult, irritable commander in a completely different light. All of his first real conversations with Lord Wellington had occurred at Anne van Daan's table and it had enabled Richard to see past Wellington's defensive and often sarcastic manner to a man whom he actually quite liked.

Richard was not sure that Wellington reciprocated the feeling and he was genuinely surprised when he was informed that as the rest of the army settled into winter quarters to recover from the appalling hardships of the retreat from Burgos and Madrid, Wellington required his company on a visit to Cadiz and Lisbon to meet with the Spanish and Portuguese governments. He suspected his surprise had shown on his face because Wellington looked amused.

"I will not be taking my household staff, Captain Graham, just one or two servants, a cavalry escort and Lord Fitzroy Somerset. We will be riding as fast as possible as this cannot be a long trip. I have observed that you are an excellent horseman, you do not complain about difficult conditions and your Spanish and Portuguese are both very good. Please be ready to leave in two days."

The citizens of Cadiz greeted Wellington with joyous enthusiasm, which may have been an expression of gratitude for all that he had done so far in helping to drive the French out of Spain but might also have been a useful excuse for parades and parties. The streets were illuminated at night in a way that reminded Richard of their arrival in Madrid earlier in the year. Wellington's every public appearance was greeted with cannon salutes, cheering crowds and women throwing flowers from balconies or running to lay their shawls and scarves before his horse's hooves. Wellington accepted the adulation with dignified restraint. He had chosen to wear a Spanish uniform in his capacity as Duque de Ciudad Rodrigo, probably to reinforce his new position as commander-in-chief of the Spanish army.

One of the reasons Wellington was here was to address the Cortes and to negotiate the terms of his new command with the Spanish government. It was also a family reunion as his younger brother, Sir Henry Wellesley, had served as ambassador to Spain for several years, negotiating the stormy waters of Spanish politics through the years of the French siege and beyond. Richard had never met Sir Henry who had followed a diplomatic career alongside Wellington's military success. He decided, on introduction, that there was a strong family resemblance but that Sir Henry seemed easier in his manners. There was obvious rapport between the two brothers and Richard wondered if it was a relief to his generally reticent commander to have a trusted member of his family beside him.

It relieved Richard of many of his duties. Lord Fitzroy Somerset was called upon to take notes at a number of meetings, and there was the usual enormous amount of correspondence to manage, but most of Richard's time seemed taken up with dinners and receptions and balls as the Spanish government and their ladies vied with each other to provide the most lavish entertainment. There was a formal dinner on the day of their arrival followed by an evening reception in one of the gleaming white mansions which overlooked the bay. The English community in Cadiz consisted of the officers commanding those troops remaining in the city, diplomats and a few hardy merchants who had not fled during the long siege. Richard made small talk with a collection of Spanish politicians, paid compliments to their wives and daughters and smiled until his cheeks ached. Across the room he could see Somerset performing the same duty. There were several pretty girls clustered around him and Richard grinned. There was to be a full ball the following evening and he suspected that his fellow ADC was being importuned for dances. Somerset's excellent manners and sunny disposition made him popular with the ladies.

"Captain Graham."

Richard turned quickly, saluting. Wellington was accompanied by a young woman dressed exquisitely in a dull yellow gown with gold embroidery which looked as though it must have cost a fortune. She was small and delicately made with mid-brown hair curling around an appealing heart-shaped face. Richard was not at all surprised to find a girl this pretty on Wellington's arm. He also recognised with some puzzlement that Wellington was desperate to get rid of her.

"Captain, allow me to present Miss Honoria Grainger. Miss Grainger was here with her Mama who has most unfortunately been taken ill and had to leave. I promised her we would take care of her daughter and see her safely home when she is ready to depart. I need to have a word with Sir Henry and one or two gentlemen before our meeting tomorrow, may I ask if you would be my deputy?"

"Of course, my Lord."

Wellington bowed and departed at speed and Richard dug into his memory for a time when conversing with young ladies at elegant receptions had been part of his normal life. It must have been ten years ago and since then he had married and been widowed and killed men on a battlefield, but he thought he could still remember how it was done.

"It is very good to meet you, Miss Grainger. What brings you to Cadiz, is your father an officer or a diplomat?"

Miss Grainger turned a pair of frosty blue eyes onto him. "What makes you think that I am here with my father at all, Captain Graham? Do you suppose that a young female is incapable of travelling of her own accord and must remain entirely at the beck and call of her father or husband?"

Richard stared at her in astonishment. "I beg your pardon, ma'am," he said stiffly. "I made an assumption based on Lord Wellington's introduction and also, I confess, on my own experience so far. I would be delighted if you would tell me how you do come to be in Cadiz since it is probably a far more interesting story."

The girl looked at him for a long moment. "I believe I was just very rude," she announced finally. "I apologise, Captain. I am not quite myself this evening."

"Has that to do with your Mama's sudden illness or is that another assumption?" Richard asked.

To his surprise she bestowed an approving look on him. "How very astute you are, Captain Graham. My Mama is not at all unwell, she was simply unbearably embarrassed by her daughter and fled the field in confusion. If she had been ill, I would have gone with her."

Richard stared at her. He was completely bewildered. "Miss Grainger, it is a very long time since I regularly attended occasions such as this, but I am sure that this is not the conversation that normally follows an introduction. Perhaps the rules have changed."

Honoria Grainger regarded him thoughtfully and then suddenly gave a broad smile. It lit up her face and gave a sparkle to her eyes. It also displayed a wide gap between her front teeth. Richard was utterly charmed. "The rules are exactly the same and I am breaking all of them," she said. "My mother is appalled and my father would give me a stern look if he was here. The trouble is that he is not here. And he is supposed to be."

Richard had begun to wonder if Miss Grainger was a little mad but her last statement caught his interest. "Are you saying your father is missing?"

"Yes, I think he is. I have been trying to have this conversation with Lord Wellington but he was either disinterested or unwilling to share information with me. It is very frustrating."

"Given that this is Lord Wellington, it could be either or both. But to do him justice, he has a great deal to do here in a very limited time. Is there not somebody else who could assist? There are a number of diplomats present, Miss Grainger…" Richard broke off at the expression on her face. "And I am treating you like an idiot, which you are very clearly not, I'm sorry. You've already spoken to them, haven't you?"

Miss Grainger let out a long breath. "Many, many times," she said. "We have been in Cadiz for four weeks, Captain. We received a letter from my father from Toulouse, suggesting that we meet him here…"

"Toulouse?" Richard said, bewildered. "What in God's name was he doing in France?"

"He was on a diplomatic mission," Miss Grainger said in exasperated tones. "Did I not tell you that he is a diplomat?"

"No."

"Oh. I thought I had." The girl was silent for a moment. "I'm sorry. I am being very ill-mannered. None of this has anything to do with you, and you are probably wishing me to the devil. And I am sorry for my language as well. I think I should probably go home, my mother was right, there is no purpose to this."

Her tone was flat and Richard saw suddenly that she was close to tears and trying very hard not to shed them. He had no idea at all what was going on but he felt a sudden need to comfort this odd, likeable girl which overrode his strong sense that he should take her home and forget about this.

"Miss Grainger, I have no idea at all what is happening here, but I can see that you are genuinely upset and more than a little angry. I can probably do nothing to help you, since I am with Lord Wellington and we shall very likely not be here much above a week. But if you wish to tell me the whole story, I'm very willing to listen and to give any advice that I can. A room full of people isn't the best place for this. May I have permission to call on you tomorrow morning and you may tell me whatever you wish?"

197

Miss Grainger lifted grateful eyes to his face. "Truly? Captain Graham, thank you, that is so kind of you. I cannot remember the last time anybody actually listened to me, it is driving me mad."

"If it helps, you'll have my undivided attention," Richard promised gravely. "Let's get you home. Have you a carriage or a maid...?"

"My maid escorted my mother home, but she will have returned by now. And I am afraid we walked here, we are staying with Sir John Marlow and his wife and their house is only a few doors away. I refuse the ridiculous notion of calling for a carriage to drive a few feet."

"Then I shall walk you home. Let me send one of the servants to find your maid."

***

Richard presented himself promptly at Sir John's house the following morning. He had wondered if he might be expected to run a gauntlet of concerned chaperones, but the girl was alone in the small salon when the servant announced him. Richard bowed and she came forward to shake his hand.

"I'm very grateful you came, Captain. You must have thought me a madwoman last night, I made no sense at all. I think, very foolishly, I had convinced myself that if I could just speak to Lord Wellington he would take my concerns seriously and I was very disappointed. Please, sit down."

Richard sat opposite her on a brocade sofa. "Tell me about your father, Miss Grainger."

"My father is Sir Horace Grainger. He is a diplomat and has served the foreign office in various capacities all his life. Often, my mother and I travelled with him. I have lived all over the world." Richard thought that probably explained her surprisingly self-assured manner for such a young woman. "Why did he go to France?"

"He was to visit several towns and cities where English prisoners of war are being held, particularly those civilian prisoners who were caught in France when the war resumed in 1803. He went as far as Verdun and held discussions about possible prisoner exchanges in the cases of several high-profile prisoners. He told us that the French were being asked to send a similar mission later this year."

Richard frowned. "That surprises me. I know that the French are seldom willing to exchange prisoners and there have been repeated attempts to get the civilians released, always unsuccessful."

"Yes," Honoria said neutrally. "Anyway, my father travelled as usual with his valet and his groom, both of whom have been with him for years, plus a French escort. He visited the prisoners and attended a number of meetings, it was a lot of travelling. During that time, he sent regular letters home, both to the Foreign Office and to us. He told us a great deal about the countryside and the food and very little about his work but that was not unusual. His last letter was from Toulouse. He told us that his mission was over and that he would be travelling into Spain to board a Royal Navy ship from Bilbao which would take him to Cadiz. He was expecting to be detained here for some time on business so suggested we sail to meet him here."

198

"And he did not come? Have you had word?"

"Nothing. It is very unlike him, Captain, he is a very affectionate husband and father. He and I are especially close. He always writes. But what is even more worrying is that the Foreign Office have heard nothing either. He did not board the ship as expected."

Richard did not speak for a moment. He realised that he had been hoping he could allay her concerns, but instead he shared them. The situation on the northern coast of Spain had been volatile for months and in many places the partisans had seized control of entire areas of the countryside from the French. Richard had seen letters describing guerrilla raids and skirmishes and he could offer this girl no real reassurance. He wondered if he should lie but discarded the idea immediately. She was far too intelligent to believe him.

"Do you think he might have been detained in France?"

"I don't know. I have spoken to Sir Henry and he assures me that the Foreign Office are making enquiries, but he will not tell me more. Letters can take many weeks and are frequently lost, especially given that it is the stated aim of the Spanish forces to disrupt French lines of communication."

"What does he suggest that you do?"

"He suggests we go home and wait." Honoria's voice was bitter. "After all, that is what women are supposed to do, is it not?"

"I suppose so. It isn't easy though."

She studied him for a moment. "Is that what you expect your wife to do, Captain?"

Richard hoped that he had not flinched. "My wife died, Miss Grainger, along with our child. Six years ago now. I wasn't there, I often wonder if I had been…but I'll never know."

Honoria Grainger went very still and Richard was horrified to see her eyes fill with sudden tears. He was annoyed at himself for blurting out so much information to a virtual stranger and one with troubles of her own. After six years it hurt less but he still hated having to explain about Sally and he felt that he had done it clumsily.

"Oh, I'm sorry. That is so very dreadful, and I've made you think about it. I am the worst person, I always ask the wrong questions and I never know when to stop. I'm so wrapped up with my own worries, I didn't think."

Richard got up and moved to sit beside her on the other sofa, reaching for her hand. "Stop it," he said firmly. "This is not your fault, and I'm perfectly fine. I will miss her until the day I die, but I can talk of it now. In fact, I'm glad that you know, because when people don't, there is always that uncertainty…is he married, is he a bachelor, should I ask about his family? I'm glad that you know. And probably because of Sally, I understand a little of what you feel. She hated waiting at home."

"Sally? What a pretty name. What was she like..no, I'm sorry."

"She was lovely," Richard said, to his considerable surprise. "She was witty and kind and gentle and very loving. She wanted a home and children and all the things I wanted too. I felt very cheated."

The girl's hand squeezed his. It startled him because he had forgotten he was holding her hand. "I'm very envious, Captain. Firstly because I could never be all of those things and secondly because I suspect I want all of those things too. I'm sorry you lost her, but you must be so happy to have had her."

Richard could feel himself smiling. "Miss Grainger, do you always say everything that comes into your head?"

"Far more often than I want to," Honoria said fervently. "Have I offended you?"

"Not at all. Talking to you is a genuine pleasure, I don't feel as though I need to be on my guard at all. Look, I don't honestly know if there is any way that I can help you, but I would like to try. May I share your story with Lord Fitzroy Somerset?"

"That charming young man who asked me to reserve a dance this evening? I suppose so, but why?"

Richard was surprised to realise that he was thinking uncharitable thoughts about Somerset. "He is a senior officer, and very close to Lord Wellington. He may have an idea of how best to approach him."

"He is your senior officer?"

"He is a lieutenant-colonel and his Lordship's military secretary, ma'am."

"I expect that is because he is a lord," Honoria said sagely. "My father has often commented on some of the odd choices for promotion within the army."

Richard laughed. "Your father is right, but not in this case. Lord Fitzroy is both an excellent officer and an excellent fellow. Also, he is my friend and will take the matter seriously. Between us, we cannot solve your problem, but we may be able to ensure you are given full information."

"That is all I can ask, Captain."

"Do you think you will go home?"

"I barely know my home," Honoria said sounding suddenly lost. "We have a house in London but I have never lived there for more than a year at a time. My mother is talking of returning there while we wait for news, but I don't want to leave without knowing."

Richard felt an irrational lift of his heart. "We are probably going to return via Lisbon but we are here for at least another week. I am really hoping you hear good news soon, Miss Grainger. It may be nothing more than an illness on the road."

Steady blue eyes regarded him. "I hope so too. But it may be very much worse."

***

Honoria was not sure why her conversation with Captain Graham made her feel so much better, since he had promised nothing and she knew that realistically he might not be able to help at all. At the age of twenty-one, she had moved in diplomatic and military circles all her life and understood very well that Captain Graham's position was relatively lowly. What he did have, however, was the advantage of access to Lord Wellington, and temporarily to his brother, the

Ambassador. Honoria was not naïve enough to assume that either of the Wellesleys would be able to produce her missing father out of thin air, but she did think that between them they possessed enough influence to push the Foreign Office into pursuing more rigorous enquiries.

Lady Grainger shook her head when Honoria told her of her conversations with Captain Graham. "It was not well done of you, Honoria. Captain Graham is not in a position to make demands of Lord Wellington and should not be pressured into doing so out of kindness."

"Captain Graham is not obliged to do anything at all, Mama. But somebody should be doing something. Father has given his entire life to the service of his country, they cannot just shrug their shoulders and pretend he did not exist."

"I am sure they are not doing so, my child. It is just they have not yet informed us..."

"It is just that we are two silly females who cannot be trusted not to swoon at the implication that something may have happened to him," Honoria said furiously. "I wish I had been a man, they would not have fobbed me off like this then."

"Of course, if you had married Mr Derbyshire last year, he would have had the right to enquire on our behalf," her mother said archly. Honoria set down her tea cup with an unnecessary clink.

"If I had married Mr Derbyshire last year, Mama, I would have died of boredom by now, so it would be of no concern to me."

Lady Grainger laughed. "He was not that bad, Honoria. I thought him very charming, and he has a very promising Parliamentary career ahead of him. I think you would do very well as a politician's wife."

"I think I would do very well as a politician, but we know that is not possible." Honoria sighed. "I am not set against marriage as you seem to think, Mama. I would like all the things that go with it – a home of my own, children, a position in the world. But I cannot marry I man I neither like or respect. Marriage lasts too long."

"I know. And neither your father or I would try to force you. It is just that you have led such an unusual life for a young girl, following your father around the world. And he has always shared so much with you, as if you were the son we did not have. I wonder sometimes if that makes it harder for you to find a man you like."

"If I did meet a man I liked, the chances are we would have moved on before I could form an attachment," Honoria said. She was surprised to realise that she was thinking about Richard Graham. Whatever help he might be able to give her in her search for her father, he would be gone before she really got to know him, and Honoria was faintly depressed at the thought.

"Honoria, will you at least attend the ball this evening? There is nothing more you can do now, and while we are here, I would like to see you enjoy yourself a little."

"I must attend, since I have promised several gentlemen that I will dance with them. Mama, how long must we stay in Cadiz?"

"I was hoping to remain until your father arrived, but I wonder now if we should return to London," Lady Grainger said. Her voice shook a little on the words and Honoria took her hand. She knew that her mother was trying to maintain a hopeful manner for her sake, but Honoria was not deceived. Her mother was as worried as she was.

"I think we should remain here a little longer. Why don't you write to the housekeeper giving her a date for our arrival, she'll need time to prepare. We can always change our plans if Father suddenly turns up with the news that we are all off to Cape Town."

"I rather liked Cape Town," her mother said wistfully. The memory made Honoria laugh.

"Apart from Sir Home Popham."

"Oh that terrible man. He talked to me – no at me – about some kind of nautical chart for an hour or more without taking a breath. I was never more relieved than when he sailed off to South America and got himself court-martialled."

"Father said it was the closest he'd ever seen you to failing as a diplomat's wife."

"Your father was no help at all, he just laughed." Suddenly there were tears in Lady Grainger's eyes. "Oh Honoria, where is he? What if he doesn't come back at all?"

Honoria put her arms about her mother and held her close, trying hard not to cry with her. "We'll be all right, Mama. I just hope he will too."

The ball was hosted at the embassy and the rooms were crowded with both British and Spanish dignitaries. It was very warm, despite the season, and there was a smell of cigar smoke which made Honoria wrinkle her nose. Both Lord Wellington and Sir Henry greeted her pleasantly in the receiving line with no indication that they had held any conversation about her that day, but Honoria supposed that Captain Graham had not had time to speak of the matter.

A regimental band played and Honoria danced with several gentlemen she already knew, including a dark eyed young Portuguese officer who had been assiduously pursuing her since the day she arrived. Honoria quite liked Lieutenant Souza but had no interest in any form of dalliance and she was relieved when Lord Fitzroy appeared to claim the promised waltz.

"You are a capital dancer, Miss Grainger, I am very happy you decided to attend. I was a little concerned after Captain Graham spoke to me of your father."

"He spoke to you?" Honoria said quickly. "Oh. I had not thought…that was very quick."

Somerset grinned. It was different to the social smile she had seen so far and it made her like him suddenly. "One of the reasons I begged Lord Wellington to bring Captain Graham on this visit, ma'am, is that he is a man who gets things done. Generally, I am very over-worked, but when I need help, he is the man I call on. Have you met him before?"

"No," Honoria said, surprised. "Lord Wellington introduced us yesterday. I do not…I have no idea why I told him about my father. He is very easy to talk to."

"He is a thoroughly good fellow. I asked because he approached Lord Wellington and Sir Henry this afternoon about the matter and I was a little

202

concerned. He was very plain spoken, which Lord Wellington does not always appreciate."

Honoria was appalled. "Oh my goodness, no. I had no intention of him doing any such thing. I hope he has not got himself into trouble."

"I think it will be fine. Lord Wellington was very irritated and I tried to intervene, but as it happened, Sir Henry was there before me. It seems he has been very concerned about the fact that nobody is talking to you about your father. But I do not intend to say more, I will let Captain Graham tell you himself."

Honoria danced with her mind on anything other than her partners. Her dance with Captain Graham was a country dance with frequent changes of partner and no possibility of rational conversation. She enjoyed the dance, and the few words she exchanged with him, and tried not to make it obvious that she was desperate to question him. She was not sure she was successful, because as the dance ended he bowed over her hand and said quietly:

"Thank you, Miss Grainger, that was a very enjoyable dance. May I hope for another? A waltz, if you have one free?"

"I should be delighted, Captain."

"May I also ask if we might speak alone for a moment. Or with your Mama present, if you prefer. We could step out onto the terrace if it is not too cold for you?"

"I am not engaged for this next dance, Captain."

Graham placed her hand on his arm, leading her through the long doors at the end of the room. The terrace was well lit and not entirely deserted, with several couples admiring the view over the lights of the lower town and out towards the lighthouse. A man stood alone at the stone balustrade. He turned as they approached and Honoria was surprised, and a little alarmed, to realise that it was Lord Wellington. Captain Graham saluted and Wellington returned it, then bowed to Honoria.

"Miss Grainger. I hope it is not too cold for you out here?"

"No, my Lord."

"Excellent. We should keep this brief, however. Miss Grainger, I took part in a very acrimonious meeting earlier with Captain Graham, Lord Fitzroy Somerset and the Ambassador. I have to tell you that during the course of that meeting, I dismissed the Captain from his post as my ADC."

Honoria was appalled. She shot a look at Graham, who appeared completely unmoved by this statement.

"Twice, I believe, my Lord."

"It would have been three times if I had not been outrageously bullied by my brother and my military secretary," Wellington said crisply. "I have, however, been brought to believe that the Captain may have a point. Despite the urgent requests by the Foreign Office in London for complete secrecy about your father's disappearance, it is not acceptable to keep his family so much in the dark. Your distress and that of your poor mother is understandable and your determination to discover what has happened is both commendable and extremely irritating."

"I had no wish to annoy your Lordship. I was just frantic to know, even if the news is bad. My father has never before failed to write to us for so long. I know something is wrong."

"Very well," Wellington said. Honoria had the impression that he wished nothing more than to get this interview over with. "You are correct in your assumption, Miss Grainger. Your father has gone missing and we have no idea where he is. I will tell you as much as I know. Like you, Sir Horace's employers at the foreign office have not heard from him for more than a month. There has been an exchange of letters between diplomats in Paris and London. The French authorities are being extremely cooperative and appear to be as keen to discover the truth as we are. On his arrival in France, Sir Horace was met by a small escort of French cavalry. Over a period of two months, he travelled widely, visiting various prison facilities. His reports arrived frequently and were factual and very much as expected. I presume during that time he was also writing to you?"

"Very regularly, my Lord."

"Sir Horace concluded his visit in Toulouse and his last report was written from there. He set off for the Spanish border, where a Royal Navy frigate under a flag of truce was waiting off Bilbao, to take him home. Nobody has heard from him since. Naturally, when Sir Horace failed to appear at the ship, enquiries were made, in case he had met with some accident that had delayed him. What is worrying, is that according to our French sources, his entire escort has also disappeared along with his servants and his Spanish guide."

Honoria felt a hollow sickness settle into her stomach. She could not speak for a moment. Somebody took her hand and held it and she realised it must be Captain Graham.

"I'm very sorry, Miss Grainger. I realise this is not good news."

"At least it is news," Honoria said. "Is anything being done to search for him, my Lord, or is that not possible? I know that the northern provinces are in open revolt."

"They are, and it is essential to my campaign that they continue to be so. Given the circumstances, we cannot send a battalion of troops into the region and I am not sure what good they would do anyway. I am going to write to the various Spanish leaders in the area to ask if they have any information about your father. I am also authorised by the foreign office, to send somebody else."

Honoria studied him and realised that Wellington was uncomfortable sharing this piece of information. She watched him struggle for a moment, then said:

"My Lord, I understand that there are aspects of this matter that you cannot discuss with a civilian and that you are probably unwilling to discuss with a female. I just need to know that something is being done."

For the first time, Wellington's face softened into an expression that was not quite a smile. "It is not because you are a female, Miss Grainger, I have an enormous respect for intelligent women. Indeed, on occasion I regret that I cannot employ them, I am sure they would outstrip some of the men. Why do I suddenly begin to wonder if your father shared more of his work with you than he should have done?"

"He did not," Honoria said quickly. "That is exactly why I know there is more. My father and I were very close. He never had a son and in some ways, he treated me as if I had been a boy. We talked of everything and my mother and I travelled the world with him for many years, but there were always moments when he would say nothing at all and I learned not to ask. I don't know what my father was really doing in France, but I know it may have been far more dangerous than inspecting prison camps, which is why I am so worried."

Graham squeezed her fingers sympathetically and Honoria returned the pressure gratefully. After a pause, Wellington said:

"Very well. I am instructed to send two of my intelligence officers along with a guide into northern Spain to try to find information about your father. I have written the letter, it will go off in the morning. Nobody here knows anything of this, other than my immediate party and Sir Henry. I am trusting you not to discuss it with anybody other than your mother."

"I shall not, my Lord, I give you my word. Mother is not a gossip, she has been a diplomat's wife for too many years and she will not ask any questions if I just tell her that a search is being made. I cannot tell you how grateful I am to you for telling me all this. I'm very well aware that there may be no good news, or even that we may never find out at all. But just knowing that an attempt is being made is very helpful."

Wellington bowed. "You may thank Captain Graham, ma'am. My instinct was to share no information at all, but he argued your cause with great passion and won over Sir Henry who in turn convinced me. You may be pleased to know that Lord Fitzroy has also persuaded me not to dismiss him. You should go inside now, you are becoming cold. It may be weeks, possibly months before we have news. I do not know what your mother's plans are, but if you will allow me to give you some advice, I believe you should return home to England where you will have the support of your many friends."

Honoria dropped a small curtsy. "Thank you, my Lord, I imagine that is what we will do. Will you…that is to say, how will we be notified if there is news?"

"The reports will come directly to me, ma'am, and I will keep you informed with any progress." Wellington shot a slightly malicious glance at Graham. "I believe I will make Captain Graham my deputy in this matter, since he has interested himself to such purpose. Will you excuse me, ma'am, I must return to my social duties. Captain."

When he had gone, Graham touched her arm. "He's right, you're shivering. Come inside and I'll find you a glass of wine."

Honoria allowed him to lead her back into the house and through the hallway into a dim room which seemed to be a library. He seated her on a leather sofa and went to summon a servant, requesting a fire, candles and wine in fluent Spanish. Honoria felt numb with misery but it occurred to her that there was something very pleasant about Richard Graham's enormous competence. She could not imagine him paying a girl flowery compliments or promising to worship at her feet, but within five minutes she was seated before a small fire with a glass of wine on the table beside her, studying her companion in the light of several oil lamps.

"You are very free with embassy hospitality, Captain."

"Sir Henry will not mind, ma'am, he is very concerned about you. Without his help and that of Lord Fitzroy, I am not sure that I would have been able to persuade Lord Wellington."

"I'm very grateful to all of you, Captain, but I know I owe the greatest debt to you. Nobody was listening to me. I cannot believe you have managed this so quickly."

"I wish it had been better news."

"It is the news I expected," Honoria said honestly. "Since we are quite alone, and very unsuitably so, by the way, I need to tell you that I have known for a number of years that my father's diplomatic career is often a cover for something less respectable. He is a spy, and probably a very useful one."

"Did he tell you that?"

"No, but I'm not stupid, Captain. Sometimes one can learn a lot by a man's silence."

"This must be incredibly hard for you, Miss Grainger. I wondered about the wisdom of doing this in the middle of a ball, but I knew how desperate you were for news. Would you like me to find your mother to be with you?"

"In a moment. I'll need to tell her and I imagine she will wish to go home immediately. I do myself. But if you do not mind very much, I would just like a few minutes to recover myself, before I have to..." Honoria broke off. She was horrified to realise suddenly that she was about to cry. She put down the wine glass hastily, fumbling in her reticule for a handkerchief. "Oh dear, I'm so sorry."

"Don't be." Graham took the bag from her hands, retrieved the handkerchief and gave it to her. He sat beside her on the sofa, and Honoria gave up and began to cry in earnest. After a moment she felt his arm go about her shoulders and she forgot about propriety and leaned into him, sobbing. Graham held her, stroking her back soothingly, murmuring comforting nonsense as if she was a small child.

Eventually Honoria's sobs died away. She knew that she should move, but she remained still in his arms. She needed to dry her tears and tidy her hair and be ready to face her mother's grief when she told her the news but she was unexpectedly enjoying the sense of being taken care of, even if it was by a man she had known little more than a day. That thought made her blush and she shifted reluctantly away from him. He did not move away, but studied her with concerned dark eyes.

"I'm so sorry," Honoria said again.

"I'm not sorry at all, I'm very glad that I'm here. You shouldn't be going through this alone. Give yourself a moment while I find your Mama. I'll leave you alone with her and make sure you're not disturbed and I'll call for your carriage."

"We don't keep our own carriage here, Captain, we came with Sir John and Lady Marlow. I don't wish to disturb them..."

"Don't give it another thought, I'll arrange something. I'll wait in the hallway for you and I'll escort you both home. Call me when you're ready."

***

Richard slept badly and rose early, taking himself down to the shore to watch the dawn spreading its rose gold light over the choppy waters of the Atlantic. He could not stop thinking about Honoria Grainger. Her dignified reception of Lord Wellington's news had touched his heart, but the sobbing misery which followed had broken it. Richard could remember how much he had cried in the months following the loss of his wife and child and he would have done anything to ease Honoria's suffering, but he knew that there was nothing that he could do. He wandered aimlessly as the streets of Cadiz stirred into morning life around him and returned to the house on the Calle Veedor to find Somerset eating breakfast. Richard joined him at the table and Somerset regarded him thoughtfully.

"You look terrible, didn't you sleep?"

"Not much." Richard accepted coffee with a murmur of thanks to the maid and reached for the bread. "I'm sorry, sir, I went for an early stroll and went further than I intended. I hope I wasn't needed?"

"No, he doesn't need us this morning apart from to sort through his correspondence, the packet came in. But I can do that. Are you going to call on Miss Grainger?"

"I'd like to," Richard admitted. "I don't want to shirk my duty, sir, but they were both in a terrible state when I took them home. Do you think he'll mind?"

"He's left specific instructions that you're to make yourself available to them and help them in any way possible, Captain. I think he's feeling guilty. We have this gala dinner with members of the Cortes this evening. You should be there for that, but why don't you finish your breakfast and go and see if they need anything?" Somerset studied him with sympathetic eyes. "Those poor women. I'm guessing they're not holding out much hope?"

"No, and they shouldn't. I'm not sure how much Lady Grainger knows, but Miss Grainger is very well aware that her father is a government agent and she knows that if he isn't dead, he may have been imprisoned by the French. They shoot spies, sir."

"He could have been taken ill somewhere."

"Along with his servants, his guide and his entire French escort?" Richard shook his head. "If there was a simple explanation we'd have heard it. Do you know who has drawn the short straw for this very unpleasant assignment, sir?"

"Giles Fenwick. I think his Lordship has asked Colonel Scovell to find another man to go with him in case one of them is killed but I don't know who that will be."

"They really want to find him, don't they? I wonder what he was carrying?"

"I don't think even Lord Wellington knows that at present. Give the ladies my compliments when you see them, Captain, and if there's anything I can do, please let me know."

Richard sent in his card and was surprised when the servant returned immediately to escort him to the same small salon where he found Honoria Grainger alone. She looked calm although rather heavy-eyed and she shook his hand and asked him to sit down.

"I'm so glad you called, Captain. I wanted the opportunity to thank you for your kindness last night. I don't know what I would have done without you."

"You're very welcome, Miss Grainger. How is your Mama this morning?"

"She has remained in bed. I don't think either of us slept very much."

"I hope you did not come down just to see me."

"No, I promise you. Although I would have done. I am far better to be up and around. Mama will be the same in a few days. I think it is more of a shock to her, since she had been convincing herself that it was all a mishap and that he was going to turn up as though nothing had happened. But she is a sensible woman and she just needs time to come to terms with this."

"What will you do now?"

"I don't know. Eventually we will go back to England, but at present Mama is very reluctant to leave, since it is obvious that news will reach here first. I will talk to her when she is a little calmer and we will decide. It may be that we look for a small house to rent in Cadiz or even Lisbon for a month or two, if that will make her happier."

"Have you no male relative who might be able to support you through this?"

"Do you think the presence of a man would make this any easier, Captain?" Honoria said frostily.

"No, not at all. But forgive me, your Mama is obviously very distressed and in matters of business and finance, your father must have had someone in mind who could assist her should anything ever happen to him. It is usual."

Unexpectedly there was a gleam of amusement in the girl's eyes. "Oh yes, he did," she said smoothly. "He was very farsighted about such matters since he always knew, I suppose, that he could die suddenly and a long way from home. He was very frank about it, we talked everything through."

"Is it somebody you could write to? Perhaps we could arrange…"

"It is me, Captain Graham. I am of full age and my father taught me to understand business some years ago. He always knew that my Mama is not of a practical bent, so he arranged that she should be paid a very generous jointure and the expenses of her household are to come out of the estate, but everything else is in my charge."

Richard stared at her and she looked back defiantly. "Have I shocked you, Captain?"

"You have certainly surprised me," Richard said. "Your father clearly had immense faith in you, Miss Grainger, and since he knew you far better than I do, I am sure he was right. But I think this is a lot for any one person to manage alone, especially when you are still reeling with the shock of this news."

Unexpectedly her eyes filled with tears again. "It is," she said. "I have no wish to shirk my duty, Captain. Until we know for sure that he is dead, I will continue to manage things as I always have in his absence. But it feels very difficult today."

"May I help?"

Honoria eyed him uncertainly. "I do not see…"

"Not to do it for you, ma'am. But just to think through what might need to be done, who needs to be notified, how to manage finances if you intend to remain in Spain for a while. I have worked for Lord Wellington for more than a year, if there is one thing I am very good at, it is managing lists and correspondence and administration. Just while I am here, of course."

"Of course. Captain – could you?"

"Yes," Richard promised rashly. "Give me time to speak to his Lordship, and I'll join you. He will not object, I know, since he is keen to be of service to you and your mother, but I should ask as a matter of courtesy. After that, you shall make a list and we shall decide what needs to be done immediately and what can safely be left until later."

It was the beginning of a very strange and curiously satisfying week. Relieved of all duties by a rather amused Lord Wellington, Richard presented himself at the house each morning where he found Honoria Grainger ready with her note tablets, paper and pens. They made a list of what needed to be done immediately and another, rather more painfully, of what would need to be done if news came of Sir Horace Grainger's death. Honoria wrote letters to Grainger's lawyer and man of business, his banker, the land agent who managed his estate in Hertfordshire and the housekeeper of his London home. She also penned more personal and more difficult notes to several relatives.

"You had better read these, Captain, to ensure that I have not said anything indiscreet. I cannot hide the fact that he is missing, since people will soon be asking questions, but I have simply said that we fear some mishap and that enquiries are being made. Will that do?"

"It will indeed, ma'am. Very well-worded and very discreet. You are your father's daughter."

Honoria smiled as though he had paid her a compliment. "Thank you. I'm proud to be so."

After lengthy discussions with Mrs Grainger, and some hasty research on Richard's part among the English community in Cadiz, Honoria inspected a small house on the edge of the old town, which had previously been occupied by a Scottish major and his wife. It was conveniently situated although in need of a good clean. Richard asked the embassy housekeeper to help him find servants and watched admiringly as Honoria ruthlessly supervised operations. He thought it was rather a shame that she had not been a boy, since she set about every task with a military precision that Lord Wellington would have loved.

Neither Honoria nor her mother felt able to attend the many parties and dinners being held in honour of Lord Wellington, but Richard insisted that she leave the house each day to take the air. He asked her to show him the town and after a little hesitation, she did so willingly. They were fortunate with the weather, which was unusually dry for early January, with several warm afternoons. Followed at a considerable distance by a bored Spanish maid, they walked through the narrow streets and explored the castle, various churches and the old lighthouse which was situated on the long, dangerous reef known as Porpoise Rocks.

The town overlooked a bay which was around twelve miles long. They walked up to Fort Catalina, its cannon pointing solid defiance at the French or anybody else who might try to take this Spanish island city. There were spectacular views over the surrounding countryside, dotted with villages and criss-crossed with vineyards, orange groves and grazing cattle. Honoria pointed out the distant spires of the town of Medina Sidonia.

"You are a very knowledgeable guide, Miss Grainger," Richard said, leaning on the stone parapet. "How do you know so much about this place, when you only arrived a few weeks before I did?"

"Lieutenant Sousa," Honoria said, pulling a face. "He was here during the siege and is now stationed here. He is a most estimable and very romantic young man, who believes it is important to learn as much as possible about every place he visits."

Richard gave a choke of laughter. "Which he then conveys to you?"

"With inexhaustible detail. I have heard things about the stonework of the cathedral they are building that I hope never to hear again. Have you seen enough, Captain? The wind is growing cold up here."

"Of course. It's beautiful though. Would you like to go home?"

"Not yet. I thought we could walk down the Alameda."

She took his arm as they turned onto the broad avenue, lined with ornamental trees and plants and blessed with wide views of the open sea. The Alameda was the main promenade of the city and the wealthier citizens of Cadiz could be found strolling there on any dry afternoon. Honoria asked him questions about his home and his family and Richard told her about Sally and his hopes for their future which had been cruelly snatched away. He wondered if it was wrong of him to speak so freely of loss to a girl who was experiencing it herself, but Honoria seemed genuinely interested. In his turn, he asked her about her father, and she made him laugh with stories of Sir Horace's illicit passion for Spanish cigars.

"My mother loathed the custom and would never allow him to smoke them, so he used to sneak out to the garden in all weathers and with the most flimsy excuses. I used to cover for him from a very young age."

"It sounds as though you were very good friends."

"We were. Are. I don't know, of course. I think he is probably dead, but there is a part of me that dreams of him arriving unexpectedly with some horrendous tale of danger and narrow escapes. He is a very good storyteller."

"I think you've inherited that from him. I'm afraid we must go back. We are to attend a concert after dinner and I should not take too much advantage of his Lordship's goodwill."

"Does he enjoy music?"

"Very much, as it happens. I believe he used to play the violin in his youth, although I find it hard to imagine."

"Do you like him?"

Richard thought about it. "He is a difficult man to like," he said after a moment. "He's a very private person. He can be irritable and sharp-tongued and when something has displeased him, he is appallingly sarcastic. I've seen him reduce an officer to tears. He's hard to know. But…"

"Go on."

"But he can be very kind and thoughtful at unexpected moments. He has very few close friends and I don't count myself among them, but when I see him with those people, he is like a different man. And he's funny. Even on his worst days, there are times when he makes me laugh aloud."

Honoria was studying him with a little smile. "I think you do like him, Captain Graham. What is more, I think he likes you too."

Richard grinned. "Honestly? I have no idea, ma'am."

"We were supposed to be attending the concert," Honoria said, and Richard caught the wistfulness in her voice.

"Are you musical, ma'am?"

"Very much so, it is my greatest love."

"Then come. It is not the same as a ball or a reception, you will not be obliged to speak to many people, and it will do you good."

"My Mama is not well enough."

"Come anyway. Join our party, I'll speak to his Lordship, I know he'll agree."

"I feel guilty for wanting to go out when my father is…when I do not know if he is alive or dead."

"What would your father say?" Richard asked impulsively.

She looked up at him and he could see that he had said the right thing. "He would tell me that it was stuff and nonsense and that I should do as I liked."

"Your father is a very wise man. I will call for you at seven o'clock."

***

Two weeks was not enough.

Lord Wellington's departure for Lisbon was delayed once again by appalling weather and reports of a flooded road, and Honoria and her mother were unexpectedly invited to dine at the embassy. Lady Grainger had barely left the house during the previous week but she studied the invitation then looked up at her daughter.

"Would you like to attend, Honoria?"

"Yes," Honoria said honestly. She was trying not to think about Richard Graham's departure. He had spent the previous day with her, going through the rooms of their new temporary home and confirming when the carters would arrive to convey their belongings to the house. He had been kind and funny and helpful and the thought of the next weeks, miserable about her father and trying to comfort her mother, without his steady presence at her side, was unbearable.

"I think we should. Lord Wellington has been so kind in our trouble, I would not wish…"

"Lord Wellington?" Honoria exploded. "Allow me to tell you, Mama, that if we had left the matter to Lord Wellington we would know nothing about what happened to my father. Lord Wellington was perfectly happy to treat us like two empty-headed females who cannot be trusted…it was Captain Graham who intervened on our behalf and it is to him that we owe all the help and comfort we have received this past fortnight. I must say…"

"No, dearest, do not say it again, I think I have understood," Lady Grainger said. She sounded amused. "I presume if we are to dine with Sir Henry and Lord

Wellington that Captain Graham will also be present. It will give me an opportunity to thank him again and to say goodbye."

The meal went very well. Lord Wellington was unexpectedly entertaining and put himself out to be kind to Lady Grainger. As the group finally broke up, a servant went to call for the carriage and the ladies' cloaks and Sir Henry drew Lady Grainger to one side with a question about her new residence. Honoria found herself face to face with Richard Graham.

"Will you be all right?"

Honoria nodded. "Sir Henry has been very kind and has said we may call on him for any assistance."

"How long do you think you will remain here?"

"I am not sure, Captain. I think perhaps until we have news. Or until we are told that there is no news. You promised that you would write to me…"

"Everything that I know, you will know, I give you my word. Should I address my letters to your Mama or to you?"

"To me," Honoria said. "If there is distressing news, it's better that she hears it from me."

"I understand. You are, after all, the head of the household."

"You are teasing me, Captain Graham."

"No, I'm not. You're the most extraordinary young woman…may I write to you about other matters?"

"Other matters. What kind of other matters?"

"I don't know. Anything. What the weather is doing and where we are marching and what kind of mood Lord Wellington is in that day. And you shall tell me if your new harp has been delivered and if the stove in the kitchen is working properly and whether you think of me at all as you are shopping in the Calle Ancha with your maid."

"I will think of you and your kindness in every street in Cadiz, and I would very much like to write to you, Captain, if you will promise to reply."

He smiled, reached for her hand, and raised it to his lips. "You'll get sick of reading them," he said.

**

Freneida, May 1813

With the preparations to march complete, Richard rode out through the dusty little village which had housed Lord Wellington's headquarters for two winters and wondered if they would come back. Wellington seemed convinced that they would not. He had spoken to his staff on the previous day, giving orders and explaining his plans in more detail than Richard was used to. There was an energy about the Commander-in-Chief which made Richard believe that this time, Wellington did not expect to have to retreat again.

There was little to see in Freineda, so Richard rode further afield, through small villages and stone walled towns where people had begun to return after long months of exile. Farmers were planting again and houses battered by shot and shell were being gradually rebuilt. Richard absorbed the sense of hope and renewal and prayed that it would last and that the war had finally moved beyond these people so that they could resume their lives.

Much of the army had already moved out, and Lord Wellington's staff were packed and ready to go the following morning. Riding back into the village, Richard dismounted, handing his horse to a groom, and went into the long low house which Wellington had occupied through winter quarters. His chief was in his combined sitting room and study with Somerset, Colonel Murray, his quartermaster-general and the tall fair figure of Major-General Paul van Daan of the Light Division. Wellington turned as Richard entered.

"There you are," he said irritably, as if he had sent a summons which Richard had failed to answer. "I have been waiting to question you about that blasted female."

Richard was completely at sea. "Blasted female, sir?"

"Yes. She has just arrived, completely unannounced, apparently on her way back to Lisbon to join her unfortunate mother. What can have possessed her to make such a journey without any warning, I cannot imagine, but I did not know what to do with her, since I cannot delay my departure for her."

"Who, sir?"

"Miss Honoria Grainger, Captain," Somerset said. He was grinning broadly. "It appears that she journeyed by ship to Oporto to visit her father's grave."

"Oh my God," Richard said appalled. "Is her mother with her? What on earth is she doing here?"

"That is a question to which we would all like an answer," Wellington snapped. "I presume you wrote to her telling her how he died?"

"You know I did, sir, I told you. She replied, thanking me. I've not heard a word since, I thought they'd be on their way back to London."

"Which is what any normal female would have done."

"Where is she?" Richard said. His voice sounded very strange in his own ears and he wondered if the others could tell. "I mean, where is she going to stay? There's nowhere here…"

"Evidently not," Wellington said. He sounded slightly calmer. "I see that you are as surprised as I am, Captain, which is most reassuring. Fortunately, I have found a solution. Or rather, General van Daan has. Mrs van Daan and her household have not yet left the Quinta de Santo Antonio as there was some delay in transporting the final patients from the hospital. They will follow the army in a day or two, with an escort of the King's German Legion under Captain Kuhn. Miss Grainger has gone to join her, she can rest her horses for a few days before resuming her journey to Lisbon and then on to London."

"Why is she here, my Lord?" Richard said.

"I think it's something of a pilgrimage, Richard," Paul van Daan said quietly. "She went to Oporto to see where Sir Horace was buried and then she travelled here overland, because she wanted to speak to Captain Fenwick and Captain O'Reilly about her father's last days. She'd hoped to be here days ago but she was delayed on the road, a broken carriage wheel, I believe. It's unfortunate, but I've told her that I'll ask them both to write to her."

213

"Did she receive his effects?" Richard asked. There was a hollow pain in his stomach. He knew that on the night before the march he could not possibly ask for leave to visit her. He had no formal relationship with Honoria Grainger, and a dozen or more letters, stored carefully in his baggage, would not be considered reason enough. Richard had thought himself resigned to not seeing her again and found himself praying that she would remember him and that he had not imagined the connection between them. It might be several years before he could return to England and during that time she would emerge from her mourning and into the world and there would be many men, younger and more handsome and wealthier than he, who would find Sir Horace Grainger's outspoken daughter to their liking. His chances were very slim but he allowed himself his dreams anyway.

"Yes," Paul said. He was regarding Richard sympathetically. Richard wondered if he was that obvious. "She was very surprised to discover that he'd written two letters during his last days, one to her and one to his wife. It seems he was too weak to write properly but he dictated them to Brat, Michael O'Reilly's servant. He managed to sign them himself. I've no idea what they said, but it seemed to affect her very strongly. I only met her briefly, but she's a fine young woman, her father would be very proud."

"Yes," Richard said numbly.

"Very well," Wellington said. "General van Daan, my compliments to your wife, please thank her for her assistance. We will be ready to move out at dawn towards Ciudad Rodrigo, you will join us then, and you may ride on to your brigade from there."

"Yes, sir."

Richard turned miserable eyes to the general. "Please give my respects to Miss Grainger, General, and tell her how sorry I am to have missed her."

"I will, Captain. Goodnight."

It was barely light when the headquarters party, including Major-General van Daan, assembled in the square outside the church. Richard checked the baggage wagons and spoke to the muleteers and grooms while Wellington and Murray gave a pile of letters and some instructions to a courier. It was already warm, with the promise of a hot day. Richard looked around with an odd feeling of finality, then went to his horse and swung himself into the saddle. Vaguely, he was aware of the sound of horses' hooves and he turned to look. Two riders were approaching at a canter. All the men in Wellington's party turned to watch and the swirl of dust resolved itself into a woman mounted on a pretty black mare, dressed in a striking wine coloured riding dress and followed by a dark haired groom. The woman slowed her horse and trotted into the square. Nobody spoke for a moment, then Major-General van Daan said pleasantly:

"It is very good to see you, bonny lass, but I thought we'd said our farewells for the time being."

The woman flashed him a dazzling smile. "We had. You are safe, General, I am not here for you. Lord Wellington, good morning. I'm so sorry to interrupt your departure, it will take just a moment. I need a word with Captain Graham."

Richard jumped at the sound of his name. He stared at Anne van Daan in some surprise. "Ma'am?"

"Don't 'ma'am' me, Captain. Did I, or did I not tell you that I wanted to see you in the clinic before you rode out?"

Richard searched his memory and drew a blank. "Erm...I do not perfectly recall..."

"Ha!" Anne said triumphantly. "I knew you would say that. Men! You are all the same. You will not admit to the least discomfort, but if you attempt to ride out without treatment, you are going to be completely incapable of continuing beyond Ciudad Rodrigo. It is utterly ridiculous that you refuse to submit to a small operation that will make you much more comfortable. And I can see by his Lordship's face that you have not even told him."

Wellington stared at her then turned an arctic glare onto Richard. "What has he not told me, ma'am?"

"Boils, sir," Anne said, triumphantly. "Given the size and position of them, I am surprised he can sit that horse at all. Let me tell you that of all the boils I have treated these are..."

"No, indeed, ma'am, do not tell me anything about them at all," Wellington said, sounding revolted. "General van Daan, are you aware that your wife has been treating this gentleman for...oh dear God, could anything be more unsuitable?"

"I knew nothing about it, sir," Paul said. Richard thought that his voice sounded rather muffled as though he might be trying hard not to laugh. "My dear, do you need to see Captain Graham before he leaves?"

"Yes. I'm sorry, but if he tries to ride like that, he's at risk of serious infection. He's just trying to hide it because he doesn't wish to miss the start of the campaign."

"Utterly ridiculous," Wellington snapped. "Captain Graham, not another word. Go with Mrs van Daan and get this problem dealt with. Preferably by a male doctor, if one is available. Join me as soon as you are able, I need you."

Richard met Anne van Daan's lovely dark eyes gratefully. "A day or two, no more, sir. I'm sorry, it was stupid. I didn't want to let you down."

"You never let me down, Captain. I value you, your health is important to me. I will see you as soon as you are fit."

Anne van Daan said nothing until they were out of earshot of the departing headquarters party then she shot Richard a sidelong look. "I'm sorry it had to be boils, Captain, it is just that I needed something that Lord Wellington would not wish to discuss in detail. I was right too, did you see the look on his face?"

The study at the Quinta de Santo Antonio looked oddly bare without the litter of ledgers and correspondence of brigade headquarters. Honoria Grainger was seated in a wooden armchair reading a book. She looked up as Richard entered, then rose, setting the book down. The mourning black made her look older and rather more lovely than Richard had remembered.

"I cannot believe you are here. I thought I'd missed you."

"I thought I'd missed you too," Richard said.

"How did..."

"Why did..."

They both stopped, smiling. Then Richard said:

215

"Miss Grainger, I'm so sorry you had a wasted journey, but I promise you I'll speak to Captain Fenwick and…"

"I didn't have a wasted journey. I didn't travel all this way to speak to Captain Fenwick. I wanted to see you before I returned to London. If that seems too forward or too…"

"No, it doesn't. Oh God, it doesn't. Honoria, please tell me I have not misunderstood you."

Honoria smiled and Richard felt his heart turn over. It was ridiculous. "No," she said. "Although I've been terrified all this way in case I had misread your feelings. I just needed to see you. To say…to ask…"

Richard stepped forward and took her into his arms. He kissed her for a long time, and she clung to him, convincing him beyond all doubt that he had not made a mistake. When he finally raised his head there were tears in her eyes.

"I went to his grave," she said. "I sat there for a while, talking to him in my head."

Richard's heart melted. "Oh, love, I'm so sorry. It's so awful for you and I can't even be here to take you home and look after you. And we've so little time."

"Mrs van Daan said she thinks we can have two days."

"Two days?" Richard thought about such bounty and found himself smiling again. "I thought I'd have to wait two years. I've a lot to say to you in two days, Honoria. Will you marry me?"

She was laughing and crying at the same time. "Yes. Yes, of course I will."

"Thank God. I've read every one of your letters a hundred times, trying to decide if I was being a fool or if you might feel the same way. I even thought of trying to say it in a letter, but I couldn't find the words. Besides, it didn't seem fair when I've no idea when I'll get back to England. And even now…it's so long to wait, love."

Her smile was luminous. "Richard, do try not to be an ass, it is very unlike you. Do you seriously think I would have made this mad journey in the worst conditions if I was not very sure?"

Richard kissed her again, deciding that she was right. For a time, it was enough just to hold her, revelling in the sense of her in his arms, but Honoria had an inquisitive nature and he was not surprised when she finally stepped back and asked the question.

"Richard, how did you manage this? I asked to see you but Lord Wellington said it was impossible, that you were about to march out and that you would not have time. I truly thought I had missed my opportunity."

"What did you say to Mrs van Daan?" Richard enquired.

"I couldn't say much at all. I was so disappointed, I'm afraid I cried a lot, and then I told her the truth. Did she do this? But how?"

"Boils," Richard said. "Let us sit down. It is rather a painful story."

By the Same Author

The Peninsular War Saga

An Unconventional Officer (Book 1)

An Irregular Regiment (Book 2)

An Uncommon Campaign (Book 3)

A Redoubtable Citadel (Book 4)

An Untrustworthy Army (Book 5)

An Unmerciful Incursion (Book 6)

The Manxman Series

An Unwilling Alliance (Book 1)

This Blighted Expedition (Book 2)

Regency Romances

A Regrettable Reputation (Book 1)

The Reluctant Debutante (Book 2)

Other Titles

A Respectable Woman (A novel of Victorian London)

A Marcher Lord (A novel of the Anglo-Scottish Border Reivers)

Printed in Great Britain
by Amazon

27894257R00136